INCOGNITA

JAIMA FIXSEN

Copyright © 2018 by Jaima Fixsen

All rights reserved.

No part of this book may be reproduced in any form or by any electronic or mechanical means, including information storage and retrieval systems, without written permission from the author, except for the use of brief quotations in a book review.

Cover design by Emily Skinner

To Regina
For the upward lift, for the nudges on, and for reading everything first.

1

EMBARASSMENT IS A FEARFUL TRIBULATION

THERE WERE WORSE things than being spectacularly jilted, Alistair knew. Losing one's leg, for instance. Losing a fortune—or worse, never having one in the first place. Of course, he didn't have a fortune of his own, but since most of his relatives did, it was almost the same thing.

Malaria. That would be terrible. Or tying yourself to a wife like the one Captain Fitzhubert had so recently acquired—plaintive and spotty. Better to be jilted than to marry one like that.

"Don't forget pox. Most uncomfortable, I'm told," said his cousin Jasper.

Alistair grimaced. Yes, there were plenty of worse things. Trouble was, none of them had happened to him, but he had been jilted by Sophy Prescott.

"This isn't helping," he growled.

"Really?" Jasper looked down at the list he held in his hand. "What about bad fish? I had some once . . . . " He caught Alistair's dark look and pulled his mouth shut.

Voices from the direction of the door warned of newcomers making their way into the room. Alistair sank deeper into his chair as Jasper set down his pencil, signaling the waiter to bring them another bottle. Once his glass was filled, Alistair reached for it, taking the opportunity to dart a glance at the new arrivals. Two of Jasper's cronies . . . and a ginger-haired fellow sporting scarlet regimentals. Didn't recognize him, but the other two were cowards. They'd laugh at his expense in private, but would give him a wide berth here.

"Stop glaring at everyone," Jasper muttered. "You just give them more to talk about when you sulk like a wounded bear. You said you were going to pretend like it didn't matter."

Indifference had sounded like a good plan when he and Jasper set out for the club, but acting the part was harder than expected —watching the sideways glances and discreet whispers.

"You aren't the only scandal in London," Jasper said, a little wearily, as Alistair's hand tightened around his glass. "Well, you won't be for long," he amended. "But if you pick a fight with Protheroe, I'm dropping you. He's a friend of mine."

"I know," Alistair said, swirling the wine in his glass. Better if he just didn't look at anybody.

Jasper gave a low whistle. "Looks like someone just lost another thousand." Over at the card table, one player was rummaging through his pockets for a scrap of paper to scrawl out another IOU. Two hours ago he'd been up nearly four thousand pounds, but now he was plunging deep and scribbling vowels, doggedly playing on, convinced his luck would change. His opponent was unmoved, despite the pile of coin and paper in front of him. Undue excitement was gauche, of course, but this fellow looked bored . . . indifferent even. And why not? Word was, he'd dipped worse himself just last week. Such reversals were fairly commonplace at Watier's.

To tell the truth, Alistair wasn't especially fond of the place— ran into his brother here far too often for his liking. It was a problem. Stifling a sigh, Alistair turned back to his cousin. "What?" He was tired enough to be provoked into words, instead of using his usual lifted eyebrow.

"I didn't expect you to mind so much," Jasper said. "Didn't think you were that attached to my sister."

Alistair hadn't thought so either. Oh, he liked Sophy well enough. She was an admirable choice. Marrying her would allow him to sell out of the army, and he was tired of getting shot and killing the French—cowardly impulses, but ones he couldn't deny in his private thoughts. Unfortunately, his arm was mostly healed and he wasn't marrying a comfortable fortune, so he'd have to return to his regiment. Alistair didn't shrink at the thought—thank God—but it made him incredibly weary. Almost made him wish he'd gone for a career in the church.

It would be nigh impossible to find himself another bride, embroiled in Sophy's scandal. True, there might be other ways out if he were desperate, but was he? He couldn't tell. It was hard to know exactly how he felt under the smart of Sophy's rejection. He was too proud, that was the problem. Never in his life had he expected to be thrown over by a girl like her—ladies usually went out of their way to oblige him.

Not Sophy. He'd courted her, kissed her, said all the right things, but she'd run off instead with a tradesman, giving up the house and the income her father had offered to settle on her, a bribe to compensate for her illegitimacy. It was a humiliation of gargantuan proportions, and it hurt too, more than he cared to think about.

He liked Sophy. She was pretty, with laughing eyes and a quick tongue, never at a loss for words no matter who challenged her, and swift with wry retorts that had as much charm as they had sting. She was wary and young and inexperienced, and probably the finest horsewoman he'd ever seen. In his mind, they would have done very well together.

Besides, women liked him. He wasn't a braggart, but it was no secret that the gentle sex had a habit of smiling beguilingly at him. He was barely more than a boy when they started tapping him teasingly with their fans and kissing him in dark corners, sending him smoky glances and conniving ways to get into his bed. And now, to be spurned by Sophy Prescott—fresh out of the schoolroom and a bastard to boot. The entire world was laughing. It might never be safe for him to look in the papers again. Just this morning he'd recognized himself in another cartoon, his nose steep and sneering, his chest puffed out like a balloon. They'd drawn him fingering a pile of money, saying 'Yes, Fairchild, she'll do . . . . ' while Sophy (a decent likeness, capturing her pert smile) escaped out the back door. Just thinking about it made his neck burn.

"Let's go," he muttered, rising from his chair, not waiting to see if Jasper was going to follow. There was no help for it: until a new scandal broke, his would be talked of everywhere. He could hide or he could brazen it out, but he was done brazening for today.

He collected his hat and was at the door of the club before he heard Jasper hurrying after him. "You're becoming maudlin," Jasper complained. "Slow down." Alistair stopped and looked back. Jasper was a step behind, frowning at having to don his hat without the aid of a mirror. He set it carefully on his head, waiting for Alistair's affirming nod before taking another step. "Just where are we going?"

"Expect I'm going to the devil," Alistair said. "I don't know about you."

"It's only Tuesday," Jasper sighed.

"What does that have to do with anything?" Alistair demanded.

Jasper shrugged and threw a coin to a straw-haired, gap-toothed crossing sweeper, who cleared their path across the street while lisping thanks.

"In here," Alistair said, turning into the inviting quietness of Green Park. Perhaps he'd feel better with more space around him —he was done with snug rooms and smug stares.

"She's happy, you know," Jasper said. "It's almost repulsive."

He was supposed to smile, but couldn't manage it. "I'll be spared the sight of that at least. I expect I'll soon be back in Spain." He cast a sideways glance at his cousin, worried Jasper might have divined some of his feelings about returning to the Peninsula. "I'm anxious to get back," Alistair said, for good measure.

Jasper regarded him through narrowed eyes. "A miraculous recovery. You couldn't reach over your head last week."

He still couldn't. The hole bored into his right shoulder by a French musket ball, sending him home from the Peninsula last winter, was exasperatingly slow to heal. Alistair could raise his arm about two thirds of the way now, but not without considerable wincing and cursing. With a saber in his hand it was worse, but he felt no pain the rest of the time, so long as he didn't try to raise his arm higher than his shoulder. "I'll be fit by the time I get there."

Jasper made a noncommittal murmur and changed the subject. "He's not a bad fellow. Tom Bagshot, I mean. Not any more oafish than he looks."

"Ham-fisted, probably." Alistair said, remembering the slope of Sophy's back as it disappeared under the muslin of her gown. The temptation of those warm shadows still plagued him. Too often he'd imagined sending his fingers there, watching her eyes growing warm and wondering. Perhaps it was her skittishness around him that made her so attractive.

Jasper grimaced. "She's practically a baby."

"You would think so. She's your sister," Alistair said, with something more like his usual smile. "She might be a baby, but she's a pretty one."

"Ugh. Be quiet." Jasper said.

Alistair was, for a minute, but now he couldn't get it out of his head. He'd been so sure he could persuade her to love him. She'd have forgotten Bagshot in a matter of weeks. "I'd have changed her mind, if she'd given me a chance," he muttered. "Seduced her so thoroughly she'd forget he existed."

Jasper hauled on his arm, dragging him to a stumbling stop.

"Wha—? Let go of me!" Alistair snapped, snatching his arm free.

"Be careful how you speak of my sister," Jasper said, his mouth a tight line.

"Take a damper," Alistair grumbled. "I'm not doing any harm."

"You are," Jasper insisted. "I'll hear your apology and I'll have your word not to speak of her again."

That was too much. He was the jilted one. Not once had he reproached Jasper for helping Bagshot get the special license allowing him and Sophy to wed. "Not today, you won't," Alistair scoffed. "Your man isn't here to help you out of your coat."

"Not overly fond of this one, actually," said Jasper, frowning at his left sleeve. "Sophy's a topper. Worth any number of coats."

"Glad you think so," Alistair said crisply, peeling out of his own. It was new, a claret-colored Bath superfine, but he tossed it onto the grass. He and Jasper hadn't scrapped since they were boys, but when they had resorted to fists, Alistair usually won. With his shoulder, they were probably even.

"Ready?" he asked, shifting his feet, trying out the ground.

Jasper swung his arms in a wide circle, the crack of his splitting coat seams ripping through the air. "At your convenience," he said.

"Excellent." Alistair shot out a fist.

"We'll see," Jasper said, swerving left and grunting as he thrust his left at Alistair's chin. Alistair answered with a quick jab that Jasper blocked. Before Jasper could swing again, Alistair threw out with his left, thumping Jasper solidly in the chest, the breath whooshing from him as he leapt back a step.

Jasper rattled in again, swinging so fast he got one in on Alistair's side, a rock-hard jolt that nearly sent him over. "Had enough?"

"Not nearly," Alistair replied. Nothing felt better than a turn up in a mood like this. He ducked. Jasper was better than he'd expected—like most gentlemen in his set, he was competent, having taken lessons with celebrated boxers—but Alistair wasn't worried. His cousin was too punctilious. He'd never had to bludgeon a man to death with an empty pistol, leaned from a wheeling horse to unseat a ferociously screaming enemy, or stumbled through smoke, carrying a bleeding friend only to find he was dead. Bad shoulder or no, he could take him.

Best do it quickly though. He couldn't swing without the joint feeling like it was ripping open. An uppercut with his left caught Jasper on the chin, but Jasper merely took a step back, cleared his head with a shake, then launched himself at Alistair, fists flailing.

"Apologize for Sophy!" Dodging right, Jasper landed a jab on Alistair's right shoulder. He buckled with a howl, but staggered up before he met the ground, catching Jasper with a swift punch right in the middle.

"Bastard," Jasper gasped, stumbling backward.

"No, that's Sophy," Alistair countered, but before he finished Jasper was grappling him around the waist. They were striplings again, gangly, furious, determined to win by foul means, which were always faster than fair.

"Get off!" Alistair yelled, tugging Jasper's hair, earning a grunt and a leg hooked around his own. Before Jasper could push him over, Alistair threw himself forward, shoving Jasper to the grass, but Jasper held tight, pulling him down. Evading a fist swinging heavily as a flying anchor, Alistair rolled sideways and froze. Five yards away stood a neat pair of boots—red leather with cheeky curved heels.

Alistair couldn't move. Jasper had grabbed his hair and was lobbing insults with immense satisfaction.

"Jasper—" Alistair began, jerking his chin at the boots.

"Good God!" Jasper's stream of profanity came to an abrupt

halt as he released Alistair's hair. "Erm—" He fell into incoherent sputtering.

Before Alistair could lift his eyes above Miss Red Boots' skirts, someone stepped out from behind them—a mop-headed boy in nankeen trousers and a blue coat.

"Ass-wipe!" he pronounced triumphantly. "Bloody—" Before the child could fire off more of Jasper's choice words, a gloved hand clapped over his mouth and Red Boots hoisted him onto her hip. Alistair was on his feet in an instant, brushing blindly at his waist coat, his apologies a messy tangle. Jasper was stunned silent.

No wonder. She was beautiful. Tall. Slender but shapely. Abundant black curls under a bonnet of golden straw. Ruby lips, winched into a tight frown and dark-lashed eyes pouring hot coals over him. Alistair flinched. Jasper, still unable to speak, nevertheless saw a way to redeem himself and pitched forward, snatching up a rubber ball lying in the grass.

"Forgive me," he said. "Is this yours?" Red Boots snatched it from his outstretched hand, then spun about in a volte-face any infantry commander would admire. Alistair didn't know how she could march so rigidly with a child wrapped around her waist, but it was impressive, a crushing snub—at least until the child piped up again. "Filthy ass-wipe!" he crowed, loud enough to carry to the other side of the park. Miss Red Boots—or Mrs., rather—halted for a split second, silencing the child with an admonitory finger, then hastened through the park gate.

Even Sophy hadn't run from him that fast. Alistair tried to laugh, but it hurt. He winced and rubbed his shoulder.

"She'll hear you," Jasper hissed.

"Doesn't matter. No way we can recover from that." Alistair reached down and snatched up his coat.

"Let me," Jasper said, stuffing Alistair's arms painfully into the sleeves and hoisting the coat over his shoulders.

"Easy does it," Alistair croaked. He glanced round. Curious

ladies vanished behind parasols. Beyond them a gentleman hustled his lady out of earshot, looking back with a censorious frown. Devil take it. At least six people had seen them.

"Let's get out of here," Jasper said, trying to straighten his coat, forgetting the seams at the back and shoulders were torn, revealing flashes of white shirt.

"Right." Alistair was already aiming for the gate to the street, pretending they weren't grass-stained and disheveled.

Jasper fingered his bleeding lip as they walked, letting out a grunt. "Who was she?"

Alistair shrugged, reviewing her features: red heels, white dress, little brat behind same, bonnet tied with a pert bow. Mortification grew as the pieces began fitting together. Hair: dark. Eyes: angry. Mouth: luscious. He had no idea who she was, but he felt certain he had seen her face before.

2

CONSCIENCES ARE TIRESOME TOO

ALISTAIR UNSTOPPERED his short bottle of whale oil. Moistening a greasy rag—once part of a French soldier's coat—he pushed it through the barrel of his pistol, twisting the rod as he went. Cleaning his gun almost always helped his mood, and tomorrow he might be too sore for the job. His shoulder felt like a lump of pastry who'd tried disagreeing with a rolling pin. At least Jasper hadn't gotten his face.

Better if he'd stayed home. Or written his colonel, saying he was ready to return to Spain. With his name already splashed across London's scandal sheets, getting caught brawling in the park only made things worse. Anyone would know he and Jasper had been fighting over Sophy. Alistair picked up a clean square of cotton. It went through the barrel as well, with more force than necessary, a kind of self-punishment—his knuckles hurt too.

He was sitting cross-legged on the floor of his bedchamber, balancing the dirty rag on his boot so it wouldn't stain the carpet. He fitted the pieces of his pistol back together, buffed the whole thing with a cotton square, and raised it to his eyes, taking inventory of each familiar scratch. He had a good memory for names and faces, but he couldn't place hers. Easy enough, though, to imagine her leaning in to a jewel-adorned ear, whispering what she'd seen today in the park, her lips twisting with contempt. He and Jasper might each nurse their bruises in solitude all day, but their families would hear about this afternoon's turn-up before dinner.

Perhaps he'd met her at that al fresco luncheon in Richmond? Might explain it. He'd drunk liberally of the champagne there, enough to blur the edges of his memories a little. No, that couldn't be right.

Alistair rose, dusted off his grass stained-breeches and hobbled to the dressing table, his muscles protesting though he hadn't been sitting on the floor long. He needed a bath, but that would require his man, Griggs, and he wasn't in the mood for any kind of company. Instead, Alistair sprawled across the bed, pulling out a battered book. It was his favorite, his good luck charm, a volume of Horace. The pages were feathering at the edges, the cover water-stained. Someday soon the book would fall apart completely, but he didn't know if he could bear to replace it. Horace had been his companion in Portugal and Spain, at Talavera, Buçaco, Fuentes de Oñoro and in the little medieval town of Tarifa, where he had finally taken a bullet in his shoulder.

Alistair started with the odes, enjoying them as he always did, until he tripped on the line, *who now enjoys thee credulous, all gold.* He instantly thought of Tom Bagshot.

Sophy, a captivating innocent, couldn't be likened to Pyrrha of the poem, but Bagshot—he fit nicely as her lover. Credulous, yes, and as rich in Methodist morality as he was in merchant gold. And he, like the writer of the poem, was jealous, sick with injured pride. Alistair flipped the page, turning his shoulder against a boiling cloud of anger, reading half a page without understanding a word. Bagshot was still in his head, Horace failing to evict him. Yet beneath envy and offended dignity there was something else . . . Alistair chewed the inside of his lip, straining after an elusive wisp of memory. Something about Bagshot, or Bagshot's morality. Yes, he had it now. It was more than just Tom Bagshot. It was the memory eluding him since he'd left the park, trying to recall just where he had first seen Madame Mouth.

He knew he'd seen her before! It was the demure dress and the little boy hiding behind her skirts today that had thrown him off. She'd looked much more dashing, and even more delicious, the first time he'd seen her at one of the opera house's scandal-making masquerade balls. Ladies of Quality might flit in and out —discreetly, if they valued their good names—but they didn't remove their masks, especially when their lips were decorated with paint. He'd noticed her early in the evening, but it was later, when she was glaring at the masked fellow dancing in the pit with his own Sophy, that he sauntered over to lean against the side of her box.

"Is he yours?" he asked. "The tall one, dancing with the lady in blue?"

She wilted for a fraction of a second before taking firm hold of her pride. "Obviously not." Her mouth tightened.

"I wouldn't worry. No harm will come of it," Alistair said. Sophy could play her games and try to avoid him, but he didn't like that she was waltzing with this fellow after refusing to waltz with him. He'd make sure she was back at his side after this dance. It was time he made his intentions plain.

"Too late. Here I stand, defeated," she said. A glimmer of humor would have softened her words, turning them into the kind of self-mocking jest that was both acceptable and wearily elegant. But there was no lift of an eyebrow, no lurking smile. She meant what she said. She cared far too much.

"Is he your husband then?" It was always best to make generous assumptions about females.

"No." The word was bare, forlorn. He felt a twist of pity, enough that he had to look and see if the beautifully packaged

12

woman was still there, or if she'd been replaced by a girl in braids and a dimity frock. No. This was the same one, brittle and alluringly varnished.

"Then he won't object if you dance with me?"

"No. More's the pity." She pressed her lips together. "He's of no use to me now, not even for dancing. I might as well take the floor with you."

"Such enthusiasm," he said, smiling at her as he walked around the front of the box. He expected she would wait for him collect her, but when he came to the door of the box she was already there. Hungry for a protector, he surmised. She was lovely to look at, but desperate and not, in any case, for him. Probably best to avoid her, but he'd already asked her to dance. He could at least use the opportunity to position himself near Sophy on the dance floor.

They dropped into the swirl of dancers without making a ripple. Alistair shifted his hand on her back, pulling her a fraction closer than was respectable. A test—one she failed. She didn't resist, or appear to even notice. Her eyes were fixed over his left shoulder.

"There is something arresting about the way she moves, isn't there?"

He moved her through a turn so he could see what she meant —it was Sophy, floating back into the circle of her partner's arms.

"I think it's more in the line of her shoulders," he said, unable to hide his frown. "She's much too young to be traipsing around with strangers."

She caught the shadow in his voice and leaned closer. "Does it tear your heart? Or just displease you? I can't tell if you love her or not."

Her sharp probing surprised him. True, his own thoughts of her were not kind, but he'd kept them to himself. Smarting from the sting of her words, he started to let go of her, intending to leave her where she stood. The smirk on her face changed his mind. There were better ways to discomfit her. He tugged her closer, so they were nearly touching, his mouth a handbreadth from her ear. Her breath quickened. She was probably waiting for words, but he didn't speak. He didn't intend to answer impertinent questions.

Tired of waiting, the woman in his arms supplied an answer herself. "Hmmmn. Not heart broken. Not yet." That, too, he decided to ignore, stonily returning her gaze as she searched his face, trying to see past the mask around his eyes.

"What is your name?" he asked.

"You first," she said.

"Rushford. Jasper Rushford," he lied.

"I am Mrs. Morris." She seemed to be waiting for him to ask after her husband, but Alistair was not such a novice. If there was a Mr. Morris, he was clearly a complaisant man, and therefore of no consequence.

"You're a nice armful, Mrs. Morris, but I'd like a look at your legs again," he said, propelling her into a spin so her shape would appear beneath the swaying skirts of her high-waisted gown. Very nice. Wherever she had come from, she looked like a thoroughbred at least—close to his own height and perfectly formed from her neck to her wrists to her ankles.

"You shouldn't say such things to me," she said.

"Why not? Don't you like it?" He slid his thumb along the edge of her hand, kindling fire in her eyes.

"Your lady won't like it," she said, radiating angry heat. Surprising. You'd think she'd have overcome such scruples.

"I don't think she'll ever know," he said.

"Probably not. Her eyes are all for Tom. Look, he's very taken with her."

If she meant to goad him, it was a weak attempt. Sophy could have her one waltz. It was of no consequence.

"Bad luck. She's not for him," he said.

"How do you know?" she asked.

Alistair grinned, happy to retake some ground. "Because she's for me. If I want her, that is." The music slowed, sinking in heavy pools between dancers approaching stillness, a heartbeat of a pause to exchange courtesies before breaking apart and leaving the floor. Alistair lifted his hands from her as the last note swam into the air. He sank into a bow. "I'm quite sure that I do, so don't give up on him, Mrs. Morris. The lady in blue is unavailable, and you are not without some attractions." He let his eyes travel slowly down below her face. "Thank you for the dance. May I escort you to your seat?"

"No." She didn't curtsey, returning instead a look that might have smelled of sulfur. Just as well. He shouldn't have offered to return her to her place—force of habit, he supposed. He needed to fish Sophy out of this crowd, not squire this jade back to her seat.·

"Good hunting," he said, speaking low.

Her quick spin away was more eloquent than words. He couldn't help admiring her as she stalked away, disappearing into the crowd of dancers, a brilliant catalogue of persons collected from every known land and point of history. It almost hurt his eyes, this collection of scandalously fragile skirts, golden collars, loose Eastern trousers and embroidered slippers with curled up toes. He stepped out of the way of a stiff lace ruff worn atop a set of panniers as wide as barrels. Not for the first time, he thanked his stars, happy to be born in a more rational age. But he'd lost Sophy. He could see every imaginable color except her domino cloak of bright blue.

It took two or three dances before he could reclaim her and steer her onto the floor himself. In the days that followed, Alistair kept watch for the tall fellow—Tom, she'd called him.

He only spotted him once, ogling Sophy through a quizzing glass at the theatre, looking singularly awkward, so he dismissed the fellow. A mistake. He shouldn't have forgotten about Mrs. Morris either. Sophy might not have married Tom Bagshot, if he'd told her what he knew about him and Mrs. Morris. He could have destroyed Sophy's love before her eyes, reducing her hero to clay, instead of telling her she'd outgrow this infatuation with Bagshot. Too late now. Sophy was married and she wouldn't like learning about her beloved's connection to that dark-haired female. It would break her heart. Might be best, in fact, if she never knew. But Jasper, who took up arms so quickly in his sister's cause, would want to hear of this.

It was his duty to tell him, Alistair decided, squashing a faint flutter of conscience. Jasper would buy that reasoning. Alistair could almost believe it himself, but for the trickle of vicious, subterranean satisfaction oozing inside him. He was no saint, after all, and it was hardly fair that he should shoulder all the misery of this affair.

Alistair shut his book with enough force that it ruffled his hair. He must wash and change his dress. And hope Jasper's temper had cooled enough so he could speak with him.

3

RELATIVES ARE WORST OF ALL

ANNA MORRIS, née Fulham, felt ready to scream, but it hadn't occurred to her once to wash her son's mouth with soap. She'd had few opportunities to confront the practicalities of child-rearing. After an hour chasing Henry in the park, where she'd torn her flounce and given herself a headache, she wondered why she bothered. Wringing permission from her brother-in-law to spend time with her son was wearing enough—and then one actually had to spend the time with him.

She'd been pleased with her appearance when she'd presented herself at the door of the Morris home, and proud of the way she had airily dismissed Henry's nurse. She didn't need more tale bearers watching her. If she so much as sneezed, her brother-in-law knew of it. But Henry had dragged his feet ever since leaving the park, dropping bonelessly to the ground in protest, dirtying his clothes and trying to kick off his shoes. She'd carried him most of the way, but they would still be late. Frederick had only granted them an hour and a half—and she'd argued hard for the extra half hour. Returning dirty and disheveled with a fretful child chanting obscenities was not going to help her cause.

"Aaasss—" Henry started up again. Anna could feel heads turning in their direction.

"Hush!" she whispered, laying a firm finger on Henry's lips. He stopped for a second, eyeing her hand. Before he could bite it, she whipped it away. There was little she understood about her son, but she needed less than a second to decipher that calculating look. Her mother claimed she'd been a biter too, before progressing to pinching. They'd cured her of that, eventually, but really—she'd be so much happier if she could succumb to impulse and give a hard twist to her brother-in-law's nose, snarl at her well-meaning mother and burn the grass covering her dead husband's grave.

Perhaps that last was a little much.

It was probably just as well the Morrises didn't want her near Henry. This short afternoon outing had nearly done her in. Nothing had gone as she'd imagined: no loving gazes, no jammy kiss (she'd decided she could tolerate jam), no trotting companionably at her side. Just another failure. No matter how she tried, everything she touched turned to dust and ashes.

You've gotten maudlin again. How contemptible.

"We're late. Your uncle won't like it," she said to Henry, probably sounding as plaintive and disagreeable as he did. At least she wasn't yowling. Yet. "We don't want—" she grunted, hoisting his slipping bottom back onto her hip, "to do anything—" Goodness, he was heavy! ". . . that your uncle will not like." Not that Frederick was disposed to like anything she did. He only tolerated her because of the money she had brought his brother. On Anthony's death, everything but her jointure passed to her son. Frederick was Henry's guardian and trustee, which put both her money and her boy beyond reach. She'd known Anthony hated her, but she had underestimated how much.

She looked down at Henry's tousled head and surly bottom lip, a hot lump rising in her throat. She'd bungled again. "Next time will be better," she promised.

Henry stuck out his lip. "No."

They were still ten houses away. She could bundle him into a hackney and take him to her parents' home, feed him tea and try to win that jammy kiss, but she had only a faint likelihood of succeeding. Henry didn't like her—and why should he? She had brought him to the park and gotten annoyed with him for ruining her clothes, for scampering away from her and finding new, appalling vocabulary. Instead of following him as he capered across the grass or taking him to stare at the milk cows up on the hill, she'd turned peevish, sure they were drawing disapproving eyes. Instead of laughing with him at the spectacle of two grown men tussling it out like a pair of schoolboys, she'd gotten angry. Yes, it was true that Henry would probably end up calling someone in the Morris house some colorful names, but what of it? If he used them on his uncle, she was in perfect agreement. Unfortunately, Frederick the Ass-wipe didn't need more excuses to bar her from Henry's company.

Ignoring yet another pitying look from the elegantly dressed strolling along Mayfair's pavements, Anna swiveled Henry to her other hip, hoping to ease the burn in her right shoulder. Her back was sweaty and her face hot. It was fitting, she supposed, that even an afternoon in the park turned into a struggle—everything else was. Her parents felt badly for her, but they were of little help. She ought to be used to helpless frustration, to containing the feverish plans that circled round her head like a mill wheel. These ideas seemed good in the small hours of the morning, but they always proved weak and flimsy against Frederick once the sun filled the sky. That wasn't what filled her with despair. Defeat at Frederick's hands was nothing compared to today's, from Henry. He didn't like her. She might as well give up trying.

But Henry's dark hair and petulant mouth . . . they were exactly like her own. And though she couldn't remember ever sharing his sturdy legs, round knees, and impudent smile, those were hers too. He was her son and she would have him. Someday.

Soon. She caught his round pink hand and pressed it to her cheek. "I'm sorry," she said, but he pulled his hand free, impatient with her caressing. "Next time we can go to Grandpapa and Grandmama Fulham's. You'll like the kitty." Someone had to, besides her mother.

Henry narrowed his eyes. "Does he have teeth?"

And claws, Anna thought ruefully, remembering a pair of gauzy silk stockings.

"Boris has teeth. Boris chewed my dit," Henry said.

She knew Frederick's poodle, Boris, but she didn't recognize the other thing. "Your dit?"

He nodded, expecting that to be answer enough. "Next time can I bring it? But not if there's a kitty."

She nodded, dumbfounded, but willing to agree to anything he suggested. He settled himself complacently, pointing to his own door once she began climbing the steps. The door swung wide, revealing the butler and the nurse, poised with waiting hands. Henry wriggled free and scampered into them with such eagerness that Anna felt her stomach widen into a cavernous hole. For a moment she wished he was back inside her, where he might bump and nudge, but no one could take him.

"Were you a good boy?" the nurse asked Henry, eyeing Anna's dress.

"Next time I'll wear a dark one," Anna said. Maybe Frederick would allow her to take Henry for a drive and they could get ices. That might go better. He couldn't run away from her if he was in a carriage. She would bring a maid with her. Or a leash.

"I'm hungry," he said to the nurse.

"Your tea is waiting for you," she said, taking his hand and leading him up the stairs. Anna tried not to mind when he didn't look back. Alone with the butler in the hall, she waited a moment, but was not invited inside. "Give Mr. Morris my apologies for our lateness. Henry had a hard time walking all the way home."

He bowed, acknowledging her message, and she left, realizing once she was outside that she should have paused to straighten her bonnet in front of the hall mirror. She gave one futile brush at her skirts, but the prints of Henry's shoes were plainly marked. At least Henry had temporarily forgotten his new words.

She turned in the direction of her parents' house, wondering when, if ever, Henry would notice her absence. On the whole, it might be better if he did not. They would never let her have him.

ALISTAIR WAS NEARLY FINISHED the transformation from grubby ruffian to society gentleman when Oakes summoned him.

"Lord Fairchild is waiting for you in the drawing room."

Alistair looked away from the mirror and the folds of his cravat. "My uncle's here?" Lord Fairchild always said the only good thing about Lady Ruffington, Alistair's mother, was that he could avoid her more successfully than her sister, his wife. Of course, Alistair's mother was gone now, fled from London, unable to face her friends, but Lord Fairchild couldn't know that. They'd hardly spoken since the day Sophy ran off. "I'll be down shortly," Alistair said, deftly shaping the white waterfall foaming at his throat.

"Perfect," said Griggs, from behind the hand mirror.

"It'll do," Alistair said, holding out his arms so Griggs could brush off any specks of lint. Alistair didn't have many coats to his name, but all of them were irreproachable.

He found his uncle in the drawing room, poking at the charred remains of a newspaper fluttering at the edge of the grate. Alistair decided to ignore this evidence of his own bad temper—the cartoons this morning had been unendurable. "You honor me," he said, bowing to his uncle. "What brings you?"

Uncle William gestured at the black tissue crumbling onto the floor. "I feel that I am in some way to blame."

"You did try to stop her," Alistair said, tightening his mouth and glancing at the window.

"Yes. But I don't think we'd have faced the problem if I had . . . done differently," he said.

Alistair lifted an eyebrow.

"Sophy told me she was reluctant, but my wife wanted the marriage and I wanted to make her happy," he said. "We pushed you both too hard."

Alistair picked up the medal he'd been presented after the battle at Fuentes de Oñoro that his mother liked to keep so prominently on her occasional table. He turned it face down. "I know Sophy didn't love me. Told me as much. But did she tell you why?" He wanted a reason. Something he could refute.

Lord Fairchild sighed. "She wanted to be loved."

"And she didn't think I could?" This was worse than he'd expected. He'd fully intended to make her as happy as a woman could wish.

Fairchild shrugged. "It's probably as much my fault as yours. I don't think I've convinced her that she isn't a mistake—she's born out of one, certainly, but—well, I value her for all that."

Perhaps Sophy would have responded to a more single-minded pursuit, though when he had tried that, it hadn't gone well. She had kissed him, he had laughed, and she hadn't forgiven him for it. She hadn't understood that he had laughed because she'd delighted him. From then on she had refused to believe he was courting her, never crediting him with sincerity. Or honor.

"I'm sorry I couldn't convince her," Alistair said, a little stiffly.

"I just said it wasn't your fault. But I would have liked the match. I'm sorry for all this—inconvenience," he said, gesturing again at the fireplace. Which was a mild way of putting the whispers, jeers, and scandal sheets.

Alistair moved to pour himself a drink, offering one to his uncle. He refused. When Alistair sat down and sipped his, he remembered why. The liquor in this house was pigswill.

"I'm sure the entire episode will be forgotten in a few days," he lied. He wouldn't forget, though. Neither would his uncle, even when society tired of it and moved on to something new. But since there was nothing to be done, he must tough it out. A man must consider his dignity—especially when he had so little remaining.

"Have you heard from her?" Alistair asked.

Lord Fairchild shook his head. "I don't expect to after the way we parted. Jasper has seen her, but he refuses to say if she is well. She's Bagshot's wife and there's nothing now to be done, but I worry for her. I know almost nothing of the man she's chosen. I've driven out twice to Suffolk, but never made it all the way to Bagshot's door."

"She was determined to have him," Alistair said carefully. Confiding his suspicions of Bagshot's perfidy to Jasper was a simple matter, but he wasn't certain he could mention them to his uncle. Jasper might deceive most with his sophisticated airs, but Alistair knew the jealously guarded secret of his cousin's private convictions. He might ogle bosoms and flirt and tell warm stories, but if Jasper had ever pursued a flirtation to its natural conclusion, Alistair didn't know of it. Jasper would expect Tom Bagshot to love his sister honestly, but Lord Fairchild's example suggested he would be satisfied with kindness and circumspection. Indeed, their world expected nothing more from husbands, who frequently got away with even less.

"He's indecently wealthy. Nothing to complain of, I suppose, though it all smells of the shop. I hear rumors of mills in dockside taverns though. Fellow's a real bruiser, apparently." Lord Fairchild's forehead creased and he stared with bleak eyes at the ugly landscape hanging on the opposite wall. "A violent man. Suppose one day he hits her?"

Alistair swallowed. It wasn't something anyone liked to speak about. "Would you take her, if she came back?"

"God, yes."

Shamed by his own feelings—hadn't he taken secret pleasure at the prospect of shattering Sophy's illusions, of paying her in kind for the pain she'd given him?—Alistair spoke. "I've seen him on occasion. Once with a dark-haired woman. The wrong sort, of course, but she seemed more affected than he. It was a chance meeting, one I'd temporarily forgotten. I was about to find Jasper, to tell him of it."

His uncle's face closed, hiding distress that seemed all the greater for being buried out of sight. "When was this?" he asked.

"Earlier in the season, the night Sophy and I went with Lord and Lady Arundel to the masquerade ball," Alistair admitted, loath to mention that mistake. If he hadn't agreed to escort Sophy and her older, legitimate sister to that vulgar spectacle, Sophy would never have crossed paths again with Tom Bagshot, and none of this would have happened.

"Fairly recently then." Lord Fairchild rubbed his cheek. "I can scarce get Jasper to speak to me. You'll tell him? See what you can find? There's little we can do, but if Sophy needs help—"

"I'll speak to him," Alistair promised.

Lord Fairchild's lips twitched but they were incapable of forming a smile. "I seem to always be thanking you of late. You've been terribly decent about all this. I wish you knew how sorry I am."

"It's nothing," Alistair said, uncomfortable with undeserved gratitude. He hid behind a quick swallow of brandy, forgetting it was vile.

"Tastes like horse piss, doesn't it?" Lord Fairchild said, as Alistair grimaced.

Alistair could only nod, glad he was spared the indignity of blushing. The economies forced on the family by his eldest brother were becoming even more shameful.

"Cyril's a careless fellow," his uncle said, neutrally, like he was commenting on the weather. "Another reason my wife liked the

24

match. You were always her favorite nephew. She worries about your future."

"She needn't," Alistair said.

Lord Fairchild leaned back in his chair, carefully preparing his words. Alistair braced himself. A charitable offer was coming. He could feel it.

"I could help. Buy your next commission or help you find a place in the foreign service if you're tired of the army." Lord Fairchild looked up from his steepled fingers to meet Alistair's eyes. "You held up your side of the bargain. I owe you something."

"Don't be ridiculous," Alistair said. If there was one thing he couldn't abide, it was pity.

"Think about it," his uncle said.

He ought to. Now that he'd lost Sophy and her comfortable portion, he needed some plan for his future. Even if the war did last forever, he wouldn't be so lucky.

"I couldn't. And there's no need," he said.

Uncle William looked at Alistair's glass. He set it down, annoyed. "I shall be quite all right, I assure you," he lied. The longer he stayed in England the more he realized his family was in trouble. Despite his mother's prophecies of disaster, no one had seriously attempted to check his brother. How could they? Their father was ailing and Cyril was nearly at the point of stepping into his shoes. There would be no gainsaying him then, and he knew it.

"You know where to find me if you change your mind." Lord Fairchild stood, reaching for his hat and gloves, still reposing on the sofa cushion. "If you could make time to call on my wife in the next day or two, I'd be grateful. She misses you." No doubt Aunt Georgiana felt guilty.

Well, he might not mind commiserating with her. They'd always been in tune, and unlike Jasper, her loyalties were with him. Alistair promised to make a point of it. His uncle left and a

25

minute later so did he, setting out to find Jasper, more depressed about his errand than before. He cared for Sophy. Truly. He always had, warming to her elusive light and her laughter, not just the comfortable life she promised. But his face didn't look like her father's, worn and without hope and weary, which told him a sad thing: he cared, but not nearly enough. Sophy, with all her talk of hearts—filled and lost and breaking—had surely known.

4

A FRIEND, OR A THORN IN THE SIDE?

OF COURSE JASPER could never be found when he was needed. It was true to his nature, Alistair supposed: self-indulgent and thoroughly annoying. Returning home, late and unsuccessful, Alistair committed himself to more aggressive tactics and told Griggs to make sure to wake him before nine.

A circuit round the park on his black gelding the next morning also failed to turn up his cousin, so Alistair rode directly to St. James Street. Jasper, the lucky dog, had sufficient means to keep his own rooms there. Dividing his time between London, a hunting box in the country, various jaunts to Newmarket, and—just the once—a walking tour in Scotland, Jasper managed to spend very little time within sight of his parents, a policy he'd pursued since first being sent to school. Alistair sympathized. A career in the army did much the same thing for him, but without setting up his parents' backs.

He found his cousin presiding over a magnificent breakfast, just as a gentleman of leisure should: ale in one hand, the racing form in the other, and a plate piled with sliced beef in between.

"Look at this," Jasper said, forgetting yesterday's quarrel and jabbing a finger at the paper beside him. "Fancy Piece beat Gordon's Zephyr by a length—a length, I tell you!"

Alistair paused before taking the proffered chair. "I'm glad to see you. Yesterday—"

"All forgotten," Jasper said, with an impatient wave. "But this upset! Wish I had seen it. Williams will be flying high—and Gordon ready to chew nails. We'll see them both at the club today, if Gordon can stand to watch Williams gloat."

"I doubt he has the choler for it," Alistair said.

"Pity. 'Twould be amusing." Jasper glanced up at Alistair and realized he had something on his mind more important than horses. Or horses belonging to other people, at least. He took a fortifying gulp of ale. "It isn't nice to come so early on serious matters," he complained.

"I'm afraid it's important," Alistair said. "The woman with the boy who saw us yesterday. I've seen her before."

"Hmmn." Jasper was only mildly interested. "Fine looking lady, I admit, but no hope for either of us. Unless she felled you with that disgusted glance, I don't see any problem—hey, aren't you still in love with my sister?"

Sometimes talking to Jasper was like walking through heavy brush. You couldn't take a step without picking up irritating burrs. "That's not why I came."

"It would be a good thing for you to fix your attentions elsewhere," Jasper said, pulling a pencil from behind his ear to circle the name of a horse.

"I dare say." Alistair glanced across the table at the paper. It wasn't a horse. The listing was promoting a cockfight.

"Well, who is she?" Jasper finally asked.

"A chère-amie of Bagshot's."

Jasper froze, his ale halfway to his mouth, frown lines gouging his forehead. Silently he set down his glass. "Can't be," he said. "Bagshot's too much of a reforming bent for that. Methodist. You know the type."

"Wouldn't be the first time a good Christian got his feet dirty," Alistair said.

"I don't believe it," Jasper said. "What makes you think so?"

"I saw him." Alistair told him about the masquerade, and the proprietary way she had spoken of Tom.

Jasper fidgeted with the paper. "Too late to do anything now, even if he was mixed up with her," he said. "Sophy's stuck with him, and he knows better than to carry on with prime articles now. New one for you to come out all prunes and prisms. Would you have told Sophy of your Spanish beauties?"

"That's different. I haven't gotten any children," Alistair said. "And you know I haven't done more than dance with another female since Sophy came to town." Jasper's gaze didn't soften, so Alistair added, "I would have told her, when the time was right." It was an uncomfortable, ridiculous notion, but it was only fair.

"How do you know Bagshot didn't? Dalliance doesn't seem his style, but I suppose it's possible," Jasper said, his intense study failing to char the meat remaining on his plate. He shook his head. "No. Sophy wouldn't fall for a dirty dish like that."

"She's very young," Alistair said gently. "He can't have told her —she'd have raised a hell of a dust."

Jasper flicked him a skeptical glance.

"The boy in the park?" Alistair prompted, knowing this was the crux of the matter. Tom Bagshot probably had given up his mistress—he seemed to have forgotten her presence entirely the night of the masquerade. Mrs. Morris—if that was her name— was probably pensioned off, dismissed. But Sophy wouldn't stand for Tom hiding a child from her. She knew the plight of illegitimate children too well.

Jasper understood at once, but he struggled with himself, not wanting to admit it. "Just because an incognita was marking Tom doesn't mean he let himself get caught. You sure she's in the game?"

"I spoke to her. She's a lightskirt. I'm sure of it." He couldn't say which of them had turned the conversation down shady paths, but she hadn't pulled back. She'd matched him, step for step.

Jasper picked up his fork, turning it in his hand so the light from the window danced across the walls as his face darkened. A thought came to him, clearing his countenance. "Normally I'd believe you. You're a good judge of these things. But this one can't be. Lightskirts don't parade their brats around the park. Whatever she is, I'd lay money she isn't that."

Alistair clenched his teeth. "How much?" he demanded, unwilling to back down.

"A pony," Jasper said.

Alistair snorted. "You can't be that sure then." Twenty five pounds was a paltry stake.

"I don't steal from my relatives." Jasper gave him a steady look. "You're taking Sophy's rejection too hard. Not thinking straight. Have some breakfast." He got up and went to the sideboard for a plate.

Alistair waved it away. "You named your stake. Let's settle this thing. If it's true, Sophy ought to know."

Jasper thought for some moments, drumming his fingers on the side of his thigh. "All right then. Haven't anything better to do."

He waited, all easy complacence, provoking Alistair to snap, "It won't be easy. I doubt Morris is her real name."

Jasper shook his head, breezily confident. "We'll know the truth by luncheon. And when I relieve you of your money, you can thank me I didn't take more." He met Alistair's look with a grin. "Come on. I expect Bagshot's mother knows the lady and this is all a mare's nest. Sophy loves Tom and she's a right one. She wouldn't fall for a man who wasn't of solid worth."

"We'll see," Alistair said, picking up his gloves. Yesterday's fist fight was more than enough. He must keep his temper, no matter how pressed.

"Well, he must be something, if she preferred him to you."

It required self-control of heroic proportions, but Alistair limited himself to a single muttered curse. Of course Jasper only laughed.

～

OF ALL THE things Jasper might have anticipated today, paying a morning call on Mrs. Bagshot was not one of them.

He had been to the house on Russell Square before. Both the address and the style of furnishing shouted that the family was new money, but Bagshot's mother surprised him today. They found her in the drawing room, bundled into the corner of a green brocade sofa. Instead of obscuring her dumpy figure with an invention of silk, lace, and ribbon, she wore a calico gown suitable for a housemaid. Unnerved, Jasper paused on the threshold. If she wasn't prepared for company, she shouldn't have let her servant show them up.

"Forgive me," he said. "Do we find you indisposed?"

Her cheeks flamed and she jumped to her feet, curtsied and took her seat again, weak apology and stout defiance warring across her face. Jasper held back a laugh. She was vibrating between the two like his mother's dinner gong.

"Forgive me," she said. "I am being comfortable today. I didn't expect visitors." She was clearly incapable of unkindness; a species of woman he had heard existed, but never chanced across. For a half-second, Jasper wished he could introduce her to his own mother. Useless, that. Lady Fairchild would never see past such eagerness to please, or that shabby cap.

"Do not let us trespass then," Jasper said, preparing to remove himself as delicately as he could.

"You're here already," she said, picking up her knitting from the cushion beside her. "You may as well say your piece." With a pudgy finger she pushed her gold spectacles off her forehead and onto her nose.

"You are too kind, ma'am," Alistair said, swiftly crossing the room and taking a seat. "Jasper, would you be kind enough to present me?"

Jasper made careful introductions, realizing it would have been better if he'd come alone. Alistair was still angry and that made him liable to act snappish, beneath the most exquisite manners of course. Mrs. Bagshot, a simple soul, might not detect —no, a vain hope that. When Alistair meant to slight, his targets felt it. Damn. There was going to be trouble.

Mrs. Bagshot offered refreshment, which they both declined. Then Mrs. Bagshot remembered someone's advice and straightened her back, moving to the edge of her settee. The room was still, so heavy with green velvet and mahogany Jasper feared he would soon be growing moss. It was time for some words, quickly. He'd get lost in this jungle without them.

"Have you heard from Tom?" he asked.

"Only a note saying they were safely arrived. Has your sister written?"

"Briefly." Sophy had dashed off a letter, thanking him for his help in obtaining the marriage license, followed by several anxious queries about his parents—would they ever forgive her? Had they spoken of her at all? He had no happy answers.

Seeing Jasper's reluctance to share the contents of Sophy's missive, Mrs. Bagshot turned her eyes to Alistair. "Forgive me. I'm afraid I missed the connection between you two."

"Captain Beaumaris is my cousin," Jasper filled in.

"And his sister's discarded fiancé," Alistair added, ignoring Jasper's glare.

"Oh dear," Mrs. Bagshot murmured, her needles jerking to a stop.

Stupid ass. Jasper hastened to smooth things over. "But we

both realize it's for the best. To stand in the way of a couple in love—"

"True. Not to be thought of," Alistair interrupted. "Sophy will make a wonderful addition to your family. You must be very happy."

"Ye-ess," Mrs. Bagshot said, her eyes flicking between them both. "She loves my boy, and he—well, he was taken with her from the start."

"So spirited," Alistair said, and Mrs. Bagshot untwisted her knitting and raised her spectacles.

"She's young," she said firmly, after measuring Alistair with a glance. "But she chose well in the end. It sounds like she would have tried your patience."

Jasper's shoulders softened and he smiled at Mrs. Bagshot unguardedly. She might have reservations about Sophy, but she would stand between her and all comers, it seemed. This pleased him, even though he suspected she took Sophy's part more out of love for her son. Sophy was a clever minx. It wouldn't take long for her to cajole her way into her mother-in-law's heart.

"True enough, true enough," Alistair acknowledged, unruffled. "Her larks have thrown me into temper—oh, once or twice. Pray tell me, does she try yours?"

Jasper frowned at his cousin. That detestable face let him get away with all kinds of impertinence. Jasper had spent a lifetime watching Alistair charm his way around the weaker sex, and today he was heartily sick of it. Good for Sophy! Jilting Alistair was a kick in the head that had been too long in coming.

"I might have been vexed with her, if she wasn't such an engaging scrap," Mrs. Bagshot said, her smile telling Alistair she was prepared to include him in this description. "For one thing, I don't hold with lying. The whole affair could have been managed better. It's a sad day when parents see fit to throw off a child, and a broken engagement is no nice thing either. But all's well as ends well, and the less said about it the better."

"An excellent notion," Jasper said, looking hard at Alistair.

Mrs. Bagshot lowered her spectacles onto her nose to inspect her work, counting stitches under her breath. Having reached a satisfactory total, she resumed knitting, the needles' steady chatter filling the room. The piece was too broad to be a stocking, too small to be of use for anything else, but it was clearly meant for something—a neat stack of the things were folded next to the balls of yarn in her basket.

"So why did you come then?" she asked without looking up, before Jasper could inquire after the purpose of her diminutive project. Jasper hesitated a moment too long. He couldn't say they were here to settle a bet.

"Vulgar curiosity, I'm afraid," Alistair, said, his smile taking the sting out of the words.

Mrs. Bagshot chortled, answering in kind. "Came to see what you lost out to?"

"Exactly." Alistair looked around the room. "You must forgive me."

"I suppose no man likes to be second best," she said.

Alistair laughed smoothly, not revealing anything. "Oh, I'm well down on the list, ma'am. Sophy much prefers her brother to me, and probably her horse too. We won't injure my vanity by following that line."

The anger behind yesterday's fistfight might never have happened, but Jasper couldn't ignore the reminder of his tender bottom lip, still a little swollen, even after the lengthy application of an oozing beefsteak. He listened warily. By all appearances, Alistair and Tom's mother were getting along like a house on fire, but this made Jasper more nervous, not less. All week he'd been waiting for Alistair to laugh off his broken engagement. He hadn't imagined it happening like this. Alistair was ever one for evening the score, and though Mrs. Bagshot showed a fine sense of humor for a pudding-faced biddy, there was a glitter in Alistair's eye he could not like.

"He's a good man, my Tom," Mrs. Bagshot said.

"Indeed. I think I may have met an acquaintance of his the other day," Alistair said. "Mrs. Morris? I saw her once with your son and then again in the park, with a little boy."

Mrs. Bagshot sighed and because she was turning her knitting, she didn't notice their waiting breath, their watching eyes. Too late, Jasper realized this wager was for much more than twenty-five pounds. If he was wrong . . . .

"That would be Anna," Mrs. Bagshot said. "Anna Fulham, as she used to be." Relief broke over Jasper with startling intensity and a genuine smile spread across his face. Of course he was right. If Tom had ever trifled with loose women, he wouldn't have made them known to his mother. Whoever Anna Morris might be, she was no impediment to Sophy's happiness.

Mrs. Bagshot's eyes flicked up to Alistair. "Beautiful, isn't she?"

Alistair nodded woodenly, apparently having swallowed his tongue. Jasper tried to contain his triumph behind a malicious smile, but couldn't resist mouthing, "Twenty-five pounds!"

Alistair didn't notice. He looked almost sick, or maybe that was just an effect of the upholstery. "A widow, is she?" he asked, his voice hoarse.

"Yes. Our families are old friends. Thought she might do for my Tom, but that didn't turn out so well."

"What happened?" Alistair asked.

"He crossed paths again with your sister," she said, nodding at Jasper. "I don't think he really saw anyone else after meeting her. I wish he could have handled it better. I'm afraid Tom was a trifle thoughtless and Anna was hurt. I daren't speak to her mother."

"You've known them a long time then?" Jasper asked. It wasn't nice to bait a defeated man, but he couldn't resist. No real harm in it. He was the one who would have to nurse Alistair out of this sulk, after all. And he'd do it cheerfully, now he knew Sophy's peace was assured.

"Ages, yes. Known the Fulhams forever and Anna herself since she was a wee thing." Mrs. Bagshot smiled apologetically. "Never saw a child with such a nasty temper, so perhaps it's just as well Tom never took to her."

"She is widowed," Alistair said again, gone deaf or stupid with surprise. "With a son?"

"Yes," said Mrs. Bagshot patiently. "Terrible shame. Been a couple of years now. I never met her husband. Well, naturally that wouldn't have happened. I gather the Morrises were none too pleased with her family." She looked pointedly at Jasper. "It's a bad business, you know, weighing down a man and wife with family censure."

"I am all agreement. Sophy is pleased with Tom, and that is good enough for me," Jasper hastened to assure her. He cast about for a new subject, since Alistair sat paralyzed on the couch. "What is that you are making?" His mother never did anything so common (or practical) as worsted work.

"You cannot tell?" Mrs. Bagshot leaned over to the basket at her feet and unfolded one of the little squares. "See, it's a little jacket. I've made caps too, to go with them. And covers to go over the nappies."

Mercy. That basket was huge, and suddenly full of dreadful significance. "You've made a good many of them," Jasper said weakly.

"Only seven, so far. I'm only starting. Babies go through so many changes a day."

Just one, or was she expecting a whole litter of them?

"Who are the Morrises? Where can I find them?" Alistair said, breaking Jasper's stunned silence.

"I wouldn't know," Mrs. Bagshot said, smiling apologetically. "But Anna and her parents live in Hans Town. On Basil Street."

"Do you know the Morrises?" Alistair asked, turning to Jasper.

He tore his gaze from the basket. "Well, there are the Warwickshire Morrises and some other ones, who claim a connection to Penderwick. Don't know those ones. But the Warwickshire lot have a house on Mount Street." These kind of details stuck in his head like barnacles. Pity his memory for Latin wasn't nearly so good. He turned to Mrs. Bagshot. "Are they the right ones?"

Mrs. Bagshot shrugged.

"Anthony Morris died in a carriage accident, I think, but there's a younger brother," Jasper prompted, searching his memory for anything else that might cue her.

"Might be the ones," Mrs. Bagshot said. "I heard Anna's husband died in an accident, but I don't know what kind."

Alistair nodded once—a sharp movement of decision—and bounced up from the sofa as if his knees were springs. "Thank you, Madam, for sparing me your time," he said, bowing to Mrs. Bagshot. In another instant he was nearly out the door. "Forgive me, Jasper. I've some business to attend to."

Jasper settled back into the sofa. Might as well, since he was being abandoned. Besides, Mrs. Bagshot might take it as permission to let herself be comfortable. Jasper suddenly had a burning desire to find out everything she'd heard from Tom. He brought out his most engaging smile.

"Between you and me," he said to Mrs. Bagshot, after the reverberations of the front door had stilled, "I think Sophy had a narrow escape."

She smiled at him. "I can't persuade you to take tea?"

Why not? Jasper accepted her invitation and set to work gently prying—few could do it better—while inwardly composing the letter he must dispatch to his sister. Hopefully it wouldn't arrive too late. He might lack experience in the matter, but he'd absorbed enough to write a treatise on the subject. Vanquishing the urge to squirm—it was entirely wretched, having to mention these things to a sister—he accepted Mrs. Bagshot's offered cup, refusing to look at that hideous basket. He must tell Sophy every thing he knew about preventing conception.

5

MORTIFICATION IS THE WORST MEDICINE

ALISTAIR RUSHED FROM THE HOUSE, cursing himself for a complete dolt. How had he mistaken Mrs. Morris for a lightskirt? He thought he understood women.

Better hope she didn't understand you.

But of course she had. Beneath the barbs, there had been that teasing pull of invisible spider threads between them, the way he had looked at her sideways and smiled suggestively, and—Heavens, what had he said? Not what one was supposed to say to a respectable woman, at any rate.

Alistair hailed a hackney, ordering it to set him down in Basil Street. He didn't know the right house, but after being misdirected by a drippy-nosed kitchen maid, he was pointed to the right one by a baker's boy.

"I've come to call on Mrs. Morris," he said, handing his card to the shy housemaid who came to the door. She turned it round in her hand like she didn't know what to do with it.

"She isn't here," the maid said.

"Please tell her I called," Alistair said.

Alistair went home. His own pistol was clean, so he took care of his brother's handsome dueling pistols, nestled inside their mahogany case. They hadn't been cleaned (or touched) in an age. No doubt Cyril had purchased them because of their gleaming barrels and the way they balanced sweetly in the hand, tried them once or twice, discovered he wasn't able to culp a wafer on the first go and decided to buy himself fishing tackle instead. Or a new horse. Either way, he seemed to have forgotten the pistols, which was fortunate, since the last thing the family needed was for Cyril to challenge someone while in his cups.

Tucking the pistols into the case with one last caress, Alistair restored them to the cupboard under the library window, pushing the case back into the shadows, wishing he hadn't left his card with Anna Morris's maid. Avoiding her for the rest of his life would be much easier than cobbling together an adequate apology, but it was too late to change his mind now. Consciences were tiresome things.

The next morning, there was a note waiting for him at the breakfast table. It wasn't from Jasper. Inside the folded paper was his card.

You've made a mistake. I am certain we are not acquainted.

The blunt hostility took him by surprise, but he supposed there was something to be said for going straight to the point. He kept his reply similarly brief.

Perhaps not acquainted, but when you see me, I think you will know who I am. May I see you?

The answer came two days later, addressed forcefully in thick black ink, resting beneath another letter from his colonel. Alistair opened the colonel's letter first—it was his marching orders. No surprise there. Anna's reply, though, was unexpected. Her letter had only three sharp words, gouged into the paper:

No. Go away.

She'd probably ruined her pen. Alistair tapped his lip thoughtfully with the folded paper. He'd tried. Really, there was little point in forcing himself upon her notice, and every reason to forget the matter entirely. Except he could not. Why was she living in a shabby genteel part of town instead of with the Morrises? And why did she refuse to meet him?

"Who's that letter from?' Cyril asked from across the table.

"A lady."

Cyril hooted softly, but Alistair didn't notice. He read the three word message again and downed the last of his coffee. He'd tried conventional means. It was time for something different. Forgetting his toast, Alistair plowed out of the dining room.

Cyril set down his fork, staring at the empty door long after his brother was gone. "Lucky sod," he muttered.

HANS TOWN WAS south of Mayfair, and it was a presumptuous kind of place. Nice enough, but it wasn't the best, no matter how it tried. The house on Basil Street was a three story brick building, as like to its neighbors as a row of uniformed soldiers: warm brick, thick white trim, a bow window on the second floor. The only thing different about this one was that it had no topiary on the steps.

Alistair stationed himself across the street. A swirly iron railing belted the house beside him, like a bad waistcoat on a man carrying too much flesh. The railing had too many embellishments for his taste, but it looked clean, so he settled against it to wait. In the peninsula, one made up for the terrifying rush of thunder and blood with twenty times the waiting, so he was used to passing time. He took out his Horace.

He read without interruption for an hour or so, until a maid from one of the houses tried plying him with questions. He gave her a smile that made pink erupt in her cheeks. Losing courage, she scurried inside. Silly thing. She'd get into trouble if she wasn't more careful.

His legs grew stiff and his shoulder complained, but he kept his post, one eye on his book and one on the door of the house where Mrs. Morris lived. Occasionally he noticed the passers-by: a nursemaid towing a trio of fair-haired boys, and a kite big enough to fly away with at least one of them, two ladies confiding in the shade beneath their parasols, a grocer's man pushing a wheelbarrow with carrot tops sticking from beneath a ragged tarp. A natty looking tilbury rattled by, earning a longer look. If he could, he would buy one just that blue color.

Still no movement from the house. He shifted again, debating whether he ought to try knocking. Perhaps she didn't intend to go out today, though he couldn't for the life of him understand why one would choose to stay penned inside on a warm day like this. Drawing his flask from his pocket, he took a long swallow. His hopes lifted when a shiny carriage drawn by a nondescript pair of black horses rolled up, but it stopped in front of the house next door, which opened to admit a portly man in a striped coat, his old fashioned wig dusting his shoulders with hair powder. Alistair started forward as the door to her house finally opened, but again was disappointed. The woman who issued forth wasn't Mrs. Morris. She was a tall, bracket-faced woman buttoned into a sober pelisse and wearing dark gloves.

"Anna!" she called, and Alistair straightened from the railing.

Anna Morris stepped outside, almost a mirror image of the woman who must be her mother. Her gown was so plain she might have vanished into the brick work, her face hidden by a close fitting bonnet trimmed with a single wide ribbon in an uninspiring rust color. The low heeled boots she wore slapped against the steps as only sensible shoes can, nothing like the clipping of the pretty red heels she had worn the week before.

"Mrs. Morris," he called, hastening across the street, dodging a dust-covered landau in need of a wash. If he didn't move fast he would miss his chance. "Mrs. Morris!"

She heard him the second time and turned her head. Under the brim of her bonnet, that lovely mouth was almost invisible in her bleached face. Her eyes were twice the size he remembered. For a moment he thought she was about to faint. Her hand shot out to halt his approach, but then she seemed to recover, turning to her mother with a straightened spine.

"This is an old friend of Mr. Morris," she lied without blinking. "Well, sir, what brings you this morning?" There was nothing welcoming in her face or words—unsurprising, given their previous meetings. He'd expected disdain, but this wasn't that. It was fear.

"Have I come at a bad time?" he asked.

"You can see we are just going out," she said, tugging on her gloves, which was hardly necessary. The York tan fit as closely as her own skin.

"May I bear you company a little while? I hoped to speak with you." He turned his smile from Mrs. Morris to the mother. Her firm mouth softened and her eyes flicked anxiously to her daughter. Seeing his way now, Alistair addressed himself to the older woman. "I've been searching your daughter out for days."

"I must arrive at the church early to mark the attendance," the mother said, glancing from him to Anna. Alistair couldn't tell if it was his attempts to charm or her daughter's obstinate frown that swayed her, but he read in her eyes the instant she made her decision. "Anna, you can spare a moment. Why don't you walk with—"

"My name is Beaumaris," he said with a bow.

Anna Morris turned to her mother. "I thought you needed my help."

"I'll have it, if I need it," her mother said. "You won't be more than a few minutes behind me." Despite her sugar-glazed smile, the message to her daughter was still a command. Anna Morris scowled, but she did not protest. Her mother gave a satisfied nod. Opening her sunshade with a snap, she marched down the steps and into the street. Anna watched her depart with flinty eyes.

"I'm sorry to displease you," Alistair said, approaching and offering his arm. She ignored it, clasping her hands behind her back as she thumped reluctantly down the last two steps.

"If you were really sorry, you'd leave. I told you to stay away."

"Why? You didn't even know who I was. Whom were you expecting?"

Her eyes tightened. "I had no notion. At the masquerade you told me your name was Jasper Rushford. I didn't recognize Beaumaris, which is the name on your card and your letters."

Damn. He'd forgotten about that.

"Which one are you?" she asked. "Or have you a third name you keep for Sundays?"

"Beaumaris. But why should my letters scare you?" He hadn't written them to sound threatening. Only someone with a dire secret would read a threat in a courteous letter from a stranger.

"You're imagining," she snapped.

He wasn't, but he would leave it for now. Ahead, her mother's dark blue umbrella wove left and right, moving forward at twice their pace. Soon they would be well behind. Alistair stepped over a dip in the pavement where a puddle congealed, dark as ink. His mouth was dry and he'd been standing too long in the sun. It made his fingers feel tight and swollen. He was getting soft. The sun today was mild compared to the blistering heat of Spain.

Explanations first. "We were at a masquerade," Alistair said. "I didn't think you were telling the truth."

"No, I see honesty isn't at all the thing," she retorted.

"I've done badly," he acknowledged with a nod. "I mistook you for something quite different. I came to apologize."

She stopped and turned toward him, lifting her chin, ignoring the shop boy who skidded around them with a curse. "Whatever for? Apologies are unlikely to change my opinion of you, nor should you care whether I think ill of you or not. If you hadn't intruded on me, I wouldn't have thought of you at all. We are strangers."

"Who share one thing, at least—a grievance with Tom Bagshot. You lost him, and he waltzed away with my intended."

"Yes, I heard." Her lips twitched. "I didn't love him, so I have no reason to be grieved, merely offended that he preferred another. I admit I was upset that evening at the masquerade, but it wears off, I assure you."

"Thank you for the advice," he returned, just as sweetly.

"My pleasure. It's always gratifying to see the mighty humbled."

He grunted. They waited for a gap in the line of passing carriages and this time he took her arm instead of waiting for her to bestow it. Letting her step alone into a busy street would make him look bad, so she did not protest. Out loud anyway. Her hand was stiff.

"They don't draw you very well in the newspapers," she said. "I hadn't realized it was supposed to be you."

"I like to think I'm much better looking," he said, trying to make light of it.

She turned her head to look at him better, and her eyes were not kind. She ought to be softening by now. "Why are you apologizing? I wouldn't have known you'd lied about your name if you hadn't come."

His ankle teetered on the edge of a deep rut, reminding him of the need to mind his steps. Before he answered he looked at her. He'd been certain that night at the masquerade that she knew perfectly well the subtext of their conversation. Now that she'd been identified as a respectable, if déclassé widow, he wasn't so sure. Was she naive enough to have missed his rather brutal innuendo? Or was she taking revenge by playing him now, making him come out and admit it?

"I insulted you and mistook your character," he said, deciding to go with the truth.

"Oh? How, exactly?" she prompted.

She was baiting him, so there was no need to say it.

"Nothing complimentary," he said, hedging.

"I understood that at the time. You thought I wanted Tom for a protector, didn't you?"

Cornered, Alistair had to fight back a blush. It was uncomfortable, having their dance floor banter rehashed in a Hans Town street.

She laughed, but it was bitter. "You weren't that far wrong. I thought he would make me a tolerable husband, chiefly because he'd be a good protector. The duties aren't that dissimilar, you know."

"True. But one is sanctioned and one is not. I misjudged you. I can only offer my profound apologies."

"I'm afraid they are far from profound," she said.

Alistair grinned. Her ready comprehension didn't put him in any better light, but he was relieved all the same. "I'll try to do better. Let me rephrase. Will you forgive me and endeavor to forget my gross errors if I plead guilty to being a scoundrel-dog?"

She looked at him, then away, fastening her eyes on something in the distance. "I can't see that it matters. It is kind of you, I think, to offer me an apology. But I'm afraid I have little use for it."

A dismissal, clearly. They walked in silence for some time, then Alistair asked, "Does your frown have to do with me, or your brother-in-law?" She didn't seem to have been taken to the bosom of her husband's family, and now that he was dead, Alistair imagined the situation was fraught with difficulty. A good reason to be on the lookout for a husband like Tom Bagshot.

"Neither," she lied. "My mother thinks I will be cheered by doing good works, but I'm afraid the prospect of them only makes me gloomy." That explained her simple dress.

"It doesn't cheer you?"

"Not at all. I'm entirely selfish, though it is a worthy endeavor."

"What are you doing? Sewing for the poor?"

"Not today." She made a face. "Collecting for the Aldgate dispensary."

Aldgate was as a particularly insalubrious part of town, but he hadn't heard of a dispensary there. A wagon rumbled by, stirring up a cloud of dust. He nudged her clear of it, raising his hand to shield her face.

"No grazes," she said, looking at his fingers. "No bruises either. Remarkable, given the turn up I saw the other day."

"I'm a swift healer," he grinned. "But I have a few marks left. Just not where you can see."

She stiffened and withdrew her hand from his arm. "I don't know what you think you will gain by approaching me. I'm not interested in casual amours, and have no intention of inspecting your bruises."

"I didn't invite you to look," he countered.

"Didn't you?" she asked.

"No. I was only stating that they were there." But he shouldn't have mentioned them, not to a respectable lady he'd already offended. Usually he was more adroit.

Her stride quickened. "Don't be obtuse. I understand you perfectly well, but since I prefer plain speaking, I will tell you this: I am not to be imposed upon. Not by you, or anyone else. I won't fall for flattering smiles and pretty compliments."

"Have I given you any?"

She ignored him. "It doesn't need to be in what you say—"

"Mrs. Morris," he interrupted, reining in his temper. "You are a beautiful lady. I won't deny that. But there's a difference between admiring a painting and wanting to buy it. You assume too much."

Her lips pinched together and her chest rose, but he wasn't

done saying his piece. "I made a mistake and am honor bound to correct it. You said Tom Bagshot could have helped you. I wanted to find out why, because perhaps I might be able to assist you. I was rather an ass that evening, after all. That's all. No more. Finis."

"You've made yourself perfectly clear," she said, with a brittle smile. "So will I. I don't need your help."

"Just mine? Or have circumstances changed? Do you not need help at all?"

"If I did, I wouldn't turn to you," she said, stopping in front of the church on the street corner. "My mother is inside. Thank you for your escort. I wish you a good day." Without waiting for him to bow, she spun away and stalked off.

ANNA HASTENED over the flagstone path, her eyes fixed on the heavy chapel doors, her feelings as jumbled as her own bureau drawers. If she picked through the tangle she might find a reason to make sense of it all, but she doubted it. They were a magpie hoard: everything soiled, broken and cheap.

He had guessed the truth about her, right from the first. If she wasn't so angry, she'd be terrified. Instead of listening to his apologies she should have congratulated him on his perception. And if Captain Beaumaris could sense her secret in a three minute conversation at a masquerade, her problems were bigger than she thought. She'd never get Henry back.

She shivered, despite the sun pressing hot against her shoulders. Ignoring the greasy feeling in her middle that always accompanied these reflections, she ducked into the shadowy church without even glancing at the rose windows. Her face wore a trained smile, but she didn't trust it for more than an exchange of nods with the soberly dressed crowd inside. Her mother sat at a table, recording the names in a book in her precise hand. As she passed, Anna picked up one of the pamphlets stacked to the side.

"Ah-ah," her mother said, and Anna's hand halted in midair.

"This isn't included in my five pounds?" Giving her mother a look (which she ignored, naturally), Anna dug a shilling out of her purse. "I'll take three of them," she said.

Clutching her handful of papers, she found a seat on the far side of the room.

Today they were listening to Dr. Henry Clutterbuck, one of the physicians working at the Aldgate dispensary. Anna had nothing against the poor—her visits to the dispensary had shocked her more than she could say—but it depressed her that she was blue as megrim, when thousands of souls faced privation, disease and ignorance. Real problems. What was the matter with her?

Dr. Clutterbuck and the vicar were moving among the attendees—there were a good number gathered today. Her mother would be pleased. Knowing it would be some time before both the earnest and skeptical found their seats and the vicar and Dr. Clutterbuck began speaking, Anna glanced down at her pamphlets. She stopped after the first paragraph. Vaccination again. She was already convinced of the advantages conferred by the procedure, and though it seemed miraculous, she'd heard it discussed so often the topic was now only mildly interesting. Last month the pamphlets had been about phlebotomy. Anna was ashamed to admit it, but she'd read them over twice with ghoulish satisfaction. She'd been bled only a few times in her life, but it had been hard to muster the correct look of suffering, when all she wanted to do was watch and prod the creature on her arm. The fact that he—there must be female leeches of course, but Anna felt the male pronoun was more accurate—was disgusting did not make the animal any less interesting.

She turned the pamphlet over on her lap and glanced out the wavy glass of the arching windows. She ought to be cheered by the sunshine but all she could think of was how hot the sitting room at home would be by the time they returned. She would stay with her mother as long as possible. The old stone church never warmed much.

If Captain Beaumaris could peg her correctly after a single dance—she could ignore whatever had happened since to change his mind—her brother-in-law probably knew Henry was a cuckoo's egg. Her husband had known, she'd made sure of that. Even if Anthony hadn't confided in his brother, a man didn't usually go to the devil without a reason. Frederick had to suspect. He wasn't stupid. Sometimes she'd considered telling him the truth, but she knew it would make no difference. He hated her already and nothing would make him give up Henry. Not while he had all that money. She'd miscalculated terribly.

Anna clasped her hands tighter and firmed her lips against the sudden desire to cry. Someone tapped on her shoulder and she managed to compose her expression enough to greet Mrs. Longswill, who'd just taken the place on the pew beside her.

"How are you, my dear?"

"Well. How kind of you to ask." Only half attending, Anna brought out the required questions, learning that Mr. Longswill was again feeling poorly, that Mrs. Longswill had been terrified to vaccinate her family, but had trusted Edward Jenner, even with half the doctors in London calling him a fool. And now, years later, Dr. Clutterbuck said the same things, and wasn't she glad—so glad—she'd had it done to all of them.

"A great thing, my dear. A great thing, if we can get a lancet on every one of the poor. Of course so many resist the idea," said Mrs. Longswill. The plume of her bonnet was askew, swaying lopsidedly as she nodded.

"I don't think many of them can read the pamphlets," Anna said, looking down at the stack on Mrs. Longswill's lap.

"But they can listen. Hear the testimony of their betters. What more can they need?"

"Nothing, I'm sure. Will you assist with recruitment at the dispensary?"

Mrs. Longswill turned even more solemn. "My dear, I really think I must."

Much longer of this and she would crack. Mrs. Longswill was a good woman, a worthy soul, and all Anna could feel was a curdling self-pity. It blanketed her like a dark cloud, never mind the sun filling the windows.

"How is your boy?" Mrs. Longswill asked.

Anna nearly closed her eyes, but saved herself at the last moment. "Full of frisk. I took him to the park the other day and nearly toppled over from fatigue by the end of it."

The happy light in Mrs. Longswill's eyes would kill her if she didn't look away. "I think we should encourage them to get started, don't you?" Anna said and set her face to the front of the room, saying nothing until the vicar took his place.

SHE'D ALWAYS LIKED the vicar's gravelly voice and the way his white wig and clerical collar stood stark against his dark robes, but try as she would, she couldn't hold on to his words today. They slipped by her ears like pebbles through water, splashing and rippling, nothing more. Anna shifted on the hard bench, reflecting that at least the note writer had turned out to be him—the man from the park and the masquerade, who'd told her his name was Jasper Rushford. She liked Beaumaris better.

Her first thought on seeing that unfamiliar name, scrolling across his neat pasteboard card, had been much worse. She'd been reckless in choosing her lovers, very reckless, and it would be no more than she deserved if some man exposed her. Never mind that it was long ago. You couldn't wash that off with a splash of soap and water. Captain Beaumaris was insulting and a nuisance—luckily the nursemaid was blaming Henry's foul language on the footmen—but he wasn't dangerous to her.

Had he told her his Christian name? No, but it was written on his card. She cast her mind back. Alistair Beaumaris. He'd signed his letters in that style, closing with 'Yr obedient servant.' Well, she got the joke there now. The man was none of the three: not hers, not obedient, and certainly no one's servant. It hardly mattered. She wouldn't see him again. There would be no more elliptical notes to terrify her.

Anna paused, her eyes tracing the edge of a leafy shadow moving across the whitewashed north wall. Lovers didn't feel like the right word for those men. They might have used it for her, but she'd viewed them more as stud horses, chosen for convenience and a single purpose. She'd been all kinds of a fool, but she really should have taken better note of who they were—then she wouldn't have panicked upon receiving Beaumaris's card. Of course, at the time, she'd been so wild with rage at her husband, she hadn't really cared who she bedded—she only wanted them for the child they could give her, a child she could flaunt in Anthony's face.

That fit of temper should have cured her of all others, the same way a blistered chest drew phlegm from the lungs. There'd been a good pamphlet about that once.

She couldn't call those men lovers—not when she could hardly remember their faces. She hadn't needed that many. Four had been enough. They'd all been rather the same, save for the footman. Despite his lustiness, he had been sweet, smoothing her hair back from her face and looking at her with a steadiness that threatened to make her cry. Certainly he was the handsomest of the lot. Also the most tender, but in theory, as dangerous as the others. No lawyer in his right mind would represent her claim if the truth got out.

When she'd spied Captain Beaumaris's dark silhouette in the street today, fear had turned her innards to water and stolen the air from her chest. Relief followed once she saw his face, but he could have been one of the four. The footman, James, was still employed by Frederick. He'd never told, but who knew what the others might do if they ever turned up? Hopefully they'd forgotten, but she could never be sure. Thankfully, it had only been Beaumaris and his misplaced apologies this time. She couldn't afford any trouble.

If only she had resigned herself to her lot, accepted imprisonment in the country and behaved herself. She would have no secrets to hide then, only the continual shame of her husband's disgust. Of course, she never would have had Henry. She couldn't regret him. Even if she never got him back, she would still have those early moments—the elbows and knees jabbing from inside her swollen belly, a tight purple face and a feeble first cry. Warm milky skin and fuzzy down hair and a pulse beating on the soft crown of his head that she watched carefully, afraid his soul might spill out. Before tears could roll past her lashes, Anna sniffed, blinked and focused on the earnest face of Dr. Clutterbuck. No help there. Her eyes followed the arched roof heavenwards, tempting her with thoughts of lifted burdens and soaring wings, but the memory of her sins kept her mired to the earth. She was failing. She'd lost her son, and he was her heart—or what was left of it. She felt like she'd been bleeding since watching him skip up the stairs of her brother-in-law's house.

No doubt she deserved it.

6

A SAD TANGLE

ALISTAIR WAS NOT USED to being dismissed by women, particularly when he was exerting himself. Despite his recent failure with Sophy, he should have managed better with this one. Something was wrong with Mrs. Morris—his behavior at the masquerade and the park couldn't explain all of hers. No reason she should be afraid of him, and she'd looked terrified at first.

Ignoring the temptation to linger in the churchyard and confront her when she came out, he walked back to Mayfair, coating his boots with dust. Lacking a better plan, he decided to visit his aunt.

"My uncle in?" Alistair asked the butler, late in remembering that he owed an apology to Lord Fairchild. Admitting his mistake would be awkward and embarrassing, but his uncle would be relieved to know there was nothing untoward between Tom Bagshot and Anna Morris—so relieved, he probably wouldn't give Alistair the roasting he deserved.

Alistair could supply the taunts he'd earned himself.

Jenkins shook his head. "But Lady Fairchild is at home."

"Any other callers?" Alistair asked, glancing to the mirror as he removed his hat.

"Just yourself, sir."

That was bad. If his Aunt Georgiana was still being scorned by the ladies of London, it would be a long time before they cleared this cloud of scandal.

"I'll announce myself," Alistair said, heading for the stairs.

Before he reached the drawing room door, Lady Fairchild stepped into the hallway.

"William? Oh, Alistair. It's you." Her smile was too slippery to stay on her face. "Not too wretched, I hope?"

To anyone else, he would have given a light reply, something to do with the virtues of fortitude. It was a profound relief to give a weak smile instead. "I'm not faring too badly. It's been days since I've read the papers."

"I as well."

"I hope you don't mind me intruding today."

"Not at all. I'm more likely to fall upon your neck with grati-tude. Too much of my own company." She reached out and took his hand. "I was afraid you wouldn't want to see us anymore."

"I'm here for a few days yet," he said. "You won't be able to avoid me."

Her eyes sharpened. "Just a few days? Have you been recalled to the peninsula?"

"It isn't so bad." This was a patent lie, and one his aunt didn't believe for a moment. She just waited in the way that adults do for children to confess the truth.

"How can you tell?" he asked. He'd said nothing to her—or to anyone—of his reluctance to return to his regiment.

"I'm sure you acquit yourself honorably, but I never thought the army a good choice for you." Warned by footsteps coming from the other end of the hallway, she motioned him into the drawing room. "Come inside. The maids don't need to hear."

Alistair walked to the far wall, pretending to study the portrait of his cousin Henrietta. The artist hadn't flattered her—

Henrietta didn't need it. But the painting couldn't turn his mind from his aunt's words. "You don't think I'm fit for it?"

"Of course I do!" she protested, realizing she had stung him. "You're much too fine for it. I wouldn't want a son of mine in such danger."

"You weren't blessed with a superfluity of them," he said, turning. She'd arranged herself neatly on the sofa, but he didn't sit down.

"You mustn't feel that way," she said. "We can think of something. Charlotte Grayson isn't engaged yet. Or Eliza Wrexham."

"I wish you wouldn't. One foray is enough for me this year. I'm not desperate," he said.

She considered this. "Too much speed would look ill, but you're running out of time. And who knows if next year you'll be given leave?"

Or be alive to take it? But it didn't help to think along those lines. "I expect I shall be leaving London within a fortnight. Won't be so bad," he said. "I won't have to avoid looking in the newspapers." It took three weeks or more for London news to reach Spain.

"When were you recalled?" Aunt Georgiana asked, a crease between her brows.

Alistair reached into his pocket, drawing out the letter from his Colonel—it was marking his place in Horace. He passed it to his aunt. She scanned it, returning it to him with a steady enough hand, but pained eyes.

"I don't know this surgeon. Thought I'd see him tomorrow," Alistair said. "No point in putting the thing off."

"Will he say you are fit?"

"I don't see why not." The lingering weakness in his shoulder he could blame on the fistfight with Jasper. "I'll be fine," he said, for the benefit of his aunt, who scowled at a flower that had fallen from the vase and lay browning on the table. She pinched it up and rolled it between her fingers.

"Is that why you came? To tell me?"

"Actually, I was hoping to ply you with questions. May I?" Anna Morris was something of a riddle. If he wanted answers, he must lose no more time.

"What about?"

"Oh, scandal, of course," he said, pleased to see her expression going from grave to interested. "I think it's high time we started talking about other people's instead of our own."

She nodded assent and though she was plainly curious, she didn't let him begin straight off, ringing for tea first and motioning him to take a seat beside her on the sofa. While he settled himself she arranged her hands prettily in her lap, tilting her head to a confiding angle. He could almost see the girl she had once been, sitting down to whisper over the failings of others —a wickedly enjoyable pastime for the young and blameless, and a comforting respite, even for them. They waited for the tray to come up, talking nothing but nothings as Aunt Georgiana poured out the tea and offered him a dish of confits that she herself ignored, since it was fashionable for ladies to content themselves with bread and butter. He only took one raisin tart, knowing his stomach had a limited tolerance for things composed primarily of butter, sugar and cream.

"I'm still waiting for your questions," she said, peering at him over the gilded rim of her cup.

"I was only waiting for leave to begin," he said. "You will think them strange."

"Dear boy. You know our family. I ceased long ago to think anything strange."

He doubted the truth of that—Aunt Georgiana had a very precise sense of what was acceptable and what was not—but plunged ahead nevertheless. "What do you know about the Morrises? The Warwickshire ones."

She frowned for a moment, setting down her cup. "Anthony

Morris died some years ago—'09 I think. It was after you wrote us about Corunna."

He didn't care to remember that battle, or the subsequent retreat, so he kept his face still and waited for his aunt to continue.

"He was what your father terms a loose screw."

Alistair snorted. "If my father calls him that, he must have been loose indeed."

"Yes, one gathers they had difficulties. His father lost heavily in a canal scheme about twenty years ago and I think the family only managed to limp along since. It didn't look as if they'd be able to bring out the daughter at all."

"Oh?" Without realizing, Alistair took another tart.

"They did in the end, of course. Five or six years ago it was. Lucinda—I think that was her name—did quite well. Married someone from the north. Quite a bit older, as I recall, but she wasn't especially handsome. Burlington? Beauchamp? I can't recall his name. Haven't seen either since the marriage, but the rest of the Morrises come to London every year."

"I gather the family succeeded in putting their difficulties behind them."

"One assumes so."

"How?"

"The usual way." She lowered her voice. "Marrying into money. I think they said it came from the colonies. Furs and timber. Never saw her though, so she must have been dreadful. Anthony Morris died of course, but there was a child, so the money and estate passed to him. Frederick Morris, Anthony's younger brother looks to be holding the reins now."

"Until the child is of age?"

"One assumes so."

"You know nothing of Mrs. Morris?"

"Why should I? The veriest nobody. I may have heard she was tolerable to look upon, nothing more."

Alistair flattened the crumbs of pastry littering his plate with the back of his fork. "I've seen her." He smiled at his aunt. "She's a good deal better than that."

Lady Fairchild shook her head. "My dear boy, she'd do you no good at all. I expect her money is tied to Morris's child. You wouldn't want that, pretty face or no."

"Who said I was interested?"

"You mentioned her. That means you've thought it, if only for a moment. If she's as lovely as you say, no doubt you couldn't help it, but man was blessed with reason for a purpose. I'm in favor of any course that sees you respectably established, but she isn't it."

"You're very definite," Alistair said.

"Isn't that why you came to me? I know what I'm about."

Nine times out of ten, she did, but he couldn't help remembering how they'd both erred with Sophy. But on that point, he suspected it was best to keep his own counsel.

WILLIAM RUSHFORD, Lord Fairchild, left his club in an unhappy mood. An hour in his favorite chair, deep in a brown study, hadn't made him better, or eased his mind about the conversation he needed to have with his wife. One of his children was already lost to him—Julius, more baby than boy, resting beneath the patch of sod that had covered him nearly nineteen years. Sophy had come to him late, after the death of her mother—not his wife. It didn't feel like Sophy had ever belonged to him, not until recently. And now she had flown.

This loss was different than the bewildering pain after Julius died that had felled both him and his wife—a wound this time, not an amputation—but it still pained him. He should have done so many things differently.

Another glass of your usual drink, he thought, meaning to

console himself. He was used to living with regret. But it would be easier to swallow this dose if he knew what he was supposed to do about his wife. Lately it had been borne upon him that Georgiana needed care and—more strangely still—that he wanted to provide it. It was an impulse he could hardly remember feeling throughout the twenty-six years of their marriage, which was probably why he had no idea how it should be done. Chances were she wouldn't let him, but he wanted to try.

It wasn't far from the club to his townhouse, a swift drive in his curricle. He let himself inside and quietly made his way upstairs, thinking. He and Georgiana weren't close, but that didn't mean they didn't know each other. You could afford to be careless among friends; enemies you needed to know better than your own self. Perhaps that was why his wife's inexplicable behavior lately was so unnerving. For all he knew, she was preparing to deliver the coup de grace.

He snorted, stripping off his gloves with unnecessary emphasis. This wasn't a blind; Georgiana was helpless and adrift. He had never seen her like this, not when he took Sophy into their home (cold compliance, but she took her pound of flesh), not even when Julius died (paralyzing grief, then attacks, swift and sharp-clawed). He owed her something. She and Sophy had grown close. She had been better to his bastard than he had any right to expect. But Sophy had fled and married her merchant, thumbing her nose at them.

He was still angry, but guilt was reasserting itself. If he studied this sad mess long enough he knew where to lay the blame: he was a devil of a father and a worse husband. Given their history, Georgiana was unlikely to accept any help he offered, but he felt he must try, if only to ease his conscience. So instead of disappearing into his library and the comforting world of the racing form book, he trudged into the drawing room. She was alone, with her embroidery.

"Yes?" she said, looking up, her needle poised in the air like a fencer's sword.

He sat before he spoke, knowing he'd persist longer if it was harder to retreat. "How are you?" he asked, looking at her over his steepled fingers.

The question should have disconcerted her. He never made inquiries like this. "My days are a little flat," she admitted. "There is not much to do."

"You have your sewing," he said, glancing at her embroidery.

"Yes. I always do." She frowned at the piece in her lap. If he troubled himself to discover how many cushions and seat covers and whatever-the-hell things she'd stitched over the years, he expected the total would be prodigious. He knew she was skilled —there was a frightening perfection in most things she did. But she never smiled, never paused to admire her work.

"Do you enjoy it?"

"Not even a little," she said. Her needle pierced the silk with a barely audible puff, then her wrist, fingers and arm floated up, trailing a coral-colored thread that pulled through the cloth with a sound like a long, deep breath. He watched her make two more stitches. She had a way of moving that made the work seem calming, almost meditative, but a sharp furrow stood between her brows.

"Why do it then?"

A muscle in her cheek twitched. She opened her mouth, started to speak, but couldn't finish the word. Whatever she had been about to say died on her tongue. She tilted her head, tried again, but he'd had enough. She had no reason.

"You should stop." Before she could counter his demand with a caustic reply, he pushed himself out of his chair. She flinched as he leaned over her, but made no move to resist when he plucked the embroidery frame from her nerveless fingers. Without noticing the design, he raised it, then cracked it over his knee. The frame splintered.

"Have you lost your senses?" she demanded.

"Probably." Three strides brought him to the fireplace, but his hand halted above the screen. It was too warm a day for a fire. No matter. He would tear up the thing.

His first tug failed. He tried again. A third time. Swore.

A nervous giggle escaped her before she could clap her fingers to her mouth.

"Just what is this?" he grunted, failing again. The square of cloth was too strong to tear, reinforced as it was by her stitching.

"A footstool cover."

"Not any longer." Before she could stop him, he snatched an evil looking pair of scissors from the basket beside her.

"Don't," she said, reaching for his arm.

"Have you changed your mind? Do you like it?"

"What else am I to do?"

It was the desperation in her eyes that decided him. "Anything you like," he said, opening the scissors. His fingers were too large to fit into the handles further than his first knuckles, but despite his awkward hacking the blades devoured the cloth, snipping through the wadded folds and littering arrow shaped bits onto the carpet. Georgiana stared at him, her hands stuck to the arms of her chair. "I see no reason why you shouldn't do anything you please. You could travel. Learn to paint. Form a dramatic society. Write a novel—clever or disgusting, whatever you choose." He swallowed. "Take a lover. Or join the Quakers. Anything, if it makes you happy." He dropped his hands to his sides, his aching thumb still trapped in the scissors.

She swallowed.

"I miss her too," he said. "Let's leave." Until London recovered from the news, neither of them could be happy here. When he went riding he missed Sophy, and he suspected the parties were no better for his wife. Jasper wasn't speaking to either of them, and though their daughter Henrietta was trying to be diplomatic, she was too occupied with her young children to give her mother more than occasional company.

"Together?" Georgiana asked. "Just what do you think we would we do?"

His heart, which had been thumping so wildly, turned to a lump of lead. On the eve of Sophy's desertion he had promised his wife he wouldn't let her be lonely. He hadn't been thinking. Outside of plans for Sophy, they hadn't had a real conversation all year—and for a good number of years before that.

Defeated, but still unwilling to desert the field, he slumped into his chair, staring at the fragments of silk scattered between them. He couldn't imagine how many hours she had spent, stitching flowers or fruit or birds. "You deserve to be happy," he said.

On her second attempt, she managed to speak. "I find it is very seldom that people get what they deserve."

He felt the barb, but he didn't flinch. "I'm sorry. You know I tried to keep her."

"I can't speak of it," she said, raising a warning hand. This was her usual response to disappointment and conflict, but it was troubling him more and more. Beneath her disarranged flounce —she had started in her seat when he seized her embroidery— she was wearing two different colored stockings, one white, one the palest blush. She did not make mistakes like that. Ever. The lines around her eyes made her look tired, and she seemed ready to break at the lightest touch.

"Let me take you away," he said without thinking. "We'll go to Brighton."

Her hand fell. "You can't be serious," she said, failing to hold back a bitter laugh.

"Of course I'm serious. Forget Sophy. Forget everything. Let's go away." Maybe it would be miserable. He hadn't travelled with her for twenty years. She refused to admit that she got sick in carriages. In fact, she refused to get sick, mastering her stomach by sheer will. It made her about as friendly as a basilisk. But perhaps this trip would be different. He would be patient and they could travel slowly. Away from town, she could think of other things—the sun on the sea, the breezes that would play with her curls and pull at her skirts. She was still as slim as a girl. If she smiled . . .

"I don't want to go to Brighton," she said.

"What do you want?"

She looked at him with desolate eyes. "I don't know. I don't want to sew. I don't want to eat. Or sleep. Or walk, or drive, or—or see people. I don't want to go to Mrs. Fanshawe's ball and I don't want to buy a bonnet to match my new pelisse."

"What about furs?" he asked, but she only shuddered. Most unlike her.

"I can't have what I want. The rest is nothing," she said, her wrist turning restlessly in her lap.

"Would you like companionship?" he asked, looking down at his hands.

She laughed, short and sharp. "And what would we say to each other, pray? Five minutes and we would use up every civil comment we had."

He swallowed. "You wouldn't necessarily have to choose me. Though I would be honored if you did," he added.

She looked at him, a crease forming between her brows. "No," she said, shaking her head. "No." She rose from her chair.

"Where are you going?" he asked, before she could escape through the door.

"To count the household linen," she said.

William sighed. She had done that just last week.

7

HIDDEN REGRETS

It was early in the evening, and Lady Fairchild found herself in Sophy's empty bed chamber. Again.

Sophy's brushes were missing, and her pearls—trinkets, only —but everything else was set out in a line on the dressing table: the perfume they had bought together, a painted fan, a new pair of gloves. The day she left, there had been a letter too.

I cannot marry him. I am sorry.

She had said nothing more.

Regrets were mawkish and beneath contempt. Lady Fairchild despised herself for sitting here, for comparing this dreary week to the way it should have been. Planning flowers for the wedding, and a menu for the breakfast afterward. Purchasing bride clothes. Perhaps a drive out to Barham to look over the house. Letters arriving, a sheaf of them, bearing the congratulations of family and friends. She and Sophy, their heads bent together, side by side.

Behind the glazed exterior, Lady Fairchild's face threatened to crumple, so she sniffed and straightened the fan so it was at right angles to the edge of the dressing table.

Bagshot hated her, she was certain of that. Sophy was young and trusting; whether he deserved it or not, Bagshot was first in her affections. And now there was a knot of worry in her brow that was too tight to unpick. Better to avoid looking in the mirror.

She swept across the room to the window, but the rustle of silk as she moved was no longer comforting. Lady Fairchild had always taken pride in her bearing, in the arrangement of her tapered fingers, in the gleam of her hair and her clothes. She had arranged Sophy's debut and Alistair's proposal as carefully as an artist's tableaux. She'd put herself into the scene—a confidante, a friend, a companion. Not the protagonist, but someone important to the happiness of all. It wasn't a lofty part, but she wouldn't have minded. Sophy would need her, and they would be close.

It was a sad thing to discover, even when you'd cast yourself in a supporting role, that you weren't needed at all.

Lady Fairchild moved the curtain aside with a finger to peer into the street. She had no interest in the goings-on below, but she was tired of looking at the things Sophy had left behind. She may as well tuck herself away too, with the slippers and riding habits and gowns. She did not wish to go out, but she ought to go somewhere this evening. One had to support appearances. Talk would die down eventually, and she would continue on as before, entertaining, going to the theatre, viewing the newest spectacle, defining the mode. It was a bleak prospect. If she were not doing those things, someone else would. No one would notice the difference.

As she let the curtain fall, her eyes dropped to the window sill, where a blue book sat propped against the window frame. She picked it up, noting the title with surprise. Sophy was an adequate student, but it was unlike her to read a book of sermons. Frowning, she flipped open the cover and thumbed through the pages.

This was no sermon, she realized, her eyes falling on familiar words. This was a description of the Marchese de Montferrat! Lady Fairchild stopped reading. She examined the cover again and the frontispiece. Sure enough, this sedate cover concealed the first volume of *The Orphan of the Rhine*. The cuts were scarcely noticeable, the new endpapers pasted in with niceness and precision. Only a careful eye could see these were not the original pages. And someone expecting a treatise on the sacraments.

Lady Fairchild snapped the book shut—she'd read this one already, and knew the fate of Julie and her children. She also knew how good Henrietta was with scissors and a glue pot. The only question was how many more proscribed books Henrietta had sent Sophy's way. With a swiftness her servants learned to fear, Lady Fairchild's eyes darted to the bureau. The next moment she was lifting out two more books from beneath a pile of gloves.

Hmmmn. Volume two of *The Orphan of the Rhine* looked unread, but there was a letter marking a place in *Lady of the Lake*.

No wonder Sophy had run away, with her mind full of this sort of romantic fudge. Lady Fairchild intended to have a few words with Henrietta. Without hesitating, she pulled out the letter. On the outside at least, it was addressed to Betty, Sophy's former maid. The inside was another matter entirely. It read:

Dear Sophy,

I saw you and your mother driving in the park—alas your yellow sunshade told me you did not need to be rescued. I'm not sure exactly how I would have accomplished it, with myself on foot and you in your carriage. Also, your mother seems a formidable lady. I expect if she looked at me, she'd know at a glance if I'd said my prayers and cleaned my teeth. One wonders how you honed your propensity for mischief. Don't take that as a criticism. I like that about you.

I will remind you that formidable or no, I am no coward, and ask again to have the honor of making your mother's acquaintance—no, don't get that pained look. I've asked once, and will hold my piece now on that head. Until tomorrow. After all, it is persistence that lets wind and water shape the hardest stone.

Thank you for your compliments—I despise my quizzing glass a little less, now that I know you favor it. I only like that it allows me to send messages to you. Here's a new one: if I hurl the thing into your box at the opera tonight, it means I like the production. Since I have no expectation of enjoyment, you should be safe.

Unless I spend the evening looking at you. Is that allowed? Never mind. I shall do it anyway, with or without your permission.

Your devoted,

Tom

Censoriousness, outrage, chagrin—these emotions vanished by the time Georgiana reached the last paragraph. When she set down the letter, she almost felt envious. She searched her memory, trying to find a letter like this addressed to her. She couldn't. She remembered Sophy chuckling over letters from Henrietta and Jasper, sometimes reading aloud the funniest bits. The letters she received from her son and daughter were recitals of facts in Henrietta's case, and polite taunts in Jasper's. More than once, she'd fought the desire to crumple his letters. One could—and did—occasionally answer in kind, but it was hard to best him. Impossible, really, shielded as he was by indifference.

And the letters she exchanged with her husband . . . well, when they did write, it was usually through the medium of his secretary.

Please inform my husband that I will stay a week longer with Lady March . . . .

Lord Fairchild bids me write that he will return from Scotland the second week of November ...

She could no longer say with certainty why things had gone so wrong. Other husbands took mistresses, other couples lost children. It didn't always make them hate each other. She and William had been at war so long, neither of them knew how to sue for peace.

Wearily, she replaced the letter and the book, closing the drawer. She had to go out this evening, or people would laugh even more. Sophy wasn't her daughter. No doubt people expected her to shrug off both the girl and her mésalliance. Never mind that she could not. She cared horribly for Sophy, her only willing companion, and felt her absence like an ache in her joints.

She would go to the theatre tonight and force herself to sit through one act. Alistair had offered to escort her, knowing she couldn't depend on William or Jasper. She was about as eager for the excursion as she would be for a purge—a horrid business, but necessary sometimes to maintain one's figure. Hairdressers, slimming diets, nail brushes, silk and lace and subtle cosmetics: with their help, she looked like a different species than the sharp-boned gutter trash that littered London's streets. But she knew hunger too—it was a terrible thing, a hopeless, desperate craving. It consumed thought, destroyed every other comfort, leaving one with nothing but want—and not all kinds could be answered with food.

～

IT WAS A SAD THING, Lord Fairchild thought, when a man had to bribe his servants to obtain news of his wife.

"Nothing ails her, my lord, though it's plain to see she's lonely without the young miss," Dawson, his wife's maid, reported reluctantly. It had taken persuasion and a considerable sum to convince her to keep him informed about her mistress, and even then, she scowled at him like he was an unscrupulous ruffian. She found the arrangement as distasteful as he.

"You could discover this yourself, sir. All you would have to do is ask her. Lady Fairchild has never made a habit of confiding to me."

"But she complains about me, yes?"

Dawson glanced down, her frown deepening. "Not lately. And why not, is what I'd like to know!"

He couldn't help a laugh, but he sobered quickly. "I'd like to know why too." He ignored Dawson's disgusted snort. "She goes to the theatre tonight?"

Dawson nodded.

"Who escorts her?" he asked with studied unconcern.

"Captain Beaumaris."

Some of his tension left. He took out the promised pound note and placed it on the dressing table.

"She's dining at home tonight," Dawson admitted, compelled to full disclosure by the money resting between them. She didn't pick it up.

"Unfortunately, I am not," William said. Pity, but he was expected at a dinner with Sir Samuel Romilly to discuss his latest bill. William didn't support the Whigs in all their endeavors, but he agreed with Romilly that something had to be done for the hordes of injured soldiers and sailors. Currently, unless they had a written pass, if they were caught begging it was a capital offense. No, Romilly and his bill could not be put off, but with any luck, he could meet Georgiana at the theatre.

"Thank you, Dawson." He left before the words held back by her bitten lips escaped her. Dawson's loyalty was well only to a point; if she spoke out of turn, he would have to dismiss her and he really didn't need any more reasons to anger his wife.

. . .

WILLIAM ESCAPED the after-dinner political debate early, knowing he wouldn't be missed. After voicing his support for Romilly's bill, he'd said little and his attention had wandered. No one questioned his excuses as he departed.

He'd left no instructions for his coachman, being unsure what hour he would be free to leave for the theatre. It would only take him a quarter of an hour to walk from Russell Square to Covent Garden, so he engaged a link boy to light his way. The streets were insalubrious, but so were hackneys, and at least he wouldn't have to sit, waiting for his hired coach to advance through the press of carriages choking the street in front of the theatre.

The skinny, tow-headed boy holding the light was ragged and grimy, but he owned a pair of shoes. He chattered incessantly as they crossed the square and turned down Drury Lane, undeterred by William's rare, one word responses. He was a resourceful scamp, offering to fetch a whore if William liked, or show him the best flash houses.

"Just take me to the theatre," William said, glancing over his shoulder, lest the boy be drawing him into an ambush. No one seemed to be trailing them, but best to keep a sharp eye out.

Under the first floor overhang of a building clad in grimy timbers and plaster, a woman minding a tea wagon thrust a cup in his way. He darted by, careful not to touch her. No good if he arrived at the theatre with smudges of goodness knows what on his clothes. The garbled cries that followed him were indecipherable. He knew without looking that the tea seller had a mangle mouth of black, peg-like teeth. Though not an especially fastidious man, he shuddered at the thought of swallowing tea sold by such a creature. Probably wasn't tea at all—just old leaves bought from kitchens like his own and dyed black again.

"Almost there, me lord," panted his little street sprite. The boy had to take two steps for every one of William's, but he never flagged, hopping over ruts and puddles of slops like a small bird.

The market was closed, the stalls cleared away. Orange sellers lingered on, selling fruit and flesh. The link boy waved at a flock of boys busy leaping and turning cartwheels in hopes of winning a chance coin. William kept his purse shut. Encouraging the children's antics would only lead to broken limbs and carriage accidents. His guide's face fell just a little as they passed—no doubt he was paid a portion of any take that came from the men he led by. On Bow Street, the Royal Opera House loomed on his right, gleaming in the smoky dark. It was still new, only a few years old, the last one having been burned in a fire.

He paid the boy, who'd slowed his patter, interspersing it with muttered comments since William had neglected to bestow largesse on the lad's acrobatic friends. The offered coin redeemed him. In the blink of an eye, the boy snatched it and darted away, blessing William loud enough for all to hear.

Share if you want, but better to save for your next pair of shoes.

The second act was well begun when William entered his box. It was empty. Disappointed, William deposited himself in a chair —a welcome relief after the hurly burly in the streets outside. True, it carried on in the theatre too, but up here he didn't have to smell it quite so strongly. He could sit back and enjoy the drama on stage, though the scenes played among the spectators were often more amusing than the show. Even the best actors were occasionally upstaged by the crowd, especially those along fop's alley, where dandies and still more whores strutted up and down between the rows of benches. The women parading below were better packaged than the ones outside, but still not as brilliantly plumed as the high fliers perched in the boxes, trying to look like Quality. Of course, the Quality had their own drama, too. If he wasn't careful, he and Georgiana might be it.

Where was she, though? The heat from the crowd in the pit, the candles, and the oil lamps made it stuffy, even in his almost empty box. At least when Georgiana arrived, she'd be carrying a fan. It was always best to seat yourself next to a female for that reason, if for nothing else.

The second act ended and the curtain fell, but he resisted the urge to wander during the interval, though the performing dogs on stage did not interest him. Two of his friends stopped by to exchange brief greetings and then Jasper appeared, coming up from the pit, looking a little worse for wear.

"Here? Alone? Father, what is the world coming to?"

"I expect your mother will arrive shortly."

"And you came to see her. How charming. I'm touched."

"In the upper works, perhaps."

Jasper grinned, but it lasted only a moment. "I almost think I should help you home and call for the doctor. You're not getting caught in her web, are you?"

William sent his son a warning look.

"A harmless inquiry. I like to know the lay of the land before I venture into it," Jasper said, raising his hands appeasingly.

"You haven't come to the house since Sophy left."

"No, I haven't come by since the wedding. I thought I should give you and mama time to reconsider your decision."

A muscle jumped in William's cheek. "She's made her bed—"

"And as Alistair so kindly reminded me, she's probably lying in it. Give over, father. She's happy. Be happy for her."

William glanced at the dog twisting through hoops on the stage, then looked back at his son. "I'd like to. But I worry. I know nothing of her husband. And your mother—"

"Yes, she's known to hold a grudge, but that needn't stop you from apologizing. You shouldn't have done that to Sophy."

William hesitated. He wanted to, but knew Georgiana would see it as another betrayal. He couldn't afford that. And if Jasper learned he was trying to smooth things over with his wife—well, Jasper would laugh first, then tell his friends, and next thing he knew they'd be wagering on it in the club's betting book. That would be considerably off-putting, never mind the fire and brimstone that would descend on him if Georgiana ever found out.

No, matters between him and his wife were none of his son's concern.

Jasper liked to pretend his mother was incapable of feeling, but William knew better. She couldn't have hated him this many years if she hadn't a heart to wound. More fool him, for injuring her so deeply. But she was lonely since Sophy's defection and there was a chance, however slight, that she might be vulnerable enough to turn to him.

"Why are you here?" he asked Jasper.

"An actress. She's playing Lydia. Chestnut curls and lovely elbows."

"I didn't notice," Lord Fairchild said.

"Pity. Well, mostly it's just a game to cut out Protheroe. I don't really want to catch her so much as prevent him from doing it. Boz bet me a monkey I couldn't."

William looked at his son with growing irritation. Jasper had never lost his head over anyone or anything, or showed any sign of possessing a serious nature. His affection for his sisters might be deeper than the desultory interest he affected for appearances, but even then . . . he was indolent all the way through. William almost wished his son had a blazing infatuation for this actress, instead of a merely sporting interest—it would change him from this slippery creature into something human.

There was motion at the back of the box. William turned his head. His wife had arrived at last. Her hand was on Alistair's arm, a smile frozen to her lips. His presence wasn't expected, or welcome, apparently.

Both he and Jasper rose and bowed.

"Good evening," William said, stretching out his hand. "I'd hoped to find you here this evening." He must begin as he meant to go on if there was to be any hope of peace between them. She didn't refuse her hand, but it took just a moment too long for her to bestow it, enough that any interested watchers would see her reluctance.

She's just saving face, he told himself. Things would go better in private.

"Pouring balm into my cousin's wounds?" Jasper asked her. "Or has he been attending to yours? I hear an injury to one's vanity can be crippling."

Ignoring sharp looks from both his parents, Jasper made to leave, but Georgiana stopped him with a question. "Do you hear from Sophy?"

"Yes."

"How is she?"

Jasper's face turned colder still. "Ask her yourself." Bowing once more, he exited the box.

In the loud silence that followed, William quickly settled Georgiana in the chair at his side before she could think to resist. No doubt she had many friends who would be glad to offer her a seat for the remainder of the evening—a ploy she had used before, though not for a good many years. Still, William wasn't going to take unnecessary risks.

Alistair took the chair on Georgiana's left. "A pleasant surprise to find you here, uncle." He waited for an answering nod before continuing, more slowly than before. "Jasper mentioned in my hearing that Mrs. Bagshot was doing well."

It took a moment for William to realize that by Mrs. Bagshot, Alistair meant Sophy. It sounded utterly wrong.

"What a dreadful name," Georgiana shuddered, apparently feeling the same.

Alistair gave him a guarded look. "I've looked in to that matter we recently discussed. It appears I was mistaken in my reading of Bagshot's character. The connection I thought was unsavory appears to be entirely innocuous."

Georgiana looked curious, but William wasn't about to go into that conversation here. "I'm glad of it." One less worry—a significant one—but he still had many.

They sat in paralyzed silence for some time, pretending to

watch the stage. The next act began, but as none of them knew who any of the characters were, or what the preceding action had been, it was more labour than it was worth to reconstruct the tangled story. The types were there: a villain, a foolish maiden, a pair of vulgar comics—he thought they were supposed to be husband and wife, but couldn't say for certain.

"I'm ready to go home," Georgiana said, "I don't feel up to waiting for the farce."

"I'll join you," William said, rising.

She paused, her fan halfway into her reticule.

"I left no instructions for my coachman," he added. "If I don't go with you, I'll have to take a hackney."

Acquiescing with a faint lift of her shoulder, she followed Alistair from the box, William behind. Inside the carriage, she and Alistair kept up a gossipy conversation about one Frederick Morris, whom she had happened to see across the theatre. He seemed an unpleasant fellow, from their talk. They dropped Alistair at his family's townhouse, where he thanked them for the evening and the convivial company, managing not to sound sarcastic. "Do you ride tomorrow, sir?" he asked.

"I'm not certain. Probably."

"I'll hope to see you in the park," Alistair said, and turned away.

The footman shut the door with a snap and the carriage shrank to half its size.

"Am I crowding you?" he couldn't help asking.

"A little," she said, so he moved to the seat opposite. A regrettable move, but it did thin the air that had congealed around them.

"Why the interest in Frederick Morris?" he asked.

"I'm not certain," she said. "Alistair was curious about him." She confided nothing more.

"You look lovely this evening," he ventured.

"Thank you."

They turned the corner—not quickly, but she reached for the strap nonetheless.

"Sophy would have liked the play," he said.

"Yes, she would." Georgiana turned her head to the window, though it was too dark to see anything. The small lantern inside reflected her face off the glass back to him. Her expression was familiar—unhappy.

"Do you ever think," he began slowly, "that we may have been wrong?"

"I don't think about it," she lied, and set to work straightening her long evening gloves. Her cloak fell open as she moved. Beneath its dark velvet, the silk folds of her gown shone in the dim light.

"I'm considering the idea," he admitted. "Not that it's a new one. I have been wrong so many times before." He watched her, hoping she'd take the offered opening.

"Everyone makes mistakes," she said.

"Georgy." She didn't frown at the use of his old nickname, so he went on. "You know what I mean."

"It's an easy thing to say, when it comes too late."

His throat tightened. "Is it?"

She didn't answer, just knotted her fingers together. The carriage halted. He'd been leaning forward, but the sudden stop swung him back into the padded seat. He heard the footman jump down onto the pavement.

"Not just yet," he called. "Drive us round Grosvenor Square and back." That would give him a little more time. He'd need it, he realized, countering Georgiana's outraged stare.

"Do you have any idea what they might think?"

"Not particularly. I don't propose to care either. I expect they think we have something to say to each other."

"I don't know why. We never do." The carriage swayed as the footman climbed into his seat. Georgiana's hand found the strap again.

"It has often been borne on me, over the years, that I haven't been the husband you might have wished."

She snorted. Good. He was getting somewhere. She might be preparing to verbally eviscerate him, but at least she wasn't doing it yet.

"I would like to change that," he finished.

They rolled on in silence. "I don't know what I'm supposed to say," she said at last.

"Whatever you like," he encouraged. Just not some polite nothing, for God's sake. Form had always been one of her strongest weapons. "The children are gone. It's just the two of us now. If we don't try, think how hellish it will be."

She flinched, and he knew he should have chosen the word wretched instead.

"What makes you think," she said carefully, "that it hasn't been hellish for me already?"

Her thrust went home, sliding right through him. He grappled for words, knowing it was too late for a defensive parry. "You haven't seemed unhappy. Until recently, I mean."

"Because I had Sophy." Her voice turned reedy, her control as crumbly as a fragment of chalk. Facing the elopement was hard for them both, but Georgiana's grief only grew stronger as the days passed. "I thought she and I—I thought she cared."

"I'm sure she does. Much more than she ever cared for me." It was the truth. Only recently had he found a way past Sophy's guard. He'd been watching Sophy and Georgiana with their heads bent together, planning wardrobes and dinners and goodness knows what else for years.

"She didn't care enough," Georgiana said. He had no answer for that. It was true. She'd chosen Bagshot in the face of both their displeasure.

He leaned forward, his hands clasped together in the space between them, his elbows on his knees. "Perhaps, in time—"

"Don't. Just don't," she said. From under her hood, she sent him a freezing glare. "I don't know why you trouble yourself. Surely it can't be that hard to buy congenial company."

He reminded himself he deserved that. "Don't want it," he said. "I only want yours. Congenial, or otherwise."

"Really," she said, her face skeptical.

"Why don't you take me on trial?"

She wasn't smiling, but the sound that slipped out might have been a laugh. "Of all the—we are already married. I can't get rid of you, which I've often found a great pity." She sobered. "I can't refuse you either."

"Haven't you, though? For years and years?"

"You haven't asked," she countered.

"I am now."

She let out a shaky breath. "I have to think about it."

William leaned back in his seat. "Do." And for the remainder of the drive, he rested his eyes upon her. He felt it might be a good sign, the way she fled into the house.

8

STALKING AND WALKING

THERE WAS no harm indulging a little curiosity, Alistair decided the next morning. He was awake anyway.

"No, not riding dress," he said, when Griggs brought him his clothes. "I'll wear my uniform."

The sight of a hussar's jacket was said to soften female hearts so Alistair thought he would give it a try. With Mrs. Morris, he needed every advantage he could get.

"It's a pleasure, Captain, seeing you properly kitted out again," said Griggs, as he moved behind Alistair's back, brushing his coat. "The fellows would be glad." Alistair didn't know if other officers gave their batmen such tremendous license, but Griggs was remarkable in many ways and a certain degree of familiarity was unavoidable after enduring the rigors of campaign. Griggs was proud, ugly, and foul-mouthed, but Alistair liked him much better than Cyril's valet, a long-faced man with obsequious manners who spoke in gravelly whispers.

"They'll see for themselves soon enough," Alistair said. The brush stopped.

"Orders have come?" Griggs asked.

Alistair nodded.

"You make my heart glad, Captain," said Griggs, resuming work with cheerful zeal. "London's well enough for a spell, but it will be good to be back where we belong."

Lord, Griggs was a bloodthirsty fellow. Alistair was a dreadful employer, only managing to pay Griggs' wage at spotty intervals. Griggs made up the difference, however, picking off the dead, and doubtless did very handsomely. But even when pickings were slim, Griggs was entirely happy with the army. The dampest billets, the dreariest rations never disheartened him. If Alistair were half as stalwart, he'd set off for Spain with a light heart.

"Going to headquarters?" Griggs asked.

Alistair shook his head. He'd seen the surgeon there yesterday after calling on his aunt.

"Why the rig out then? No one's out and about this early," Griggs said, scrutinizing Alistair's uniform.

"Thought I'd go to church."

Griggs laughed. When he realized that Alistair wasn't hoaxing, he composed himself, pretending he'd never lapsed. "An excellent notion," he said, his voice bland, but his eyes suspicious. As well he might be. The last time Alistair attended services, he'd gone on a dare. Today's challenge wouldn't net him fifty pounds, but on the bright side, he was less likely to be arrested for disturbing the peace.

THE CONGREGATION GATHERED in the church on Basil Street was a large one. A good number of eyes followed Alistair as he found a seat, but none of them belonged to Anna Morris. No one ventured to speak to him and he didn't recognize a soul. The sermon was well begun before he finally found Anna and her mother. He couldn't see their faces, for they sat at the front of the church and wore simple, close-fitting bonnets. The memorial plaque on the wall above them was the telling clue. It was for one Richard Fulham, lost at sea, 1804. A brother, probably. An older man, the right age to be her father, sat beside them on the pew. Alistair couldn't see well enough to note much more than his abundant side whiskers and thinning hair. His shoulders were a little stooped, unlike the ramrod posture of his wife and daughter.

Their combined attention didn't waver the entire sermon. Watching it was exhausting, for someone used to letting his eyes travel over the congregation, waiting for the tinted light from the stained glass windows to make a man's nose turn blue, or give a prim spinster a rosy blush. Alistair joined in the hymn singing, thinking it ought to go some way to offsetting his complete lack of attention to the sermon. He had a fine baritone and performed well in drawing rooms. He'd hoped—ignominiously, to be sure, that the sound of his voice might make Anna Morris glance over her shoulder, but the congregation sung with such enthusiasm he doubted she would hear him. The woman down the row from him warbled atonally, and ahead of him a passel of children sitting between their parents, orderly and well-behaved as a wall of bricks, sang in rousing unison.

It wasn't until after the service that he caught Anna Morris's eye, while fielding questions from the local Divine—a worthy gentleman who accosted Alistair the moment he exited the chapel.

"And are you connected with any of the families in this flock?" the vicar asked.

"Er, no," Alistair answered. "Merely acquainted." Anna dodged his eyes, but her mother smiled at the sight of him.

"Captain Beaumaris. What a surprise." She took her daughter's hand. Anna couldn't escape, but she'd apparently decided against looking at him. Well, he could charm her mother instead. Alistair bowed over Mrs. Fulham's hand, wishing her good day, being generous with compliments—he'd hoped to have the pleasure of seeing her here, and how fortunate this was, that his wish had come to pass.

"You must dine with us today," Mrs. Fulham said, ignoring the start given by her silent daughter. "Unless you have other plans?"

"You do me too much honor," Alistair said, "But I am happy to accept. I have no other engagements."

"How fortunate. Now, if you'll excuse me, I must speak to the vicar." She turned away, marooning him and Anna on a silent island amid the chatter of the dispersing crowd.

"Using my mother isn't fair," Anna said, her face devoid of expression.

"Yes, but I make much better progress." Time was slipping fast.

"Ahem!"

Alistair turned. It was the father, side whiskers and all, frowning at him. Anna made introductions while Mr. Fulham looked him over, unimpressed by the lacings of gold braid crossing Alistair's (he was told) admirable chest. "How do you come to know my Anna?" he demanded.

Interrupting Anna's lie about a friendship with her late husband, Alistair said, "I met her at a dance. It was quite unforgettable."

Fulham snorted. Anna sent him a kindling look.

"You knew Morris then," he said. Plainly, that was no endorsement.

"Not really."

Fulham harrumphed something that sounded almost like 'ruddy blighter.'

"Do you mean me, or Mr. Morris?" Alistair asked, making a lightning decision. Better to ride to the charge than try flattering this fellow. "Because if you mean me, I must inform you that I'm generally referred to as a bang-up cove. I won't presume to classify the late Mr. Morris."

"Well, I will. He was a rogue," Fulham said.

It was a toss up whether Anna was preparing to snarl or swallow her tongue. Alistair forestalled her with a raised hand.

"Flying to your husband's defense? Very proper. But I can't say I wish to hear about him."

"You wouldn't want my tears spotting your coat," Anna interjected sarcastically.

Alistair pretended to consider. "Well, as to that, I'd hazard that most men would put up with a great deal to put an arm around you. Spots are not too bad, weighed in the balance."

Fulham choked back a laugh and Anna's cheeks bloomed with color—angry or embarrassed, he couldn't tell.

"I'll say no more on that head, sir," Alistair said. "Your wife has been kind enough to ask me to dine. If I infuriate your daughter too much, I won't get any dessert."

This time Fulham allowed himself a chuckle, looking at Alistair with a kinder eye. Anna, on the other hand, looked ready to slice him into quarters. Before her mother finished talking with the vicar, she attached herself to her father, leaving Alistair to take her mother's arm. They set out for the Fulhams' house, Anna walking ahead with her father and Alistair and Mrs. Fulham following behind.

He managed to evade her close questioning about the sermon by agreeing with everything she said and quickly turning the conversation by inquiring about her activities at the church the other day. Her half-hidden smile suggested she knew he was dodging, but she didn't seem to mind. By the time they reached the house, Alistair had learned a great deal about the Basil Street Benevolent Society, but nothing at all about Anna or her secrets. Mrs. Fulham turned to her daughter at the door. "Do you intend to walk more today?" she asked. Anna hesitated, and Alistair was too quick to let the opportunity pass.

"Allow me to accompany you," he said.

"I'd hoped to call on Henry," she said, stalling, her eyes on her mother.

"Who is Henry?" Alistair asked, looking round.

"My son," Anna said.

He blinked. The boy didn't live here? "Where is he?"

"He lives with his guardian. My brother-in-law."

Ah. This must be the source of her difficulty. "I'd still like to come with you, if I may," he said. He turned to Anna's mother. "We crossed paths in the park once, Master Morris and I, but at the time, his mother didn't see fit to present me."

"I can't think why," Anna said. The edge in her voice made her mother glance between them.

"No reason why you can't bring along the Captain," Mr. Fulham said.

"I can see no reason why Captain Beaumaris should be interested in my concerns," she said.

"Can't you?" her father asked, giving her an admonitory look. "Go on, both of you."

It was a subdued Anna who took his arm.

"We'll take a hackney," she said. "I'm not being seen with you in the park."

"Are you always so decided? I thought I looked rather well today," he said. "My man assured me of it."

She gave him a look as he took her arm and steered her down the street. "My parents already think you are courting me. If we walk together through the park others will too." The paths by the serpentine would be busy on a Sunday afternoon.

"Yes, but that's less remarkable than you climbing out of a hackney with me in the middle of Mount Street." Walking with a lady in the park was nothing singular. Being alone in a carriage was. Surely she knew that.

"I'm not dressed for a promenade," she said, still scornful.

"Yes, you don't show as well in that drab gown. What happened to the red boots? I liked them," Alistair said, using the smile that usually let him get away with impudence.

"My mother doesn't think they are appropriate for church," she said.

"Do you agree?"

"It wouldn't matter how I look if you weren't done up like a peacock. No one would notice us then."

"I don't mind being noticed," he said. "I usually am—so are you, I expect, even done up like a Quaker." He'd rather have people speculating about unfamiliar beauties on his arm than hashing over his broken engagement.

They turned north onto Sloane Street. "Why doesn't your son live with you?" he asked.

"Frederick Morris doesn't permit it. He is Henry's guardian and his trustee."

Aunt Georgiana had told him this, but he hadn't expected Morris would keep the boy from his mother. Alistair waited for a gap in the carriage traffic and stepped off the pavement into the street. On the other side the park unrolled before them like a bolt of green velvet. A stream of Sunday strollers progressed down the paths, congregating in patches of shade. "Is that why you wanted Bagshot? To get your boy back?"

Her eyes darted up to him. "Yes. My father—he's tried, but he's too pliant and Frederick Morris too determined. He's within his rights, after all. The lawyers who would talk with me wanted more money than I could afford. My widow's portion isn't large, you see, and Henry has the bulk of my fortune. Or Frederick, rather."

"Your father wouldn't pay a lawyer?"

She sighed. "He did try, until I told him not to waste his money. Legal action would take years and I'm unlikely to win. My father already settled most of his money on me when I married. He kept only a modest sum for himself. My husband oversaw the contracts, and my father was too awed by the Morrises to haggle for a better bargain. I was too in love with Anthony to allow it, if I had considered the matter at all. I was young then, you see. Father feels badly about it now, but I was more taken in than he was."

He covered her hand as they passed into the dappled shade of the park's giant trees. "I'm sorry."

"Not as sorry as I am," she said, drawing in a deep breath and straightening her shoulders. "Live and learn, they say. Are you certain you want to accompany me? I can always give my parents your excuses."

"Why don't you want me with you? I've behaved admirably today."

She didn't smile at his jest. "Why waste your time? I can't afford you, and you need a wife with money. That's why you were engaged to Sophy Prescott, wasn't it? I may not have caught all the intricacies of society, but I did absorb enough to know the plight of extra sons. And I read the newspapers."

He stopped walking, taking a moment to iron his face smooth, managing to keep his tone civil, if not his words. "You've a lovely mouth. It's fascinating—like a viper's. Did you talk to Morris this way?"

"My marriage isn't your concern. Nothing to do with me is."

"You have a very low opinion of me, ma'am."

"What of it? Need I remind you of your first opinion of me?"

She had him there. "Pax," he said, lifting his hands. "It means peace. A truce," he explained, seeing her blank look. "Let's pretend none of that happened, that we met today at church, not at that ridiculous masquerade—"

"What of your bout of fisticuffs in Green Park?"

"I'd appreciate you forgetting that too." He offered his arm again, and a conciliatory smile. They walked on, the gravel crunching softly beneath their boots.

"What was your fight about?" Anna asked.

A pause, while he led her into the softer grass. "I can't get you to believe it never happened?"

"No. Henry loves his new vocabulary."

He sighed. "My obligations grow and grow. We were arguing about his sister, Sophy. The new Mrs. Bagshot."

She peeked at him sideways. "You cared about her. I'm sorry."

"I don't know why you and everyone else should be so surprised," he grumbled.

"You cannot blame me, the way you spoke at the masquerade —you seemed quite heartless."

"I expect I was trying to be, then. Not your fault. What cuts deep is that I couldn't convince the lady I was anything else."

"Perhaps it's your habit of looking remote and superior. No, forget I said that," she said, when he looked up quickly. "I'll keep the peace."

"It's not the done thing, wearing one's heart on one's sleeve," Alistair said coolly.

"I know that much," she said with a sigh. Alistair watched her, wondering if she was thinking of her husband.

Ahead of them the water shimmered white under the high sun. Anna turned her face, shielding her eyes, but Alistair was used to brighter glare and hotter suns. Perhaps she didn't care for the bedecked crowd clustered around the reedy shore. He changed course, seeking more shade. They found the footpath again, weaving deeper into the trees, their regular tread measuring out his remaining time. He wished he had more of it, but he was for Spain. That couldn't be changed. Outside their quiet space, beyond the screening trees, the Sunday promenade went on; light muslin gowns and long tailed coats as flat as the French paper puppets his cousin Henrietta had favored when they were children. They looked like figures, not real people, prim young ladies with their maids, dandies with entire bouquets fixed in their buttonholes and—dash it, that one was Cyril.

Before they were seen, Alistair veered towards the carriage way, slowing their pace once they were clear, waiting for her remark. His behavior was too singular to avoid comment. But when she spoke, it wasn't what he expected.

"Is that why you wanted to see me?" she asked. "Because we both lost what we wanted? I, Tom, and you, Sophy Prescott?"

He swallowed. Perhaps it was. He was hard put to explain his compulsion otherwise. "You must be right." They'd both played and lost. How depressing.

ANNA DIDN'T TRUST Captain Beaumaris or like him, but it wasn't terrible having a handsome gentleman walk her through the park. At the very least, it kept down her nervousness as they approached the Morris door. Captain Beaumaris rapped the knocker.

"Master Henry's not at home, I'm afraid," the butler said. "Driving with his grandmother." He didn't suggest she come inside to wait.

Anna bit the inside of her lip. This wasn't the first time a Morris had slighted her. It would happen again, perhaps as soon as the coming week, for Frederick derived particular satisfaction from these taunts. So did her mother-in-law. The last thing Anna wanted was that woman in the vicinity. A hundred miles was too close. "I thought she was visiting her daughter up north," Anna said.

"I believe she was," Arden said uncommunicatively. Well, Charlotte Morris probably tried even her daughter's patience after too long.

"Do tell them we called," Captain Beaumaris said, extending his card into Arden's hand.

"Does Morris often do that?" he asked, once they were outside. "Keep your boy from you, I mean?"

"We aren't on friendly terms," she replied, dreading the questions that would follow. But Captain Beaumaris said nothing more until they reached the end of the street.

"Are you tired? Is the heat too much?"

"It's not a long walk. I'm neither an invalid nor a cripple." The words came out more scornfully than she intended, but he didn't comment.

They said less on the walk home and it was her fault—she still smarting from another Morris jibe. She knew most of them by heart: she was too coarse, too credulous, too plain in her tastes or else too lavish. The litany rattled round her head, whipped faster by anger that again he'd stolen her time with Henry. Unable to drive the thoughts away, she missed one or two of Captain Beaumaris's remarks, replying at random. She was, however, sufficiently alert to take in his occasional nods or words of greeting to some of the passers-by. His acquaintance seemed to consist entirely of sporting gentlemen, recognizable by their conservative clothes and lack of paunch, and beautiful women. A particularly lovely one with silvery blonde hair, driven in grand style in an enormous barouche, looked like she expected conversation with him. Anna didn't like to speculate why. And wasn't she a little old for him? Captain Beaumaris couldn't be more than thirty.

He did not seek conversation from any of his friends, keeping to quieter paths and inoffensive subjects, trying one after another, for they had little in common. She hadn't seen Kean's Hamlet, heard Catalani sing or read Mrs. Radcliffe's new novel. "That's a relief," Captain Beaumaris said, capturing her attention at last.

"You don't like novels?"

"No."

Anna had no quarrel with that, preferring pamphlets and newspapers herself. She figured it best not to tell him she'd fallen asleep last night reading a soothing description of wounds, their debridement, and the consequences of festering.

But it was distracting, and rather nice, being pelted with questions. She hadn't been to Carlton house, but she liked hearing what Mrs. Goring wore when she was there. "Is she the one the papers call 'the Ethereal?'" Anna asked.

"The very same," Captain Beaumaris said.

"Is she so very lovely?"

"Exquisite, and well aware of it. It's fashionable to affect modesty, but she never does. I believe I prefer it when a lady doesn't pretend to be unaware that she's immoderately attractive."

She ignored the quick glance over her bonnet and plain dress. "Was Miss Prescott—forgive me, Mrs. Bagshot—that way?"

"Not at all." He smiled. "She was a Genuine, and rare at that. I don't think she considered herself beautiful at all. She isn't really, next to her half-sister."

"Is that what makes her attractive?"

He considered. "It goes a long way towards it, certainly. She tries on intimidating looks like my aunt, but it never works for her because she spoils it by being a complete wretch."

"She's amusing, then," Anna said, forcing herself to sound interested, not wooden.

"Entirely. But we needn't speak of her. It's very rude of me to bring her up with you."

Curiously, now that he was ready to put this lady away, she wanted to talk about her more. What was it about her that made men like Beaumaris and Tom Bagshot fall at her feet? The only thing Anna's looks had won her was an indifferent husband and a string of lovers she didn't like to think about. And she wouldn't.

"I don't mind hearing about her," she said, with a rueful twitch of her brows. "I'm curious—what is it she has that I lack? The person I should ask is Tom, I suppose, but I can't imagine doing it. I'd blush so deep I'd scorch my ears. And it might be something I cannot change," she finished, more soberly. She had no reason to confide in Captain Beaumaris—plenty of reasons not to, in fact, including her pride—but the words were coming easily and she didn't care enough to stop them. His original opinion of her had been so terrible it was impossible to fall in his esteem.

"You could smile more," he said at last. "I'm sure you have one, but I've scarcely seen it."

Feeling a pinch of annoyance, she flashed him a dazzling array of teeth.

"Gracious, are you going to eat me?" he asked.

Anna wrinkled her nose at him. "Not if you speak nice." She looked him over, taking in the magnificent uniform and the fine looking set of shoulders. "All that braid and button work would disagree with me."

He laughed, loud and light. "Frederick Morris should be more careful. You're a dangerous enemy."

Yes, just ask my dead husband. "I've contemplated revenge a time or two," she admitted aloud. "Gratifying to the imagination, but impossible. He has every advantage."

"What would you do to him?" Beaumaris asked, steering her away from the morass of self-pity as lightly as he'd edged her around the uneven pavements.

"Not certain. My mother doesn't hold with witchcraft."

"Thank heaven for that! If I found myself alone with you, a belle dame sans merci—" he broke off, seeing her confused face. "Are you unfamiliar with French? Or is it poetry?"

"Both," she said, unashamed, for there was no censure in him.

"She is the beautiful lady without mercy. I'll lend you the poem and you can tell me what you think," he said, his eyes warm with a light she knew had imperiled many hearts. They were so good at saying one thing while his lips said something else. "I'll bring it round tomorrow."

"Tomorrow?" Anna asked, her voice dry, though she was secretly pleased. "There's no need—"

"I leave almost immediately for Spain," he inserted quickly. "Matter of days."

Oh. She shouldn't be surprised. He was interested in her because they'd both been slighted, that was all. Besides, he needed to marry money and she no longer had hers. "I'll have to read quickly. Is it a long poem?"

"Don't sound so resigned! It's not long at all, and very beautiful." His eyes were speaking again, saying things he wasn't going to say aloud. Unless she was a victim of her own imagination.

"Tell me about your family," she said. He knew more than enough about hers.

"My father's seat is in Kent and he spends most of his time there due to poor health. My elder brother is currently in town, but he'll take himself off to Brighton shortly," he said.

She nodded so he would go on; not hearing what he was saying so much as sharpening her liking for the cadences of his voice. A woman could grow tipsy listening to those perfectly enunciated words.

Reciting the names, titles and whereabouts of his relations took the rest of the walk home. "Will I have to repeat this performance over dinner?" he asked good-naturedly. Of course it was boring him.

"No," she said quickly. "My parents won't ask about that kind of thing." They had little use for gentry. If her mother hadn't decided a year ago that the best thing for Anna was a second marriage—a happier one—they would probably have given Captain Beaumaris short shrift.

The rest of her confidence deserted her when they entered her parents' drawing room. Oh, it was fine enough; well-furnished, with no hint of anything shabby, but nothing was fashionable or lovely. The drawings on the walls were maps and indifferent watercolors done by her father's surveyor friends on voyages to the Americas, and her mother still insisted on displaying Anna's first, badly-executed sampler. *Blessed are the pure in heart*, it intoned ironically from the wall in crooked red letters, only slightly less wobbly than the parade of yellow birds in the row beneath. Then there was the miniature of her brother, framed with a lock of his chestnut brown hair, and her mother's books, all sermons and essays, scattered on the tables.

"You have a talent for organization, I see," Alistair said to her mother, glancing in an open memorandum book where she recorded the minutes of the Benevolent Society. Her mother accepted this topic of conversation as happily as always, describing the Society's mission, her hopes for the dispensary, and her opinions of the medical profession. No matter how often Anna peeked at Captain Beaumaris, he never looked bored, though his responses took on a rehearsed quality. It was subtle, though. If she hadn't been jumpy as a cat, watching for things he might store up to laugh over in private, she wouldn't have noticed.

Dinner, of course, was unfashionably early and hearty too. Neither of her parents cared for French sauces or foods they couldn't recognize or pronounce. Anna marked how much he ate, trying to judge if he was pleased with the meal or merely being polite. She couldn't tell. At least the wine was good. Too late, she realized she hadn't been watching, and might be on her third glass. Admonishing herself to be more careful, she ate quietly, letting him laugh with her parents, who had never been told, in Anthony Morris's iciest accents, that immoderate feelings were not displayed in company.

"They worry about you," he whispered to her, when her mother purposely asked her to walk him alone to the door. It was late now. They'd talked long after dessert.

"I know," Anna whispered back, feeling harassed by their embarrassing expectations. "It can be something of a trial."

His expression told her immediately that she'd spoken ill. "I would be happy to claim affection like theirs," he said, and Anna caught a glimpse of a home like the Morris's: chilly, polite, and no place for a boy.

"That's not what I meant," Anna said hastily. "I'll explain to them why you called. In friendship—they'll understand. I don't want their expectations to make you uncomfortable—" She should stop now before embarrassing herself further.

Alistair turned away from her, darting into the boot room to retrieve his hat. Anna followed him, despite the uncomfortable motion in her stomach.

"I understand what you mean," he said, keeping his back to her. Impossible to say for certain in this dim light, but his neck might have been flushed. He set the hat on his head, carefully adjusting the angle, then turned and walked past her, heading for the door. Before the breeze of his passing died, he was back at her side, pressing her hand. "I'm not uncomfortable. I should be, but I'm not. Thank your parents again for dinner."

9

NEVER RUSH YOUR FENCES

ANNA TRIED to explain after he called again the next day. "He's just being kind."

"That's why I like him," her mother said.

"Mama, he's leaving almost immediately for Spain," she said, setting down her pen.

"Careful. I don't want any blots," her mother said, glancing at the Benevolent Society's neat ledger. She reached out and brushed a dry thumb across Anna's chin. "Who can say what will happen?"

Anna scowled down at the paper. Perhaps her mother would understand if she wrote it up as a balance sheet. On her side, a column of red debits: little money of her own, a son she couldn't have, and an unholy temper. His interest might make sense if she accounted for her looks—most gentlemen seemed to like them— but she'd made it plain she wasn't interested in romantic liaisons. So had he.

There's a difference between admiring a painting and wanting to buy it.

She felt her cheeks coloring. And on his side . . . well, he was nice to look upon, it was true, but she wasn't making the mistake of throwing all away on a handsome face again. He was proud—too well born to be content with a bourgeois wife, dependent on the generosity of another man's son. Besides, she'd be a fool to trust a man so skilled at caressing with his eyes, so easy with his entendres. He was too shady to be trusted.

Of course, so was she. It was a useless proposition, not even worth thinking about, with nothing but liabilities on every side.

The next day, he called again.

"Why do you keep coming?" she asked, after an evening of penny-point whist with her parents. He couldn't be amused by such games.

"I keep hoping you'll change your mind. I could help you."

"With Henry?" She shook her head. "I can't see how." But she slid a smile across the space between them like she was about to pass him a point. He'd played his cards incredibly well tonight, barely managing to lose. "You might have fooled my father, but I know we should have won."

He put his lips on the very tips of her fingers, more a nibble than a kiss. "That wasn't the game I was playing."

IN FRONT OF HER PARENTS, he was the soul of respectability, but when the two of them walked alone, he took all kinds of liberties, without ever touching her: approving her dress, her figure, the lazy curl that wound along the side of her neck, her rouge, scent, and her dove grey lace gloves. Easy enough to mistake such candid admiration for something more, but he was a connoisseur, not a collector. She must remember that.

"How about Frobisher? He'd do for you. Likes beautiful women," Captain Beaumaris said, tilting his head at a man trotting by on a bay horse. "Shall I make the introduction?"

She refused, of course, blushing and flustering.

"No? He'd make a tolerable husband, so long as you can stand his mother," he said, inadvertently snuffing her warmth.

Anna stared into the trees.

"You're chewing your lip again—what must I do to make you stop that?" he asked.

"It won't harm them. Or you," she added, seeing he was about to protest.

"Don't be obtuse. Having trouble with the Gorgon?" he asked, using the name she'd given her mother-in-law, the other Mrs. Morris.

"Just more of the same," she said, smoothing the wrinkles in her forehead.

But it wasn't. Two days later, she went again to appeal to Frederick, hoping she might at least glimpse Henry from the bottom of the stairs. Frederick received her with his usual solemnity in the library, the Gorgon at his side. The air was thick with antipathy, making it hard to move. Anna listened. Pled her cause. Asked for leniency, but of course there was none. She had her pride, though. She did not cry until she was facing her own door.

IT TOOK some days to arrange, but after an examination by a second surgeon—the first one insisted upon it—Alistair was permitted to return to active service. "Give Colonel Halketts my best," said Mr. Wethers, the surgeon, smiling as he affixed a tight signature to Alistair's orders.

"That I will," Alistair said. His daily practice with pistol and saber was still unsatisfying and painful—he tired with alarming speed, but could manage Wether's brief examination with a cheerful face. Distracting the surgeon with talk through most of the appointment helped.

Alistair left Wethers' office at the hospital, thinking about Spain and his shoulder, resolving to pass an hour (if he could stand it) at Manton's shooting gallery. He made a quick stop at home, then set off to Davies Street, his brother Cyril's duelling pistols tucked under his arm. They'd been tempting him too long from the back of the library cupboard, finally overcoming his scruples. He culped only three wafers before he started missing.

"Problem with your piece?"

It was Jasper, lounging against the wood-paneled wall, looking very indolent for a man who, most days, could hit fifteen of twenty wafers.

"Wish it was," said Alistair, calmly reloading. "It's this shoulder of mine."

Jasper shook his head. "Nasty business."

Alistair nodded, unsure if Jasper's summation should amuse or irritate him. Squaring off, Alistair fired again.

"Might have clipped it," Jasper suggested, to be kind.

Alistair didn't bother taking a second look, just shook his head. "A clean miss, and not the fault of the equipment."

"Nice looking piece," Jasper said. "One of a pair?"

"Filched them from my brother," Alistair admitted.

Jasper made a face. "Wasted on him. Forgive my plain speaking."

"Oh, I'm with you," Alistair said, quickly wiping down the pistol so he could tuck it back in the case.

"Come by Tatt's with me?" Jasper suggested, seeing he was preparing to go.

He ought to. If he was to find himself another decent horse before leaving . . . .

"Love to, but I'm afraid it had better be another time." Alistair closed the case with a snap. If he went to Tattersall's he'd have to forego walking with Anna.

Jasper followed him outside Manton's, frowning as he straightened his cuffs. "Gone back into hiding? Haven't seen you at the club."

"No, just preparing for my journey. Lots to be done," Alistair said.

"Evidently." Jasper narrowed his mouth. "Where're you off to?"

"Business," Alistair said, but something in his face must have given him away.

Jasper exhaled in a huff. "You can tell me about her next time. Or not." He touched his hat, perfectly polite, but plainly displeased.

Alistair held in a sigh, watching Jasper stroll away, headed to his tailor or his clubs. There really wasn't anything to tell. And while he had, on rare occasions, hinted to his cousin about a particular lady's charms, his knowledge of Anna Morris's predicament was not for sharing. She bore up tolerably well, but someone ought to help her. He didn't know exactly how or why he'd become convinced the someone should be him.

It was past the time for afternoon calls when he knocked on the Fulham's door, but the maid who answered the door reported that Anna was upstairs.

He found her in the drawing room, alone, her forehead resting in her hands. She lifted her face as he approached, brushing her cheeks, unable to hide her red-rimmed eyes.

"What's the matter?" he asked, mired in place, his hand frozen above the table where he usually dropped his gloves.

She smiled weakly, corrected her posture and lied. "Nothing."

"My dear, when your eyes look like that, you'll have to come up with something better." He held out a handkerchief. "Tell me."

She dabbed her face obediently, then set the folded square on her lap, smoothing it with her fingers. Her lips clung together, holding everything in.

The roundabout approach, then. "Come walking with me," he said, stretching out his hand to forestall arguments. "Very pretty," he said, admiring her soft blue walking dress as she rose. "You visited Brother Frederick today?" She always dressed with care and circumspection when meeting her in-laws.

Anna caught her lip with her teeth, answering with a sharp nod. Something painful then. Her bonnet was beside her on the sofa, trailing grey ribbons onto Mrs. Fulham's carpet—the serviceable, quiet design couldn't have been Anna's choice. "Don't forget your hat," he said.

She was close to his height, their eyes nearly level as he fitted it onto her head and fastened the ribbons, wishing he could tell her she didn't need to hide behind damp eyelashes.

"Are your parents out?" he asked, for he didn't see anyone on their way out of the house.

"Father is home. He's resting." Instead of turning north, she took him past the church to Hans Town Gardens, a pocket sized bit of greenery compared to Hyde Park.

"You won't see anyone you know here," she said.

It wasn't something that concerned him, but he'd failed to convince her of the truth of it. "What's the matter? Is it your son?" Her eyes flashed to his and he knew he'd guessed the truth.

"You needn't—"

"I want to know," he insisted. It had been satisfying, picturing Frederick Morris standing behind his wafers earlier today. His family treated Anna abominably, stealing her money and keeping her from her son. He didn't like to think how her husband might have behaved, after seeing the scorn the Morris butler had heaped on her when she'd gone over to see Henry that first Sunday.

Her lips folded together, then she said, low and careful, "My mother-in-law is taking Henry back to Warwickshire."

"What will you do?"

"I can't go there. They won't have me in the house. I'll have to find a place nearby, or I'll never see him. It's just—I never wanted to go back to Warwickshire."

"How—"

"I've money enough," she said quickly. "I'll have to keep to a simple style. A cottage. No more lace gloves or shopping on Bond Street." She gave a fleeting smile.

"Why won't they let Henry live with you?" he asked.

"He needs to be brought up properly," she said, with a lightness that accentuated the pain in her eyes. "It won't do to forget that no matter who I am, Henry is a gentleman's son. I can't be trusted to teach him what a gentleman ought to know. Nor can my parents."

Alistair did not doubt that she would follow the Morrises to Warwickshire and that she'd be ignored there even more effectively. If, in desperation, she turned to a town lawyer, she might be able to buy herself costly hopes, but nothing more. She needed an ally, someone able to beat Frederick Morris at his own game.

His mother would refuse point blank to help her, no question of that, but perhaps Aunt Georgiana might . . . Uncle William said he wished to help him. Of course, one never took up people on offers like that, or asked them to transfer their kindness to another. But it needn't be for very long. All in all, it wasn't an enormous favor to ask. They would need a clear reason though, something better from him than pity for a striking face.

"Let's sit down," he said. One needed to, for conversations like this. He'd done this once before, but it hadn't frightened him like this. Sophy had been well prepared to hear his offer.

"If you were living with respectable people—no, the best people—would Morris let you have Henry?"

She turned her palms up fatalistically. "In theory. But Frederick would find a reason to say no. Something about the situation wouldn't be right enough for him, and besides, I haven't one. Frederick doesn't approve of any one I know."

"He'll approve of me. Of my family."

She faltered, her lips falling open. "Bu—"

He stopped her with a lifted finger. Time for that later. He had to take this at full gallop or he'd find a reason why it couldn't

JAIMA FIXSEN

work. "You wouldn't have to live with my mother. Dreadful situation. My father is dying and her theatrics over it would infuriate a saint." Anna, bless her, looked far too tempting to be one of those. Besides, he didn't trust Cyril to keep the line.

"I'm thinking of my aunt, Lady Fairchild. She's perfect," he said, before Anna could argue. "She's a notable hostess, a bastion of respectability. If she's deigned to notice a Morris within the last five years they'd remember it. No one would dare say her house isn't a good place for Henry. My aunt could get you started, introduce you to the right people." She'd opened society's doors for Sophy. Anna had her husband's name, if not his family's support. She could find a way in as part of his aunt's train.

"But she wouldn't do it. Why would anyone?"

Being a guest of Lady Fairchild wouldn't be enough. Anna needed a stronger foothold. And Aunt Georgiana wouldn't take Anna without an excellent reason. "She'd do it for me," he said. *Probably.* "Suppose we told her you were to become my wife."

Anna's breath left her in a surprised huff. "But I'm not!" she said. Her eyes turned accusing. "You can't afford to marry me."

"True. But we could be engaged. I'm off to Spain in a few days. There will be plenty of time for you to meet someone who suits after I'm gone. You can break off your engagement to me whenever it's convenient. There's plenty of reasons. No one will blame you. My career, all the time apart—it's perfectly understandable." He smiled lopsidedly. "Always possible I'll turn up my toes and you can save yourself the trouble."

"Don't joke about that." She scowled at the ground in front of them.

"The important thing is that in the meantime, you'll have charge of your son."

She knotted her fingers together, looked at him once, then glanced swiftly away, to the walking path where a skinny housemaid with a giant basket of shopping listed by. They remained silent, waiting for her to pass out of earshot.

"You can't want this," she whispered. "I'm all wrong for you."

Oh, but she wasn't. She was so right that— "I want to help you," he said. "I'm not usually troubled with benevolent impulses. You may as well give me my way on this one. Who knows if it will happen again? I should have at least one good deed credited to my name."

"It's too much to ask of you. And your aunt."

"You aren't asking. I offered."

"Then it's too much to accept," she said. "I can't."

"You'd rather go to Warwickshire, where they can continue stalling you at the front door?" It would happen, he was sure of it.

She ironed her lips into a stiff, starched line. "I haven't anything to offer you."

He understood exactly what she meant. No tumbles, no brush of skin on skin, no raking his fingers through her hair. He hadn't let himself consciously explore the idea too far, but it had taken shape anyway, in the shadowy backstairs closet of his mind. Well, she was honest, so he wouldn't pretend to be high-minded. If she'd been willing, he would have accepted. Gladly. With a boy's eagerness, and perhaps even the shaking hands.

Thankfully, he had sufficient presence now to keep them perfectly still. "Anna, I haven't asked for anything. I won't. We don't do things that way, you know. Keeping personal ledgers."

Blood flooded into her cheeks and she retreated, shamed, behind the dusky shade of her eyelids.

"You're uncomfortable with chivalry," he said. "Fair enough. As an impulse, it's new to me too. If you'd rather, we can stick to exchanges. Let's start with a smile."

Her eyes snapped up, confused and not a little suspicious.

"Well, I won't object to a kiss or two, if I can get them," he said. "But I'll consider myself amply repaid if I see more smiles on you, and know that when I leave, you'll be happy. No," he said, stopping her again with a finger on her lips. "Don't expostulate about refusing pity and charity. Just say yes."

She struggled, her chest rising as if her heart were trying to climb out of it.

"You're too proud, my dear," he said.

"Fine! Yes! And don't blame me when you regret it." She scowled at him, now the words were wrung out of her.

"My smile?" he asked, hiding his jubilation behind a careful examination of his fingernails. There was no reason for it, after all. Their agreement was only pretend.

Her expression was more of a grimace.

"Your parents will think I frightened you into marrying me if you show them a face like that."

"No, just that you browbeat me, and that's the truth," she said.

"I don't think we want anyone to know that," he said. "This won't work if people think it a mere business arrangement."

"I thought most marriages between your kind were," she said, with acid sweetness. "That has been my experience, certainly."

"Choose more carefully next time. I'd like to see you happy." And because it seemed appropriate, he leaned in to kiss her. Pretend or not, she'd still accepted him. At the last second, courage failed him, and he limited himself to a brief, brotherly salute—an action as businesslike as franking a letter. She didn't lean in, or hide her eyes from him when he pulled away, but her cheeks burned. He was satisfied.

"We can be friends," he said. "Allies."

"All right."

He studied her expression, tilting his head. "Nearly there. Let the smile show a little more in the eyes. Yes. That's right. We want your parents to think you're delighted with our engagement."

"Are you?" She eyed him suspiciously.

"Of course I am," he said, gathering up her hand and pulling her to her feet. Throwing away caution for just a moment, he pulled her close, until their bodies were nearly touching—close enough that the space between them turned alive and quivering.

He held her there, letting that silent hum grow, consuming every other sense until he could stand it no more.

"Why wouldn't I be happy?" he said, letting go of her hands and retreating a step. "I'm engaged to the most beautiful woman in London." She would catch any man fool enough to look into those dark, dilating eyes. He'd have to take care.

"How old were you when you married Anthony Morris?" he asked. A beauty with a handsome fortune should have done better than Anthony Morris, no matter how plebeian her birth. "Why did you choose him? You must have had other proposals."

She shook her head. "I was eighteen and just out of mourning for my brother. A lawyer friend of my father's invited us for dinner practically the first evening we put off our blacks. Anthony was there. He must have arranged it all with my father's friend, because he never ate at that house again once we were married. I think the lawyer worked for his family."

Huh. Plucked her before she had bloomed even. Selfish bastard.

They stepped out of the dappled light of the park, back into the dusty glare of the street, Alistair moving to shield her as a coal wagon trundled by. Even the air around her was potent, making it nearly impossible for him to pretend to be unaffected when their shoulders brushed together. Yet it didn't sound for a minute that Morris had lost his heart to her. "Was he dreadful?" he asked.

She mirrored his easy tone, slipping him a sideways smile. "Oh, quite. You can be sure I repaid him in kind."

Before he could inquire, she went on. "If this were a real offer, I'd advise you to reconsider. You should, you know. What if I changed my mind and decided to keep you?"

Once they were engaged, he wouldn't be able to call it off. Only ladies had the privilege of changing their minds. It was a tempting thought, but marrying Anna was no way to provide for his future. Their children would be practically paupers. And unless Anna turned shrewish and lost her looks—God forbid—they'd probably have about a dozen. Completely impractical.

His silence chased the humor from her face. "I wouldn't repay you with such an ill-turn, you know," she said, softly.

"Of course not," Alistair said. "I'd make a bad bargain, you know, if you were stuck with me."

She laughed at that, but he hardly heard. If Anthony Morris had never found her . . . if he'd come to her first, when she still had her fortune, it could have been different.

There was no point in thinking of it. A man could waste his life, lost in the world of might-have been. He couldn't afford to be a dreamer.

"We are agreed then?" he asked.

"Yes." She glanced at him, more tentatively than she had before. "Thank-you."

CONCEAL YOUR HAND

THE NEXT MORNING when Anna sat down to breakfast, her father took the unprecedented step of folding his newspaper and setting it aside. He didn't even notice the daily puzzle soaking up butter from his toast.

"Are you sure about this?" he asked.

"I'm sure," she said. It was the same answer she'd given when she'd come running home without Henry, certain she'd soon have him back in her arms. It hadn't been as simple as she'd expected. "Perfectly sure."

She took a pear from the bowl on the table and sliced it in half with one clean stroke, laying it open and flicking away a stray seed with the point of her knife. It landed on the tablecloth, but she ignored it.

"It's very sudden," her father said.

She wished he'd pick up his fork, or find his way back to his coffee cup. Her engagement couldn't stand this kind of scrutiny. The hopes that had prompted her acceptance last night seemed foolish this morning, but the fact was that most of her dreams evaporated while she slept. Happily ever afters only seemed possible in evening—by candlelight, over the dessert course. That was when she'd fallen for Anthony. Even now, she could remember him, smiling at her across the table, playing with his fork. She should know better. Dreams were always lost at breakfast, evaporating as soon as your eyes fell on the toast rack. No wonder so many ladies thought coming down to eat the meal was insupportable. You could cling to fiction in bed, with a cup of chocolate in your hand.

"He's a handsome dog," her father said.

She agreed silently. Captain Beaumaris was far too handsome for his own good, or hers. But—"That's not why," she said.

"It isn't? You fell head over ears for Morris." He didn't need to finish the thought. They both knew how that had turned out.

"This is different," Anna said. "He cares about me, not the money."

"He better. Won't get more than a pittance from you, will he?"

She lifted a slice of pear to her mouth and chewed slowly. Alistair was getting nothing at all, except trouble. Hers. Of course, there was the possibility that he might still be hoping for —intimacies, she thought, quashing the sudden skip of her pulse. Last night he'd claimed he could be satisfied with smiles and perhaps a few kisses, but Captain Beaumaris was a man of the world, and she was a widow. He might expect more from her in exchange for the help he was offering than he would from a lady who'd never married. Well, if he did, he'd be disappointed. As far as he was concerned, she was as respectable as she ought to be. She wasn't, of course, but she could kiss and be careful.

"He seems right enough. Of course, so did Morris," her father said.

"I'm not rushing into marriage this time," she reminded him. "There's plenty of time for us both to consider the matter. He thinks he can help me with Henry."

Her father fiddled with his knife. "That so? I hope he may. Frederick Morris is a slippery fellow."

"We are going to speak to him today," she said, looking down at her plate so she needn't see her father blush. He wasn't to blame for her current situation—she had her own foolishness to thank for that—but she felt an ache every time he retreated behind a shamed face. He had tried to help her, but he was too kindly a soul to trump the Morrises. He was a retiring sort of man, a persistent organizer who managed small details, not the god of her childhood.

Yet another vanished illusion. It had been many years since she and her brother had skipped fearlessly in their father's wake, through dockyards or across the decks of Henry Bagshot's clippers. No matter how rough the sea or how primitive the port, their faith in their father had been unshakable. It wasn't fair, really, to trust a mere man like that. Her father's shoulders were stooped now, his brown eyes turning cloudy at the edges. Every year since they'd lost her brother, he seemed to shrink a little. Her mother, on the other hand, took on more and more—organizing flowers for the church, sewing shirts for the parish poor, chairing the Benevolent Society. Her virtue shone bright as the plaque beside their pew, in memory of Richard.

Anna poured herself another cup of coffee. She hadn't slept and now her eyes felt gritty.

"Let's hope Henry doesn't take after the Morrises," her father said, unfolding his newspaper and reaching for the last point of toast.

"Little danger of that, I think," Anna said, setting down her cup. It didn't even clink against the saucer. "He doesn't look like his father." Praise God for that.

∿

ALISTAIR SET out to call on his aunt the next day as early as he dared, mulling over Anna's qualms, and wondering if his weary muscles of persuasion were strong enough to bring another person round. Convincing Anna again had been hard enough.

She'd suffered a second attack of conscience after telling her parents last evening, which worsened when he explained that he felt it best if he broke the news to Lady Fairchild alone. "For I don't doubt she'll be surprised."

Anna had cast him an anguished look. "Don't try putting a pretty face on it. She'll think you've lost your senses. She'll never go along with it!"

It had taken him a good quarter hour of soothing words to get her to agree to the engagement all over again.

"Trust me. We'll have Henry tomorrow," he said. She'd quieted then, believing his promise. He wasn't as sure of himself this morning.

Despite the relatively early hour, Alistair arrived at Rushford House and discovered he'd missed the chance to corner his aunt alone. She was already entertaining her country neighbors, the Misses Matcham. Alistair entered the room with a broad smile, concealing his inward groan. One Matcham was bad enough. When confronted with the pair, he generally opted for strategic retreat.

The eldest greeted him with something of a gloat. "So you are not to be married after all, Captain Beaumaris."

"Not to Miss Prescott at any event," he said, with awful heartiness. Miss Matcham's answering smile was so predatory he had to fight the temptation to make his excuses and bolt. *They can't stay for more than a quarter of an hour.*

Unfortunately, from this angle, he couldn't read the clock.

"Have you heard from Sophy since her marriage?" the younger edition, Miss Eliza, asked Lady Fairchild.

"I have not," his aunt said, in a voice that could have chipped ice. She looked to Alistair, closing that subject. "Has the news come, then? Are you for Spain once more? I hate to see you go."

"You must not have read about our victory at Salamanca," he said, her concern coaxing hints of a genuine smile from him. He'd heard rumors at his regiment's headquarters yesterday while arranging his journey, but hadn't gotten the full account until reading it in the papers this morning. "Marmont's wounded, the French in retreat. By the time I arrive, Wellington will be across the border and into France."

"Then you won't be away for long," Lady Fairchild said, a smile flooding her face.

"With any luck," he said lightly, hiding how well he knew the changing fortunes of war. For every advance, there was a retreat.

"You must dine with us again before you go. This evening," she said, then glanced apologetically to the Matchams. "You understand me well enough to forgive my rudeness for leaving you out of the invitation. An evening like this one can only be for family."

"Leave takings are always rather dreadful," said Miss Eliza. "We wouldn't want to intrude."

"Of course not," said his aunt, her eyes sharp above her smile.

Silence fell. Lady Fairchild made no move to speak, drumming her fingers on the back of her other hand, until the Miss Matchams realized they'd been dismissed. At the same instant, they leapt from their seats and bundled themselves out of the room, a frothy, muslin-clad, chittering cloud, swept out by a chilly wind.

When the door clicked shut behind them, Lady Fairchild turned to Alistair and sighed. "I'm going to have to cut them, but I haven't decided if it should be at Almacks or the park. I'm leaning towards Almacks. How dare they ask me about Sophy!" She sniffed. "I detest plain girls. They always think they can make up their deficiencies by being arch and sly."

"Leave off the delicate shudders," Alistair said. "I understand you perfectly."

"And the way they looked at you! I don't care that Miss Matcham's father has settled a round sum on her—no one would take her, else—you are not to have anything to do with her."

"Done."

"I wish Jasper were half so biddable," Lady Fairchild said, souring.

"It's easy for me," Alistair said. "You never ask me to do anything I don't like."

She lifted her eyes to his, but he didn't let himself warm too long in her understanding glance. Too premature. "Are you well?" he asked, not quite ready to charge across the field.

"Of course I am. Just a surfeit of my own company and a revulsion for everyone else's. Nerves. Maybe I'll finally have to break down and try that Russian Vapor Bath they are always going on about." She lowered her voice. "Though I can't see that —that sweating—you will excuse the indelicacy—could be thought to have any benefit. It sounds most unpleasant." Like so much else, his aunt considered perspiration an affliction to be suppressed and ignored. He'd never seen her with dew on her forehead or a shine on her nose. But he hadn't come to swap tales about slimming regimes and unsavory Russian baths.

"I leave on Friday," he said, knowing he might only have a few minutes before other callers intruded. "There is a matter for which I must beg your help."

"Come here," she said, motioning him to join her on the settee. "Of course I will help you. What is it?"

He grimaced as he sat himself down. "You won't like it."

"Then I am particularly well-suited for it. I excel at doing what I don't like," she said. Despite her smile, the grim certainty in her eyes made him lower his own to study the contours of his knees. Jasper often said his mother was a monster in female form, and every once in a while, Alistair half-believed him.

"I'm engaged to be married," he said.

"No! Again?" she said, starting forward when he didn't contradict her.

"I'm afraid I am."

"Who?" she asked. "Not Miss Lucas. An act of desperation if there ever was one. You—you didn't—" She narrowed her eyes, and he realized his life would be completely different if he'd gotten Lady Fairchild for a mother, instead of her feather-brained sister. That life would probably be better than the one he had now, but it would be much more uncomfortable.

His aunt drew herself up in her seat, her back a curve of steel rising from the cushions. "Who was the lady you were walking with?—I saw you with her one Sunday afternoon."

"Mrs. Morris," he said. "Now, happily, my fiancée."

"No," she said. "Leave it to me. I'll get you out of it."

He was quite sure she could. Best to make a clean breast of it. "Aunt Georgiana. I don't need you to get me out of it. We aren't really going to marry."

"Of course you are. That sort of nonsense only happens on the stage. You're engaged, aren't you?"

"I was engaged to Sophy."

She flinched, but said nothing.

"Both me and Mrs. Morris admit freely that a marriage between us would be an impractical disaster—"

"So you haven't completely lost your senses," she said.

She was being generous. He suspected he had. "You know enough about her to know she's been treated appallingly by the Morrises. They've taken her money and they won't let her have her son. They claim she can't raise him properly."

"Well, of course she can't. He's to be a gentleman, isn't he?"

Alistair paused, trying to construct the right words while his aunt looked blindly at the window. "She's his mother. She wants him terribly."

"So?" She spoke calmly, but she was twisting the ring on her littlest finger.

"It would be cruel not to help her when I can. I must do this."

"Must! You need do nothing at all. And neither do I. That's what you're asking, isn't it?"

Alistair looked down guiltily. "Yes."

"The world abounds with tragedy. Sometimes one just has to harden one's heart."

"I want to fix this."

"Why? No, don't tell me. Even under that rubbishy bonnet she wore on Sunday I could see she was appallingly pretty. But what's the point? I'm not furthering your dalliance."

"I'm not bedding her," Alistair said, and his aunt's face froze. "I wouldn't ask you if this wasn't respectable. I'm not doing this for —that," he said, softening his language at the last minute. "This is to make her happy. Why shouldn't she be? And I—I could be satisfied if I accomplished that."

Lady Fairchild's retort died on her lips. They were too much alike—not in looks, not in coloring—it was the desolate expression on her face that Alistair recognized, the one he tried to show only to his mirror. Yawning emptiness with no break in the horizon. "What exactly do you want me to do?"

"I can get her boy for her and wrest some money from Morris, more than the beggarly portion he currently gives her. But I can't leave them at her family house in Hans Town."

"Certainly not." She mouthed the name of the district with a moue of distaste.

"It's not so bad," Alistair said.

"I wouldn't know. I never go there."

He decided not to argue. "Once I leave, there is no one to stop Morris from taking the boy back. But if I left her with you—"

"He wouldn't dare try." She said it simply, without pride. It was a fact, nothing more. "Your uncle would make sure she and the boy got the right settlements."

"On her own, no one would trouble to look at her. With you—"

"If she weren't with me, no one would believe this engagement story. I still don't."

He needed her help. He couldn't think how to make it work, else. One more try. "Will you help me? Let her and the boy live here. Give her the standing she would have as my affianced wife. Introduce her to the right people, so that when she breaks our engagement, she can find herself a husband who will be kind to her."

"That's what you want?"

The clock chimed, but neither of them turned to look.

"Yes," Alistair said.

"Even though you love her?" She forestalled his denials with a flicked finger. "Oh, I can rephrase if it makes you more comfortable. You certainly aren't indifferent to her. I know what that looks like. You don't even resemble it."

He hadn't the temerity to lie, so he dismissed her assertion with a shrug. "It doesn't matter if I do." Admitting his irrational and unseemly interest only exposed him for the fool that he was. Nothing could come of it, save this small thing: an engagement of a few months or maybe a year, and restoring to her that which was her own. And that would be enough, if she were no longer snubbed, lonely, and pretending she wasn't afraid. His feelings would eventually dilute to a comfortable fondness, until he'd be able to think of Anna Morris with the mild nostalgia one felt for any missed chance.

At twenty-eight, he had a collection of those already, and it didn't scorch anymore, to visit his family home or ride over his father's lands. It didn't hurt to remember the first young lady who captured his heart, or the fact that she'd married a grey-haired baronet with somewhat circular geometry. The widow who consoled him afterward had taught him to love well but lightly.

"The Season is over," Lady Fairchild frowned. "I can't find her a husband if there's no one here."

There it was: a near-invisible fissure. Alistair pressed harder. "But you don't intend to go back to Cordell. You'll probably stay through the Little Season, then find your way to one of the spas. You needn't find her a husband tomorrow."

"The sooner I take care of that, the better I'll feel," she said, eyeing him carefully. "You can't afford to be such a romantic."

He glanced down at his fingernails, ignoring her reproving eyes. "So you'll do Brighton. Perhaps autumn in town. It will be almost tiresome, on your own."

"What if I don't like her?"

"That would be complicated, but not exactly tiresome," he said. If she hadn't learned to relish domestic conflict, she should have by now. She was terribly good at it.

"Perhaps." His aunt leaned her head, letting her fingers play with the pearl hanging from her ear. "She's not a watering pot, is she?"

"She's got good armor," Alistair replied. He'd never have considered bringing her here, else.

"I'm in no humor to like anyone," Lady Fairchild said. "I'll probably dislike her from the start, simply because she isn't Sophy. And it's ridiculous, letting yourself be engaged to this girl. Suppose she doesn't let you go?"

"I'm not worried," he said.

"You should be. She wouldn't be the first to lose her head over you."

"I almost wish she would." He hesitated a fraction of a second. "I thought Sophy was going to be my good luck charm. New wife, new life—all that. She really didn't like me at all, did she?"

Lady Fairchild looked down at her hands. "She's a fool," she said.

"I'm not so sure," Alistair said. "At any rate, she's a happy one." *And I can't say that for either of us.*

He thought she might have sighed, but couldn't be certain. It seemed as if a shadow passed over her, falling into the tired spaces in her face, around her mouth, beneath her eyes. It startled him. He was used to his aunt looking beautiful and bloodless, not wan, like a blown rose ready to fall.

"Does she know how to behave?" Lady Fairchild asked.

"Yes. You can polish away the last of the rough edges. Think you can manage it?" he asked. He'd planned this question to prod her into accepting Anna as a point of pride, but now he wondered if he'd asked for more than he ought.

His aunt raised her eyebrows, letting them voice her affront. Alistair backtracked into a conciliatory smile. He knew better than to doubt her ability. "Bring her along with you tonight," she said. "But I don't want to see the boy until tomorrow. And I won't take him unless he comes with his nurse. I can put her in the way of the right people, but I won't endure the headache of finding more domestics."

Fair enough.

11

KEEP YOUR NERVE

NOT FOR THE FIRST TIME, Anna wished she could get rid of the cat. He was fat, lazy, ready with his claws, and doted on by her mother. He'd stolen one of her handkerchiefs after luncheon, shredding it along with Anna's nerves. Indifferent to Anna's dark looks, Danny batted the torn linen and smoothed his whiskers. Still no word from Captain Beaumaris.

A polite knock sounded at the front door, a muffled lub-dupp she wouldn't have heard if her ears weren't alert for every sound. Flinching from the noise and from the sudden stab of her needle, Anna sprang to her feet, sucking her injured thumb.

"Get out!" she said, chasing the cat with flapping hands out the connecting door.

"Is that really necessary?" her mother asked.

"Yes." Anna wasn't going to have Captain Beaumaris looking at damp, chewed up rags or her mother's thick-legged pet, who was forever hissing at strangers. She gave the door a hard thump, silencing Danny's yowling.

"I don't like seeing you fretting about appearances again," her mother said, looking at Anna over the shirt she was hemming, another project for the poor. A diligent seamstress, her mother did not consider Anna's engagement sufficient reason to alter their schedule, even though Anna's progress on the garment assigned to her was pitiful. It was so bad, she should probably just give it to Danny. He might smother himself as he clawed it apart.

"You are sufficient just as you are. This family has nothing to be ashamed of," Mrs. Fulham said.

"I know," Anna said, unable to help cataloguing her mother's calloused hands, the books of sermons spread over the tables and —horror—one of her own garters, half concealed under the couch. She snatched it up and sat down, jamming it between her chair and the cushion. The ribbon, in her favorite shade of red, was ruined. "Why can't that cat stay out of the laundry?"

"I'll remind Hester to keep the door closed," her mother said, unruffled. This was probably the twelfth time she'd made such a promise, but Danny's thievery never stopped. There was no time to argue; Anna could hear Captain Beaumaris in the hall.

"Alistair," her mother said, rising from her chair with a wide smile. Anna followed a second behind. Ignoring the anxious question in her eyes, Alistair addressed himself to her mother with his usual charm. He had her tamed like a puppy. All he needed was a bell. How he managed it, without ever turning weaselly . . . Anna stopped herself, shamed. She never used to be this spiteful. It shouldn't bother her that people liked him. She should be grateful he was willing to exercise his talents on her behalf.

"What does your family say?" Anna interrupted at last, tired of the niceties batted back and forth between her sham-fiancé and her mother. Left to themselves, they'd never stop. If there was bad news to come, she wanted to hear it.

"Lady Fairchild is delighted. We'll dine with them tonight and get you settled there in the morning. Why don't you set your maid to packing your things while you and I fetch Henry?"

Relief hit her like the sea's cold spray, but before her skin could pebble with the chill, a new worry took hold. Heaven help her. She hadn't thought about her maid. Hester was yet another of her mother's projects, a fourteen-year-old orphan of the parish. Anna couldn't bring her to Rushford House.

"I'll look after it," her mother said. "You go. Henry must hear the good news."

Her mother's assistance would probably make things worse, but it was impossible for Anna to feel more rattled than she already was. Henry. She must think of Henry. Running upstairs for a bonnet and gloves, she rejoined Alistair in the hall, tying the ribbons under her chin with clumsy fingers that felt thick and stiff.

"Let me," Alistair said. In a moment's time, she had a jaunty bow tied under her ear and a kiss dabbed onto her lips. Her mother, standing on the stairs, was smiling.

"That kiss doesn't count, you know," Alistair explained once they were outside the door. "That was to please your mother, not me."

Anna said nothing, having a good idea of the kind of kiss that might please him, but knowing she would never dare admit it. A carriage was waiting for them on the pavement.

"My father's," Alistair explained, helping her inside. He took the seat beside her without comment, possessing himself of her hand.

"You don't mind?" he asked, when her fingers twitched involuntarily.

"Of course not. I'm just anxious about Henry is all. What if Frederick—"

"Leave him to me. That's what you wanted, isn't it?" He was smiling, but the laugh had gone from his eyes. "I'm no Tom Bagshot, but I won't disappoint."

They rounded a corner, causing Anna to sway into Alistair's shoulder. He didn't move, but of course he was holding the strap. Anna quickly flung out her free hand to the one hanging on her side of the carriage.

"Frederick can be—unpleasant," she persisted. She didn't like to think of the things he might say about her to Alistair. Despite telling herself that she would endure anything to have Henry, the idea of Alistair learning the truth wasn't something she could think of without her stomach dropping a foot lower than it belonged.

Alistair was unfazed. "I'm sure his manners are most unpleasant. It needn't concern you."

They rolled to a stop in front of Morris house, Anna's heart dancing a faster version of its usual jig.

He promised to help, and he will, no matter what Frederick says, she reminded herself, dizzily climbing the front steps.

Alistair rapped on the door. The lag before it opened was much shorter today. Usually the door swung wide so portentously, she felt like she was waiting to be admitted into one of the more undesirable circles of hell.

"Madam." Arden bowed, showing her in.

"We've come to see Morris," Alistair said, sweeping her into the hall. "We are expected."

His boots were loud on the shining tiles. Her slippers made no sound. She passed the bronze Hercules on the table without her usual shudder; the hero's death throes didn't interest her today. Henry's bronzes, she thought, straightening her back. Henry's pictures. Henry's floor. Even the mice hiding behind the skirting board were Henry's, and he belonged to her.

When they entered the library, Frederick rose from his desk, a courtesy he didn't usually offer her, but any hope she might have felt was exterminated by the expression on his face. He might as well have been wearing armor with the visor down.

"Anna. Captain Beaumaris. Do sit down."

They did. She wished she could do it as easily as Alistair. She felt like a school girl ready to have her palm switched, but he seemed to expand even as he folded himself into his chair, looking as if he were calling on Frederick to fulfill a tedious favor.

"Such startling news. You must know," Frederick said, addressing himself to Alistair, "how strange it is to imagine our Anna marrying again."

"Not strange, surely," Alistair said. "It has been some years."

"I must congratulate you," Frederick said. He was still looking at Alistair, but Anna recognized the tone of suppressed anger—it was reserved for her, and uncannily similar to her dead husband's.

Alistair ignored the brittle tone, responding with a nod. He crossed his legs and leaned back in his chair, glancing meaningfully at the brandy decanter resting on the table between the windows. "Anna love, why don't you run up and see Henry. I'll come up in a moment so you can introduce us."

"I—"

"Do let us sort this out between ourselves," Alistair said, overruling her protests. "One gentleman to another." It was almost frightening how implacable he looked, behind that amiable smile. Anna turned to the door, sure that whatever Frederick said to him, Alistair wouldn't desert her, not until she had carried Henry from the house. What might come after, she couldn't say, so she escaped from the room, grateful she needn't stay to watch her brother-in-law break a molar. His smile was so hard, it looked ready to shatter.

HENRY WAS UPSTAIRS, sprawled across the braided rug on the nursery floor, throwing pebbles at a rank of tin grenadiers.

"Wait until my hand's clear!" exclaimed his nurse, as a stone bounced off the back of her wrist before flying across the floor.

Henry gave a little squirm of delight, then lowered his head, sighting the last three soldiers with one eye winched shut.

"Hello, Henry," Anna said, dropping onto the rug behind the scattered ranks of Henry's miniature army. "Are you Napoleon today?"

His look was blank.

"Are you pretending to lead the French?"

Still nothing.

"Are you a canon?"

With a wicked grin, he chucked a pebble at her chest.

"Ow!" Too late, she twisted away, her hand clapped to a spot beneath her collar bone. "That's going to leave a mark!"

"Time to put the toys away, Master Henry," said the nurse, Lucy, raking up fallen soldiers and spent shot with her fingers and dumping them haphazardly into a battered tin. Anna rubbed her skin. No wonder the paint on Henry's soldiers was so chipped.

"Give a kiss to your mama," Lucy prodded, snapping the lid shut.

Henry clambered to his feet, plodded to Anna's side and leaned in to plant a sulky salute on her cheek. She caught his hand. "How are you?"

He didn't answer. Lucy stowed the war-in-a-box in the cupboard under the window, retreating to the rocking chair and her basket of mending. Anna and Henry eyed each other in silence, hardened scouts assessing the enemy's defense. "You look well," Anna said. His dark hair was unruly, but the color in his cheeks was bright. The room, with its starched curtains, sparkling windows and bedcovers drawn tight at the corners, strove for meticulous order, but Henry's mark was everywhere, random and irrepressible. A pile of pine needles and pebbles were gathered in a corner and a soggy sock peeked out from under Lucy's footstool. He had smudges on his white ruffled collar and leftover jam beneath his right ear, evidence that he moved faster and pulled harder than the hand with the washcloth.

His ferocious scowl was a little off-putting, but Anna slogged on. "I've good news," she said. "I'm getting married, and you are going to come live with me."

Henry only cocked his head. It was Lucy who froze, the motion of her rocking chair arrested mid-swing.

"We are going to stay, both of us, with—with my fiancé's family. You'll like him," she added desperately, not that it would matter much. "He's a captain of hussars."

"The kind on the horses," Lucy filled in, when Henry looked to her for an explanation.

Henry's eyes lit up, making Anna slightly more wretched. She'd planned to present Alistair to Henry as his new papa, but it felt wrong now.

"Is the captain handsome?" Lucy asked.

"Very," said Anna, trying to sound like this pleased her.

"Does he wear a sword? Can I see it?" Henry asked.

Anna didn't think that was a good idea.

"Perhaps tomorrow," Lucy said, lifting up a frilled shirt and examining a rent in the collar, as the storm brewing on Henry's brow blew away. Anna swallowed her chagrin. If Lucy hadn't spoken, she'd have refused, probably goading Henry into a tantrum.

"Should we pack your things?" Anna asked Henry.

Lucy shifted in her chair. "In a few minutes? I'd feel better once we have your uncle's permission," she said to Henry, avoiding Anna's eye. She whispered loudly to Anna, "I shouldn't like Master Henry to be disappointed if nothing comes of it." Clearly, she was of the opinion that nothing would.

Anna agreed with the best grace she could muster, telling herself that while Lucy might doubt, she hadn't met Captain Beaumaris. They'd soon be sending for Henry's trunks.

~

ALISTAIR WAS silent until the door shut behind Anna and Morris pressed a glass of brandy into his hand.

"Nice, this," he said, letting the flavor uncurl slowly in his mouth. The best brandy, new rugs, new draperies . . . no stinting of Anna's money in this house.

Noting his silent inventory, Morris raised his chin. "You're not getting the money."

"Of course not. Belongs to Henry, doesn't it?"

Morris nodded uneasily. Bastard was obviously skimming.

"Hard to see this all go to your brother's boy," Alistair said. "I know. I'm a younger son myself. Still, that's the way of it." He stared into his brandy, swirling the glass.

"She's got no right to complain of me," Morris said, breaking the silence and setting his drink onto the desk. "The faults of her breeding, her character—"

"Are no longer any concern of yours," Alistair interrupted, freezing Morris with a look. Choler rising, Morris pushed back his chair, but Alistair stayed in his seat. Mr. Wart-Morris might be more quick tempered than he'd expected, but this defensive rattling only confirmed his suspicions. "Reasonable men have ways of resolving problems like this," Alistair said gently.

"Do they?" Morris leaned his knuckles on the blotter, hiding from view a ring Alistair thought he quite liked the look of.

"Assuredly. A reasonable man in a situation like myself would see a lawyer and get him to audit your accounts. It might take a while—or it might not," Alistair said, smiling as he gestured with his brandy, "but a good lawyer would find me something to complain of, eventually. A suit would be filed in Chancery Court. I know nothing of such matters, save that they tend to take a devilishly long time to settle."

"You're welcome to try it," Morris sneered.

"I don't think I will," Alistair said. "Instead, I suggest that you give Anna custody of her son, and sufficient funds to provide him a lifestyle suitable for his means and station. There should be no need to touch the principal."

Morris laughed. "And I suppose this house and Henry's estate will fund themselves?"

"They ought to," Alistair said, looking around the room at the walnut panelling and tall shelves filled with books. "This house is nice—the desk by Sheraton? Yes, I thought so—but no reason to keep it open when the owner doesn't live in it. Perhaps Henry could rent it to you."

Morris looked ready to explode. "And why should I—"

"Your life will be more pleasant if you do," Alistair said. "I promise." When Morris said nothing, he decided to elaborate. "You wouldn't like being cut by society. I could arrange that, if I wished. But I think the neatest solution by far would be simply to shoot you."

Morris swelled like the sails of a frigate, but Alistair didn't break the careful inspection of his fingernails.

"You wouldn't dare!" Morris finally burst.

"Why not? It's much simpler than you suppose. I kill people all the time," Alistair said. "I'm rather good actually. Compared to wafers at Manton's, there's nothing to it. Simplest thing in the world, if I caught you unexpectedly."

"You're mad!"

"No, no. We haven't any of that in our family," Alistair said, slowly rising from his chair.

"I'll report you to the law!" Morris said wildly, spittle flying across his desk.

"But I haven't done anything yet," Alistair said. "And I assure you, if I did, no one would see me. None but you know what I've said. Who would believe it? I don't look unreasonable. And I'm not entirely without sympathy for you. I don't object to you keeping some small portion of the interest for yourself as compensation for ensuring Henry's properties are kept up or for any other sundries that may occur. I do object to robbery, to keeping Anna's son hostage out of avarice and spite, and to your manners. But if you meet my demands, I'll be quite satisfied."

"Will you, by God!" Morris slammed a fist into the desk, sloshing the brandy in his glass. "I won't endure these accusations! I demand satisfaction—"

"Splendid," Alistair said, straightening his left sleeve. "My seconds will wait on you in the morning. I choose pistols."

Morris strangled off his tirade, his jaw hanging open. "But—but you—"

"My dear Morris, you've just provided me a perfect opportunity. I'm not one to let it go to waste."

"I didn't mean—"

"You mean when you demanded satisfaction that you weren't challenging me to a duel?"

Morris's face turned scorching red. "I—I—no, I did not," he said, spitting the words reluctantly onto the desk between them.

A bemused smile lit on Alistair's face for a moment, then fluttered out of sight. No good trying to press the matter, not with a coward like Morris. "How disappointing," he said. "Then we are agreed? I'll join Anna packing up Henry. In future, you may send your correspondence to her at Rushford House. Have your man of business send me your proposal for Henry and Anna's allowance by Wednesday."

Morris was too apoplectic to respond to his farewells. Alistair left the room and mounted the stairs, wondering idly about the possibilities of Morris expiring naturally. But Anna's husband had died in an accident, so no luck there. The Morris breed didn't seem short-lived.

Anna's voice guided him to the nursery door, but he lingered outside, nervous. It had been an age since he'd been in a room like this. He wasn't sure how to manage it, so he'd taken the precaution of bringing a gift. A tiny box rested in his pocket.

"Hallo," he said, striding into the room with a heartiness that would have made Jasper snigger.

Anna struggled to her feet, hauling Henry up from the carpet, in spite of his legs, which flopped like empty coat sleeves. "Alistair, this is my son. Henry." Her smile was brilliant, but not blinding enough to hide the panic in her eyes.

"How do you do?" Alistair said, bowing to Henry. The boy looked him over. Recognized him.

"Ass-wipe!" he exclaimed.

"Master Henry!" exclaimed the girl in the corner, springing out of her rocking chair as Anna's cheeks drained of color. "I've told you a hundred times—"

"No matter," Alistair said, forestalling the nursemaid with an outstretched hand. He probably deserved it. He dropped to a crouch, where he could receive the full force of Henry's impudent grin. "You look"—and talk, but no need to mention that —"like a proper soldier," Alistair said. "Ready for your marching orders? You and your mother are going on a visit." Best to get him out of the house quickly, while Morris was still in shock. They could bring him back to Anna's parents' house for the night.

The boy scuffed his toe on the carpet. "Are you really a soldier?" he asked.

"I'm a captain of hussars," he said, knowing this was the pinnacle of every small boy's dreams, until they outgrew such foolishness. For him the dream expired long before he became a captain. Others weren't so lucky, and died first.

"See what I've brought you?" He reached into his pocket. Henry slipped free from his mother's grasp to snatch the box, sliding open the lid before Alistair could blink. "Wahoo!" Henry shouted, executing a triumphant leap when he saw the figure inside. It was a tin hussar riding a charging horse, his saber drawn.

"Lucy! Look! I've got a new one!"

"He hasn't any with horses, sir, just plain soldiers," the nurse explained.

128

"I have a uniform just like it," Alistair said, "But no mustache. See?"

Henry looked from the soldier clutched in his fist to Alistair, then back again. "Why not?"

"It wouldn't suit him," Anna said quickly. "He's handsome enough without one."

"Maybe you should try one," Alistair said. "It seems I don't have permission."

Henry cocked his head to one side. "All right," he said. "How?"

"Stop shaving," Alistair explained. He reached out and thumbed Henry's chin. "No whiskers yet? Never mind. Give them a year or two."

"Or twelve," Anna said, when Henry turned to her for confirmation. His shoulders slumped. "I'm sure when they come, they'll be glorious," she added. Henry perked up at that.

"You'll look after the packing?" Alistair said, glancing at the nurse.

"Of course, sir."

"I hope you'll come with us, Lucy," Anna said, stumbling a little over the words. "To Rushford House. Henry will miss you, and I—"

"Mr. Morris has given his full approval," Alistair added, smiling, since he didn't want the bother of finding a new nursemaid either.

"Oh." Lucy's cheeks turned pink. "Well, I couldn't leave the young master."

"Excellent," Alistair said, tucking Anna's hand into his arm. "Something tells me that Master Henry is in dire need of an ice. Let's remedy that, shall we?" In his own ears, he sounded over-inflated, uxorious. But he'd chosen the right words. Henry jumped into his jacket and soared down the stairs, Alistair holding one hand, Anna clutching the other.

"So far, so good," Alistair whispered, and Anna forgot her anxiety long enough to smile.

12

KEEP YOUR ENGAGEMENTS

NEVER BEFORE HAD Lady Fairchild let sympathy and guilt urge her to support such an unqualified disaster. No matter how matters eventually settled, there were problems ahead. Still, it was more comfortable involving herself with Alistair's troubles than examining her own. She sat at her writing desk, nibbling her pen—a habit she'd have to give up, now that she couldn't blame the damage on anyone else—trying to think of the best way to share the news with her sister. Alistair would write, no doubt, but he wasn't sharing the entire story. Nor would she. If they were to carry the thing off, the secret must be kept as close as possible.

Unused to keeping secrets from her sister, Georgiana crossed out line after line, struggling against her hesitant pen. She was on her third sheet, the failed attempts torn in pieces, when the front door opened and she heard footsteps on the stairs. William. She'd have to tell him too. Best not put it off.

He was in his study, of course, the sporting papers sticking out of his coat pocket and a stack of letters in his hand. Greeting her with more of his troubling friendliness, he invited her to join him. She took the proffered chair, her eyes flying involuntarily to the watercolor painting above the mantel. It was a view of their gardens at Cordell, and it never failed to heat her blood to a boil —it had been painted by Sophy's mother. Tightening her lips—it was wisest to remain cool to him as long as he sported trophies like this on his walls—she prepared for battle.

William shifted in his chair. "Perhaps it's time I updated the furnishings."

"It's no concern of mine how you keep your rooms," she said with a venomous smile.

"I trust you've passed a pleasant afternoon?" he asked.

"It was interesting, certainly. Gave me a great deal to think upon. I've taken your advice and gotten myself a new project."

"Oh?"

"Yes. I'd prefer to help him, since I failed signally the last time, but Alistair's requested my help for another instead. His fiancée, in fact."

William was a refined man, restricting his astonishment to a fractional lift of his brows.

"He's in love with her," she said. Eventually she'd find the right words to deceive her sister, but William knew her too well. She had to give him the truth. She would never approve an engagement to such a pitiful nobody, no matter how lovely of face and form. If Mrs. Morris still controlled her fortune, it would be different, though even then, she would prefer a marriage that wasn't quite so degrading to her nephew. "He'd marry her himself, if he could—"

"Didn't you just say they were engaged?" William said, stopping her with a raised hand.

"A ploy, nothing more. He can't foist her on us without some kind of connection."

"And the purpose if this is to . . .?"

She knew she'd end up feeling ridiculous. Too late now for regrets; she had given her word, and was bound to see the thing through. "She's a widow. Anna Morris. Married to Anthony, of

the Warwickshire family. Took her for her money, of course."
William showed no recognition—she didn't expect him to, since
Anthony Morris hadn't ordered his life around his stables. Most
of the time, William didn't even recognize their neighbors in
town, though he knew every farmer, hound and horse for miles
back in the country. "She wants her son, and Alistair has taken it
upon himself to get him for her."

"How noble of him."

Georgiana ignored his flat tone. "She'll need a husband eventually, and unless I help her to a suitable one, Alistair could very well
end up married to her. He's kept his head so far," she said, ignoring
William's skeptical eyebrow, "but who knows what he might yet do."

"I've heard of Anna Morris," William said. "But she hadn't
roused his pity then. I suppose it's a commendable emotion, but I
don't see why either of us should embroil ourselves in Alistair
Beaumaris's concerns. I'm happy to help his career, but this is—
strange. You're overtired, my dear."

"You said I might do whatever I pleased," Georgiana said.

"If it made you happy. Will this meddling accomplish that?"

"I don't require your permission. I can befriend anyone I like."

"True. But you never have before." He glanced at the bundle of
letters in his hand. "I've just had word from John. Fortis is ready
to foal. I'd hoped to be there—I've hopes for this one."

Horses. Always the horses. "I thought you wanted us to spend
more time together," she said.

"I do. But it's been twenty-seven days since I broached the
subject and you haven't given me an answer. What was I to
think?" Before she could answer, he moved again. "So you are
accepting my offer?"

No. But she couldn't say that. "Life would be more pleasant,
certainly, if we had fewer quarrels," she equivocated.

"Is that what we do?" he asked, the corner of his mouth lifting.
Quarrel was a mild word for the sterile wasteland between them.

"I don't like to exaggerate," she said. "Plenty of married persons disagree from time to time. I daresay—" But she didn't, floundering into silence. William's proposed experiment terrified her.

"All right," he said. "We'll both stay in town. When do you meet this girl?"

"This evening," Georgiana said. "She's coming to dine."

"I'll have to send Somerville my regrets," William said. "Assuming you're wishful of my company?"

She was, but would prefer he expressed the sentiment in less romantic terms. His presence would be useful. "I'd like your help, if you are willing," she said carefully.

"Then you have it. Bring on Alistair's charity. Bring on whatever you like." He smiled mockingly, tapping his letters with his forefinger. "What kind of husband would I be, denying such a pretty request from my wife?"

Georgiana rose from her chair. "The worst, undoubtably. I'll see you at dinner."

∾

"WHAT IS THE MATTER BETWEEN THEM?" Anna whispered, once she and Alistair had withdrawn to the relative safety of the drawing room sofa. Dinner with Lord and Lady Fairchild was an experience like no other.

"The mood is thicker than usual," Alistair admitted, reaching over her lap to turn the page of the book of engravings she was pretending to read, letting his hand brush her arm. "Quite a costume," he said.

Bridling at his criticism of her dress—her mirror didn't lie, and she'd looked very well in this floating lavender gauze—she followed his eyes down to the book and discovered he was referring to someone else, a woman in baggy trousers and some sort of blouse on top that left her midriff bare. "That would be very chilly," Anna said, turning the page.

"Not if she were next to me," answered Alistair.

"Unfortunate then, that I am here instead."

He laughed, a low chuckle that brushed against her ear. Anna turned the page again, finding a much safer drawing of a man in robes and a turban. She glanced across the room, where Lady Fairchild sat at the pianoforte. She was out of practice, clearly choosing the instrument because she was tired of maintaining the flow of conversation. Her husband stood at her shoulder, turning the pages. Every time he reached forward, her fingers skipped along a little faster, but at least this was easier than watching them speak—that was a regular game of tug of war. Neither one had been dragged through the mud yet, but even she could tell they stood on slippery ground.

"They are old campaigners," Alistair explained, following Anna's eyes. "They've been at war as long as I can remember. Don't worry. They are excessively polite about it."

Anna swallowed. "They don't like me." She was used to bearing up under the perceptive glance of her mother, whose affectionate heart blinded her to Anna's hidden sins. Lady Fairchild was another matter. Anna wasn't sure if adultery or bourgeois opinions rated worse in Lady Fairchild's books, but when she felt that lady's gaze, she was convinced she'd revealed everything. Lady Fairchild surely knew how she'd watched in trepidation before choosing a fork.

"You've lived with worse," Alistair said.

True, but that didn't make this any easier.

"Something tells me you didn't let Morris bully you," he said.

"After the first year, not much," she admitted. Though he had won every battle that mattered.

"I'm sure you can cope with my uncle and aunt. Come, it's late. I should take you home."

Relieved, she rose from the sofa. All evening she'd been

thinking of Henry and the dusty nursery upstairs, emptied now of trunks and storage cases, and void of nearly anything else. The toys and books that had been hers and Richard's were long gone. Only their little beds remained, and a creaking rocking chair, evidence of the forlorn hopes of her parents that they might have grandchildren (who were allowed to visit them) someday. That nursery furniture, cleaned of years of dust, would only be used for one night. She wished they didn't have to come back here, where Henry's noise would rattle through the house, jangling the ornaments on the tables and the sapphires hanging from Lady Fairchild's ears.

Alistair announced they were leaving, thanked his uncle and aunt, promising to ride with his uncle in the morning. "If you could point me to a good horse, I'd be grateful."

Lord Fairchild nodded, his brow creasing as he considered this profound problem.

"Until tomorrow," Lady Fairchild said. "Jenkins assures me that all is ready."

Anna thanked her, thinking how much better it would be if she and Henry could hide themselves away in her parents' empty nursery instead. She could take the other bed. They could line Henry's soldiers along the windowsill, where Richard used to put his ships—battered miniature vessels with stained sails. He'd lugged them everywhere, even into bed, unlike Anna who had never brought playthings with her, tucked under her arm. The soft doll sewn by her mother always slept upon the shelf, because —though she'd never admitted it—she'd been afraid of smothering her.

Alistair took her arm after the butler had helped her into her cloak. A moment more and they were outside, closed into a carriage full of heavy night air.

"This hot weather can't hold forever. There'll be a storm soon enough," Alistair said, arranging his cloak around his knees.

Anna felt smothered by her own. She'd hoped escaping into

the relative cool outside would lesson the pressure squeezing dew out of her forehead, but she felt sticky as ever. "Think you will be around to see it?" she asked.

"Maybe, if it comes tomorrow. I travel to Portsmouth the day after that, and I'd rather leave before the city is awash in mud."

It made sense, and she could fault him for nothing, not when he was exerting himself so greatly on her behalf. But she felt wronged nonetheless that he was pitching her into Rushford House and then abandoning her. "I wish you didn't need to leave so soon," she said, playing with the edge of her cloak.

"So do I," he said. "I left Spain hoping I'd never have to return." He shrugged, as if going back was a minor inconvenience.

"Sounds as if you don't care for soldiering," she said, reaching for the carriage strap as they lurched to one side.

"Can't think of anything I like less," he said, copying her light tone. A warm beam slid from a streetlamp outside through the carriage window, pushing the shadows from his face. His eyes were bleak. Unaware of her furtive glance, he stared at the cushions opposite. Neither the velvet (dark grey) or the buttons (black) deserved such scrutiny. Anna didn't know what to say, only that she must speak, quickly, before the silence exposed him even more.

"I wouldn't venture to understand how hard it must be."

"Good. You could not."

"I'll pray for you," she offered, hating how feeble it sounded. "Henry too," she added, though she realized she had no idea what exactly he'd been taught.

Alistair huffed a laugh. "Did you pray for your brother —Richard?"

"Of course."

"Then do you think it helped?"

She didn't lean away, though she wanted to when he wounded her with words. A gingery retort danced on her tongue.

"My mother is sure of it," she answered, finally. "And on the worst days, that's usually good enough for me." They endured, and if they felt the loss of Richard's easy smile, they did not speak of it. Anna dropped her chin, hiding from Alistair's scrutiny, but saw from the corner of her eye how he lifted his hand, letting it hover beside her cheek. At the last moment, he changed his mind, dropping his hand to his lap.

"Stop fending back tears with your eyelashes," he said. "I'm sorry. I should know better. My profession makes me churlish sometimes."

"I can understand why," she said, blinking to clear her eyes. "I often feel churlish too."

"Well, you aren't acting that way in return. You're very kind. Too good for me—don't laugh!" he said, cutting off her hmmph of disgust. "I'll take the prayers, but I'd hoped for your letters, too. To keep up the fiction, you know."

"I can do that," she said.

"Good." He settled deeper into the cushions. "You're a good woman, Anna."

He took her hand, lacing her fingers in his own, sparing her the need to reply. The way his thumb slid along her own told her he'd prefer a response that wasn't words. It felt so good, that little sweep on her hand, warm and soft and tempting. It made her insides quiver, especially when she met his eyes. She wished she wasn't wearing gloves.

It was delicious to look and touch, but this was how trouble started—a shifting leg, a sideways glance. Even innocuous words sounded risqué when exchanged in breathy whispers. Before you knew it, you were giddy, in a delirium of pressing fingers and greedy mouths, thinking only: I am wanted.

She hadn't thought about trying to get a child until after the first big slip, when, after letting Mr. Gormley slide his hand too low in a dance, he offered to drive her home. Mr. Gormley was widowed, and forty if he was a day, but handsome enough she'd happily followed him into the hallway, slipping away from the shabby village assembly where Morrises didn't go. Exultant over his heated kisses, tingling with desire and the heat of revenge, she'd made no protest when they'd fallen together in his carriage, thrashing around each other's clothing for a brief moment that left them sweaty and panting for breath. Frightened by her intensity, Mr. Gormley hadn't argued when she asked him to let her out at the bottom of the drive.

Anna returned to herself, skin scalding, as Alistair began walking the fingers of his other hand up the bare skin of her wrist. He was nothing like Mr. Gormley. He was much more dangerous.

Kisses. He just wants kisses. They were all right, surely.

Except he hadn't kissed her yet. She was sure he intended at least that, but he was taking his time about getting there. Not that she was complaining. His fingertips tripped past the crease of her elbow as delicately as a dancer on tiptoe, moving under her cloak, climbing upwards, over the bit of lace edging the bottom of her sleeve. When he reached bare skin again at her shoulder she was already leaning toward him. She paused, enjoying the warmth of his breath on her cheek—it smelled like cardamon—before letting him close that last half inch to her mouth. Their lips melted together and she held back a sigh, succumbing to her favorite weakness.

She loved kissing. Even the slobbery ones and the demanding mouths that tried to uproot her tongue, though Alistair was neither. He was warm persuasion and gentle insistence, but he kept his word even when she wished he wouldn't. No wandering hands, no climbing on top of her. Anna slid her hand over his cheek to trace the curve of his ear, resolving to get rid of her gloves.

No you don't. You know better.

She couldn't ignore her conscience this time, or, after lurching round a sharp corner, the reminder that this carriage was much the same as Mr. Gormley's, and therefore too dangerous a place for the removal of gloves. With infinite regret, she made her hands relax and drift back into her own space. Her greedy lips didn't want to stop playing, but Alistair got the signal and slowed, disengaging with a smile.

"I remember. Only kisses," he said.

Thank goodness she had dignity enough not to sigh. *You are not that person,* her conscience scolded. And she knew she wasn't. Not anymore.

If thine eye offend thee . . . . Really, if she cut out and cast off her sinful parts as the bible said, she'd be a pitiful, maimed thing. Eyes, skin, fingers, lips . . . .

This carriage was far too warm, but it didn't feel like hell at all. If she didn't stop kissing him though, it would take her there, sure as Wednesday followed Tuesday. She looked at Alistair, who was sober now that the smile had fallen off her face.

"God won't wink at this," she mumbled.

His arm slid round her shoulders, comforting, brotherly. The rumble of the wheels rolling over the cobbles filled the silence, punctuated only by an occasional creak from the springs. "Should I apologize? I will if you want, but I'd be lying. I'd do that again in a heartbeat."

It was silly of her, but his admission made her glad, widening her mouth into a lopsided smile. "Better not. We've lies enough already. Best if we don't take unnecessary chances."

"No more kisses?"

Was it wrong of her to rejoice that he seemed as forlorn at the prospect as she?

"I didn't say that. You'll still be here tomorrow." It was practically a promise, but for the rest of the drive, she kept her hands clasped primly in her lap.

13

FAIRY TALES AREN'T TRUE

ONE MORE DAY and he'd be gone. Still, it was impossible not to float up the stairs after Alistair's kisses. They were good—more than the usual mind-wiping distraction. She was too fuddled to know if it was his skill (superlative), his looks (arresting), or the newness of this kind of chaste longing, but she drifted into her room, aware of one difference she'd never experienced before: a feeling of serenity, that all would be well. Clearly, she'd been without kisses too long. She was drunk on them, deluded. Anna fished a nightdress out of her clothes press and ascended the last flight of stairs, finding her way by the light of her flickering candle—stubby now, after waiting so long for her return. Her father had left it in the hall for her, along with a note.

He's a good lad. So is Henry. Sorry for doubting you.

Somewhere her mother had found a rug for the nursery. The room had been swept, the corners cleared of cobwebs and dust. No curtains in the windows, though. Since she didn't want to put out her candle and undress in the dark, Anna moved to the corner and crouched down out of sight, which made it even harder to struggle out of her clothes. She nearly lost her balance and had to fling out an arm to grasp the wall, but Henry didn't stir. He lay face down in his pillow, his mouth open, his face flushed. The toy hussar was beside his bed on the floor, where it had fallen from his limp hand.

Papa's right. He is a good man, she thought, creeping across the floor to right the tiny figure and slip her son's hand back under the sheet. Returning to her corner, she laid her dress over the back of the rocking chair, winced as she yanked her stays from back to front so she could unpick the laces, and unrolled her stockings. Bare and shivering now, she dove into her heavy nightdress and jumped into the second bed, pulling the covers up to her chin. The sheets were cold but crisp, smelling of soap and lavender. Anna drew up her feet, hugging her knees because her toes were cold.

"Night, Henry," she whispered, blowing him a kiss. A simple gesture, but it gave her a surge of warmth, knowing he was there, waiting for her kiss to waft across the room and land on his cheek.

She dozed, waking with a start when her arm fell off the side of the bed, which was smaller than she was used to. Edging closer to the wall, she shifted to her back, then her side. The mattress was thinner than she remembered.

After a few minutes she rolled onto her back again. It was too dark to see the ceiling. The lingering taste of cardamon in her mouth had to be her imagination. It made her think of Alistair, and kisses, where he might be now, and what his face would look like if he was sleeping. Did he pull himself into a small space, with the sheet drawn up under his chin, or did he sprawl across his bed with his arms flung out and his palms wide open? Did he sleep in a nightshirt or in his skin? And how pale was he where he wasn't tanned? Her lips quirked. Hard to say. Once he left England, he'd probably end up sleeping in his uniform—perhaps even his boots. By all accounts, campaigning was harsh.

Of course, it wouldn't be all bad for him. A week at sea, a short stop in Lisbon or Oporto—she should find out where he'd disembark—and then a trek through Portugal and into Spain, where he'd rejoin his battalion. If Wellington continued his advance, the army might be in Madrid by the time Alistair caught up with them. She hoped so. He'd get a decent billet there. Anna didn't trust her own luck, but Alistair's seemed better. Perhaps he'd arrive just in time to chase the French back where they belonged.

There would be ladies, if the army was in Madrid.

Idiot! She punched her pillow and settled back down again. *It's an army. There'll be women about, in Madrid or no.* Alistair was a fine man. Women would want him.

She frowned into the dark, aware that she shouldn't be pettish about it. She wasn't marrying him, after all. He was just loaning himself temporarily. Pity. But then, she'd already had one handsome husband. She couldn't expect to snare another. Anthony always knew how to cut a dash.

That's what he'd done too. Sewed up her fortune in the marriage agreements, wed her in a quick ceremony at her parents' church and bedded her, just as promptly. Not at the inn where they'd stopped on their journey to Warwickshire, though she'd lain awake half the night, hoping, wondering why he didn't come to her. Anthony waited until they arrived at the family pile, then he took care of it. He couldn't allow an annulment, after all, and he was the kind of man who attended to details, however unpleasant. She, poor fool, still had stars in her eyes when she'd tripped out of her bedroom to find him that morning, dressed and ready to return to London.

"You aren't dressed!" he'd hissed at her, frightening her with severe eyes. He returned his attention to his coffee, but not before she saw his disgust. "My mother's coming. She'll teach you what's what."

"Can't you?" She'd never met the other Mrs. Morris.

"I'm returning to London. No," he said, stopping her with an upraised hand. "Please. No scenes at breakfast." She waited silently, too shocked to sit down, while he finished his coffee. He left while she was still without words, frozen by the sideboard in bare feet and a night gown.

It took three whole months before she gave up hoping for letters. By then the other Mrs. Morris, a she-dragon fond of jewels and the town of Bath, had informed her of her purpose in the family—providing money. At first Anna cried, then she wrote her papa and discovered she was trapped. Trapped with a critical and keen-eyed rheumatic woman, caught up in the come-out of her own daughter. Abandoned in an isolated country house, with servants who laughed at her, neighbors who knew nothing about her, or were too aristocratic to care. When Anthony came home in the fall to shoot his birds, she screamed at him, but all he did was shoulder his gun and go outside.

He was content to wait until she was broken—after all, time was on his side. He thought.

Even before the sister got married, Anna was escaping to the village. It wasn't long to walk. Wary at first, she did little else than poke her head into the shops, purchasing unnecessary ribbons and bottles of miracle cream. Then she let one of the shop boys walk her home and ended up kissing him in a haystack—a much more beguiling way to spend her afternoon than wandering from room to room in the Morris house. The she-dragon was busy redecorating.

Later, when Anna returned to her room—she preferred taking her meals there, on a tray—she stared into the mirror for a long time, practicing a bland face, convinced the kisses would show. The next day, when she chanced across her mother-in-law in the hall, she trembled, expecting her sin would be seen and that she would be promptly devoured.

The other Mrs. Morris saw nothing, telling her only to stay

out of the upholsterers' way, but it was still a week before Anna braved the village again.

No one noticed. Not the apothecary, the vicar, or the village gossips. Anna spoke with them all, and no one named her a scarlet woman or harried her out of town. The shop boy, David, winked at her, but that was all.

A week later Anthony returned, having some business with his steward. She grimly allowed him his rights, hoping it would get her a child at least. The attempt was unsuccessful, the only satisfying thing being that he enjoyed it as little as she did. Two weeks later, Anna went to the village assembly—the dragon had returned to Bath—and ended up in a carriage with Mr. Gormley. She'd met him a month earlier at church, after deciding to attend the local Methodist congregation, instead of the one frequented by the Morrises.

She learned two things from David and Mr. Gormley—one, that it was much more enjoyable receiving embraces from men other than her hateful husband, and two, that men liked embracing her. Anna might not have gotten a baby from that fateful carriage ride, but she did conceive an idea, a way to get her revenge. It was easier than she thought, getting men to tumble her: a medical student, studying with the local physician, who liked sharing his knowledge of anatomy; a tall gentleman she saw only the once, riding through the lanes, who stopped to help her carry yet another package of ribbons. He introduced himself as Clarence Fitzjohn, but the letter on his signet ring was an R. And James, the footman, who knew her mischief and the reasons for it, but was good enough to give her what she wanted and keep her secret. Anthony came and went, oblivious to it all.

But he wasn't blind. When she was in her fifth month, he realized he'd made a mistake. He screamed then, forgetting he'd declared it vulgar. Anna fled and James showed her where to hide, behind the cold frames in the back of the gardener's shed.

"Maybe you should go home," he whispered, coming out later with a plate of supper. It was simple fare, so it had to be his own.

"I'm staying," Anna said. "He'll divorce me, and I'll get back my money."

"Don't be so sure," James said. "You should be careful." He was right.

Anthony left the next morning, despite consuming three bottles of brandy through the night. By all accounts, three bottles was nothing for him in the months that followed. He drank, whored, fought three of his friends, and injured two horses, while the dragon watched Anna and frowned.

Henry was born, and Anna forgot her unhappiness for a little while. She wrote her mother, inviting her to see him christened. Her parents came, but prudently stayed in the local inn, missing Anthony's arrival that evening, the drunken shouting, the shattered vase of flowers. The spilled water lay all night, ruining the new pianoforte.

The next morning, Anthony received her parents when they came to bid Anna and Henry farewell before journeying back to London. He waved them off politely from the door, then turned to his wife and told her never to send for them again. He was so still, so calm, and so cold that Anna began to tremble. She tiptoed around the house for two days, never leaving Henry's side, sleeping in a cot in the nursery, but Anthony didn't seek her out or speak to her again before dashing off to London.

She breathed easy again.

A month later, Anthony returned. "I'm taking the boy to London."

"I won't let you. Henry's mine," Anna said, clutching him closer, fighting off her sudden dizziness. In that instant, the room had lost its air.

"I don't know whose son he is, or which ditch you laid in when you conceived him, but as he is to be my heir, I'll see he's raised properly."

"You can't—"

Anthony cut her off with a laugh. "Didn't think of that, did you? You might have played me, but I've always held the trump card, Anna. Hand him over."

Movement caught her eye; a plainly dressed woman standing in the hallway. And a footman—not James—with a wooden face and wide shoulders.

"Don't make me take him. He'll only get hurt," Anthony warned.

She looked at his gloved hands, lean and sure, and felt her insides churn. There was no softness in his face, in his voice, in the grimly competent servant waiting to take charge of her son. She stuttered protests, incoherent pleas, but he lifted Henry away and deposited him in the arms of the wet nurse, who headed for the door. Anna's legs broke like straws and she crumpled to the floor, throwing up a hand to catch Anthony's coat.

"Please—"

One look was all she got. One look that made her shiver, that chilled her in her bed even now. Uprooting her sheets, Anna wrapped the bedcovers round her shoulders and hopped across the cold floor to Henry's bed, exhaling a jagged breath at the sight of his tousled head. Afraid of waking him, she lowered herself carefully to the floor, her heartbeat slowing as she measured the pace of her son's breath, a stir of air that curled around her face, warm as the steam from her morning tea.

I thought I'd never have you back.

That, of course, wasn't strictly true. She had followed Anthony to town, quaking with rage and fright, haggard from lack of sleep. Was Henry feeding? Did they leave him to cry in his crib? Did they swaddle him with one hand free, so he could suck his fingers?

Anthony's servants didn't let her past the door. Anna's father, white and wrathful, didn't get in either. Nor did his lawyers, his influential friends. Every day, Anna walked by the house on

Mount Street, peering at the upstairs windows, wondering where her son was, watching Anthony come and go, but mostly go. When he saw her in the street he nodded at her like an acquaintance or a passing stranger. Only now, years later, did she realize that in those last months he'd grown lines around his eyes, that his careful dress had turned slipshod—a cravat askew, his gloves crushed in his clasped hand, scuffs on his boots. Before Henry was a year old, Anthony died of a broken neck when his curricle overturned on a race to Brighton.

Ever mindful of appearances, the dragon invited Anna back to Warwickshire for the funeral. Anna went, forsaking pride since it meant seeing Henry. He wasn't there. Frederick had left him in London. "No point bringing the child," the other Mrs. Morris said. "Unhealthy."

She and Anna both donned new blacks and sat in the drawing room, not speaking, as Frederick and Anthony's friends stood witness while Anthony's remains were consigned to the family crypt. "I've something to show you," she said to Anna, when evening shadows finally shrank the room to a reasonable size, a small bright circle around the fireplace. "Come."

Anna followed her mother-in law with a stuttering heart, upstairs and down the passage to Anthony's chamber. She'd gone in only once—to smell the coats he left behind that first time, before her heart was broken. The room was desolate and clean, waiting for an occupant who would never return. The other Mrs. Morris walked straight to the bedside table and opened the drawer, lifting out a small packet wrapped in grey silk.

"Look on this," she said.

Anna took it from her outstretched hand, pulling back the silk to reveal a miniature in a gilded frame. It was of a young lady— blonde, and not even very pretty. "Who's this?" she demanded.

The other Mrs. Morris raised herself an inch. "This is the lady my son loved. They couldn't marry. There just wasn't enough money."

Yes, money made people do hateful things. Sometimes Anna wondered how her life might have been, if she hadn't had so much of it, once. She traced a circle on the sheet next to Henry's shoulder.

It was wrong of you, Anthony, to marry me for mine. I wouldn't have played you false, if you hadn't done it first.

14

PARLOUR GAMES

IT WAS ENTIRELY possible that Lord Fairchild knew more horses than people, and unquestionable that he liked the horses more.

"We won't go to Tatt's," Lord Fairchild said, setting out with Alistair in the early morning. "Friend of mine has one I think you'll like. You can save yourself some blunt if we offer him direct."

She was a beautiful horse, with long lines and strong quarters, but it was her soft mouth that decided Alistair. She moved at the lightest touch.

"She'll do," Alistair said, nodding at the groom. "Why is Somerville selling?" he asked Lord Fairchild in an undertone.

"Opera dancers are expensive," Lord Fairchild said with a grin. "Right now Somerville has one with a temper."

Alistair squared things with Somerville, who said he'd send the mare round with the groom. Lord Fairchild was watching the retreating horse. "I'd have liked her for myself," he said to Alistair, as they left. "Try not to get her killed, will you? If I could breed her with Ajax . . . . " He hummed to himself, imagining leggy foals.

"I should collect Mrs. Morris and Henry now," Alistair said, nudging his uncle into reality.

"Right. I'll come with you. Let me drive you there. That is— does her family keep a carriage?"

"I expect so," Alistair said, keeping a straight face.

"Good. Can't bring her back in this curricle—not unless she sits on your lap."

"And I don't know where we'd put Henry," Alistair said.

Lord Fairchild laughed. "Where's the house?"

Alistair gave the direction, sitting back while his uncle spun the curricle round corners, threading it through traffic with considerable skill. It was a well-tuned vehicle, drawn by horses few men could best. They shaved past a crested town coach with little more than an inch between their wheels.

"I can't think of a tactful way to ask, so you'll have to pardon me. I know something of ruined marriages, after all," Lord Fairchild said, diverting his attention from his horses long enough to flash Alistair an apologetic smile. "How damaged is she?"

"Mrs. Morris? She's not—"

"I don't know if I can stand to live with two of them," his uncle interrupted. "And I can't leave Lady Fairchild, not yet. Do you think they'll like each other?"

Alistair wanted to say yes, but felt compelled to be honest. "I've no idea."

Lord Fairchild grunted. "Me neither. Better hope they do, or I'll—I don't know what I'd do, actually. Hunt you down in Spain, I suppose, and give you a list of grievances."

"Anna's a little sharp-edged," Alistair conceded.

"I noticed." Lord Fairchild swung them round a corner. "Dash it, I've taken the wrong turn. Where're we going again?"

Alistair supplied the direction. "You make it sound like Anna's soiled. She's not."

His uncle nodded noncommittally.

"Morris was a scoundrel," Alistair said.

"Husbands often are," Lord Fairchild said, his voice shaded with amusement. "Or so I've been told."

"That's the one," Alistair said, pointing at the house. Lord Fairchild halted his horses, surveying the surroundings with polite interest, too well-mannered to show much surprise—for an unfashionable quarter of town, it was quite pleasant. A maid answered the door. "They're waiting for you in the drawing room," she said to Alistair.

"Show us up," Lord Fairchild commanded.

Henry was sitting on the sofa, swinging his feet and scowling. Alistair suspected the boy didn't care for his jacket and starched shirt; he wouldn't have, at that age. Anna looked tired, and probably was if she'd had to stuff the boy into his clothes. Like her son, she was dressed with care, in a dark blue dress with braided trim, the masculine style highlighting how very much she wasn't. The dress and curling hair would have looked quite dashing, if they'd been paired with a laughing smile. Anna's eyes were fever bright, her hands stiff.

Alistair stepped forward to make Lord Fairchild known to Anna's parents. If they were surprised to find a viscount in their drawing room, they received the news calmly. Anna's mother was dressed austerely as ever, and Mr. Fulham wore a rusty black suit, but neither became conscious of their plain appearance, or turned ingratiating.

"Don't feel like we are stealing them away," Lord Fairchild said. "You must visit your grandson and daughter while they are at Rushford house on those days that they don't come to you."

Gratified, Mr. Fulham made polite conversation with Lord Fairchild while Mrs. Fulham called their carriage.

"I'll ride over with you, if I may," Alistair said to Anna.

"Does he usually go out of his way to charm?" Anna whispered, glancing at his uncle.

"No," Alistair answered. "So this proves he doesn't hate you. Stop worrying."

"The imposition—" she began, twisting her hands.

"Lord and Lady Fairchild don't allow people to impose on them," Alistair said. "They could've said no. How is Henry?"

She winced. "He threw his breakfast on the floor this morning and kicked his nurse."

"I'll keep my distance then," Alistair said.

Once Anna and Henry's boxes were dispatched with the carrier, along with the nursemaid and Anna's maid, Alistair finally found himself in the Fulham's carriage opposite Anna and Henry, who was less sulky now that his lips were pursed around a peppermint. Lord Fairchild, who was driving his own curricle, would probably arrive at Rushford house ahead of them by a good ten minutes, giving Alistair a little extra time to talk Anna out of her nervousness. Her gloved hands were clenched tight, Alistair's conversational sallies going almost unheeded.

When they pulled to a stop in front of Rushford house, the footmen were waiting. With one hand on Henry's shoulder and the other resting in the curve of Anna's back, Alistair shepherded them up the steps.

"As far as I know, Lady Fairchild's never murdered anybody, worshiped the devil, or spied for Napoleon," he whispered to Anna, trying to coax a smile. "You're quite safe." They stepped through the front door and into Bedlam.

A small boy—not Henry—careened around the hall, racing around like a beetle in a box. He looped around Lord Fairchild, who was smiling, his hat held in midair, expecting it to be lifted away by Jenkins the butler, who'd just deserted his post to fling out a steadying arm as the boy lost his balance, wheeling his arms in the air.

"Gently, Master Laurie. Gently now," Jenkins chided, and Henrietta's boy quieted. It would last, Alistair predicted, about twenty seconds. Before he could speak, his cousin Henrietta turned towards him.

"What's this nonsense about you getting married?" she began, stopping as she caught sight of Anna. "Oh."

Alistair knew all about crossing lightly over heavy ground. Time to move fast. "Lady Arundel, allow me to present my fiancée, Anna Morris."

Henrietta, bless her, greeted Anna with a smile. "What rubbish. He knows I'm Henrietta to family." She looked Anna over, her smile growing as she took in Anna's close hold on the small boy at her skirts. "Well, I won't call you Mrs. Morris. No point, when you're going to be Mrs. Beaumaris before long." She leaned towards Anna confidentially. "You lucky thing."

"She's hopeless," Alistair explained.

"And shameless to boot," Henrietta added. "If you can't bring yourself to use Henrietta, call me Lady A."

Anna still hadn't found any words, so Alistair filled the gap. "Just the one today?" he asked, nodding at Henrietta's son Lawrence, who was beginning to oscillate again.

"No, Will's here too," Henrietta said, glancing over to the far side of the hall, where Lady Fairchild stood beside a large potted palm. She had Henrietta's younger son in her arms, and he had a fist—and a mouthful—of foliage.

"A family party. You must forgive us or join in, Mrs. Morris," Lord Fairchild said, setting his whip and his gloves on the table. "Henrietta, next time you might give us a little warning."

"Pooh," she said. "Next thing you'll make me wait for an invitation card. Don't be absurd."

Armed with considerable beauty and an imperviously cheerful disposition, Henrietta was used to getting her way. Other young wives with her high spirits might have been labelled fast, but Henrietta was comically devoted to her wispy scholar of a husband and had never met a soul she couldn't charm.

"This is your son?" she asked Anna.

"Yes, this is Henry."

"Make sure you bring him to visit Laurie. I can't think what he'll do in this house. It's not fitted up for children."

"We've made the necessary changes," Lady Fairchild said loftily. "Mrs. Morris, if you would care to see? William, you can take the baby." She deposited the surly-looking infant into her husband's arms. Lord Fairchild's eyes widened, but he promptly took himself off, motioning for Jenkins to join him, as the rest of them trooped up the stairs.

"I've put you in the green room at the end of the hall," Lady Fairchild was saying. "It gets good light, and—"

"Will Henry be close by?" Anna interrupted.

"Just up the stairs," Lady Fairchild began.

"May I sleep upstairs too?"

"Only if you want to sleep in the nursemaid's room." Lady Fairchild's laugh hung in the empty air. "Would you prefer that?" she asked at last, prickling a little.

"You needn't fear for Henry. He'll be quite all right," Alistair said. Henry and Laurie, already cementing their relationship, pushed past them into the room and slid under the bed, wriggling like eels.

"Of course," Anna said, swallowing. "It's a very pretty room," she said, giving it a cursory glance.

"Your maid is quartered upstairs and will see to your unpacking," Lady Fairchild said, her eyes falling on the trunks resting in the middle of the floor. "I sent her to help the nursemaid unpack for Henry."

That seemed to meet with Anna's approval. "May I take a look?" she asked. Lady Fairchild nodded. They lured the boys out from under the bed and climbed up the stairs to a little white room on the top story girdled with dark wood panelling. The deep windows were partitioned from the room with blue cutwork curtains. Lucy the nursemaid looked up from the chest of drawers, where she was putting away stockings, and a scrawny bird of a girl, who must be Anna's maid, though she scarcely looked old enough to braid her own hair, paused in the act of hanging a little hat on the peg in the wall. They both dropped curtseys—the starved wren sinking deep enough to honor the queen.

"The bed's a little large," Lady Fairchild said, "But we didn't have anything smaller. Now, perhaps we might leave the boys here and—"

"Tea, by all means, mother," Henrietta interrupted. "But I know Laurie would much rather help Mr. Jenkins. Laurie?"

~

THEY WERE CLOSETED in the drawing room five minutes later, relieved of the children. Lady Fairchild brought Anna to her side by asking her to help hand round the cups.

Henrietta pounced. "So you're engaged? When were you going to tell Percy and me?"

"Hen, you're exhausting," Alistair said, pulling his eyes away from Anna and his aunt. "I fully intended—"

"Does Jasper know yet?"

"I wrote him last night," Alistair said. He'd kept back the full story. He should try to introduce Anna to Cyril, since he was the only one of his immediate family within spitting distance. His parents would have to settle for a letter. Alistair didn't mind. Telling Lady Fairchild had been tricky enough. No doubt his engagement would be blamed when his father took another decline.

"It's heartless of you, getting engaged to her and leaving town," Henrietta said, stirring her tea.

"If there was any way to avoid it, I promise I would," Alistair said. "Your mother will look after her."

"I will too," Henrietta said, laying her hand on Alistair's own.

"Mama told me they wouldn't let her have her boy. Made me feel absolutely murderous."

"That, I'd pay to see," Alistair said, touched nonetheless by Henrietta's stout offer of allegiance. She was easily the best of all of their family, the soaring waltz caught between darker sonatas. Anna brought them their cups, but was called back to take the seat next to Lady Fairchild.

"Where did you find her?" Henrietta asked, taking a sip of tea.

"Green Park," Alistair said. No need to mention that unfortunate masquerade, especially since Henrietta had been there. Might lead to unpleasant questions.

"Mother and I should leave you two alone, shouldn't we?"

"'Twould be the merciful thing to do," Alistair said. He'd be everlastingly grateful.

"Then I'll arrange it. I am still your favorite cousin, aren't I?"

Alistair grinned. "Less vexing than Jasper, but the children are a liability. Must you always bring them about?"

"Idiot." Henrietta set down her cup. "If you thought for half a second, you'd realize I brought them to be kind. Henry will do so much better if there's another boy to knock things off tables. Don't you think so, Anna?" she asked, raising her voice.

"Pardon?" Anna asked, turning towards them.

"I was telling my cousin that I think it will do both our boys good to spend time together. They only make trouble when they're bored, so it's much safer with two of them."

Alistair looked down to his cup, stirring again, though the sugar was dissolved already. He could remind Henrietta of a few choice moments he'd shared with Jasper—the latest being their turn up in the park, just weeks ago—but held his tongue. Aunt Georgiana remembered many of them, he was sure. He was treading a thin enough line as it was without calling up old misdemeanors.

"Mama, have you the latest Lady's Magazine? There was a redingote with shoulder epaulettes I quite fancied. I was

156

thinking of having it made up in a dark plum color," Henrietta said.

Lady Fairchild frowned and set aside her tea. Henrietta might be a wife, a mother, and mistress of her own household, but her mother still liked to dictate what she could wear. "I can't recall the costume you mean, and I'm not sure how you'd look in plum."

"You have a gown that color, don't you? Let's see if I can support that deep a shade."

Lady Fairchild left first, her brow creasing as she imagined Henrietta in unflattering clothes. Henrietta followed, winking at Alistair as she closed the door, signing with her fingers that he had five minutes at least.

"Well, what do you think? I can't say they won't drive you half-mad at times, but they won't persecute you. I dare say my aunt won't even trouble to sneer most days." He crossed the room, examined the cakes on the tea tray, deciding against a piece of lemon cake, then set himself on the arm of Anna's chair, slipping his arm across her shoulders. Too bad she was in an arm chair, not the sofa. The possibilities were so much better with a little more room.

"I needn't have worried so much," Anna admitted. "But if you'd seen what my life was with the Morrises, you'd understand why I was afraid."

"Put it behind you," Alistair said, pressing his fingers into her shoulder and finding the knot he'd expected. "From now on, they'll never be more than a nuisance and a letter arriving every quarter, which will at least come with a sizable bank draft." Still working on the knot, he drew the first letter from his waistcoat pocket with his other hand. It had been waiting for him when he arrived home last evening.

Anna flipped the letter open, letting the bank draft slide into her lap. She read the letter first—it was terse, but polite—then she glanced at the draft. Gasped. "What did you say to him?" she asked.

"Nothing that wasn't true. Don't worry about it. My uncle knows the amount you should receive and he will look into it should anything go amiss. He can set you up at his bank, find someone to manage things for you."

"My father can help me with that," Anna said.

"If you wish."

She folded up the papers and tucked them into the bodice of her dress, unaware of Alistair's heightened interest. He was in the perfect place to watch the papers slide between her dress and her skin.

"Is there a garden?" she asked, rising from the chair and crossing to the window. "Henry will be a terrible nuisance if he can't get outside."

"I think the house shares a small one, yes." He came up behind her at the window and let himself plant a kiss on her neck. He'd be reaching after that letter if he didn't touch her somewhere, quickly. Her neck seemed like a safe choice, but of course it led up to that delectable ear, half hidden under a wing of dark hair. It wasn't a problem until Anna turned her chin and gave him her lips—perfect lips, rouged and full. He'd developed a habit of visualizing them whenever his mind wandered, when thoughts slipped beyond control. Pleasurable, yes, but dashed inconvenient.

"Pardon. I couldn't resist," he said, relaxing his hold.

"I've given you leave to kiss me," she said. "Thank you."

"For the kiss?"

"That too," she laughed. "But I was thinking about bringing us here. Dealing with Frederick. The toy soldier for Henry."

"Don't kiss me because you're grateful," he said, pulling back a little, even though he wanted to put his lips to her soft ones again.

"Oh, it's more than that," she said, her lips curving at the corners.

"Good. Cause I must admit, I'm tempted to kidnap you and

take you to Spain. Quite a hardship, losing you when we're just getting started." But it would be better, in the end. There could be no future between them. "You're smiling," he said. "I have my uses, you see."

"I enjoy you. I don't want to use you," she said, her smile fading.

"You aren't. I want you to be happy. And being enjoyed is what I like," he said.

"I'm sure," she said with a low chuckle. "Don't kiss too many beauties in Lisbon. Just enough to keep in practice."

He lifted an eyebrow, but she only laughed at him.

"No one achieves such mastery without practice, Captain. You kiss exceedingly well, and I will miss you more than is good for you. Count yourself lucky that I am letting you escape. I'll see you off in the morning."

"I leave before dawn."

"I am awake then. Henry too, if this morning was any indicator."

He considered the virtues of subtlety a moment, then decided it wasn't worth the attempt. He wanted a kiss and he wanted it close, so he turned her around. "Has it been five minutes?"

"Why?"

"Henrietta said she'd give us five minutes."

"I don't know. I didn't check the clock."

"I should have. What poor planning. I don't mind being caught by my aunt. Do you?"

She kissed him quick, her breath warm on his face. "Yes. I don't think she likes scenes in her drawing room."

Fair enough. "Alright then. Let's put you back in your chair," he said, propelling her to her seat.

"And pretend we're talking corn prices? It won't fool anyone."

"Kiss me then, and don't be ashamed of it."

She did, though her cheeks were scarlet. When Henrietta

returned—alone, thankfully—startling them with a crow of laughter, Anna was too flushed to turn any redder.

"Alistair. So greedy! Shame on you. It's been at least seven!"

"I should go." Heaven knew he had a thousand things to do, and only hours remaining. He fought for some light words, bending close to keep them from Henrietta's ears. "I will remember you—here, in my aunt's drawing room—when I am in Spain."

He kissed her hand. And stole it again, ten minutes later, milling with the family by the door. He tousled Henry's hair and threw greetings, unnoticed, to Henrietta's boys, and kissed Henrietta and his aunt. Uncle William wished him well and they all came out to the front step to wave him off. Aunt Georgiana was blinking rapidly—had been ever since he put on his hat.

"Take good care of yourself," she said.

He always meant to, but it was difficult. He promised to anyway, smiling as he descended the steps. Anna was waiting at the bottom one.

"Good luck, Captain," she said, her low voice scarcely audible above the wishes of his relatives, the noise of the children, the ruckus in the streets. It was a worn out wish, but it settled round him like a schoolboy's scarf, warm and comforting. Even once she was safely married, he knew she'd consider him a friend—a pleasing notion. Striding away more jauntily than was his wont, Alistair decided it was no bad thing, giving help to a good woman.

15

CONTRIVING

"Come to Watier's with me tonight?" Cyril asked, late that evening, when Alistair stumbled across him in the hall.

"I'm leaving tomorrow," Alistair said. He was fighting heavy eyes already, and no wonder: he'd been to Horse Guards again, supervised his packing, seen his bankers and written a new will. He had few worldly goods, but no reason Anna shouldn't have them if he couldn't. A real fiancé would do that, he was sure.

"That's why I'm inviting you," Cyril said. "It's our last chance."

"Good of you," Alistair said. "But I'd rather not. Have to make an early start if I'm to reach Portsmouth in good time."

Cyril shrugged and started off toward his chamber—hopefully to change his cravat. The marvel at his throat was making Alistair uncomfortable.

"Look," Alistair began, stopping Cyril before he'd gone more than a few steps.

"Yes?"

"I should tell you something . . . "

"Mmmm?" Cyril waited, eyebrows raised. Alistair yanked his eyes away again from his brother's cravat. Many gentleman chose to wear the style known as the *trône d'amour*—he did himself, in chaste white. But pairing that knot with a neckcloth in the color known as *Yeux de Fille en Extase*, or Eyes of a Girl in Ecstasy, was excessive. Never mind. He had more important things to discuss.

"I'm getting married," he said in a rush.

"In Spain? I hear the women are fine, but mother will have a fit if you marry a Catholic. Don't put her through that."

"New one for you to be considering her nerves," Alistair retorted. "I'm not getting married now, just engaged. She's not Catholic." It was the only point he could think of in Anna's favor, besides her face, but his mother was too mercenary to appreciate that.

"Hmmn." Cyril thought it over for a minute. "Sudden, isn't it?"

I'll say. "Not really. She's staying with Uncle William and Aunt Georgiana. Just thought you should know."

"Has she a name?" Cyril asked.

"Anna. Anna Morris."

"Don't recognize it," Cyril said. "Sure I can't persuade you to come?"

Alistair shook his head.

"I'm off then. Try not to get shot."

It was probably the friendliest exchange they'd had in years.

On his way upstairs, Alistair found a note from Jasper.

You brute,

Just when were you going to tell me? Convenient, that you are recalled to Spain before I can force an explanation from you. I was joking, you know, when I asked if she had felled you with a glance. You are a dog, but I wish you the very best of luck.

Alistair rubbed the back of his head uneasily as he folded away the letter. His parents. Cyril. Henrietta. Jasper. Henry. Mr. and Mrs. Fulham. When he'd suggested the scheme he hadn't thought he'd be lying to so many people. It was beginning to feel uncomfortable. Henry would remember little enough of their brief meetings, but he liked the Fulhams. Henrietta, who'd accepted Anna so warmly, could only be hurt when Anna broke the engagement.

Frowning and silent, he submitted to Griggs' handling, preparing for bed. No way to fix it. Besides, he was doing his best. Yet the longer he thought about it, the worse he felt, and he had enough to contend with without brooding over his own qualms. Falling onto his pillow with unnecessary violence, Alistair shut his mind and ordered himself to sleep.

As PROMISED, Anna arrived at his parents' house early—before eight o'clock—to see him off. "You can put this in the coach," she said, pushing a basket into his hands, seeing that his horse was saddled nearby. "I asked Lady Fairchild what she thought you might like to eat." She looked doubtfully under the napkin. "There's some good Madeira, but I expect you'll have plenty of that where you're going."

He'd probably drink the Madeira, but Alistair wasn't sure about the food. He always suffered from a nervous stomach on departure days. This morning he'd limited himself to a plain cup of coffee. Griggs was looking favorably at the basket, though. The man could devour his own weight and not even burp. And never gain an ounce, either.

"You'll look after him, won't you?" Anna asked Griggs, who tugged his forelock to her like the carter's son he was.

"Always do," Griggs said. "Don't you be worrying."

Anna smiled at him. "I'm counting on you."

Like many ugly men, Griggs had a fatal weakness for beautiful women. Turning his attention from Griggs' immediate, embarrassing devotion, Alistair crouched down in front of Henry, who was scuffing his shoes on the step, clutching the little tin hussar to the front of his coat. "You'll keep watch on your mama for me?" The boy nodded, his attention on the saber at Alistair's side.

"I'll bring one home for you. A French one," Alistair promised. Henry's eyes widened, innocent of the knowledge that prizes came from dead men.

He'd had been like that too, when he wore short coats and through his years at school, his naiveté lasting even into his first campaigns. He couldn't recall exactly when his saber had changed from a beautiful, mirror-bright curve to a butcher's tool, something to be continually cleaned and sharpened. "Good lad," Alistair said, his knees cracking as he pushed himself upright. He reached out to ruffle Henry's hair. It was as silky as Anna's and of the same sooty-brown.

"Next you'll be giving him brandy and teaching him to smoke," Anna said. "I'm still terrified he might pull out some of your language in front of Lady Fairchild."

"She's heard it before," Alistair said. Like Henry, she'd heard most of it from Jasper. "Did you remember the pistols?" he asked Griggs.

"Under the carriage seat," Griggs answered.

"Good," Alistair said, guilty but unrepentant. After a long internal debate, he'd finally decided to nab them. They were far too nice to leave in a cupboard, and if Cyril kicked up a dust, he wouldn't be here to see it.

"If you've forgotten anything, write me and I'll see it gets sent on," Anna said.

"I will. Thank you." When she'd insisted on coming to wave him off, he'd feared he was in for his mother's brand of theatrics: leaky eyes, pleas to be careful, continual nervous fluttering. He should have known better. Anna was calm and solicitous—interested in his well-being, but no more. Her practical attention was much more to the purpose.

"Safe journey," she said, hoisting Henry onto her hip.

The child was an impediment, but not enough. Alistair roped them in with his arms, ignoring a kick to his hip from Henry, who was mashed between them.

"Henry, help a fellow out, will you? I can't see your mother behind that hat."

Henry let go of Alistair's epaulette and shoved aside Anna's bonnet. "Here she is."

It would be a fine thing, Alistair thought, to be smiled on the way Anna did to Henry, but her happy expression lasted only a brief moment before contracting into a pained frown. Along with the bonnet, Henry had wrapped his fingers round a piece of her hair.

"Those curls are mine today," Alistair said, releasing Anna with one arm so he could pry Henry's fingers loose. "You'll send me one, I hope. Didn't have time to ask before." In truth, he hadn't thought of it, but he wished he had now.

"I will, if you want it," Anna said.

"Good." He smoothed her hair into place with his fingers, then let them slip down her cheek, tracing his index finger over the corner of her mouth. "Glad to see you smiling, Mrs. Morris."

He leaned in to kiss her, a brief touch only, since they were standing in the street, balancing her boy between them. "Good hunting," he whispered. "Don't rush yourself, and don't settle."

"I'll be careful," she said, and stepped out of his arms.

He always made a point of whistling to himself as he left home to ride to war. Today the notes came easier. By the time he had turned the corner, he was singing one of his battalion's favorite tunes, the wildly colorful *Downfall of Paris*.

"Sir!" came the outraged protest of a ruddy nosed gentleman, leaning protectively over the perplexed lady sharing the seat of his curricle.

"Lovely song, isn't it?" said Alistair, tipping his hat. He rode on, ignoring the sputters behind him, singing until he finished the last verse.

∽

WELL, that was that. Anna helped Henry into Lord Fairchild's carriage so they could return to the house, wondering if she would ever see Captain Beaumaris again. It seemed unlikely.

"Are there cannons in Spain?" Henry asked.

"Yes," Anna responded absentmindedly.

"Can I have one?"

She looked at her son, who was peering up at her hopefully, fiddling with a button hanging from his jacket by a loose thread. All the buttons had been securely fastened when he'd put on the jacket this morning. No wonder Lucy was always sewing.

"Canons aren't for children," she said, not bothering to correct Henry's speech. The larger issue required attention first. "They're heavy, dangerous, and they shoot fire."

Henry's eyes grew round and rapturous. "Can I see?"

"Not today," Anna said. "Give me that button. If we put it in your pocket, it won't get lost." She pried it free and slid it into his pocket before he could lunge to the far side of the carriage, where she'd stuffed his ragged blanket. This was the dit she'd heard so much of—a grey, threadbare tatter of wool, patched in a multitude of places with mismatched thread.

"Is that from your uncle's dog?" she asked, reaching across Henry to finger a large rent.

"Mmmhmm," Henry nodded, clutching the dit protectively.

"I could mend it for you. Grandma Fulham would do the best job, but I can manage in a pinch."

"In blue?"

Why not? "I can patch in it blue," she said. Lady Fairchild might have blue thread; if not, she could send her maid to buy some.

Henry gave a satisfied nod from the far corner of the coach. He didn't like being squashed or coddled, and tolerated her touch with an impatient air. But he was here, within reach. She couldn't look at him for long without her throat constricting and her eyes growing hot. Last night she'd crept into the nursery again, plunking herself down on the floor by the bed, counting his breaths, watching him sleep, forgetting her irritation over his bedtime tantrum because his bread and milk hadn't come in his usual blue plate and cup. Despite Alistair's success, she didn't feel up to demanding dishes from Frederick. She might be able to buy a similar one. Or Henry could learn to accept inconvenience— no, that possibility was too remote to expect. Perhaps she could ask Frederick for the blue plate after all. He was hateful and condescending, but unlike Henry, he probably wouldn't scream at her. Henry had lasted a good half-hour last night and once again thrown the offending dishes onto the floor. She'd tried to reason with him, but failed, feeling worse every time she imagined Lord and Lady Fairchild exchanging pained glances on the floor below.

She'd find a way to manage. She had to. No matter what happened, she wasn't losing Henry again.

LISBON AND LONDON

AFTER TEN YEARS in the army, Alistair had a good idea what to expect on his journey. He wasn't disappointed. Arriving in Portsmouth that evening, he learned the HMS Gallant wasn't ready to sail.

"Two more days to finish revictualling, at least," said Jamieson, a young coronet journeying out to join Alistair's regiment. Alistair got himself a room at the Old Ship, an inn with clean enough sheets and food that earned more praise—deservedly, Alistair decided, putting away a second slice of pie. After a long day's riding, he was hungry.

Retiring to his room, he wrote his parents and started a letter to Anna. Sealing the letter to his parents and setting the one for Anna aside (he'd add more later) he descended to the public room, where Griggs was swapping stories with another campaigner. Jamieson was in another corner with the new recruits, wiry lads with smooth faces, except for one sporting an unusually luxurious mustache.

Must have started shaving when he was twelve, Alistair thought.

They spent the night tossing back bumpers of gin. Alistair, the oldest of the lot, was pressed for story after story. He obliged, and some of the ones he told were even true. Later, when these fellows knew more, they'd question his veracity, but he wasn't about to waste such naiveté by ruining the game. Fuddled by drink, he finally made his cautious way upstairs, tired enough to sink immediately into dreamless sleep.

The Gallant finished taking on supplies and sailed before Alistair could enjoy too much of the landlady's excellent pie or run into trouble with her daughter, who had an unfortunate tendency of latching eyes on him. She'd have had better luck with Jamieson, though it was probably for the best. Jamieson was young and careless.

Despite the promise of calm seas, Alistair spent the first two days miserable in his hammock, or heaving his guts over the side. Once Neptune accepted his customary offerings, Alistair's stomach declared a truce. He spent the remaining days pondering Horace, the majesty and minuteness of a ship at sea, and trading friendly insults with his brother officers in the King's Navy. The frigate was cleaner than most of the lodgings Alistair found, but he was grateful he fought his battles on land. Too much time on this floating ant hill and he'd turn mystic or philosopher. Either would be tedious, if not for him, then at least for everyone else.

The ship was crammed full of infantry recruits, a noisy, undisciplined lot that Alistair suspected he'd end up escorting across Spain. There were stores and oxen and horses—they could never get enough remounts. The captain didn't confide in him, but Alistair expected there were money chests secured in the hold too—he hoped so, for it was difficult keeping the army supplied with goods purchased from their Spanish and Portuguese allies, and the soldiers' pay was usually months in arrears. Alistair had money enough for now, even after buying the new mare, having won a pretty sum playing whist against Tom Bagshot. Of course, he still had to acquire a pack mule or two in Lisbon, so it wouldn't be too long before his pockets were to let.

In spite of himself, his spirits lifted when they reached port. His black gelding fretted in the sling as he was lifted from the ship to the docks, but the mare was unperturbed by this rude handling. She landed lightly, flicked her ears as she waited to be released and accepted a pat on the nose, looking at the other horse with mild reproach.

Lisbon was a beautiful city: houses with walls of creamy oyster and red tile roof-hats; domes and cupolas edged in stonework lace; hills clad in trees of a green like no other, since today there was no haze. Alistair spoke better Spanish than Portuguese, but it felt good all the same to shape his tongue around that language again. He wished his friends on the Gallant well, and then, since he was yet a man of means, he dispatched Griggs with the horses and baggage to one of the more pleasing hostelries. "Clean. And quiet," he ordered. No doubt he'd join Jamieson and the others this evening for a dance or a visit to the theatre, and a glimpse of Lisbon's ladies, but afterward he wanted a quiet place for himself with just a pen, paper, and a bottle of port.

Anna would not look so out of place in Lisbon, he thought, with her bright lips and dark hair, though her eyes were a perhaps too light a grey. Still, dress her up right and teach her the fandango, and she'd look as beguiling as the rest of them. Those curving lips and dark lashes would look well, half obscured by a black mantilla. Maybe he'd find one for her once he got into Spain.

Reporting promptly at headquarters, Alistair received a pleasant surprise—no tending a wagon train across hot plains for him.

"Staff's borrowing you for a spell. You know the country and right now there's no one else. Clermont tried to ride his horse up a flight of stairs and broke a leg, damn him," said General

Barnard, the depot's commanding officer. "I need you to carry dispatches. You've got good horses?"

"I'd show you them, if you had the time," Alistair said, knowing the harassed general did not. "Or you can take my word for it."

Barnard grunted. "I'll take your word. I'd send you tonight if I could, but I expect the best you can manage is tomorrow morning."

Alistair considered. Griggs would follow after him, with the mules and the baggage. If he was quick finding the hostelry, he could dash off a letter and take it to the Gallant before they even finished unloading. "I can be on my way before nightfall," Alistair said. "No need to delay. I've seen Lisbon before." One dance or play was much like another. He wouldn't miss anything tonight he hadn't had before.

Barnard's approving laugh sounded more like an artillery blast. "Not like those recruits! Lost in the gutters and fleshpots inside of an hour. Have to haul them out and shout them sober before they'll march."

"They'll have both discipline and order by the time they reach Madrid," Alistair said.

General Barnard grunted noncommittally. "Let's hope." He leaned back in his chair, appraising Alistair again. Alistair didn't flinch. No reason to—despite his inward misgivings, his record was spotless, as was his uniform, and General Barnard had a reputation for being more concerned with the latter. "Well, get going!" barked Barnard, so Alistair did.

ANNA'S first day at Rushford House was the worst. The rest were only marginally better.

The first test was an afternoon with Lady Fairchild in the drawing room. Lady Fairchild didn't accept any callers, so Anna had to endure two hours of elegantly poisonous questions, watching Lady Fairchild's Sphinx-like countenance, wondering if the next time she'd answer wrong and get eaten. Anna stumbled over her responses, caught on the idea of Lady Fairchild unhinging her beautiful jaw before coiling round and swallowing her. She'd forgotten it was possible to sweat and shiver at the same time.

It made no sense to her, but apparently it mattered that her fingers were symmetrical, that she was quick to puzzle out acrostics, and that she had all her teeth. Satisfied, Lady Fairchild closed the interview with a gentle inclination of the chin. "It's nice to get to know you. I think you and Captain Andrews will suit perfectly. Wear your green silk tonight. He'll be sitting next to you at dinner."

By the time the expressionless Fairchild footmen brought out the second course, Anna was certain of one thing—if she were ever alone with Captain Andrews, she'd do him an injury. Stabbing wouldn't silence him, so it would have to be the garrote.

The next candidate was nicer, less enamored with his own opinions, though thicker about the middle. Mr. Geoffrey Gordon-Page let her complete her sentences when she ventured to speak, even if he wore a glazed, falsely interested look.

"We didn't know what to do with the extra vaccine, so I ate it," Anna finished, just to see if he was listening.

"Really."

"Yes. Three pints of it."

He smiled indulgently, unaware that she knew he wasn't attending. Which must be why Lady Fairchild had warned her he was a writer.

And what would you say, Mr. Gordon-Page, if I told you to undress me now, at the table? 'Really?'

He probably would. Anna speared a flabby piece of macaroni and chewed it with unnecessary force. Even if she wanted to, catching this man's fancy was impossible. She'd never be as attractive as a blank sheet of paper. Swallowing mechanically (she hated pasta), she reflected that it was useless trying to please herself, in spite of Alistair's advice not to settle. She had to think of Henry. If her choice was between a good husband and a good father, she'd take the latter. Anna sat through the evening's musical entertainment with pursed lips, revising her goals.

This approach didn't prove any easier. Gentlemen only seemed put off when she tested the waters by speaking warmly about her son—much more warmly than his current behavior deserved.

"You must stop going on about Henry," Lady Fairchild chided after another evening. "You can't expect gentlemen to be interested in children—even their own. Besides, wouldn't you prefer your husband to stay out of it and leave you a free hand?"

Not really. She wasn't managing well at all. They both knew that. If Lady Fairchild would simply allow her to replace the breakfast room wallpaper, Anna wouldn't need to shrivel every time she thought about it.

EVENINGS WERE DREADFUL, but the shopping was nice. She and Lady Fairchild might disagree on everything else, but they both loved clothes.

"These are the ones," Lady Fairchild said, holding up a pair of silver mesh stockings. They'd been up and down Bond Street all afternoon, trying to match Anna's new beaded slippers.

"Worth the search," Anna said, as the shop assistant made up the parcel.

"Absolutely," said Lady Fairchild. She didn't frown until they were on their way out, the bell on the door ringing behind them. "What will you do with the others?"

"Wear them. Eventually." Anna knew her mother would disapprove, but it was comforting to be needlessly extravagant.

Lady Fairchild was perfect company to talk over the shape of a bonnet or the width of a sash. She knew the words for every color, lace pattern, and mode of dress ever invented. It took some coaxing to persuade her into a charcoal pelisse with gold frogging and a china silk dressing gown with blue and green medallions, but, "If you can't be bold, who can?" Anna asked.

Anna could have happily devoted herself to renewing both their wardrobes, if she weren't failing as a mother and faced with the wretched work of finding a husband. The more she thought about it, the sicker she felt. She didn't want any of them. They were too bald, too sleek, too broad, or laughed too much at their own jokes. No one had Alistair's white, even teeth, dangerous sense of humor, or his chivalry. None of the gentlemen who complimented her looks, or carried her fan, or called at the house to make conversation in the drawing room would ever offer her so much in exchange for so little.

In her private thoughts she admitted the truth. Alistair Beaumaris was the husband she wanted, but he was not the one she was going to get. She must be reasonable. She'd be lucky to find someone to take her part, someone who'd do right by Henry. Yes, it would be nice to find someone who loved her, or at least someone she wouldn't mind going to bed with, but she'd be content if she could find an amiable man. A courteous one. Perhaps she should have tried harder with the writer, Mr. Geoffrey Gordon—was it Clay?—she couldn't remember.

Every morning in front of her mirror, Anna gave herself a lecture, reminding herself that all she expected—all she deserved —was a friendly husband. It shouldn't be hard to find one, but it was. Lady Fairchild, noticing the fretful lines on Anna's forehead, assured her with ill-concealed impatience that in a few months more gentlemen would return to London. Henrietta, more perceptive, if less well informed, saw the same marks of worry and responded with a crushing hug.

"He'll be fine," she said, leading Anna to her untidy sitting room and patting her hand. Since it suited the part, Anna allowed herself the luxury of a few sniffles and accepted a cup of sweet milky tea. She couldn't resist Henrietta's sympathy, or her comfortable cushions, and ended up laughing more than she had in weeks.

It wouldn't do Alistair's reputation any good at all, Anna realized, if she broke their engagement too quickly. So she needn't feel guilty if she avoided Lady Fairchild's drawing room to visit Henrietta and her boys.

"Tomorrow we'll see Laurie and William again," Anna said that evening, as she tucked the bedcovers around Henry's defensively hunched shoulders.

"Fine," he snapped, in exactly the same tones as Lady Fairchild.

17

DIVERTIMENTO

LORD FAIRCHILD KNEW BETTER than to hope to see his wife outside her rooms before noon, let alone appear at the breakfast table. As far as he could recollect, she had never done so. If he wanted to speak with her he'd have to force his way in. So he breakfasted with Mrs. Morris, waved her and the boy off to Henrietta's, and waited until Georgiana's maid, Dawson, appeared in the corridor.

"I'll take that," he said, stealing the breakfast tray from her hands.

"My lord—"

"You may take the day off," he said.

Dawson curtsied and left, leaving him to struggle alone through the door, the china clinking alarmingly as he balanced the tray with one arm. The door clicked open and he shouldered it wide, sloshing chocolate onto the napkin. He winced. Georgiana would want a fresh one. Never mind. She could endure it for one day. Then he saw her severe look and almost changed his mind.

"What are you doing here?" she asked, drawing the bedcovers up to her chin. William held out the tray. Georgiana diverted her frown to it only momentarily, convinced this was a hostile invasion.

"I have a surprise for you. Be quick about your breakfast, will you?" William said, more easily than he felt.

"I'm paying calls with Anna today."

"I'm afraid not. She's gone to Henrietta's. The boy too."

She lifted an eyebrow, but accepted the tray, overlooking the splash on the napkin. She rattled the spoon through her chocolate and took a cautious sip. With her neat nightcap and plaited hair, she could have looked fragile, but for the frown. Her eyes were practically pinning him to the wall.

"I don't hurry," she informed him, setting aside the spoon.

"I know," he said, taking his life in his hands and perching on the edge of her bed. Before she could protest, he picked up the knife and began spreading butter on a corner of toast. "We needn't tell anyone. Eat." He thrust the buttered triangle—barely browned, the way she liked it—in front of her, but she didn't take it.

"I can't eat with you shoving food at my mouth," she said.

"Give it me then," he said, biting off half of the toast, licking away the drip of butter that ran down his fingers. He shouldn't feel hungry, though he had risen earlier than usual for his customary ride, knowing a good gallop was the best way to stiffen resolve. He crammed the rest of the toast into his mouth and wiped his fingers on the sheets.

"You're disgusting," she said, turning her eyes to the wall.

"Quite. Come on, eat up. No reason not to. I can't see anything under that nightgown you're wearing, not in this light."

Scowling even deeper, she reached for the toast. She ate it slowly, nibbling around the edge, sipping her chocolate, watching him. Her toes wiggled beneath the covers.

"Where's Dawson?" she asked.

"Gave her the day off."

"Who's going to help me dress?" she asked, annoyed. "Betty?

The way she brushes, she'll tug out half my hair."

"I can do it," he said.

She snorted, dabbing plum preserve on the last wedge of toast. Once it was evenly distributed (maintaining a clear border of crust to protect her fingers), she looked up at him again.

"I can," he insisted.

Her eyes narrowed. William waited, hoping she'd take up the challenge—just how well did he know the ins and outs of a lady's clothes? Truthfully, he was long out of practice, but telling her that wouldn't help. He was trying to win her back, not bring up old grievances.

Curiosity won over dislike. "Very well. Fetch the pomona green walking dress and a white point lace petticoat. You can remove the tray first."

What the devil kind of color was pomona green? It took seven trips to the dressing room to find it, and even then he still had the wrong petticoat. A pile of rejected gowns rested on the foot of the bed, a tangle of skirts and sleeves and flounces.

"I suppose that petticoat will do, though I hadn't planned for pink," Georgiana said.

"You're most accommodating," he murmured.

"I could be here till nightfall if I don't settle for this one," she said. "Put it over the chair." He did, turning to her, a smile growing on his face as he waited. She'd had her fun. Time for his. Her fingers twitched, bravado leaking away.

"I've changed my mind. Get Betty," she said.

"You aren't getting rid of me now, not after I fetched all those dresses."

"It's not my fault you can't follow instructions."

"Come on. We'll be all day at this rate."

"Fine." Setting her mouth, she rose from the bed, stripping off her nightgown herself, daring him to comment. He knew better, holding his tongue as he handed her towels and soap while she splashed herself from the can of hot water. "Just where are we going?" she demanded, her eyes fixed on the wallpaper. It was different from the paper that had decorated the walls, years ago, when he'd been used to visiting her room. Everything was. He didn't think a stick of the old furniture remained. Her bed was smaller now, too small to accommodate a couple with any degree of comfort.

"Well?" she prodded.

William backtracked, trying to remember her question. "It's a surprise," he said. She toweled herself dry, keeping her arms tucked against her chest like the wings of a baby bird.

"Chemises and stockings are in the top drawer," she said, nodding in the direction of the tallboy. "Take one from the pile on the right."

He pulled one off the top. "It will be warm today," he said, examining the thick material doubtfully.

"It's fine. Just give it to me," she snapped.

"Losing your courage?"

She grabbed the chemise and yanked it over her head.

"I like this pink one better," he said. It was a fine lawn, edged with lace and ribbons.

"Of course you do—oh, just get out. Send that useless Betty to me." She pushed past him and yanked a light corset from another drawer, groping around for a lace.

"The only thing I hear from you about Betty is how stupid she is," William said. "Let me."

"You aren't any better! You didn't even recognize pomona green!"

"We could pension off Dawson and you could teach me," he said, plucking the corset from her hands and wrapping it around her. "Pass me that lace."

"I want a blue one," she insisted.

"I know blue," he said, holding the corset with one hand and drawing out a ribbon of the correct color with the other. "Right?" he asked, pausing for her approval.

"That is cerulean," she said.

"But also blue."

He was proficient enough with her laces, hooks and pins, earning himself a sour glance through the mirror. Knowing she wouldn't believe excuses—finding your way through a woman's clothes was not a skill a man forgot—he tried for humility, offering an apologetic smile. Except for that, he avoided her eyes. There were better things to look upon: pink toes, legs that could have belonged to a ballet dancer, long white arms.

"You need to eat more," he said, rubbing his knuckle down her back. "I could almost play a tune on your ribs." She leapt away from his touch, so he pulled her back, frowning as he tightened the laces. "Don't know why you bother with this. You're skin and bones."

"Ladies my age don't disdain a little help," she said, shifting the corset around her bosom.

"If you say so. Comfortable? Sitting right?" he asked, sliding a quick hand over her breast before she slapped him away.

"Perfectly," she said, her eyes warning him to keep his distance. She glanced at his hands, then at the array of combs spread over the dressing table. "I'll do my hair myself, since I'm not in the mood to be pawed."

"I'll be very careful," he promised.

"And you'd look at me that way the whole time! I'd be better off with one—or both—of the footmen. They know to keep the line."

They better. "Spare your breath, Georgy. I've just seen you in your skin, and even though I'm not going to be able to think of anything else, I'll keep the thoughts to myself. You'll have to endure the looks. Call me whatever names you like. I'm not attending."

"Then I should ask you now for permission to redecorate your library?"

He chuckled. "My dear, I'm distracted enough you could probably get away with a good deal more than that."

"Don't tempt me," she said.

"I'm trying very hard to do just that. So far the result is humbling."

"Good."

He gave a last tug at the laces, then tied them into a bow.

"I'll do the stockings," she said, lifting them from his hands the moment he took them from the drawer.

"Don't be cruel," William said, stretching out his hand. She had beautiful legs.

Georgiana took a step back and folded her arms, the stockings clutched in one fist. "You said we were in a hurry. I'm not being ousted from my bed at this ungodly hour, simply so you can haul me back into it."

"You'd let me?" he asked flatly.

Terrifying silence. "Absolutely not," she said, a second too late.

Here goes. William stepped forward. He didn't reach for the stockings.

THEY LEFT an hour later than planned. Georgiana was too quiet.

She regrets it, William thought, wondering how on earth he would persuade her, now that kisses and caresses had failed. Once they had climbed out of her bed at least. It was a good thing they weren't going far. In this silence, a longer drive outside the city to Windsor or Reading might have killed him.

She said one word when they disembarked. "Punting?"

"Yes."

They boarded the little craft and pushed away from the river's edge without spending any more words.

He wished she'd just tell him what he was supposed to do now, but she seemed afraid to look at him, absorbed in the quiet ripple of the water. William leaned against the pole and pushed their boat under the arch of a bridge, watching the shadows swallow his wife before the afternoon sunlight reclaimed her. She was leaning away from him, trailing a hand in the water, immaculate as ever, not looking at all as if they'd rolled out of her ridiculously narrow bed a short time before. Maybe she wanted to pretend they hadn't, returning to their familiar antagonism and forgetting anything else.

"You used to enjoy rowing on the lake at home," he said, remembering how she would disappear on warm afternoons. Sometimes she'd row steadily back and forth. Other times she'd lie out of sight along the bottom of her boat for so long he'd worry she'd tipped out and drowned. "Why did you stop?"

"I didn't enjoy it any more," she said, not looking up from the water. It was murky and green, turning darker where the trees draped their shadows. Behind the growth edging the river he glimpsed great sloping lawns, rising to even greater houses.

"Do you ever go fishing?" she asked.

"Haven't in years."

"I used to, when I was small. When I'd see Sophy setting out from the house with her rod and reel I often wished I could go with her."

"Why didn't you?" he asked.

"I don't know. I never thought she really wanted me—she seemed to need her escapes. But now I think she might have needed someone to escape with more. I wish I had let myself ask."

She turned her blinking eyes to the river bank, to the swaths of tall grass. Georgiana never asked—she expected, William realized. She'd scatter rebukes, corrections, and smiling reminders, the last gently spoken, but still with all the force of command. Fetch this, purchase that, and stop wearing that ghastly color. Accompany me to the opera and converse sensibly at my parties and remind the servants not to do such and such, and just give me a moment's peace. One could comply or refuse without having to engage her personally. She'd invite Sophy to drive with her to the village, bring her up to London. But she wouldn't ask to fish with her, or to share the private enthusiasms of any of the family.

"Once we return home," he said, "you and I will go fishing."

"I'll make you bait the hooks," she said, deflecting in vain. It would take more than that to discourage him. She'd never care for horses, but she liked being around water. He did too. It felt good to work his arms, poling them along the river.

"This haze is ruining my hair," she said.

"Over warm?" She shouldn't be. She was wearing the wispy pink chemise, the one he liked, under her gown.

"No." A dragonfly darted across the water.

"I like your hair," he said. "Why did you stop enjoying boating?"

"For a time, I don't think I enjoyed anything," she admitted.

He remembered that too. After losing Julius, he'd eventually turned to Fanny, Sophy's mother—a temporary solace that lasted only until Fanny's conscience got the better of her. Georgiana had turned to no one. Her sister was the kind of person who half-listened to your sorrows and then hurried to tell you how much worse she had it herself.

"It was a terrible time," he said, knowing she'd understand what he meant.

"Eventually I came to enjoy parties and dinners—the planning mostly. It gave me things to do, to think about. More so than boats and idle drifting."

"I like drifting," he said, pushing them to the left, so they could float under the shade. Her dress—a light muslin, not the one of pomona green—wavered between white and grey in the light filtering through the leaves. There had been no solace for Georgiana. She'd gone from grief over Julius straight to fury over his affair and his bastard child, hurling herself into feats of organization, the fixing of innumerable details.

"I'm good at planning. I like success," she said.

"And now?" he probed, steering their craft into a gentle eddy, where they could spin and watch the current pass.

"It seems rather useless. I'm alone."

"You don't have to be," he said.

She pulled her fingers out of the water, flicking diamond drops over the murky depths. "It's easy for you. People like you, even when you've done nothing to deserve it."

"Sophy never liked me," he said. It was an old hurt, a deep one.

"She did in the end."

Maybe she had, but it had been short-lived. Sophy was further away from him now than she'd ever been. "I know it was lonely. I couldn't understand why you never took lovers," he said. "I'd prefer you didn't now—I want you for myself if I can persuade you—but I would have welcomed it once. I expected it, actually. You know I wouldn't have stopped you." He wasn't sure what he'd do if she tried it now.

She looked at him, then back over the water. "Sometimes I did, in my head," she admitted. "But when it came right down to it, there didn't seem much point, if it was only to even the score with you. You wouldn't have cared." She dipped her hand to the water again, stirring it with her forefinger. When she spoke, it was simply, without a hint of pride or apology. "I couldn't. That's just not who I am."

"I know," he said, around the sudden thickness in this throat. Best just to say it. "It shames me. If I had half your honor—"

"We should never have had Sophy. And she is partly my own," Georgiana said. "At least, it feels so."

"Still?"

Georgiana nodded.

He waited until his unsteady lips would permit speech. "I miss her," he said. "Let's go to her. Let's write."

"I think of it everyday," she said. "But I don't know how. She loves Tom Bagshot. So much that it frightens me. He must despise us."

William couldn't reassure her there. Tom Bagshot had no reason to love them. And he couldn't think of Sophy without remembering her broken face, pleading with them to let her have the one she loved. Pushing her to marry Alistair had been a mistake.

Georgiana turned to him, lifting her hand out of the water to shade her eyes. "Do you think we would have had other children? Together? If things had gone differently?"

"I'd like to think so." If today had happened ten years ago, they might have. They could have been out on the river today, with a little boy or girl in play clothes as rumpled as Georgiana's skirts. "Do you think we'd have been happy?"

"I don't know," she said. "We were never—you know. We were never like Henrietta and Percy, or Sophy and her Tom."

He took his time, poling them forward. "We could try to be."

She smiled at him. "I expect we are too old."

"Maybe. But today I'm pretending to be at least a decade younger."

She looked him over. "You make a good forty-seven. If you were younger you'd have to start tying your cravats like Jasper."

He shook his head, studying her in the quiet that settled between them. She'd always been lovely, but right now, with her sun-dappled skirts and fly-away hair, she didn't look cold, like a piece of blown glass. It gladdened him, that she was his wife. "I should call you Penelope," he said with a teasing smile.

"Ugh." She wrinkled her nose at him. "Why not Letitia? That's just as bad."

"It doesn't suit you. Penelope does." Not being a scholar, she wouldn't understand, but he thought it a likely comparison. It saddened him though, how close the allusion was to the truth. Eighteen years was a long time apart.

"It doesn't suit me at all." She looked at him sideways, a smile hiding in the corners of her mouth. "Stick with Georgy."

18

GOOD MOTHERS

ANNA, a city dweller for most of her life, was used to enduring the stagnant late-summer heat.

"It's more a matter of deciding not to be worn down by it," she explained to Henrietta. "It can't be changed, so one must carry on."

Henrietta made a face. "Percy and I leave for the country on Tuesday. It will be nice to have shade. And a breeze."

Hiding a smile, Anna didn't reply that both could be obtained in London. In fact, they were enjoying both now in the garden behind Lord Arundel's house. She would miss Henrietta. "I'm sad to see you go. You've been so kind to Henry and me."

Henrietta dismissed this with a twinkling eye. "It's no penance, passing time in your company. And Laurie needs a play-mate or he gets rough with Will."

Anna glanced down the garden, where Henry and Laurie were battling with sticks found on this morning's walk in the park. Henry was leaping about, slashing the bushes with the better of the two sticks. It had a knobby end and the boys had quarreled several times over its possession. Now they were handing it off every ten minutes, measured with Lord Arundel's

186

borrowed watch, resting on Henrietta's lap. It was a fine time piece, but dented, probably from being used as a toy. Little William liked to grab it when he tired of snatching at his mother's hair.

"They do get along," Anna said. Henry was manageable with Laurie. She didn't know what she was going to do when his playfellow was gone. "How do you get your boys to like you?" she asked.

"Pardon?" Henrietta asked.

It wasn't a tactful question, but Anna was out of time. A month had passed since Captain Beaumaris left, and in that time, she'd visited Henrietta most days. She'd watched, trying to mimic Henrietta's laughter, her easygoing manners, but Henry never curled into her lap or raced across the room to bestow careless pats on her legs. He held her hand when they walked on the street because she scolded when he didn't, and shied away from the rest of her touches.

"The other day, when I told him we weren't coming to see you, he threw his tin hussar at me," Anna said.

"How badly did you bruise?" Henrietta asked.

Anna showed her with her fingers.

"Where?" Henrietta asked.

"Here on my leg," Anna said, gently indicating the spot. It still hurt.

Henrietta glanced down to the boys, romping now beneath the branches of the hedge, their happy noises tumbling across the grass.

"I try to love him, but he doesn't care for it," Anna said, her words coming out in a rush.

Henrietta's forehead creased, and even that was pretty. Normally Anna would be jealous, but it was impossible to dislike Henrietta.

"He has seen so little of you," Henrietta said, troubled. "It's hard for you both."

Anna fought back her swelling throat, fingering the fraying edges of the ratty blanket Henry had left in her lap, like a gigantic dead moth. "I wanted him with me for so long, but it's not going as I planned. He doesn't like me. And he screams if he can't have his blanket, or his hussar. He'd be happier if I left him alone with his nurse." Try as she would, Anna could not summon any charitable thoughts for the insufferably competent Lucy Plunkett.

"Jealous?" Henrietta asked.

Anna nodded.

"She's had more time," Henrietta said.

"I know it isn't her fault," Anna said. "She didn't steal him from me. But they used her to do it." She didn't know when the wet nurse was dismissed and when Lucy had taken her place, or if there'd been other nursemaids in between. The first three years of Henry's life were lost to her, a closed book in a language she couldn't understand. As for the future—well, it was hard to hope for better, when her efforts were so fruitless.

Henrietta took her hand, squeezed with gentle pressure. "Henry's young. Give him time. You have all his life to do it. He'll love you before too long."

Anna blinked, washing out her lungs with a deep breath, trying to use the flood of air to push away her leaden mood. "I'm sorry. I shouldn't have—"

"Of course you should." Henrietta squeezed again and retracted her hand. "You are trying, so it will come out right. Not trying, that's the biggest mistake. But you won't do that, I think."

Henrietta pried a strand of her hair from Will's fingers, which were heading to his mouth, then glanced down at the open watch. "Time to trade sticks!" she called. Henry handed the prize over, grudgingly accepting the shorter, thinner branch from Laurie. He stomped around a bit, but within moments the two were laughing again.

"You make it look easy," Anna said.

"I have help," Henrietta said. "And I never lost them. I am so glad that you have him back again." She looked down at William and stroked his hair. "I am fortunate with Percy. I've always known that. And you will be too with Alistair," she said, looking up at Anna with a smile.

"I certainly am so far," Anna admitted. She did not like deceiving Henrietta. The longer she knew her, the more she wished they could be cousins in truth. It was all too easy to love her.

ALL WAS quiet when Anna and Henry returned to Rushford House, but that didn't mean Lord and Lady Fairchild weren't home. Wary, lest she spur Henry into another tantrum and spoil everyone's quiet, Anna nudged along her heavy-eyed boy. "Upstairs," she whispered. He was too tired to resist, shuffling along beside her, half asleep. If she was careful, she could put him into bed for a nap.

He stumbled on the second step, but she caught him and lifted him up, letting him sag against her shoulder, his cheek warm against her neck, his sweep of dark hair caressing her. She bit her lip, fighting a sudden onslaught of tears. He was so much bigger now than the bundle that had been stolen from her arms—back then he'd been about the size of a loaf of bread, and not much heavier either. There was weight to him now, sturdiness in his limbs, though now they dangled limp around her waist.

A moment to get control, then she climbed upwards again, treading softly down the hall to the back stairs that would take her up to the nursery. Halfway there, a door opened, putting Lord Fairchild in her path. He raised a finger to his lips, then closed the door behind him with a soft click. His wife's door, Anna realized. Before she could stop herself, she scrutinized his clothing: buttons, cravat, jacket. Perfectly tidy, but that didn't mean—

"Can I assist you?" He offered his arms, but she couldn't hand him Henry. This half-conscious embrace was too precious.

"I don't want to disturb him," she whispered back.

"At least let me help you with the doors," he said, moving along beside her. He opened the door to the stairs and followed her up, stepping softly, but not as softly as she. Anna already knew where the treads creaked from stealing upstairs most nights to sit and watch her sleeping son. When he was asleep, she could smooth his hair without him ducking away from her hand, bring his soft paw to her own cheek, and count the pulse that beat at his wrist. He couldn't fight or scorn her when he was sleeping.

Lord Fairchild opened the door at the top of the stairs, then the door to Henry's room. Lucy was there, putting away some folded laundry. She hastened to draw back the bed covers. Anna set Henry down, blocking Lucy with her back so she could arrange his arms and hear him sigh as he sank into the pillow.

"I'll take off his shoes," Lucy said, pushing forward. "You can leave him with me."

Dismissed, Anna turned for the stairs. She was halfway down when Lord Fairchild spoke, his voice low. "My dear, you have a tear drying on your cheek."

She turned, frightened a little by Lord Fairchild's level glance. He came down a few more steps, stopping three above. "It's nothing," she said, brushing her cheek with the back of her hand.

He was silent, not needing to contradict her lie. They both knew. Without a word he sat down on the stair, motioning her to do the same.

"Lucy—" Anna began.

"Won't find us. She has a novel sticking out from under that pile of Henry's trousers," Lord Fairchild said. "We could go to the drawing room, but you seem more comfortable here. Is it the portrait of my grandfather there that makes you freeze? I would too, if I weren't used to ignoring him."

That won a reluctant smile from her.

"Please sit down," he said.

She did, carefully tucking her skirts under her.

Lord Fairchild wove his fingers together, leaving the thumbs free to tap against each other, a quick, irregular beat. His nails were smooth and shaped, his cuffs falling over his wrists just as they ought. He watched his thumbs, perhaps counting time, perhaps choosing words, before he looked at her and spoke. "It is hard to lose a child. And more difficult than you think to get them back."

"How do you know?" she asked, her voice thick with the effort of controlling it.

"I never met my daughter Sophy until she was ten. She came to me when her mother died. Hated me for years." He smiled, the way a man does to shrug off pain.

"Does she still?" Anna asked, both curious and afraid of his answer.

"I don't know. She has more reason now. I didn't listen when she told me she didn't want to marry Alistair."

Anna didn't know how she bore up under his penetrating eyes, but she kept her face smooth, even as her hands went cold. She was too afraid to ask if he knew the truth about her engagement, so she asked, "Why didn't you? It would have been easy for you to help her."

"Yes, if I only had one person to please. I was trying to support my wife. The fact that I neither knew or trusted Bagshot simplified matters."

"That was a mistake. He can be trusted," Anna said.

"I hope you're right. Sophy is dear to me."

"And your wife?" she asked, before she could stop herself. By all accounts, they despised each other, but he had come from Lady Fairchild's room just now.

"Have you ever—" he shook his head, then looked down at his

191

hands. The shape of something important lurked in his unspoken words.

"Made a mistake?" Anna filled in. She wanted to know.

He looked at her carefully. "What do you know of mistakes?"

She dropped her eyes. "I've made a few."

She could almost hear his thoughts, fitting together in the silence. Anna pressed her lips together, bracing herself for what he might see. Maybe he'd throw her out, but her instinct—and she was wagering heavily on that—said that he would understand.

"I remember Anthony Morris," he said at last. "Was he a mistake?"

"One of them." She swallowed. "I'm trying to do better."

"So am I," he said. They passed a smile between them the way weary friends pass around a drink, but then Lord Fairchild asked, "Does reform include Captain Beaumaris?"

"He's a perfect gentleman," she said at last. "Much too good for me, but I'm not in a position to refuse his help, not yet. I promise you needn't worry. I think too much of him to do him any harm."

"Then you don't intend to marry him?"

Her cheeks burned, lighting up her neck, even her ears. "I told him myself I wouldn't serve him such an underhand trick."

"Even if it was what he wanted?"

Anna banished her blush with a laugh. "He likes me, but I'm not afraid of that. Besides, there is a great difference between what we want and what we can have. You and I both know that. Look at our children."

"True. I'm in no position to give advice," he said. "I've been the single greatest impediment to my own happiness. Don't you be."

"I'll be careful," Anna said. Like him, she'd given herself too much pain already. "Thank you for telling me." She rose and smoothed her skirts, but Lord Fairchild stopped her before she could proceed down the stairs.

"Mrs. Morris?"

"Yes?" Anna turned, her skirts gathered in one hand.

"Careful isn't what I meant you to be."

ALISTAIR HAD BEEN GONE LONG ENOUGH that Anna was expecting a letter. Every day she tried not to wait for the arrival of the post, or be disappointed when it brought nothing for her. She'd sent him one already, enclosing the promised lock of hair, but unless one came from him she couldn't write again. To inundate him with letters that weren't returned would be embarrassing.

The trouble was, even though she wouldn't let herself write again, she was always composing imaginary letters, telling him of Lord and Lady Arundel's departure, Jasper's new horse (she was no judge of such matters, but Lord Fairchild was sufficiently enthusiastic), and the handsome politician who'd tried to flirt with his aunt. Lady Fairchild hadn't noticed. It would have been interesting to watch if Lord Fairchild had been there, more interesting certainly than the flagging conversation she'd failed to revive with her own dinner partner.

Anna sighed. One didn't need to talk when one could simply display an expanse of bosom. The gown she'd worn last evening was an excellent alternative to speech. She'd opted for better coverage today, since it was time to brace herself for another assault from Henry's grenadiers. The mark below her collar bone from their first battle had finally faded away, and she had no interest in acquiring another.

"Charge!" Henry roared, swiping at her line with his favorite hussar, knocking over the fortifications she'd dutifully erected from his basket of toy bricks.

"Charge!" he said again, scattering bricks across the carpet and into the corners. Henry had picked up the word from Henrietta's husband, Lord Arundel, who liked playing with his small boys, but couldn't separate himself from his interest in history.

Every game became a re-enactment of some famous battle. Young Laurence had picked up a name or two (he called his hussars after the late General Moore, but pronounced it like he was asking for another biscuit). Henry hadn't gotten past his one command.

Everything was a charge now, from his flight down the stairs to the swooping of his breakfast spoon. This morning, when Anna rushed down to the hall to stop Henry from swinging his favorite stick, she couldn't help noticing Lord Fairchild firmly closing his library door. Lady Fairchild hadn't risen yet, but Anna knew she could look forward to another quarter hour of pointed pronouncements about managing boys and the failings of Henry's nurse. What Lady Fairchild said privately to her husband (or, more likely, her maid), Anna could only guess. Now that Henrietta was gone and the days were cooler, they spent much more time at the house, where Anna felt like a bigger nuisance each passing day.

"You've won again!" Anna exclaimed tiredly, surveying the litter of toys cast about the floor. Served her right for giving Lucy the morning off.

"Did I do it well?" Henry asked, looking up. The earnest question and the hungry look in his eyes stopped her cold.

"Of course!" she said quickly.

"You can do better," he said, settling back again, frowning at her half-hearted attempt to re-pile the bricks.

"You're right," Anna said. "I should do this properly, shouldn't I? A stronger wall?"

Henry nodded.

"Perhaps a tower here?"

Henry's eyes sharpened, his face moving closer to the bricks as she stacked them higher.

"This could be a cannon," Anna said, laying a narrow brick sideways on what might pass, to the highly imaginative, as a parapet.

"That's good," Henry said, adding another sideways brick to the battery.

"Who will fire it?" Anna asked, reaching for the scattered soldiers. "This one here?"

It took longer to choose a suitable figure. Henry had no engineers or artillery, but was happy to eventually settle on a rifleman —the subtleties of uniforms, divisions and brigades being beyond him, though at this rate his ignorance wouldn't last long. Anna had never seen him so intent, or, as they raced around the room on their knees gathering bricks, so content in her company. They piled up the bricks, adding more towers, thicker walls, and plenty of makeshift guns, until none were left and Henry was back on all fours, peering under the bed, hoping to find a couple more strays. Twenty minutes must have passed with the two of them in complete accord, laughing even. Stranger still, Anna felt at ease, buoyant without the ballast of her usual worries. Following him with warm eyes, Anna waited for Henry to return to the rug. He did, but he didn't launch immediately into his assault, though the tin hussar was ready in his fist.

"Is it good enough?" Anna asked, for he was scrutinizing the fortress—a formidable objective now—with a critical eye.

Henry glanced from the foot-high walls to the hussar in his hand, and the dozen two-inch soldiers he had left on his side of the rug. "What if he can't do it, Mama?" he asked.

Reassurance died on her tongue. Henry's eyes were serious and wide. Guiltily, for she knew she was doing no good to herself or her boy, she lied. "He'll manage it, love. He's so brave."

Equilibrium restored, Henry picked up another soldier. With both hands he swept forward, smashing over the wall, laughing as the bricks cascaded into a heap between them. Anna laughed with him, keeping her smile. "Yes, again," she said, agreeing with him, privately trying to decide if it was good that Henry believed her so absolutely.

19

ADVANCES

So much for arriving in good time, Alistair thought. The rate he was going, he'd be lucky to make Burgos before the snows.

He was exaggerating—it was only September—but he was in a foul enough mood to believe his prediction, ever since his guide had wandered ahead and vanished between walls of steep scrub and sliding rock. It was miserable finding his own way through the Sierra Guadaramma, parched and sweating all day, shivering in the dark at night, as brown with dirt as the rabbit he had shot at earlier today—and missed.

At least his worthless guide hadn't stolen more than an extra flask and a haversack of food. Also, Alistair was not yet out of biscuit, though he'd had to share with his horses since they were camped on a bare slope without any forage. No wood for a fire either, so perhaps the rabbit was no great loss. He'd succumbed to necessity and eaten raw meat before—fed it to his horses too— but he didn't care for it.

London was a world away. It did no good to long for hot coffee; he might as well wish for a flying carpet. It didn't help to think of what one couldn't have, including Anna Morris. Curling up under his cloak, Alistair settled down to wait until it was light enough to ride again, wondering if, when he returned to Madrid, there might be a letter waiting for him.

And what would she have to say? Nothing good, he was sure.

Since you left I've been to four routs and fifteen parties. I've found myself another husband—a little fat, but kind and complacent. Just the man for me! He lives in Northumberland, so I don't expect we shall ever meet again. My sincere thanks . . . Best wishes . . . Yours Respectfully, Goodbye.

Maybe he shouldn't have asked her to write. If he ever got a letter where she signed herself *Yours Respectfully*, he'd go out and drown himself.

One of the horses flicked a tail and took a step sideways, hooves crunching the flaky stone track that passed for a road. Alistair shifted, but the ground didn't soften; he had. It would take a few weeks before he toughened up again. His legs ached from days in the saddle, and if he wasn't careful, he'd end up with the cavalryman's curse—boils on his buttocks or the insides of his legs. He rolled onto his stomach, setting his head on top of his folded arms.

No good. If he stayed this way, his healing shoulder would be stiff as frozen leather in the morning. Better move back on his side.

Anna would pity him if she could see him now. Oh, maybe she'd tease him for his tanned face and the destruction already begun on his jacket, asking if he was indeed the same fellow who'd squired her about the park. But she'd also take his head and rest it in her lap (if she didn't think of it, he would ask) and comb her fingers through his salt-crusted hair. Too bad he didn't approve of ladies straggling along in the tail of the army—not that Anna, who was quite sane, would ever do such a thing. He could conjure her in these mountains with his imagination, and send her back in a twinkling to London, but he could not imagine her jolting after a marching division in the spring wagons, or bringing Henry into danger.

Well, dreams weren't supposed to resemble the workaday world. They wouldn't be dreams unless they were substantially better, so he may as well make these idle thoughts worth the name. There'd be Anna, in cool white muslin, a mantilla draped over her shoulders, a secret smile curling her lips and tilting up the corners of her eyes. Henry too—one attempt at verisimilitude couldn't hurt—his hair lightened to a warm chestnut by the sun, his skin as brown as Alistair's own. Put them in a clean little house in Lisbon, on a hill that caught cool breezes and had a view of the sea. Put him there too, healthy and whole; the war won, or very nearly. He would carry Henry up the hill on his shoulders, leave oranges on Anna's pillow and make love to her every afternoon.

Alistair snorted, laughing at himself, wondering when he'd turned into such a sap skull. Shifting his hip off one stone and onto another, he pulled his cloak tighter and stared into the sky.

THREE DAYS LATER THAN PLANNED, Alistair finally handed over the dispatches to Wellington's harassed-looking secretary. "Rough going?" the Military Secretary asked.

"Nothing out of the ordinary," Alistair said, not wanting to make excuses. He was pleased to have recovered one lost day by dint of some hard riding, but it was nothing to boast about. He was still late.

"Why's one of Alten's carrying messages for the Staff?" the Military Secretary asked, looking skeptically at Alistair's black uniform.

"Just borrowed, my Lord, General Barnard being short a staff officer. I'm to rejoin my brigade unless you have further use for me," Alistair explained. He hated sieges as much as anyone, but if it was required, he'd take the blow on the chin without complaining.

"No, you're well out of this one," the Military Secretary said.

"Though perhaps you'd like to stay for today's show. You're just in time."

"Sir?"

"Blowing up the mine today," explained a nearby adjutant, straightening up from a map held down on the table with a saber and an expensive looking carriage clock. "Planned for yesterday, but of course it wasn't ready." He took a sharp glance from his superior and Alistair sent up silent thanks that he hadn't been ordered to stay. Tempers in this crumbling, low-ceilinged room were as heated as the ones simmering in the trench.

The Military Secretary thumbed through the dispatches then thrust them at the adjutant. "Do something with these, will you?" With a sigh, the fellow took them to a corner and cleared a space in the welter of papers on his desk, relieving Alistair's mind. Stacks of maps, lists and reports covered every surface, with still more papers bulging from the chests lining the walls. If his dispatches were piled with the rest, who knew if they'd ever be read? Already he could feel sympathetically-induced eye strain. The hard-pressed staff were clearly struggling with the usual issues: delayed ordnance, scanty provisions, flagging morale, unsatisfactory reports from the depots, and an ever increasing butcher's bill. Wearily, the adjutant leaned forward in his chair, kneading his temples as he started reading.

"Expect you'll need to visit the commissary," the Military Secretary said.

"I'm a little hungry," Alistair admitted. "And I should look after my horses."

"Not much forage, I'm afraid," clipped out the Secretary. "Only the regulation allotment." That would feed one of his horses. He'd have to dip into his own funds to look after the other.

They directed him to the commissary, instructing him to check with the staff when he was finished. "Maybe they'll have something for you to do." Messages maybe. In an action like this, there wasn't much use for cavalry.

It was bad news about the forage allotment; he'd have to see what he could buy in the village they'd taken outside the walled town. Rest would help the horses, but he couldn't expect both to recover when sharing feed for one. He loped along the lines where the brigades were gathering, trying to ignore the expectant haze thickening around them. Up on the hill, there was movement in the trenches. His pulse quickened.

Catching sight of the dilapidated commissary, Alistair quickened his steps, when the roar of an explosion bashed into him. Staggering, tightening his grip on the leads of his sidling horses, he turned halfway round. The ground rumbled and the black gelding reared, dragging him sideways, so he dropped the mare's lead, though she was prancing fretfully and whickering. Hauling on the black's lead, he forced the stamping forefeet to earth, cursing the animal in a steady, low voice.

"Settle down, you devil. Settle down." Accepting a soothing hand, the horse stilled, though his eyes showed white and rolled fitfully. The mare had taken herself a few paces away, but was behaving herself better. Alistair groped for her trailing leads. If the gelding couldn't get used to war's smoke and thunder, it didn't bode well for either of them.

Horses under control, Alistair gaped at the fortress and the fountain of earth spewing into the air, boulders and masonry rocketing into the sky like weightless nothings until they changed course and came speeding back to earth. Someone started a ragged cheer so he joined in—weakly, because of the icy spiders treading down his spine. Around him, hands patted cartridge pouches and shouldered rifles as preparations accelerated, keeping tempo with his rat-a-tat heart. Recalled to himself by his fidgety mare, Alistair muttered, "Come on, beauty. I'm not taking you into that." The smoke hadn't cleared from the breach yet. Alistair looked away, before the maw in the walls started grinding the men running into the rubble.

Intent on the backs of his hands, the flicking ears of his horses, Alistair collected his allotment of oats, dividing it between the mare and the gelding, blunting the whistles, bugle calls, and artillery barrage filling his ears. They must have blasted a reasonable gap. The ground shuddered—just a mumble this time—and Alistair glanced instinctively over his shoulder.

The defenders were back at work, pounding shot from the tower batteries. Twenty minutes in, and both sides were already taking a beating. Snagging his ration of biscuit, Alistair left the horses in the care of another officer's batman and made his way to the command post where he could watch and wait with the junior staff officers.

"Beau's too stubborn," one of them muttered. "We'll never take it, not with so few."

Alistair didn't comment. The breach looked to be a hundred yards wide, but there were few guns in the English batteries. Their sputtering fire was a token effort, no threat to the defenders scrambling along the broken walls.

"No proper tools, save those taken from the town, no sappers. The men will dig, but they don't like it."

Alistair grunted. "Don't know much about it," he said, knowing his cavalry uniform would excuse him.

"Lose your way?" the other officer asked, glancing at Alistair's jacket. "I daren't hope we are to be joined by *the* Division."

"Just myself," Alistair said, masking his sick stomach with a light tone. "Though we'd crack this nut soon enough if they ordered us here."

"Such humility in the Light Division," his companion murmured.

"It does look like they've given you a rough time," Alistair conceded. "Tell me the lay of it, if you will. I just arrived."

His companion pointed out the companies, enumerating the

difficulties of digging communications trenches under fire, of batteries destroyed before guns could be placed, the bivouacs, for they had no permanent shelter. "You must have drawn the short straw if they sent you from Madrid while the rest of your division kicks up their heels."

"Actually, I'm just back again from London."

"Oho!" The officer laughed. "And how are the amusements in Town? And the ladies?"

"Only the finest," Alistair smiled.

"Do tell," he began, but—

"Brown!" the colonel shouted.

"That's me." He smiled with a fatalistic lift of his eyebrows. "Looks like I'm off."

"Good luck." Alistair watched his new acquaintance jog away, then looked up the hill where a floundering mass of red jackets funneled into Burgos's stone jaws.

Chewed up and spit out, Alistair thought, watching another charge falter. The crowd around him thinned.

The next squadron made it farther, over the mound of rubble and out of sight, but the company behind them was lagging. Alistair shifted his feet. Without support, the men inside the walls wouldn't last long.

"You there!"

Alistair looked around, but the frowning colonel was looking at him.

"Sir!"

"Order Graydon's company to support the 6th!"

"Just there?" he asked, feeling light-headed and foolish, but needing to be sure.

Answered by a curt, affirmative nod, Alistair set off, cursing under his breath. Pitched into a battle, not knowing the plan or the troop's disposition . . . it wasn't the first time this had happened and unless he got picked off by a stray bullet, it wouldn't be the last. He scrambled over a silent battery, only glancing at the unlucky wretches draped across the ground or propped against the gun carriages. Grim business, this. Served him right for thinking he could play spectator.

It was a relief to hop down into the trench to make his way up the next section of hill. Progress was faster. By the time he caught up with Graydon's confused men he could feel a slick streak of sweat between his shoulders.

"Where's Captain Graydon?" he demanded of a grimy, hollow-cheeked private. All he got was a shrug.

He peered over the man's head, through a thicket of muddy coats and bayonets. "Where's your bleeding officer?" he shouted.

"Bleeding, sir!" barked out one of them. The sergeant, Alistair realized with relief.

"We are to advance to support the 6th," Alistair said. Though he had no ability to recognize them or their officers, he knew where to find them: up.

"Not your kind of fight this. Sir," said the sergeant, looking him over with a flicker of pity.

Alistair felt it like a spray of sparks. Snuffing his temper, he laid an impatient hand on the hilt of his saber. "No, but I'm not a dunce. Probably goes something like this—move forward and kill any French that get in the way until I'm shot. Right?"

The sergeant blinked under the barrage of sharp words, but gave a reluctant smile.

"I may not know how to drill your men, but I can run with them up a hill," Alistair said.

"You could come with us until we join the 6th, at least," said the sergeant.

"Thank you," Alistair said, tense with the effort of damping both fear and anger. "If you're certain you'd rather not manage it yourself?"

"No, sir," admitted the sergeant.

"Well, then."

The sergeant gave a nod, blew sharply on his whistle, then

gave a bellow that buzzed in Alistair's ears. He glanced up at the fortress, smoke drifting over the crumbling walls, the rocky slope below littered with mangled men and broken stones.

"Ready." He drew his saber, his arm hairs rising at the familiar hiss. The shining blade winked at him. Counting in unison with the sergeant, they reached three—the critical beat where you plunged in, and prayed your men would follow. *Don't think. Just go.*

Alistair vaulted over the trench, pounding up the slope, his boots skidding on the loose wash of soil and stone. A man beside him fell, but Alistair couldn't tell if it was bad footing or a French shot. The sergeant was a steady runner, swearing at the men and waving his musket with no shortage of breath. Nimble fellows outstripped them both, weaving past the dead, the ruins of some failed trench work and the masonry heaved wide by the blast.

They called a slope like this a glacis, and it felt as slippery as ice. Alistair struggled on, bent forward, grasping at handholds, each footfall sending stones tumbling below. Another fifty yards. Twenty. He was shouting—God only knew what—raising his saber like he was charging across the field, thrown off by how slowly his target came nearer. He was used to flying over the ground, sweeping over hills, crashing into column and artillery, not scrambling along, fighting for every foot.

They jostled into the tail of the 6th, close enough to the wall to be peppered by muskets and rifles from the wall and the fortress inside, but too far to blood the French. Thrust against the jacket of the man in front of him, Alistair peered over the man's shoulder, then staggered as the fellow fell back against his chest. Before the man finished screaming, he choked, his hands grabbing at his chest, then flying up to fumble at his mouth. Bloody foam flecked the corners. Cursing, Alistair pushed the fellow to his left, to avoid sticking him with his sword. There was no room to move in this press.

"Wait here. Someone will help you," Alistair lied, lowering

him to the ground. Blood spilled down the man's chin; at least death wouldn't take long. Behind and to his left, Alistair heard the sergeant; ahead he could see the French falling back to the fortress, behind the inner walls. Brandishing his saber, he shouted the advance, breaking into a run. It felt better running, though his pace was nothing to that of a horse. When he was moving he could feel detached and thrilled; not so when he was pressed up against dying men. Light danced along his beautiful sword as it played in the air, thrusting, sweeping, cutting through bone and sinew with a tug that would haunt him later, echoing through his arms before he could sleep.

"Sir!"

It was the sergeant, hollering from a small redoubt built against the wall. There were no more Frogs in killing distance, so Alistair jogged over.

"Here's Colonel Whyte of the 6th. You can bring word back to headquarters. We've taken the outer wall."

Whyte was scribbling on a scrap of paper with a pencil.

"Of course," Alistair said, feeling both relieved and foolish. "What would you like me to say?" He pushed his sweaty hair off his forehead, realizing that somewhere along the way he'd lost his hat.

"I'm not sure what we're to do next since we've no ladders, no men to climb them, and no way to bring up our pitiful number of guns, but advise them we will hold this position until they decide."

"Nighttime trench work, probably," the sergeant scowled. "More mining."

Whyte shrugged, but beneath the dirt his face was drawn. Alistair took the paper and slid it into the breast of his coat.

"You'll want to make your way back through the communication trenches," the sergeant reminded him.

"And stick to bitters until I learn to hold my liquor," Alistair said, annoyed at the sergeant's cosseting and his own relief at escaping.

"Just trying to help," the sergeant said. "That was a nice climb we had. Wouldn't mind doing it again some other day."

"I prefer the flat and the speed of a horse, but it would be an honor." Alistair offered his hand, pleased the ghoulish looking sergeant didn't hesitate to take it in a crushing grip.

The fire from the fortress was picking up now that the French were regrouping, so Alistair hastened back through the breach and down the slope. Enough shot whizzed by to give him bad dreams for days to come. Going back was worse, he decided, making his lonely way past the squadrons who were climbing, facing the sting of French fire.

He delivered two other orders, both far less hazardous. When night fell, the guns belching only intermittently, he joined Brown, the staff officer he'd met earlier, to share out the evening's ration of beef and biscuit.

"We'll see what tomorrow brings," Brown said, summing up the day's action with a shrug—the outer wall breached and taken, but at high cost. "You on your way back to Madrid?"

"First thing in the morning," Alistair said.

BEFORE THEY TURNED IN, he was visited by Whyte, who'd come to give Alistair his compliments and restore his missing hat.

"A little trampled, but you can get your man to fix that. Don't know what he'll do about the holes, though." A musket ball had torn right through, leaving two neat punctures, front and back.

Alistair laughed his thanks, vowing to keep the hat as his lucky piece. But once he found his billet—clearing out the gear of a man who was now sleeping underground—Alistair swept it from his head and took a closer look, fingers trembling.

. . .

HE WASHED and undressed down to his shirt, but he couldn't settle. After his nights outside on the ground, it was a sad waste of a bed. Finally he gave up trying to sleep, rising and throwing his greatcoat over his shoulders. The floor boards were rough and covered with layer of grit that stuck to the soles of his feet. Griggs, who liked to spoil him even in the most primitive lodgings, probably had a pair of slippers wedged somewhere in his bags, but that didn't help him now. His feet were already dirty and they weren't cold enough to make it worth soiling his one relatively clean pair of socks.

Alistair settled into the wobbly chair, his knees and elbows falling sideways like a lax-limbed marionette's. He was done dancing for one day, thank God. There was a lamp on the table— a good one even—that when lit emitted a steady glow, beating back the shadows to the corners of the room, allowing Alistair to stare again at the empty circles torn out of his hat. For a long time he turned it round in his hands, tracing the tiny voids with his fingers; empty spaces that could have engulfed him so easily. He tended to think of death fairly often, but seldom with a relic like this in his hands. It gave him pause, even more than the bullet they'd dug out of his shoulder. That trinket he'd presented to Griggs.

Well, he'd gotten away again. Impossible to say if the next one would find him. There were other possibilities too: dysentery, cannon shot, the wrong ship on a sea voyage. If he was lucky he'd find a more prosaic end: heart seizure, old age or influenza. Death might be tomorrow or a long way off. Impossible to say. The only certainty was now.

Alistair rummaged for his pen. He already had a half written letter to Anna, detailing the journey to Burgos—a sketch of the mountains, a scathing assessment of his shooting after missing that rabbit, a humorous misunderstanding with a baker from one of the villages. Instead of adding to it, he laid out a clean sheet. He started writing, his hand flying across the paper, returning after the briefest plunge in the ink bottle, when he usually liked to pause and try out different words.

Dearest Anna,

I'm a shocking liar. Selfish too. I can't stand the thought of you and Mr. Worthy, whoever he might be. When I engaged myself to you, it was because I wished it were true. I wanted you for my own but a partial loan seemed like the best I could get.

Will you marry me? I've nothing to recommend me, save that I look well in a uniform and on a horse, but I'm mad enough in love that I'm certain we could find a way. Not maybe a life of wealth and triumphs, but for me anyways, one of happiness.

I want you and I want Henry and I want to spend my days collecting your smiles. Would you mind terribly?

Say yes.

He stopped, then shook his head and laughed softly. He scrawled a post script.

I was commanding you to say 'yes, my love, I'll marry you,' not 'yes, you clod, I mind.' I might be a lot of things, but I am seldom a clod. Is that enough to make you throw your lot in with mine? I hope so.

Yours, burning and fervent and possibly half-cracked, but all for love of you.

Alistair

Before caution—or reason—could take hold of him, he folded up the letter and sealed it. No point reading it over. He wanted it just as it was, nothing but honest, unguarded sentiments. He was tired of hints and unexpressed hopes and reasonable excuses. Leaving the letter on the table, he returned to bed. This time, sleep took him quick.

20

PEACE TREATIES

ANNA HELD HER BREATH, waiting for Lady Fairchild to leave her room. She was hiding behind the door, avoiding a summons to the drawing room to flirt with Mr. Phillips. Twice yesterday she'd lost the thread of his gentle conversation, wondering what it would be like to kiss that saggy cheek. She liked the twinkle in his eyes, but if she married him she'd be kissing that fatherly face for at least a decade. Besides, Mr. Phillips might be an estimable man, and kindly too, but she would rather spend the afternoon spoiling her gown with Henry.

Once Lady Fairchild's footsteps retreated downstairs, Anna emerged from her hiding place, tiptoeing down the backstairs and into Lord Fairchild's study. Halfway to the long window, she saw him, concealed in an armchair, watching her in amusement, his book forgotten. She smiled guiltily, but he raised a finger to his lips, motioning her with a tilt of his head to proceed out through the long window. Outside, Anna squinted, surveying the garden, unable to spot her son.

"He's gone into the shrubbery again," Lucy explained, looking up from her conversation with Betty, one of the maids. They were sitting on a low wall dividing the paved walkway at the back of the house from the square of enclosed lawn. They had sewing in their hands, but seemed more interested in a pamphlet lying open on the stonework between them. It was about syphilis, including diagrams and a lengthy discussion of probable causes, so Anna had recommended hiding it from Lady Fairchild.

"I'm going to play with him," Anna said.

"Of course. I'm here if you need me," Lucy said.

Anna was determined to need no one today, especially Lucy Plunkett, and walked toward the patches of Henry's white shirt showing behind the lace of blackthorn branches stretching across the back garden wall. The grass was long and damp, wetting her feet above the edges of her slippers. In spite of the gooseflesh spreading up her arms, she left the shawl Lady Fairchild had lent her folded over a branch. Better to be a little chilly than to trail that long silk fringe through the hedges.

She stepped softly, the leaves too damp to break under her feet. Henry was burrowed deep behind the branches, murmuring to himself.

"My horse. You can't have that one. And my dog too." Intent on the row of twigs and pebbles he'd arranged in the dirt beneath the blackthorn, he didn't see Anna until she stepped in front of him, holding her skirts close and pushing aside a thick branch with careful fingertips. Before he could speak, Anna let the branches close behind her, screening them from Lucy and Betty's view. She crouched down beside Henry, tucking her hands on top of her knees.

Deciding she was no threat, Henry dropped his voice and moved a pebble half an inch. "You go there. Don't touch that one."

He spoke in a child's whisper, but the admonitions he gave his pets of stick and stone were sharp as the thorns around them. Anna watched him with a breaking heart, wondering if he'd learned that tone from her. She'd like to think it was Frederick, but she couldn't be sure. The way his brows drew close, colliding in a sharp line above his nose, was all too familiar.

The dirt would do no good to her skirts, but her legs would get sore if she remained crouching, so she lowered her knees to the ground after a quick swipe to clear it of sharp bits and sloes. There'd been no frost yet, but the berries were dark blue and plump and some had fallen to the ground. She picked up one and rolled it between her fingers, then stopped, realizing Henry was doing the same.

"Don't eat them," he said. "They taste like poison."

Anna laughed. "How do you know?"

Henry changed tactics, a gleam lighting his eye. "Try one." He stuck out his palm.

"It looks like it would be tasty," Anna said, playing along. "But I'm not sure."

"It'll be delicious," Henry promised, forgetting his warning just seconds ago.

"Give it here," Anna said, opening her arms and letting Henry climb into her lap. He reached up, putting the sloe to her lips.

"Are you sure?" Anna said, moving her chin aside.

"Try it," Henry begged, bouncing a little.

"Do you really think I should?" Anna asked, trying to keep a straight face. "I'll share it with you. You first."

Henry's face fell, but only for a moment. "No, you."

"All right," Anna said, bracing herself for the worst. It had been decades since Tom Bagshot and her brother Richard had tricked her into eating sloe berries. They couldn't taste that bad. She opened her lips and Henry pushed the berry in, his eyes locked on her face. Tentatively she moved the berry around with her tongue, then squeezed it between her teeth.

"Faugh!"

Henry rocked back and forth with laughter, his face scrunched up like a monkey's, while Anna struggled to work some spit onto her tongue. Her entire mouth was coated with dry bitterness, as if she'd chewed a whole handful instead of a single berry. She spat the rough feeling fruit on the ground, rubbing her tongue against her teeth, trying to scrape off the taste, suspecting what she really needed was a towel or a toothbrush. But Henry was grinning at her, his eyes bright, his smile so wide she could count nearly all his tiny teeth.

"You!" Her fingers clambered up his ribs like gangly spiders, all the way to his armpits, making him shriek. "It tastes awful! You should try one," she said, quickly composing her face, plucking a sloe from the nearest branch and sticking it under his nose.

"Uh-uh," Henry said, shaking his head.

"You don't think it will taste delicious?" Anna teased.

"No."

"It made my mouth all prickly," Anna said. "What if it stays that way?"

Henry didn't answer with words, just gave her a cheeky grin that flooded out of his face and lit up his eyes. Anna nearly started in surprise when he butted his head into her chest and stayed there, leaning against her breast. Before he could pull away, she moved her arms to rest around him, gently, and looked down at the top of his head. His hair needed trimming. He was a beautiful boy, with his dark, too-long hair, his shoulder blades sticking out like wings, his perpetually drippy nose smearing against the bodice of her dress. Anna pursed her lips and blew softly, shakily, just enough to stir his silken hair. It didn't wave and spring back like his vanished baby down, but the touch of her breath made Henry squirm and move closer. One breath. Two. Then he was in motion again, sliding off her lap, stepping on her skirt and rubbing it into the dirt, his fingers catching up a handful of black earth that he poured into her lap.

"What's this?" Anna laughed.

"Treasure," Henry said, like he was sharing a secret.

"Can I keep it?" Anna asked. "Or should I just hold it for you?"

Henry seemed unwilling to give it away for good. "Hold it," he said.

Anna nodded. Henry brought more treasure. When Anna suggested transferring the pile of twigs, stones and earth to her handkerchief, Henry agreed. She plucked it from her bodice, but Henry was more interested in the crackle of paper than the lace-edged linen she held out to him.

"What's that?" he said, reaching for the neck of her dress.

"Henry!" Anna laughed. "A gentleman never puts his hands—never mind." She didn't want him sticking his hands down her dress, but she didn't want to scare him away either. She quickly passed him the folded square of paper. "It's a letter. From Captain Beaumaris." It had arrived just this morning.

"From the ship?" Henry asked.

"No, he sent this one from Lisbon."

Henry settled on his heels, folded his arms around his knees and looked at her expectantly.

"You want to hear it?" she asked.

Henry nodded, so Anna unfolded the letter. The paper was soft from being next to her skin.

"My Darling Anna," she read. "That's me," she explained, seeing Henry's look. She scanned the letter, trying to chose what to say.

I'm told this style of address is permissible to one's fiancée. Even temporary ones.

No, she couldn't read that. "I read all my books on the voyage to Lisbon and most of the captain's too. Skipped the ones on navigation and South American ports. With the fine weather, we arrived even before the water on board got musty. I'd forgotten just how lovely this city is."

Wretch. She could imagine.

"The Light Division is in Madrid—"

"You said he was going to Spain," Henry said.

"Madrid is a city in Spain. It is where the false king lived, until we chased him away."

Henry liked that news, and let out a small hurrah.

"I haven't seen Madrid myself, but I'm told it too has many beauties," Anna began, then decided to skip the next part, which read:

But I'd rather you'd given me a miniature of yourself, so I could appreciate yours. No matter—memory will serve well enough.

"You will be enjoying parading around town, I hope, even at this slow time of year. You and my aunt must make a fine picture —*molto elegante*—that means very elegant," Anna explained to Henry. She left out the next bit.

I hope your Spanish stretches that far. How about this? Besas como un ángel.

Tomorrow she was buying herself a spanish dictionary.

"Give my regards to Master Henry, and tell him I haven't gotten him a French sword yet. I have every intention of doing so before we drive them back to France." There was a break, then a new paragraph, the one that made her anxious.

"Appears I won't be idling away in Lisbon, or crawling to Madrid with the newest infantry recruits. The General Staff is borrowing me and sending me on a jaunt to the siege at Burgos."

He said how glad he was to leave the provisioning and packing to Griggs, how preferable it was to ride speedily on his own, but Anna couldn't help her unease, imagining him crossing unfamiliar mountains and desert plains alone. Of course, by this time, he'd probably reached Burgos and left already. At least she knew where to get her news from.

He signed his name with a flourish at the bottom of the single sheet, styling himself her fond Alistair.

Fond. She wasn't sure she cared for that word. It sounded fatherly. Indulgent. Not the way she liked to be kissed, for certain.

"I like him," Henry said, returning to his game as Anna folded away the letter. "Will he be back soon? We could show him the steam works."

Anna carefully tied her handkerchief around the dirt treasure and tucked it into her hand. If Henry asked, she'd give it to him, but he seemed to have forgotten it in favor of snapping off thorns. "Would you like to go with Grandpapa again?" she asked.

Better to evade questions that had no happy answers. Still, she was happy a letter had come, that he was well, that he ascribed himself as fond, instead of *Yr. Obedient.* Now she had permission to write him again—keeping to her budget of one letter for each one she received, though she didn't see how she would restrict herself to a single sheet.

Half-composed sentences continually jostled in her head, waiting to be spilled onto paper. She wanted to tell him about Henry's battles with tin soldiers, tease him with the names of the gentlemen she danced with, and bore him (probably) with the results of her shopping expeditions with Lady Fairchild. She would tell him about Henry taking Lord Fairchild's book out in the rain, feeding her sloe berries and fitting himself into her arms. Hadn't Lord Fairchild warned her against being careful? Very well, then. She'd give up some caution and still keep some pride. She could abide by her decision to exchange letter for letter, but when she wrote, she would fill as many sheets as she liked.

"Yes, and you must come too," Henry said.

To the steam works, Anna realized. Of course she would go. She would accompany him to a leper colony—anywhere he chose to invite her. "All right. I've always wondered which makes more noise—a steam engine or my very own boy." She nipped his nose, leaving a smudge of dirt.

Henry pulled away, rolling his eyes. But he was smiling.

WHEN ALISTAIR ARRIVED IN MADRID, Griggs and three letters were waiting for him: two inscribed in a neat hand from Mrs. Anna Morris, and another from his aunt. Alistair endured Griggs' fussing for an hour, trying not to let his hands twitch for the letters as his batman had his way with wash towels, razors and ointment. He was worse than ever, frowning over the holes in Alistair's hat, reminding him he'd promised Mrs. Morris to look after him. Finally Alistair couldn't wait any longer. Dismissing Griggs with an oath and a hurled boot (true, Griggs had got him a very tolerable billet, but all the fussing had already used up any credit he'd earned there), Alistair adjusted himself more comfortably on the bed and reached for the letters.

"We'll apply that ointment again in an hour," Griggs said, cracking open the door.

"Let me alone with my letters, or I'll apply it to your eyeballs!" Alistair snapped. The door closed with a thud. Alistair forced himself to open Lady Fairchild's message first. It was short, written in thick, emphatic lines that might have bled through to the other side if not for the quality of the paper.

> . . . *Lovely to look at of course, but there is a Wall of Reserve I cannot get past . . . sometimes I think she is rather sly . . . it relieves me tremendously when I remember she isn't really going to marry you. The cost of maintaining her appearance would be ruinous. You wouldn't believe what she spent on stockings last week!*

Things couldn't be going well if his aunt was finding fault over such trifles. Alistair sighed and opened the next letter.

Dear Alistair—

It was a sight better than Captain Beaumaris.

I hope this letter finds you well.

That last, not so much. It sounded a good deal like the letters he'd been forced to write his parents from school.

For myself, I'm contemplating life as a monkey trainer—it appears so much easier than mothering my son. I took him to a pantomime yesterday and the woman in charge of the monkeys seemed to have an easier time of it. She had a very fine costume of silver spangles, so animal training seems to offer a tolerable style of living. Of course, I'm comfortably circumstanced thanks to your intervention with my brother-in-law. I could conceivably buy a silver-spangled costume without coaxing furry creatures through hoops, but I think your aunt wouldn't like me wearing anything so revealing in her house. She doesn't like me much, I'm afraid.

He laughed, then winced.

Your uncle has been very kind.

Oh dear. That wouldn't help.

With the Little Season upon us, there are innumerable parties. I prefer the dancing kind, though I did win a pretty sum playing silver loo the other night. Exhilarating, when I am used to playing against my parents for matchsticks. My mother, of course, does not approve. I attend church with my parents and continue working with my mother on behalf of the dispensary. I saw the most interesting rash this week.

Alistair scanned over these gruesome details. Really, his own saddle sores were bad enough. Idling around Madrid would give them a chance to heal, as would the vile smelling ointment smeared across his bare buttocks. Griggs said, as he'd been slathering it on, that word was they'd be in Madrid for a few more weeks. Alistair rolled onto his back, pulling up the edge of his blanket to cover his midsection. Griggs wouldn't like him getting ointment all over the sheets, but the stuff smelled powerfully enough Alistair thought it might be good against the fleas. He grabbed his boots from the floor and stuffed them under his shoulders, propping them up so he could read comfortably. He opened the second letter.

> More parties of course, but they are less fun now that your cousin Henrietta is gone. We visit my parents more. I miss them and they love to see Henry. He likes to go with my father to watch the ships. They also went to see a steam works—Henry was most impressed. Since the expedition he has been trying to build his own version upstairs in the nursery. I think it will be fine since I have removed his stash of coal and made sure he can't get any matches.
>
> Do all children require such extraordinary vigilance? You won't credit the number of times I've caught him a moment away from disaster. I have lurched from heart-stopping fear to wrath more times than I care to count. He listens to perhaps one word in ten when I scold, but he smiles at me. Several times a day now, though often with mischief. He fed me sloe berries. I'd forgotten how truly awful they are.

She didn't mention Lady Fairchild again. Alistair went back to his aunt's letter, frowning, aware there was nothing to be done. Anna would have to manage, and so would his aunt. If Anna's company was irksome, all the more reason to help her to another husband quickly. Though that was a prospect that gave him no joy.

He should send off his own letters. There were three in his bags, including his dangerous gamble, written after the fighting at Burgos. Alistair chewed the inside of his lip. Writing the thing had been easy enough, but sending it . . . . Once it passed from his hands, there was no going back. Asking her to give up the comforts of London was incredibly selfish. And what could he offer her? The chance to rub grease over his bottom in place of Griggs? No, sending that letter was not the honorable thing to do. He'd keep it for himself, because he couldn't burden her with a request like that.

THE DAYS PASSED, AND GRIGGS' face, as he inspected Alistair's sores, grew less grim. Alistair finally threw the jar of ointment against the wall, the resulting odor a just reward for his show of bad temper. Still, it convinced Griggs to leave him alone and let him enjoy Madrid.

The city was full of diversions for the English, even though most of them had little money. It cost only a pittance to eat and drink at the cafes lining the Prado, where strolling guitarists would play for anyone willing to spare the smallest coin. There were dances hosted by wealthy Madrileños, who filled their stately homes with music, wine, and beautiful ladies, bedecked in silks and lace. Sometimes Alistair would catch a twinkling eye or slide a hand around a slender waist, but too often he'd end up thinking about Anna and then about Anthony Morris and the morality of taking without giving. It ruined the mood, sending the stars falling to earth, turning pretty ladies into tawdry girls and flighty gallants into callous seducers. He'd given Anna his word, and though it was only temporary, it left him with nothing to give to anyone else. He was fast acquiring a reputation as the stuffiest man in the company.

Still, Madrid and her balls were a world away from weary marches and cold bivouacs, a pleasant diversion from war—until the walk home in the early morning, when wheelbarrows filled with the dead joined you on the road leaving the city. Starvation and war always kept close company. Alistair was used to that.

When he had a moment to himself, he wrote Anna or re-read

her letters. He was chuckling again about Henry's steam works when he heard footsteps on the stairs. Hastily stuffing the letters in his trunk, he dismissed thoughts of Anna in silver spangles.

"Almost ready," he called, reaching for his hat.

Jamieson blew through the door. "We'll be late," he said. "Good Lord, what's that stench?"

Alistair wrinkled his nose, though he couldn't smell anything anymore—the skin lining his nose had probably burned away. "Griggs' cure for my saddle sores, I expect," he said.

"Well, it works, from the look of you, but no wonder the ladies give you a wide berth!"

Alistair checked his watch. "Where are we going again?"

Jameson stared at him. "Hamlet. Remember?"

Now he did, but he restrained the sigh, murmuring instead, "The thespians of the 95th. Such a delight."

"I'm going to enjoy myself," said an affronted Jamieson. "Besides, not much else to do until the paymaster loosens his fist."

Alistair smiled, just to be agreeable, though Jamieson was dead wrong. Acquiring expensive mistresses was what put a fellow under water. "You aren't bringing Manuela?" Alistair asked.

"Not tonight," Jamieson said, flushing under his freckles, like he always did when her name came up. He'd arrived in Madrid, only a little the worse for wear, and promptly found himself a stunning mistress who claimed she was partial to men with fiery red hair.

Or whoever's paying. No point in being churlish about it, Alistair chided himself. He shouldn't be jealous. And he wasn't really —Jamieson's Manuela was lovely, but Alistair didn't want her. "Take care of your hide," Alistair said, leading Jamieson down the stairs. "What would I do for entertainment without your blushes?" Perhaps it was unsporting to tease him over his crimson cheeks, but Alistair liked him better because of them. It took a good five minutes for Jamieson to stop spluttering.

21

THE STEADFAST TIN SOLDIER

TWO DAYS LATER, they were ordered to retreat from Madrid. Wellington's siege had failed; they would attempt the liberation of Spain again another year. Outnumbered, with winter approaching, it was time to seek safety and gather in Portugal again. The army had almost become soldier-farmers they'd been at this seasonal rhythm so long. It was dispiriting news after the great victories of the summer.

Progress was slow, as always. They stopped in a few villages, waiting for orders under intermittent rain before finally climbing the pass of Guadarrama under an opaque grey sky. The snail's pace was torturous, especially for Alistair's brigade, who formed the rearguard, ever mindful of the reports that Marshall Soult and King Joseph's numerous force was advancing behind them. When they began their descent at last, Alistair reached up to finger the hole in his hat. No sign yet of Soult's army. His luck still held.

Two days of resting in Aravaca changed his mind. There were no houses, the tents were sodden, and men began falling ill with dysentery.

"You sick too?" Alistair demanded, returning to his tent to find Griggs white and sweating, hanging out Alistair's wet clothes.

"I'm never sick," Griggs said through chattering teeth. It had certainly never happened before.

"Forget the clothes. They'll never dry in this. Get some rest," Alistair said, pointing to his camp bed, concealing his alarm. Griggs began to argue, but Alistair cut him off with a curse. "You're no good to me ill, and you'll get worse sleeping on the ground." Griggs didn't argue when Alistair pressed him with a flask of brandy, and drifted off to sleep not long after swallowing the dose. Yanking on his heavy cloak, Alistair set out in the evening rain, but the doctors were too harassed to come.

"Bring him here if you want him seen," said the exhausted orderly, but Alistair wasn't going to consign his man to the field hospital if he could help it. Venturing into the wagon train, he bought a pot of broth from a sergeant's optimistically named wife, which he reheated in his tent over a spirit lamp and spooned down Griggs's throat.

"You must drink and stay warm," he said, knowing they wouldn't be stopped for long. Griggs needed to recover quickly. It was November, and soon the rain would become snow. Alistair passed two anxious nights dabbing Griggs' forehead and reading him Horace before Griggs recovered enough to snap at him to put the damn book away.

Alistair pocketed Horace with a relieved smile. "It's all I have," he apologized, spreading his hands.

"Just let me sleep," Griggs begged with a groan, rolling over and hunching his shoulders. "I'll give you back your bed tomorrow."

Griggs would have kept his word, but the next day they were on the march. Spain's infamous roads were worse than ever. Griggs, mended save for his leaking nose, had the worst of it, driving the mules and Alistair's spare horse around the foundering wagons. Alistair and his company ranged back and forth, guarding the flanks of the mud-covered infantry, alert for the French. Reuniting with the divisions from Burgos, they camped near Salamanca. To Alistair's relief, everyone was too wet and surly to recount stories of the victory on the same ground just four months earlier. The scouting reports of the French numbers and positions were too discouraging.

They waited nervously, but the French attack never came. Within a few days they retreated again, leaving in the dark of night. Alistair was glad to leave the plateau, where icy winds cut through his tent and his damp clothes, but the first day's march was no better. Unceasing rain swelled the rivers until men had to ford through waters up to their shoulders, and softened the roads to oozy pulp. They travelled until dark, making camp in the soggy woods, only to discover that they'd lost the baggage train and were now without food and supplies.

Sitting around a weak fire and devising punishments for the idiotic quartermaster who'd gone the wrong way was little comfort. Alistair emptied the liquor remaining in his flask and pulled his cloak closer, ignoring his alternating spells of dizziness and shivering. He shared out his remaining biscuit with Griggs and his horses, and accepted a cup of something stringy and boiled from one of the men in his company.

"It's rabbit," the man assured him with a wink.

Tasted more like horse. Alistair glanced around, but no one was admitting to losing one. The brigade major, who'd seen almost as many battles as God, passed around a hat of roasted acorns. They were scorched in places and left a bitter taste in the mouth, but it was comforting to have something to chew. "Better than nothing in the belly," the brigade major said.

Alistair woke in the morning to gunfire. Stumbling to his feet with a potent curse, he rushed for his sword and his horse, not pausing to pick up his hat.

"Wake up!" he bellowed, throwing his saddle over the gelding.

The mare had carried him the day before and needed rest. Fumbling with the girths—his fingers were half frozen—Alistair watched Jamieson vault onto a bony Spanish mare. "Get to headquarters!" Alistair ordered.

Griggs was hastily rolling blankets, hurling bowls and spoons they'd used last night into the saddlebags. Blowing on his hands to lessen the chill, Alistair quickly surveyed the rest of the company. No more than four or five troopers were mounted. The rest were reeling about like drunkards, still in a fog of sleep, or fumbling through their preparations with stiff limbs, crippled by fatigue and cold.

If they were caught like this, there was a good chance most of them would soon be dead.

"Make ready!" Alistair bellowed. It was tempting to abandon kits where they lay—a solution that saved one from the sword but not from the snow. Mumbling about the shortcomings of youth—Jameson still wasn't back yet—Alistair jumped into the saddle and took off after him, cantering toward the nearby village where the senior officers were quartered. The pathetic hamlet sagged in the ceaseless drizzle. It had about as many buildings as there were letters in the alphabet, most of them smaller than sheds. Alistair had probably seen a hundred such places, the lopsided shutters and sparse yards telling a familiar tale. This place had been trampled by so many armies it was a wonder it wasn't flat.

Jamieson was riding toward him. Alistair drew rein and waited, too experienced to feel any great relief.

"Well?" he asked.

"Nobody knows," Jamieson panted. "Could be that pack of idiots in the 28th. Maybe they saw a rabbit."

"I heard three shots," Alistair said. With rabbits, you never got more than one. "Did they give any orders?"

"Mount everyone and ride southwest to look. Infantry's going to hot foot out of here," Jamieson said. As they rode into camp, Jamieson's mouth went white about the corners. "Damn me if we aren't going to get nabbed by the French before breakfast! Before those troopers even get their trousers on!"

"At least we don't have to worry about the quartermaster's wagons," Alistair said, trying to calm him. Ready or no, it was time to move. He glanced back to his bivouac, relieved to see that Griggs had loaded the mules and was leading them and the mare in the direction of the 28th Foot. "Stay as close to the column as you can," Alistair called after him.

Griggs turned, handing off the leads to one of the starveling boys that always seemed to be hovering at hand. He could be English or Spanish or half of each, and might not even know himself.

"Course I'm staying near the Foot. D'ye think I've gone soft in the head?" Griggs said, stalking toward him.

"I like that horse," Alistair said. "Don't want to make a present of her to some Chausseur."

Griggs rolled his eyes. "No more damage to your uniform, mind," he said. "Not much good at sewing up holes." He reached up, handing Alistair his hat.

"Thanks." Jamming it on his head, Alistair turned the black around. Most of the troop was mounted now, deciding to abandon what hadn't been stowed away. The French would find themselves some cook pots today, though the heavy iron things were more of a penance than a prize.

He signaled the company to ride. A minute later they were passing between the trees. Jamieson rode beside him, growling incoherent curses—one of many ways to cover fear, and not such a bad one either. There were plenty worse. He'd seen men piss themselves or turn into bawling, gibbering fools. Listening to Jamieson with sympathy and growing wonderment—it had been a long time since he'd heard such creative profanity—Alistair remembered how it felt to be green. He could only be grateful it took more than this to get him to the profane stage. Once you'd seen enough death, you didn't get more than anxious until it was breathing in your ear.

The rushing air was cold on his bare cheeks, whistling through his coat. The ground was slippery and soft, wretched for fighting, but they didn't pause at the edge of the wood where they were forced to abandon cover. A rolling plain stretched before them, slit down the middle by a sloppy stream that in drier times was probably only a trickle. A blank hill rose on the other side. The whole of Soult's army might lie behind it or nothing at all.

Tearing across the field, they cut through the stream, spattering mud up their horses' flanks, their boots and the arms of their coats. The drumming of hoofbeats sounded through him, shaking the earth, yet he knew from experience they wouldn't be heard on the other side of the hill. Not yet at least. They might have been scouted out already, of course, but no point speculating till they reached the top of the rise—the sight from there would tell him if the French expected them or not. At his signal, half the troop peeled off with Harris, sticking to the low ground, darting around the rise. The rest drove uphill, slowing as they neared the top, a few of the horses foundering in the greasy earth. Alistair raised his hand and they slowed to a walk, breathless and silent, waiting. The creak of saddle leather, the swish of a tossed mane, fingers that tightened around reins as one readied one's sword: every detail seemed terribly important, picked out in bright colors though the sun was weak, almost lost behind the heavy grey sky.

Drawing breath almost as one, they crested the ridge, glancing down at the tight ranks moving below. It was the French. Alistair took one look, then turned back, hoping they were tucked out of sight. His orders were to engage only if necessary, but it would be, if they were to defend the 28th Foot from this horde of French Cavalry.

"Ride to the village. Tell them we've got Hussars, Chasseurs and Lancers," he said to Jamieson. "They're moving fast, so go quickly." God send Jamieson reached the 28th in time for them to form up. The stream, even swollen with days of rain, wouldn't check the French advance any more than it had halted their ride across the plain. The forest was sparse, nearly leafless. His troop and Harris's would fight, but they couldn't turn three or four times their number, not alone. "We'll fall back. Take a position at the edge of the wood."

If they were lucky, it would confuse the French estimate of their numbers, perhaps even give time for the artillery to join the party. But if it came to a pitched battle, the English foot, cavalry and artillery combined were still greatly outnumbered. He spurred his horse faster.

At the stream, he heard bugles and glanced back at the swarm of French Horse spilling over the ridge. Damn, they were fast. No time to wait in the fringes of the trees. Signaling the troop to ride on, they raced across the open fields, trying to put more space between them and the oncoming Chasseurs before they would have to turn and fight. A hundred yards from the forest's edge, Alistair gave the signal, wheeling about as his sergeant sounded the call. Within seconds they were massed and ready, sabers drawn, the colors flying bravely. A nod to the sergeant, another note on the bugle that was swallowed almost immediately by galloping hooves. Alistair leaned forward, his eyes fixed on the glinting helmets and streaming plumes of the French. A second troop was pouring over the hill; something to worry about after they collided with the first, springing across the plain, devouring the distance between them. On the right, Harris's troop swung into sight, darting along the course of the stream to the space where they would all collide. A quick hit, then away, if they could manage it, north towards the village. Alistair tensed, raising his saber, finding a line and a target—a broad blue coat and behind it, another. He could reach both if he held his course and moved quick.

"Show 'em how we fight in *The* Division!" Alistair roared, adding to the bellows from his sergeant. Behind him, Gordon was yelling in gaelic: fierce, meaningless words that always made him shiver. Kicking his mount forward, Alistair lunged out of reach of his target's falling blade. A quick thrust, a snick and a pull that momentarily caught at his sword, then he was away, nudging the black to the left, away from the wild cavorting of a riderless horse. Another thrust, the clang of metal on metal, the grunts of men and horse. On, leaping over a bad patch of ground that he spotted almost too late, his eyes watering from the speed. An oncoming chausseur marked him, galloping towards him on churning hooves. Alistair noticed the spattered brown horse, the swinging plume, the face screaming blood-curdling obscenities he couldn't make out above the pounding in his ears. Their swords rattled together; he shoved with shoulder and horse, forcing a faltering side step but tangling his own sword. Cursing, he lurched the other way, pulling himself free, then kicked his horse forward before a Frenchman turning towards him could cleave his skull in two. He felt the blade whistle by as his horse took off, screaming.

This time it was all he could do to check the black's course. The maddened animal was ready to plow into anything that crossed their path. Reining in hard, Alistair slowed to a canter, glancing back on his left. The French, deflected from their course, were veering east on a line that would soon have them skirting the village. Reforming quickly, Alistair joined his men with Harris's troop, circling west, chased by the bugle calls of a fresh squadron of French Lancers. Well, Alistair wasn't going to face them today, not if he could help it. He spurred his horse onward. Beneath him, the ground was a sickening blur. Veering into the woods, they shot through the trees, bypassing the village and laboring up another slope. "Steady!" he called out, for he was too far to reach the trooper beside him who was sliding off the back of his faltering horse. He drew in, but by then the animal had regained his feet and Daniels, a tough old campaigner, had pulled himself back into his seat.

"You fall and I'll have to leave you here for the frogs," Alistair warned.

"I never fall," said Daniels, glancing at Alistair. Daniels had been in the Peninsula since the first campaign with Moore and never gotten anything worse than greying side whiskers and a face of tough brown leather. "Worry about yourself. I don't want to have to cart you to the surgeons. That's not mud on your leg, is it?"

Alistair glanced down, surprised to find a large dark stain spreading over his knee and a slit in the top of his boot.

"Never felt anything?" Daniels asked.

Alistair shook his head.

"You're all right, then. Your man can sew you up later," Daniels said, laughing at Alistair's sudden change of face.

"I'd rather use your tailor," Alistair said. Daniels had never required stitches in his skin, so far as Alistair knew, but his wife was known for her skill with a needle. Daniel's uniform might get threadbare or soiled, but it was never in need of mending and his tent never leaked.

There was no more time for talking, or for worrying about the nick on his leg. Grateful his horse had good wind and strong quarters, Alistair spurred him to the top of the slope.

"Look at our boys!" crowed the sergeant, as Alistair broke out of the trees and onto the plain. The Foot was here—formed up in squares. Shabby, starved and worn, they were ready all the same, rousing a cheer from the just-arrived cavalry. Letting out a whoop, Alistair stood in his stirrups, waving his sword at Gregson, the brigade major, who was riding beside his tight ranks of infantry.

"So you do know how to get up early in the morning!" Alistair called.

Gregson grinned and swore at him. "D'you find the French?"

"Course! Invited them out to play—expect 'em any minute, the laggards!"

Ordered to left flank, they took off at a trot, happy to leave their pursuers in the infantry's hands for now. By the time they'd taken their position, both the Chasseurs and the Lancers were massing, preparing to charge.

"We're outnumbered," someone muttered. Alistair looked over. Another green one.

"Doesn't matter," he said. "Watch and learn." Unless the French had brought invisible artillery, their squadrons of horse would break on the British squares.

The man didn't believe him. When the French sounded the charge, he shifted in his saddle, glancing left and right at the men beside him. Alistair played with the ends of his reins, watching with a practiced air of idleness, yet still intent. Gregson's men were well drilled, but it didn't do to get careless. Alistair caught his breath—the French charge was beautifully co-ordinated, flying like wispy cloud, untroubled by the broken ground. Suppressing a shiver of envy—the French Cavalry trumped the English in numbers and glamour—he waited.

So did Gregson. The French stormed closer and closer still, until even Alistair began to wonder if—

A crack of gunfire ripped through the air and the vanguard of the French cavalry shivered. At this distance, Alistair couldn't see the holes punched through limbs and bodies, only the out-flung arms, crashing falls, and thrashing hooves that inevitably followed. Another crack as the second rank fired, and the French charge bounced away from Gregson's square, just in time to be repulsed by another.

"Mind where they're going," Alistair said, to no one in partic-ular. "Can't let them have the road."

But the chasseurs were regrouping, riding back to the squares for another swipe. Though swift and fierce, by the time they struck again, any damage they'd inflicted was already repaired, the lines of infantrymen closing ranks in the time it took to blink. Peeling away, but not giving up the field, the French reformed again, but by this time the squares were marching in formation, crawling west. Alistair motioned to his troop and they set forth with the usual jingling, holding themselves to the painfully slow pace of the Foot. Marches like this were wearisome things, interminable hours of bluffing, keeping a stoic front for the enemy. The French kept pace for a while, finally swooping in again, but once more, the squares held them off, Alistair's troop ready to pounce should the French attempt to overtake the Foot and find a better target further up the line.

"Losing interest, I think," Alistair said, when this third charge turned even quicker than the last. It was the end of the fighting season. Time to let each other alone.

Apparently the French commander had reached the same conclusion. Both companies drew off together, moving for the woods. A moment later a rider bolted out from the middle of the square, making for Alistair's company.

"We're to keep an eye on them?" Alistair asked.

"If you'd be so kind," said the adjutant, wiping his streaming nose.

They followed the French at a respectful distance, not wanting to pick a fight on their own, for a good two hours before changing course, convinced the French had had enough.

See you next year, Alistair thought, turning westward again, hoping it wouldn't take them too long to find the road. It was raining again. Alistair hunched his shoulders in his damp coat, trying to calculate how many miles to go until they reached their base at Ciudad Rodrigo. He wasn't sure of his guess, but didn't bother to pull out his map, just in case it was still dry. Besides, whether his guess was right or wrong, the number of miles remaining was too high to please anyone. Wiggling cold toes in wet boots, and ignoring the noisy pleas of his stomach (the devil knew where the supply wagons were by this time), Alistair reminded himself there was much to be grateful for. At least they'd parted ways with the French.

22

GLITTER AND GLOSS

LADY FAIRCHILD WAS ADMIRING the effect of sapphire earrings against her pale blonde curls when the door to her bedroom opened.

"Almost too pretty, I think. Don't know if I should allow it," William said, quietly closing the door. Turning on her chair, Lady Fairchild caught her maid's eye in the mirror, signaling her to vanish. By the time she was facing her husband—the word had an unaccustomed, silly warmth today—she was smiling.

"I didn't invite your opinion," she said, pleased to have it nonetheless.

William leaned against her dressing table, picking up a fan she had discarded, inspecting the carving on the ivory handle. "I was hoping you'd make time for me today."

Georgiana made a face. "Mrs. Morris took an age with her shopping. Besides, you're getting spoiled." She liked him intruding in her rooms, but she couldn't admit that. Not with words, at any rate.

"Getting rid of Alistair's fiancé is proving to be time consuming," she said, speaking her excuse aloud. It wasn't all bad. She'd never had a companion before who took shopping as seriously as herself—it was like choosing weapons, a kind of personal arma-ment. Despite sifting through shops for hours, the only worthy finds had been this fan for herself and a bonnet garnished with artificial cherries for Mrs. Morris. Instead of making her look hopelessly young and countrified, as such flourishes generally tended to do, she'd made the bonnet look . . . provocative. Geor-giana frowned, remembering the sheen of Anna's bright lips, the mocking expression she had unconsciously put on with the hat.

"You don't enjoy it?" William asked. "I think I like her."

"She's certainly beautiful," Georgiana admitted, her eyes darting to William's hands, playing with the tassel on her fan.

"And about Henrietta's age," William said, setting the fan on the table. "Don't be a goose." He was laughing at her, smiling in a way that made her think he might try to kiss her. Gratifying to be sure, but she still couldn't laugh with him about pretty women. Perhaps not ever, she thought bleakly. In spite of the care she took with her hands, her age was written there, plain to a watchful eye. The grey in her hair had come prematurely, but she had always consoled herself with the way it silvered her blond coloring. Unfortunately, she was now at an age where grey hair began to belong.

It had hit her today, watching Anna laughing at her cherries, a sight to behold—striking, with the kind of beauty that made men catch their breath. Anna might have had a hard time of it, married to Anthony Morris, but he was dead now. She had her son back and still some youth, even. Georgiana hadn't spoken of her insecurities before, hadn't even let herself think them, but William's interest in Anna's progress with the terror residing in the nursery hadn't escaped her. He and Anna fell into conversa-tion easily whenever they met. In private, Georgiana found she and her husband had plenty to say, but in company, they hadn't broken out of old habits. She was afraid to try. If this romance didn't last, she couldn't bear for anyone to know.

"Georgy . . . . " William moved closer, frowning and seeking out her eyes, which she promptly hid, searching the top of the dressing table for another pot of rouge in her favorite naked pink. She would give it to Anna. "Will you ever trust me?" he asked.

"I want to," she said, blinking twice. "It's difficult."

"Does it make you feel better, believing the worst?"

"I don't know." She hated confronting her own bitterness, but she couldn't ignore it either; it was a heavy fetter drawing her up short every time she thought herself free. She looked up, capturing William's eyes. "When I see—" She caught her breath. Started over. "I can only do this if I have all of you. I'd rather go back to nothing at all than discover I'm sharing you. And if I ever do, I swear I will cut you up and go after the woman with a fork."

"I believe you would," William said, sliding his hand over her bare shoulder, drawing her in to lean against him. Georgiana pressed her lips together to still their trembling. Threats were unlike her, but she meant this one.

"You care that much?" William asked. His hand was stroking her back, calming her in a way she could grow to depend on, if she wasn't halfway there already. She'd forgotten how it felt to have worries smoothed away, vanishing like they'd never existed at all.

"Yes," she said thickly, knowing the word was unnecessary. She scowled at his jacket buttons—she'd admitted a hopeless disadvantage, and for what? But then William exhaled a tension she'd never noticed, his hands tightening on her shoulder in a quick, impulsive hold.

"I thought I could persuade you to care just a little. I hoped, but didn't think I could expect any more," he finally said. "Someday you'll trust me. In the meantime, I'll enjoy your jealousy." He lifted one hand, laid it gently over her carefully sculpted curls, scarcely touching. "It'll do no good to my vanity, though."

She looked up at him, narrowing her eyes. "I haven't forgotten how to trim you down to size."

A laugh rumbled through him. "I wouldn't think so. There isn't a woman alive who can do it with your flair. Believe me, Georgy, I know you well enough not to be careless. You worry about my loyalty, but I know perfectly well the next time we quarrel you'll eat me alive. I'd much rather we kept it small. Perhaps something to do with the children."

Georgiana thinned her lips—rolling her eyes would be ungenteel. "There's plenty to be annoyed with there. Henrietta says she'll not join us for Christmas and Jasper is infuriating. He won't show me Sophy's letters."

"Me neither," William said, turning quiet.

"What if he's the wrong sort? I mean, he is of course, but what if it turns out worse than that? We don't know a thing about Bagshot, and she's absurdly in love. He'll break her heart."

"Anna Morris speaks well of him," William said.

"How tremendously reassuring," Georgiana said, more skeptical than ever. She reached for a new pair of gloves laid out and ready on the table. "She's just too good at—at snaring men. I shouldn't have let her walk out in that red pelisse. You should have seen the heads turn. I don't know how she does it—her husband—"

"Not such a prize after all," William interjected.

"Naturally. I never set much store by that family," Georgiana said. "And then Alistair. Jasper would probably ogle her too, if he wasn't afraid of her."

"No!" William laughed.

"Could be suspicion or his own wariness, but you must have noticed how he avoids her. And she's enslaved Mr. Phillips, not that she shows a particle of interest—" He'd sent flowers after the Sutton ball, poor man.

"She didn't have luck with Tom Bagshot, though," William said.

True. Which might be a point in the man's favor. "I really can't be easy in my mind about him," Georgiana said. "Not with the little I've seen of him." It was grossly uncomfortable having Sophy in a stranger's keeping.

"Maybe we should go home for a spell," William said. Cordell Hall, in Suffolk, was always home to him. Before she could finish shaking her head, he continued. "We could write first. We needn't call."

"He might not let us through the door," Georgiana said.

"I could ask my tenants if they've seen Sophy. Taking rides in the neighborhood, that kind of thing."

She answered with a chilling lift of her eyebrows that usually made her family scrabble for excuses—any excuses—to explain their stupidity, but she only provoked a smile.

"You can't be serious," she said. "Sophy's marriage is undoubtably the talk of the county. If we set spies on Bagshot it will only make it worse. Besides, there's Mrs. Morris. I promised Alistair."

"You should call her Anna."

"I will, at Lady Wincholme's. Maybe even 'dear Anna.' It sounds nice, doesn't it?"

"Yes, and Lady Wincholme will doubtless be taken in. Anna isn't."

Lady Fairchild's shrug was more a suggestion than an actual movement. "I agreed to help her, not fall in love with her." Alistair had done that already. She hadn't been too worried at first. Once he was removed from London, his feelings would naturally lessen, but to date, there were no signs of that. His letters to her arrived almost as regularly as the grocer's bills. Alistair! Who wrote his own mother perhaps twice a year! It had been more than two weeks since his last, though. Perhaps she could begin to hope. "She's not good for Alistair. I worry. She'd have offers by now, if she'd take the trouble to cultivate the interest gentlemen are so quick to bestow on her."

"You don't want to rush her."

"Yes I do. The quicker she's tied up with someone else, the better. Don't tell me you enjoy all of that," Georgiana said, tilting her eyes up to the ceiling. It was quiet just now, but the bumps and whoops as she'd been dressing . . . .

"I'm pleased to see the two of them happier," he said. "Her attention is on her son. No wonder she has none to spare for the gentlemen you are trying to foist on her."

"I'm not trying," Georgiana muttered, reaching for her fan. "They're eager enough on their own."

"She has good reason to be cautious," William said, sliding it to her across the dressing table. "You should be able to understand that."

"I do," Georgiana said coolly, adjusting her neckline. "No secret that Morris made a dreadful husband. Henry doesn't look a thing like him." She smiled at her husband in the mirror.

"Doesn't mean anything. Look at our children." Jasper and Henrietta took all their looks from her side of the family. Sophy was the only one of William's children who'd borrowed any of his features.

"Yes, but I am not the same as Anna Morris," Georgiana said. "We handle adversity differently." She wasn't sure and she would never ask. But when Henry got older, some people would remember Anthony Morris and they would wonder too. Anna's preference for crimson rouge didn't help.

William was thoughtful for a moment. "I hope you still intend to help her."

"I gave my word," Georgiana said. She'd always had a particular fondness for Alistair, and right now the best thing she could do for him was untangle him from Mrs. Morris.

"I warn you that I intend to dance with her this evening," William said. "Remember, it doesn't mean I'm pursuing a love affair—I'm only interested in one with you."

Maybe that was why they never danced. William was the best

secret she'd had in years. "I suppose you may dance with whomever you please," Georgiana said as indifferently as she dared. "So long as you know where to come at the end of the evening." Her eyes met his in the mirror.

"Goodnight Henry."

He was wearing his nightshirt, his toes bare and pink as prawns. His hair was still damp from his bath.

"You smell nice," he mumbled, tracing the gauze of her gown with a careful finger—permissible, now that he was clean. By midmorning, he'd probably need another scrub. Anna had promised to take him and his toy sailboat to the park again.

"Should we ask Grandpapa to come with us tomorrow? He'd love to see your boat. When I was small, he took me and Grandmama across the sea."

"To Spain?" Henry asked, perking up a little.

"America." Anna didn't bother explaining the difference. Her transatlantic voyages would never compete with the adventures of a Captain of Hussars. "Sleep well." Anna kissed him on the top of the head and propelled him into bed. He climbed under the sheets, hauling them up to his chin.

"I'll stay with him until he's asleep," Lucy whispered as Anna backed out of the room.

Whisking downstairs, Anna reached up to check her hair—no serious damage. Good. Her maid wasn't very quick with fancy coiffures, so there was no time to do this one over. Anna didn't mind if her hair wasn't perfect, but Lady Fairchild would. Tonight was an important party.

"Much nicer than the Burlington's last week," Lady Fairchild had said. They'd attended that musicale only for her sake, Anna was sure.

She hadn't disgraced Lady Fairchild—yet—and it was mainly

agreeable, spending time with her. Unlike Anthony's mother, Lady Fairchild kept Anna close, preventing her from making noticeable mistakes in company, though Anna felt so much pressure not to embarrass herself people probably thought she was made out of wood. The women at least. Men were easier to entertain: just give them something to look at and choose the right smiles. Tonight's gown was sufficiently lovely to make up for any shortcomings with her hair. It was new.

Flush with money, Anna was spending joyfully: lemon yellow gloves, this gown of plum-colored silk, and a day dress in gauzy white muslin, embroidered with red flowers growing up from the hem. Today she'd purchased a bonnet adorned with cherries, and yesterday she'd bought Henry a toy boat. Alistair, she knew, would laugh at the bonnet before moving in to murmur inappropriate things in her ear. She'd thought of him the moment she'd seen it, because once he'd said her lips were the same color—and every bit as delicious. But she was biting the bottom one now, embarrassed to find Lord and Lady Fairchild waiting for her at the bottom of the stairs.

"I didn't mean to keep you waiting," she said. "I was just with Henry."

"Did he like the boat?" Lord Fairchild asked.

"He loves it," she said. "We'll take it out every day, so long as the weather holds. It should make the mornings quieter."

Lady Fairchild smiled politely at that, which only increased Anna's chagrin.

"You look lovely. Remind me to have my maid show yours a trick she has with hair," Lady Fairchild said, pressing down one of Anna's loose pins. She reached into her reticule. "I bought this for you. A dewy pink. Your vibrant cheeks are just the thing to make the color come alive." She pressed an enameled box into Anna's gloved hand. "There's time if you want to try it now."

"I'll wait until after supper," Anna said, glancing at the hall clock. She had lingered far too long in the nursery. "I'm so sorry to have kept you waiting."

Lady Fairchild said nothing. Lord Fairchild chuckled. "You must spend more time with Henrietta. I doubt you could turn her into a punctual creature, but her family would be glad if she acquired your habit of apology at least."

There were hot bricks on the floor of the carriage, but they did little to counter the insidious chill that crept under Anna's cloak. Her ears were cold, but Lady Fairchild hadn't drawn up her hood, so neither would she.

The iciness was gone by the time they reached Lady Wincholme's—from the air at least. The hostess bestowed warm greetings on Lord and Lady Fairchild, but welcomed Anna with a voice that would have left frost on a window. "So delighted. I've been longing to meet Captain Beaumaris's fiancée," she said. Anna smiled back bravely, convinced of Lady Wincholme's curiosity and the threat it implied; the protestations of delight were a transparent lie. Anna fumbled for a reply, proving her stupidity to Lady Wincholme and whoever happened to over-hear. Finally granted a chance to escape, Anna sped after Lady Fairchild into the ballroom.

Lady Fairchild took pity on her. "Calm yourself. She's prob-ably jealous," she said, patting Anna's arm as they progressed around the perimeter of the brilliantly lit room. The heat from the candles and the miasma of perfume was stifling. Searching for somewhere to rest her eyes, but finding only gilt and mirrors, Anna tightened her grip on her fan, longing for Henry.

"This place is fine," Lady Fairchild said, stopping between two alcoves. "Count to fifty," she ordered after a minute. "Use your fan." She was working hers slowly, wafting air over Anna's shoul-ders. "For goodness' sake, get a hold of yourself."

Anna didn't answer. She was counting as instructed, passing sixty. "Lady Wincholme is nothing," Lady Fairchild whispered. "She'd have liked Alistair for herself, I'm sure, though after the disaster with Sophy it would have taken considerable adroitness to get her to marry him. She isn't in a hurry to marry now that Wincholme's gone."

Anna took in the scale of the room, crusted over with blue and gold flourishes like a hull eaten by barnacles. "Pity. She'd be a good prospect for him." But Lady Wincholme would have to wait until next year, if Alistair came to London again. Anna licked dry lips, wishing she could totter out of the room and hide in the cool dark outside. Until she and Alistair were finished, she didn't want to think about 'eligible situations' for him to marry.

"Not as good a prospect as Sophy," Lady Fairchild said, with a silent laugh. She raised her fan to shield her face and leaned closer. "Sophy is much more pliant and agreeable. Usually. I expect that when Lady Wincholme does remarry, her husband will not have an easy time of it. Of course, Alistair has considerable powers of persuasion. In a contest between him and our hostess, I would lay my money on him." She slid her eyes over Anna, appraising her minutely but saying nothing. From Anna, her eyes moved to the crowd, alighting on a slim gentleman with a dark head. Anna recognized that hair. Impossible. She started forward, but then she saw the man's face. He bore some similarity to his younger brother—clearly drawn by the same hand, but with softer lines and paler tints.

Lady Fairchild nodded, acknowledging her nephew. "Cyril, on the other hand . . . . " Her eyes flew to Lady Wincholme.

"Lady Wincholme would boil him down and spread him on toast," Anna whispered back, pleased they could agree on something.

Lady Fairchild stifled a laugh, her shoulders shaking. "Too true. Should we throw them together and see what happens?"

There was no time to answer. Cyril was before them, executing an elegant bow, presenting his compliments and asking Anna to dance.

"Enjoy yourselves!" Lady Fairchild said, sending them off with a tinkling wave.

Cyril's hands clung like tentacles. Anna decided that no matter who she married, she would see to it that Lady Wincholme never caught Alistair. She was welcome to take a bite out of Cyril whenever she pleased.

ANNA WAS DANCING with Cyril before Lord Fairchild reached the door of the card room. It was his usual haunt at entertainments like these, but tonight he didn't plan to play. He made a circuit of the room, then returned to the ballroom. Georgiana was on the other side of the room, holding a glass of lemonade, nodding seriously (though he doubted she was listening) to everything Mr. Grimpen chose to say. A tireless reformer, Grimpen, with a keen mind. Georgiana probably had ten years on him. William inspected the sleeve of his black coat, flicking away dust that wasn't there.

"Evening, sir." Jasper appeared beside him. "No games for you this evening?" Even as a child, he'd had that needling smirk.

"Perhaps later," William said.

"Will you be at Cordell for Christmas?" Jasper asked.

"Depends," he said, glancing at Anna, who was dancing a reel with a man who seemed to have no control of his elbows. They flew out from his sides like the angular legs of a crane.

"I thought you might be visiting Sophy. I am."

"Your mother and I weren't invited," William said stiffly.

"I wonder why?"

"Give her my regards," William said.

"I'd rather not." He nodded in the direction of the dancers. "You and mother are taking prodigious care of Alistair's pretty bird. Haven't spoken much with her myself." That was true. He'd dined with them twice since Anna had joined them, but exchanged no more than commonplaces with her.

"Lovely, isn't she?" William said, curious to test Georgiana's theory, more interested in provoking his son than complimenting the lady.

"Appallingly so. Alistair told me the first time he saw her he took her for a high flier."

"Yes, I heard that." With the really good ones, it was hard to tell the difference. They looked and spoke the same as ladies. Only the reputation differed. Mostly. "How stupid. He's usually keener than that," Lord Fairchild said. Of course, Alistair had proven himself not entirely rational when it came to Mrs. Morris. Which wasn't such a bad thing. William liked her.

"Thought she was tangled with Sophy's Tom. Well, I knew he must be mistaken on Tom's part, but maybe he was brighter than he knew. I passed Frederick Morris in the club today. He was hinting all kinds of things."

William stiffened. Anna had alluded to an imperfect past, but he respected her confidence, and her efforts to put such things behind her. "I hope you had the sense to silence him." He didn't give a farthing if Georgiana's suspicions about Henry's parentage were right—he was in no position to judge. They both shared a close acquaintance with regret, which was probably why he liked Anna, and wanted her to be happy with her child. He wanted it to be possible for both of them.

"I may have mentioned a foul odor and that I was thinking of giving up the place," Jasper said idly. "But who knows? If they let Morris in at White's the others are probably just as bad."

William couldn't help a half smile. "Talk like that and he'll call you out."

"I think not. The brother was a fire eater, but Frederick's a coward. Spluttered and pretended he hadn't heard me. No danger from him." Jasper's lip curled perfectly, an exact imitation of his mother's. The two of them were like magnets: so alike they repelled.

"Do you dislike Alistair's fiancée?" William asked.

"I have no quarrel with Mrs. Morris. Don't know how I feel about Alistair's fiancée."

William didn't know what to say. It was an ill-advised match, but Anna was a hardy soul. The world wouldn't think her a good prospect, but—

"Mama keeps looking at you," Jasper said, glancing from one parent to the other, his narrowed eyes asking why.

In spite of himself, William grinned. "Yes, she does." And then he abandoned his son for the refreshment table.

THE CHAMPAGNE WAS GOOD, the food tolerable, the music—well, he wasn't qualified to judge. William caught Georgiana's eye, walking past her at supper, and once again, from the edge of the ballroom. She was waltzing with Grimpen, trying not to look bored. She was a lovely dancer, but he ignored the temptation to ask her himself, knowing she wouldn't stand for it. They didn't exchange words at parties, only looks. Tonight was duller than usual, especially since he'd decided against the palliative of the card room. He danced with Anna, debating all the while if he should warn her about Frederick Morris's rumblings.

He decided not to. She was uneasy already, and had looked that way all evening. Instead, he set himself to drawing out smiles and handed her off to her next partner looking less troubled. He danced with a few more ladies and his hostess—standing in the ballroom meant he had to be somewhat obliging. Once, years ago, he had thought about kissing Lady Wincholme as they wandered too far from the rest of their party down a shadowy Vauxhall avenue. He was very glad he hadn't. Lady Wincholme's angular little chin was as piquant as ever, but he suspected intimacies between them would have been sordid and mutually disappointing. He was of a retiring disposition; Lady Wincholme, exhaustingly manipulative. Blatant about it too. Not for him, her crystal laughter, her over-bright cheeks, the arch manners and disdainful yet hungry smiles. Give him his intent, secretive Penelope. He wanted her painted again. She hadn't had a portrait done in years.

"My Lord, you aren't attending," Lady Wincholme said, teasing, but with a predatory showing of teeth.

"Forgive me. It's the music," he lied.

"Beautiful, isn't it?" she said, flashing diamonds at him.

"Lovely rhythm," he said, failing valiantly. Heavens, let the dance end soon. "Like—like the paces of a good horse."

Lady Wincholme's parting, at the end of the set, was less warm than her greeting at the start of the evening. No matter. William was searching out his wife, wondering if he could lure her into one of the alcoves.

No, this one was taken, and the next was flanked by Jasper and his least favorite nephew. No good. If Georgiana wouldn't dance with him, she sure as hell wouldn't follow him into shady corners under their son's nose. But he did catch her eye over the hair plumes of his waltz partner at the end of the evening. Georgiana's answering smile was small and quick. Dazzling.

So dazzling that he found himself humming inattentively on the carriage ride home. Tunelessly, but that went without saying. Georgiana, who was an expert on all his deficiencies, forbore comment. Anna, of course, was too polite to complain.

23

PIVOT

After hearing the hall clock chime four, Anna decided it was no use and got out of bed. She regretted it instantly. It was December and hours before dawn; her room was blood-sappingly cold. Leaping from one carpet to the next, Anna grabbed a heavy wool dressing gown draped over the folding screen and burrowed into it, adding a shawl for good measure. The fire was dead, nothing but powdery ash, but Anna knew her room well enough to find the armchair without lighting her candle. She'd been here nearly four months. It was time to stop avoiding the issue and find herself a husband. It might take a good six months or so, and she hadn't even started. She couldn't stay at Rushford House forever.

Anna leaned her head against the wing of the chair and pulled her hands deeper into her sleeves. She was as bad as Henry, balking at this like he did when it was time to brush his teeth. A sigh escaped her, wafting up like a feeble white flag. Her heart wasn't in this; it had deserted her and gone to Spain. Unfortunate, but not really surprising. Hearts were unruly things. They caused a good deal of trouble.

There must be some man out there who was sufficiently kind

and passably handsome. No, forget that. Better if he was passable company. She'd danced with a score of gentleman at Lady Wincholme's ball—surely one of them met this standard. It shouldn't be this hard to separate their faces and pull up their names. She must forget Alistair. She'd promised to release him. It wasn't the first time she'd made plans like this in her dark room, but this time, she really would put him away.

Anna had enough practice with night-time worries she could make them awake or asleep. She did both, dozing intermittently in her chair. When her maid came early in the morning to light a new fire, Anna lifted her head, smiled blearily, and shuffled back into bed to thaw under the covers and wait until the room warmed. Then she rang and dressed. Tired, but resolved, Anna was surprised to find herself alone at the breakfast table. She considered the wind scouring the street and testing the windows an excellent reason to stay indoors, but Lord Fairchild was seldom deterred from his morning ride by unfavorable weather. No matter how thick the frost, he usually beat her to the table. Not today—a fine piece of luck, Anna realized, spying the letters resting beside her plate. Lord Fairchild didn't pry, but she'd rather read them unobserved. Forgetting the welcome smells of breakfast and her night time resolutions, Anna reached for the letters with an accelerating heart. There were two: one with battered corners, the direction written in Alistair's swirling hand, and a second with crisper edges but cruder script. She broke the seal on Alistair's first, ignoring a twinge of guilt.

Dearest Anna,

It was how he addressed all his letters, but regular use didn't lesson her pleasure in the endearment. His next sentence made her pause.

I'm a shocking liar. Selfish too.

Selfish? No—he was anything but. And lies—well, his imperfections certainly didn't detract.

> *I can't stand the thought of you and Mr. Worthy, whoever he might be. When I engaged myself to you, it was because I wished it were true. I wanted you for my own but a partial loan seemed like the best I could get.*

Something was happening to her breathing—or else the room was losing air.

> *Will you marry me?*

Of course she would! Yes, and yes again!

> *I've nothing to recommend me—*

The wonderful idiot. Didn't he see?

> *—save that I look well in a uniform and on a horse, but I'm mad enough in love that I'm certain we could find a way. Not maybe a life of wealth and triumphs, but for me anyways, one of happiness.*
>
> *I want you and I want Henry and I want to spend my days collecting your smiles. Would you mind terribly?*

She devoured the rest of the brief letter, her skin alive with each word, especially his closing:

> *Burning and fervent and possibly half-cracked, but all for love of you,*
>   *Alistair*

Wasn't she also? Surely there could be no greater joy than this mutual madness. Anna read the letter again, torn between containing this unstoppable torrent of feeling and letting herself dance around the table. The merely tolerable husband of her late-night plans died unnoticed. She would have Alistair.

Still no Lord Fairchild. Anna grinned, hugging the letter to herself and sinking back into her chair. She brushed her finger over his signature, and—no one was looking—pressed her lips hard and swift against the paper. Even when she put it away, her hands still yearned for it.

She peeked at the door again, composing herself, reaching for marmalade she wasn't going to eat. She added extra sugar to her coffee and sliced open an orange and then gave up. She read the letter over again, quickly, because she already knew the words by heart, then slipped it out of sight on to her lap. She might not be able to eat, or drink more than a swallow of her syrupy coffee, but she could make a pretense of reading the other letter.

She read the first paragraph twice, her heart beating slower and slower as cold inertia overpowered her. Yes, it was from Griggs. She dragged her eyes back up to the top of the page, forcing herself to decode each word, for though the letters were neatly made and spaced, they felt as strange as a foreign alphabet. Almost, she wished they were.

Mrs. Morris,

He's bad—we all were along the retreat, sick and cold and hungry, but of course our Captain isn't one to complain. The only action was a trifling skirmish, a little thing. Wasn't even mentioned in the dispatches. But Captain got a nick below his knee and of course the only thing we regretted was the ruin of a good pair of boots. A clean cut, so he didn't get stitched until we arrived at Ciudad Rodrigo, and then it was already festering. He's too fevered to write or understand a word anyone says and he sweats and rattles with chills and shudders so bad I think he'll knock out his teeth.

I'm doing my best, as I promised, but can't say as he'll outlast the fever. He'll need help if he does, but he'd never ask you for it, even if he could. I've been with him a good many years though, and I know what he wants. Figure there's nothing wrong if I ask for him. I'm guessing you're the kind that likes to know. And I'm guessing you want to keep him on this side of the great beyond too. He'll want to see you. I've sent on the letter I found in his jacket pocket. It's at least a few days old, cause he's been too sick to write.

This explained the scuffed appearance of Alistair's love letter. Anna swallowed, trying to understand this unfathomable cruelty —rejoicing one moment in her beloved's confessions, and the next discovering he might already be a dead man, nothing more than old ink on dry paper.

She curled over her plate, struggling to breathe, watching tears spatter on the china and drop onto her uneaten toast. For minutes or seconds, she couldn't say—it felt as if the world had stopped and she was the only animate thing left in it. A stupid delusion, and one she must dismiss. Time was advancing, even if she couldn't feel it, and dripping all over the table wasn't going to help. Lord Fairchild hadn't appeared—a small mercy, and one she must use. She might be able to hold up in front of the servants, but not a friendly face. Anna rose from the table and hastened upstairs.

Lucy Plunkett was surprised to hear of the sudden change in plans—"I'm taking Henry to see his Grandparents today"—but didn't question Anna about the early hour. She was used to Anna's eccentricities. If she'd stayed to see the methodical assembly of two valises though, she would have wondered. Anna and Henry made their whispered way down the stairs and out the door.

"It's a secret," she told him. "We're going to join Captain Beaumaris."

"Then why are you crying?" Henry asked, reaching up to wipe her nose.

She'd give him the truth soon, but she couldn't manage it now. "We'll miss Lord and Lady Fairchild."

"Not that much," he said, skipping ahead of her on the pavement.

When the hackney dropped them at her parents' house, Anna just made it through the door and into her mother's arms. Tears came, and this time they were sobs, so it was some time before she could make herself understood. She gulped at a bottomless cup of hot tea, spilling her story, while her mother and father listened silently and took turns chaffing her hand. Then she cried again, because her father wanted to go with her.

"Papa, not in winter," Anna said, begging him to be sensible. His shoulders were stooped and his hands arthritic, the fingers swollen and veering sideways. "We must ride through the mountains and—" Her voice broke. "What if we don't reach him in time?"

She couldn't say that he would slow them down, but he understood. "I'll take you to Portsmouth, at least," he said. "Henry?"

"I can't leave him," Anna said. "And if I did, Frederick would snatch him."

Some parents would argue and insist she be sensible, but hers didn't question. They understood this was a time for practical action. Handwringing never saved anyone. Her mother oversaw the packing, transferring the valises into two compact trunks, adding stores of bandages, basilicum, and tinctures she thought Anna would need. Her father drove into the city to change her remaining money from paper to gold and to buy her a pistol. "Not much good with them myself, but if you at least learn to hold it right and keep it by you, you should manage."

Traveling to Portsmouth by post-chaise, he sat with Henry on his knee, drumming advice into Anna's ears and explaining to Henry how sailors were expected to behave. "It's your first adventure," he said to his rapt grandson. "Think over everything carefully and it won't be your last. You want enough to fill a lifetime."

He saw her to Portsmouth, found her a ship and didn't blink when she told the captain that she was journeying out to nurse her husband. "Wise idea," he whispered to her, when they were private. "Didn't realize you'd kept the ring."

Anna frowned at the jeweled band Anthony had given her as if it were a fetter. Her father put an arm around her and squeezed. "Too much my girl to throw away anything valuable. Tell me, has it been hidden away in the back of your bureau all these years?"

"Under the chamber pot."

He laughed. "You remember what I said to Henry. Think everything over before you act, and choose where to put your trust mighty carefully." Anna turned and put her arms around his neck, remembering when his bones had been padded with a thick layer of muscle. "Thank you, Papa."

His voice turned gruff, as it was wont to do when any of his family kissed him. "Yes, well, you'll be all right."

As a younger man, he'd confronted chaotic docks, gales, and foreign navies, reducing all to neat lines in a ledger. That counted, of course, but it was mostly because he was her papa that Anna believed him.

24

A CHALLENGING CAMPAIGN

Lady Fairchild was entertaining callers, wishing Anna Morris would finally choose to appear. Her mother arrived instead, in a gown so plain she might have been taken for the housekeeper.

"Lady Fairchild. I am sorry to interrupt, but I have some news. I'm afraid Anna was too upset to think of informing you."

"What happened?" Lady Fairchild asked, forgetting for the moment that her visitors were almost as gossipy as she was.

Mrs. Fulham settled herself tidily in the nearest chair. "Captain Beaumaris has been wounded, gravely I fear. His man wrote Anna and held out little hope."

Lady Fairchild set aside her cup of tea, keeping her face turned to the table, resting her chin on her hand to still her trembling. These things happened all the time. Handsome young men went to war and died, even though they still looked like the irascible boys they'd been not long ago.

"What happened?" she asked again.

"An injury to his leg—not a large one, but it's become inflamed. He's sick with fever."

Lady Fairchild held back a shudder. Nothing scared her more.

She could remember, clear as if it were yesterday, how her baby boy had sweated and thrashed, then turned limp and dry, his lips cracking, his skin painfully hot to the touch. It was torture to watch, but better than what had come after, when he had turned empty and waxen and cold, as lifeless as the box they had to put him in. Georgiana shut her eyes and pressed her fingers hard against her mouth. This wasn't the same. Alistair was older, stronger. Even if he died, she would not have to watch it—but she didn't need to. Her imagination was far too good.

The walls wavered, like the room had filled with water. "Does Anna wish to stay with you?" She would want comfort through this difficult time.

Mrs. Fulham rearranged her hands. "No. She's going to Spain. Left for Portsmouth already. Captain Beaumaris needs her, so she's gone to help him."

Edging away from Mrs. Fulham's sharp gaze, Georgiana shrank beneath memories of her frequently voiced objections: the time she'd called Anna a pretty face with empty pockets, and a girl with baggage and no breeding. The truth of these assertions didn't excuse her. They were ungracious and unkind. Silence pressed on her, but Georgiana couldn't speak. A hundred sniffs, slights and snide remarks made it near impossible to breathe. Why couldn't she have treated Anna with compassion? She'd been petty and proud, unwilling to acknowledge Anna's better qualities, namely that she fought for the people she loved. Georgiana realized, prickling with shame, that no fortune or pedigree could equal that. Bravery and commitment were more important, and Anna had both.

She should have been kinder. Then Anna might have told her, or asked for help. Instead, her treatment of Anna had earned her the humiliation of hearing this predicament afterward, when it was too late offer comfort or aid. And in front of guests . . . .

"Is your husband with her?" Georgiana asked, flushing.

"Just as far as Portsmouth. He'll help her find passage. Anna

255

felt, and it is the truth, though we wish it were not, that my husband wouldn't fare well in the journey through the mountains. She didn't want to leave Henry."

"She's taking him to Spain?" Fear doused embarrassment, leaving Georgiana clammy and cold. She could have kept Henry, protected him, if only she'd given Anna the least reason to trust her.

"It's not quite the Sahara," Mrs. Fulham said calmly, but Georgiana's head was spinning. Mountain passes in winter, infested with brigands and the British Army—thousands of layabout rogues culled from the slums of England. Even the officers were not to be trusted.

"Her reputation—" Georgiana gasped, glancing at her guests and realizing it was too late. "They'll never reach him—and even if they do, he might be already dead! Who will protect them?" How could the Fulhams have let her go alone, taking the boy? The peninsula was no place for a lone woman and four-year-old child. Someone must go with them. William or Jasper or—

Cyril. Of course. Yes, it should be him, because if Alistair was gone, someone must marry Anna and bring her home. Georgiana knew she'd have all manner of difficulties bending Jasper to her will, but she was confident of succeeding with her weakling nephew.

"She's gone already, you said?" Georgiana asked, rising from her chair.

"Yes. To Portsmouth. She'll sail to Oporto and go from there to Ciudad Rodrigo."

"Forgive me. I must go." She and Mrs. Fulham could wrangle over the handling of this crisis tomorrow. They might as well become acquainted, since Anna was going to be part of the family one way or other. If Georgiana was to fix things, she must act now, before Anna and Henry got too far ahead. The poor girl needed someone to help her. If Frederick Morris ever learned of this, he would have every right to take her son back.

"Where's Lucy Plunkett?" Georgiana demanded, striding into the hall. She couldn't see Jenkins, but she trusted he would appear, sensing her need.

He didn't fail her. "She may be in the kitchen," Jenkins said, materializing at her elbow. "But I'm not certain."

"Watch her. Don't let her leave the house." Anna might pay her wage now, but Georgiana didn't forget that Lucy had been hired by Frederick Morris first and couldn't be trusted. William was out—gone to Tatersalls—but Georgiana wouldn't wait. She ordered the carriage brought round.

"Take me to St. Audley Street," she said.

It was early enough in the afternoon that she found Cyril at home. "Just tell me where he is," she snapped at the butler, unwilling to give her nephew the luxury of a warning. He wasn't, as she expected, foraging at the sideboard, assembling a late breakfast. He was in the billiard room, lounging over the table. She glared at him, at his too long hair, at the cue in his loose fingers, his foaming cravat and his tasseled boots. Cyril's other hand was sliding over his watch fob, trying to tuck it out of sight.

"Don't bother. I've already seen it," she said, and Cyril flushed, as well he might. *A naked woman! Really!* "Utterly tasteless," she said.

He smiled weakly.

In crisp words, she told him what had befallen his brother. "Are you not concerned?" she asked.

"Of course I am!" Cyril set down the cue and scrubbed a hand through his hair. "It grieves me more than I can say. All my thoughts and prayers are bent on his safety and recovery."

Georgiana snorted. He should have known better than to tack on the last bit. Prayers indeed! She'd always known Cyril for a wastrel, but she hadn't expected him to prove entirely useless in this moment of crisis—it was the fault of his father's stock, no doubt. Her people were made of sterner stuff. "Prayers are very nice, I'm sure, but I'm more interested in learning when you depart."

"Depart?" Cyril looked at her in surprise. He gave an uneasy laugh. "Just what do you think my going to Spain will do?"

She stared at him until he dropped his eyes. "For one thing, if you bestir yourself, you can ensure your brother's intended bride does not travel wholly unprotected. I expect you're useless in the sickroom, but if the worst happened, you could at least bring home your brother's remains."

Cyril shuddered. "Surely not. A tasteful plaque, in the family chapel . . . ."

She slammed the flat of her hand onto the billiard table with enough force that the balls jumped. "You would leave him feverish and suffering, with only that ruffian Griggs to attend him?" She leaned closer. Overriding Cyril's protests that Griggs was a frighteningly capable fellow, she backed him to the opposite end of the table, punctuating her opinions of Cyril, his ancestors and what he deserved with an emphatic forefinger.

"You are a sorry, weak, addle-brained excuse for a man, who ought to be strung up by his heels and beaten. I'd like to think the experience would cram some sense into your head, but I own to few hopes. You would get what you deserve at least, and we needn't fear damaging your faculties, such as they are." He opened his mouth to protest as she drew breath, but she jabbed her finger an inch closer, silencing him. "You will cease your depredations on the family fortune. You will give up these ridiculous waistcoats and that atrocity you attempted to hide in your pocket. And you will arrange forthwith to help your brother, or God help me, I'll administer the beating myself!"

Immediately he began struggling out of his jacket. "Not here, you imbecile!" she shrieked, flinging up a hand to shield her eyes, realizing he intended to remove the offending waistcoat. "If you think I will stand the sight of you in your shirt sleeves, you are greatly mistaken."

"But—"

"For goodness' sake!" Georgiana snapped. "Stop gaping at me and do something! Anna and her son are already on their way to Portsmouth—halfway to the coast by now if they took seats on the Mail! Her father is too old to make the journey and she must have some male to accompany her. If Alistair dies, and there's a very good chance he will, someone must marry her and bring her home! She'll lose her son otherwise. You'll have a devil of a time, persuading her to take you, but I'm sure, when you explain—"

He wasn't catching on. Slowly, as patiently as she could, she explained that dragging Henry to Spain was an excellent excuse to remove Henry from Anna's care, and Frederick Morris was not the kind of fool to pass up such a chance. If Anna couldn't have Alistair, she must have a husband. Cyril was weak, but he would do.

"You'd have her become Lady Ruffington?"

"Yes, and you would thank your stars for it! You'd never get a lady of her mettle unless she was forced to it." She hadn't been nearly as good to Anna as she should have been. Cyril was a poor way of making amends, but it was the best she could do.

"Yes, but I've no notion how to get to Ciudad Diego," he protested.

"Rodrigo! It's Ciudad Rodrigo, you half-wit! If you can't prove as resourceful as that minx towing her child, you should be shot!"

"I'll go. This instant," Cyril said, backing towards the door as if he feared she might produce a pistol from her person any moment.

"Do," Georgiana said, impressively cool considering she was vexed beyond measure. Cyril's shortcomings defied her vocabulary. Unless she was willing to demean herself and swear like a trooper—and she was not—there were no words strong enough for such selfish idiocy.

"You may report to me once you are decently attired, with your travel arrangements in order. An hour should suffice. Since this is a case of some urgency, I will wait in the drawing room. You may send your butler to me, so I may have some refreshment."

It didn't fix anything, of course, but the general outlook always improved when she had her own way. As Cyril fled the room, she was almost smiling.

∾

EVERYONE IN HIS FAMILY—WELL, everyone but his mother, really—always gave him a hard time. Aunt Georgiana was horribly unjust. He was worried about his brother, damn it.

Still, as he rattled out of London in a post chaise, Cyril was mainly wishing his aunt to perdition, not fretting over his brother's precarious existence. The day only got worse: innumerable stops and changes, with indifferent food brought out by smarmy innkeepers. None of it was good, but the mushroom fritters were egregious and made him sick enough to forswear food entirely. Like his aunt, Cyril didn't care for carriage journeys. A sea voyage might just kill him.

Sipping cautiously from his flask, he made it to Portsmouth, surprised he was able to force himself to stand. It felt like he was permanently mangled. Tottering gratefully to the nearest tap room, he recovered there for a good long while. By this time it was well past dark—too late to chase after Mrs. Morris. Cyril put himself to bed, gingerly inserting himself between the sheets, dubious despite the assurances of the innkeeper. His valet, damn his eyes, was still in London. He'd threatened to give notice when Cyril ordered him to come along. An impertinence, but no one else could produce such a miraculous shine on his boots. At the time, Cyril thought he'd be able to manage.

He woke in the morning, repenting this error. It took an age to wrestle his way into his clothes—the thatch-haired lackwit the inn sent him was worse than no help at all. After hours trawling the docks and waterfront taverns he finally found word of Mrs. Morris, who'd sailed already on the supply ship Gloriana.

"Quiet lass," put in his informant, whose Irish brogue rendered him almost unintelligible. "Boy's a regular scamp. Off to join her husband. Some do, though I can't think why."

Enunciating his words carefully—reinforcing the way English was supposed to sound—Cyril inquired when the next ship to Oporto might be.

"The Viper sails tomorrow. Maybe the day after. Depends."

"Would you direct me to the captain?"

This was arranged. The captain, a heron-like man with ginger hair and an excruciatingly loud speaking voice, happily agreed to take Cyril on board. The price seemed high for something Cyril knew he would only regret, but there was no help for it.

"You'll want to change those," the captain said, nodding at Cyril's roll of bills. "Spaniards don't take paper. Only gold."

Naturally, the Portsmouth banking establishments exacted a ruinous rate of exchange. Grumbling over their avarice and the stupidity of the Spanish nation—he was not sure they couldn't be blamed for his current situation—Cyril stumped back to his lodging, too sour to linger in the tap room. Dinner, taken in his rooms, was excellent, but only a temporary consolation. A couple on their honeymoon had taken the room beside him.

He sailed two days later, leaving behind an acid note for Next Door—if he hadn't impregnated his wife by this time, there was surely no point trying.

DISCIPLINE

HENRY WAS A PROPER SAILOR, just as her father and brother had been. Untroubled by wind or tumult, he spent every moment he could on deck. Anna didn't mind. Except in the worst weather, it was much nicer than their snuff-box-sized cabin, whose best feature was the door. It only fully opened when she piled their boxes onto the bunk, but there were advantages to snug quarters —every night she slept with Henry curled against her stomach, his fingers wrapped tight in the folds of her nightdress. Henry was alarmingly well-behaved, so fascinated by the captain (who had a stump for one arm and a whip-crack voice) that he followed his instructions to the letter, even the one Anna had worried about most.

"Mind your mother!" the captain snapped, just once. Henry might have looked at her sideways a time or two since, but mind her he did. His interest in the captain was nothing to his obsession with the ship.

"Intent as a wolf watching a flock of sheep!" said the lieu- tenant, smiling at Anna over Henry's head as he passed them on his way below. "Studies everything, doesn't he? Has he figured out how to fix a position yet?"

Not that she knew, but Henry had learned plenty. He stored up everything he saw, narrowing his eyes with concentration each time he brought out a new word—top gallants, fo'c'sle, oakum—which was probably his favorite, since he seemed compelled to repeat it over and over in a sing-song voice. Also weevil. She wished he'd never learned that one, or discovered (and devoured!) his first specimen with such glee. But he was happy, and she could only be glad of that. It cheered her—not enough to forget the reason for their journey, but enough to lesson her worries about what they might find at the end of it. Alistair might even be well by then. She'd look a proper fool, journeying to him in such haste . . . but Griggs wouldn't have written if he hadn't been desperate.

When Henry was sleeping, it was harder to hope, or ignore visions of Alistair in a crowded hospital, lying in dirty straw, his skin fiery, his wound festering. She tried not to let herself think that he might already be dead, but the possibility felt as near as her own shadow.

The only remedy was to think of his letter, telling herself she would find him—hale or already dead or still fevered. It was the only thing to do. If he was mad enough to marry a portionless nobody and raise another man's son, her own lunacy—fleeing London, taking passage to Spain, passing herself off as his wife—wasn't so very bad. Even if it was, she couldn't make herself care. This was her chance at happiness. If all she achieved was a trip to his grave, she would have it. She would weep and curse and tell him the truth—that she loved him, that he was a fool for leaving her and for loving her in the first place.

She'd explained to the captain and to the few that asked that her husband was wounded and needed tending. Seeing that she worried, they didn't ply her with questions. Occasionally they offered hearty assurances which she smiled at—the bluff words were meaningless but kind.

"You can go out with one of the wagon trains," the captain

said to her when they were a day out of Oporto. "Quartermaster will help you arrange things."

"Only if they leave on the morrow," Anna said, smiling thinly. "I would have to possess unbelievable luck to manage that, Captain, and I think I used it all up finding you." Besides, if she attached herself to an Army wagon train, she'd eventually cross paths with someone who knew Captain Beaumaris, and that he wasn't married—yet.

The captain blustered, of course, but she was adamant. There was no time to waste. "Perhaps you could help me by putting me in the way of a guide. And some mules. I'm afraid I haven't made friends with horses." Mules made her uneasy too, but her hasty enquiries had revealed that carriage travel through Spain was both difficult and slow.

Mules would be costly, given the shortages that accompanied war, but her money should stretch far enough to get her to Ciudad Rodrigo—though it might be a push if she had to get herself back to England again.

The purchase of three mules and the hiring of a guide emptied her purse of nearly half her store of gold, but she could sell Anthony's ring if they got desperate. She wouldn't miss it.

No turning to a watering pot now, she scolded herself. The trick, her father said, to finding your way in strange places was caution and a hearty belief in your own competence. Get yourself in a dither and you were lost. Keep your head, and you'd probably be alright. Anna, gripping Henry's hand tight in her own, watched the scaff and raff of Oporto stream by: men in fraying coats, bellowing foremen, loose-jointed sailors off on a spree. The chatter of languages and the creak of cable muted as she gathered her courage. She just had to keep her head. Doubting wasn't allowed.

. . .

IN SPITE of Anna's resolve not to worry, her anguish worsened all the way through Portugal and into Spain, urging her on. Not until they reached Ciudad Rodrigo did fear immobilize her, anchoring her in the middle of the street, hidden by the evening shadows. All she could do was stare blankly at the house that held him. It was small, square and crumbling, wedged between two buildings in slightly better repair but of the same dusty stone. The windows that had shutters—rickety paint-peeled slabs— were closed, only a few of them leaking light into the street, giving the house a wary appearance that seemed typical in this town. Scars of French and Allied sieges marked the citizens and much of the stonework of Ciudad Rodrigo. Everywhere she looked she saw torn up earth, hastily repaired walls, lean faces and unnaturally still streets.

Behind her, the tavern on the corner was lavishing light on its sparsely filled taproom, the excess pouring invitingly into the square, but so far she and her little band were the only wanderers who'd been lured inside. She'd left Henry and Bartolome, their guide, polishing off dinner under the benevolent watch of the innkeep's wife. Anna wasn't hungry. Most of Bartolome's conversation with the innkeeper had flown past her ears, but the sympathetic smiles she'd understood. Alistair was here, and still alive.

She'd meant to rush across the street immediately, but couldn't somehow, a strange circumstance after five days of hard travel over a hundred and fifty miles. All throughout the journey, she'd felt threads of worry fastening round her. Now, here she was, fifty yards from Alistair and unable to move, pinned down by ten thousand Lilliputian doubts.

She tried to recall his letter, but the fervent ink couldn't free her feet, though it had hurried her on from London and Oporto, upriver and over mountains, steeling her against chill wind, thirst, and the most terrifying lodgings she'd ever come across.

She knew the feel of her pistol perfectly now, and the bruises on her bottom too.

Despite his protestations of love, the warming words, the plea —no, the command that she marry him, he hadn't sent that letter. That had been Griggs. Chances were her coming would surprise him. Until this moment, she'd never considered the surprise might be unwelcome.

What are you going to do? Go back?

No. That would be ridiculous. And she'd have to think of excuses to give to Henry and Bartolome. It was a miracle Henry hadn't finished his supper already and come chasing after her—a circumstance she could only attribute to the late hour and the long day's ride. She'd imagined this meeting with Alistair hundreds of times and was sure of one thing only—she wasn't going to do it with Henry clutching her skirts.

She hurried across the street and pounded on the tired-looking door. Before her heart could slow, the door yawned wide, coughing up a stooped figure gowned in grey and black who waved a candle in her face.

"Captain Beaumaris?" Anna asked, flinching away from the light. It dipped as the grey vulture in front of her conducted a scrutiny, protesting in voluble Spanish.

"I must see him," Anna said, trying to edge her way around the knobby veined hand barring her way.

The protestations grew louder and sharper, words Anna suspected were neither polite or kind, but she firmed her chin.

"I'm English!" Anna snapped, pushing the woman out of the way and snatching the light from her hand. It flickered, making their shadows dance like demons against the plastered walls, slopping wax onto Anna's hand and making her draw breath in a tight hiss.

"Estupido!" she spat, plowing her way to the stairs. She wasn't as quick as Henry, but she'd gathered a few words. Fury mounting as she climbed the stairs, chased by the wailing lamentations of the landlady, Anna nearly stumbled into a full-moon face that appeared suddenly in her pool of light. His eyebrows shot to the ceiling as he leapt back, untangling their elbows before the candle could set her gown on fire.

"Griggs!"

"Mrs. Morris!"

"Where is he?"

Griggs jerked his head up the stairs, pressing himself against the wall so she could pass. As she marched up the remaining steps in a torrent of swirling skirts, Griggs called down a few laconic Spanish words, stopping the woeful moaning from downstairs.

"Thank you," Anna threw back at him, as she crossed the upstairs landing and sailed through the open door.

"What the devil—" Alistair stopped. Anna froze too. His thin cheeks, pale under a few days worth of beard, the insufficiently stuffed pillows compressing as he struggled to push himself upright, his rough, tumbled hair—these details flew past her, scarcely heeded. Anna's attention was stuck on the hollow under the sheets, as deformed and jarring as a sunken furrow of lips without teeth.

His face twitched, going even whiter. "Sawbones lopped it off below the knee," he said finally, with painful bravado.

"I see." Her hands banded together. She couldn't make this worse by reaching out to steady herself on the nearby ladder-backed chair. And her face—she must do something with it, find a better expression than paralysis. Anna struggled for a moment, then gave up. Impossible to hide her shock. She had to speak. "Griggs wrote that you were ill, so—"

Alistair relieved her. "I certainly was. But they managed to save most of me. Don't know what they did with the rest, though —" he huffed a silent laugh. "I was going to say part of me wonders where they put the trimmings. How apt."

Anna pressed down on her unsteady lower lip and dropped

herself onto the edge of the bed. She took up his hand, turning it over in her own, as if she were just discovering his elegantly formed fingers. The tip of one pressed softly, almost unnotice- ably, against the inside of her wrist before he deftly slid his hand away, hiding it under the sheet.

"Where is my uncle?" he asked.

"I came alone," Anna said.

Alistair swallowed convulsively. "Dear God. Why?"

The room was over warm, the fireplace piled high with coals. A dizzying wave of heat lapped up from her toes, swirling around her ears. Anna stared at the cracking plaster behind the bed, wishing she could simply dissolve, shimmering out of sight like a desert mirage. "Griggs sent me your letter."

"I think I know the one," Alistair murmured. "It was never meant to be seen. Forgive me. I'm just—surprised. You came from London alone?"

"I brought Henry, of course."

"Of course," he said weakly.

"We hired a manservant in Oporto. Bartolome. He's quite invaluable." He'd brought her here, so he could bring her back, presumably.

"I'm sure." He seemed to choke, unwillingly drawing Anna's eyes from her inspection of the scarred walls. Alistair was leaning forward, hiding behind his hand, his shoulders shuddering as he cursed softly, desperately. Perhaps it was her own extremity that made her reach for—or fall on—familiarity.

"Save the Lord's name for prayer," she said, shocked at how exactly she sounded like her mother.

"I am," Alistair said, looking up at her with wet eyes. "This is as good as I can manage."

His hands were clutching the sheets like he meant to shred them. She was too afraid to touch him. His eyes were strange and glassy, and he'd never looked at her like this before.

"Why did you come?" he asked.

"You were dying. And you'd asked me to marry you."

"That letter." Instead of cursing he exhaled. Somehow he managed a smile, but it was mocking, unkind. "Thought you'd be sensible. Dismiss my ramblings. Suppose you'd arrived only to find me at death's door?"

"I would care for you until you mended. I'll do it now, if you'll let me," she said, defiance setting her spine.

"I'd no idea romance was so catching," he said softly. "I should never have written that."

"Are you withdrawing your offer?" she demanded, stung and burning.

He looked away, smoothing the edge of the sheet with his fingers. "I think you should choose a man with better symmetry. Coming here . . . I'm honored by your sentiments. But it's a declaration I can't accept. No one would hold you to it."

Anna set her teeth, clinging to pride, trying to forget the aches of long days in the saddle, thick mountain fog with icicle fingers, the vile substance she had downed when one innkeeper claimed it was stew.

"So you lied."

He opened his mouth, but she didn't let him speak. She couldn't stand another word of protestations or abasement. "You don't love me." The words of his letter echoed in the pause, his promise that he loved her to madness.

"I don't think how I feel matters anymore. I could have found a way to support a wife with two legs, but not as a truncated cripple. You wouldn't want—"

"Don't tell me what I want," Anna snapped. "I came to you. Doesn't that say enough? Of course I'd rather marry a whole man, but I don't have that choice. I want to marry you. You weren't thinking about money when you wrote me that letter."

"It's different now."

"Of course it is!" Her fingers were shaking, so she pressed them against her skirts. She would never watch him ride again,

JAIMA FIXSEN

secretly admiring the shape of his leg. He would never again sweep her around a room to the tune of a waltz—that one long ago dance was all they would ever have. A cruel twist, for back then she hadn't even known she would love him. Well, life seldom unfolded as you wished it.

"Only a cold heart could make you an ineligible husband," Anna said, trying not to let her lips quiver. "I know. The rest doesn't matter as much as you think." She'd come, undeterred, to this gritty room in a war-shattered town—and he thought he could deter her with warnings of twice-turned dresses, bargain cuts of meat, and the puny deprivations of the shabby-genteel? *You should know me better than that.*

Of course, it was one thing for her to forsake pride—by now she had very little. For him, it was all he'd ever had. Without money or a pedigreed lady-wife, he could scarcely be considered a gentleman, and without his leg he couldn't be a fighting sword. "You are enough for me. More."

He studied her for a long time with wet eyes. "Our children will be poor," he said.

"Henry will help them." He had money enough. It was an uncertain future, but was there really any other kind?

"He'll have to keep me too."

"You'll be his papa. He'll like nothing better," Anna said. Henry had a warm heart, once you found a way in.

Alistair stared at the place beneath the covers where his foot should have been. "I've always been superfluous. A hanger-on. I've never been able to snap my fingers at the world, and I suppose now I never will. It isn't easy, consigning yourself to leeching from a stepson."

Anna reached for his hand. "But we need you. I'm not made to be alone. And Henry needs a papa to teach him."

"Anna, you could find someone else."

She shook her head, willing to be as stubborn as needed. He was weakening. "You've ruined me for anyone else."

270

He swallowed. "You're a fool, Anna." But he was reaching for her shoulder and there was a wobble in his voice. Before he could move too far, she inserted herself in the warm hollow by his side.

"At least I'm a pretty one."

He took her hands and pressed them to his stubble-roughened cheek. "What kind of lady goes traipsing through Portugal alone?" he muttered. His cheeks were damp, but she preferred him using her hands to a handkerchief.

"I'm not a lady." Thank goodness, because ladies probably didn't demand to be kissed and she was about to. But before she could speak, Alistair pulled her close, hiding his face in her hair. Her fingers tightened on his and her heart skipped, even as her eyes burned with tears. Whole or broken, he was hers, and she wanted him.

"You'll marry me tomorrow," she said. No excuses.

"Today," he whispered back, his chin rasping her cheek and making her laugh.

It was delightfully impossible. She chuckled and shifted closer, her knees sliding onto Alistair's lap as she raised herself to be level with his eyes. He pulled his face away. Winced.

"Oh, I'm sorry," Anna said, horrified.

"Stitches are still oozy. And the—the stump is swollen. Bruised."

Anna swallowed. She would ask to see it, but not now, when all she wanted was to hide her face and leap back behind the chair. She'd hurt him. "Is it agony?" she mumbled, hiding behind her falling-down hair.

"A special kind," he said, pulling her closer. "It hurt when they cut the leg off too. I was too fevered to understand. Thought I was in hell." His words were light, but she'd never seen his face so shadowed, or felt so desperate and powerless to smooth away pain. She wanted to hide his hurts away in gently-cupped fingers, but they were too vast and formless to fit in her hands. As the first stirrings of fear shifted in her stomach, Alistair traced a finger down her cheek along the curve of her bottom lip. "If you'd look up, I think you'll see I'm blushing too."

He was, but it showed in his ears more than his face. It made him look younger and foolish, so Anna kissed him. He tasted faintly medicinal, but she liked it, continuing until she was breathless and almost raw from whisker burn. She'd never kissed an unshaved man before, let alone considered the hazards. Her face was probably redder than a case of the measles.

Perhaps if I kissed him only on the lips . . . .

"I'm a broken fumbler," he cautioned.

"Maybe at first," she grinned, taking his mouth back. Wounds healed, even the kind beneath the skin.

"Where's Griggs?" Alistair asked.

"On holiday? I don't care," Anna said.

"Well, we should fetch him. Or someone. Before I really do ruin you."

It would be more comfortable to laugh at him or simply ignore his words and enjoy the feeling of resting against his warm chest. This was an opening though, and she must take it.

"I'm sure traipsing here—you make it sound much easier than it was, you know—has done that already. But you see, I was ruined years ago—I warned you I was a bad bargain, remember? You needn't fear for my reputation. I deserve none."

"What do you mean?" Alistair asked, unconvinced and more interested in playing with her hair.

She paused before beginning, working moisture back into her mouth. This confession was essential, something she'd practiced, but no easier in spite of it. Anna flattened her slick palms against her skirts. *Tell him. You're done with secrets.*

"Alistair, what did you think when you first saw me?"

He shifted. "I apologized for my error."

"You needn't have. You were right. Or not far wrong anyway."

He shook his head. "I don't believe you. I thought you were a lightskirt, remember?"

"Not that bad, but—a fast piece, definitely. I had lovers. Henry isn't Morris's son. I did it to hurt him." Her lips faltered around the words. "Of course it only made things worse. He took Henry from me. Anthony was wild before, but after that he was truly reckless. The accident was almost inevitable." She ducked her head, unable to continue, but Alistair didn't speak and the hand was still in her hair. No choice but to press on.

"You picked me out of the crowd in that masquerade, and knew from a look exactly what kind of games I once played. Can you wonder that I was terrified when you discovered who I was and where I lived? I was trying so hard to be respectable, hoping to get Henry back. Not just for that, though. For myself too. Oh, Anthony deserved something, but what I did—I hurt myself and Henry as much as I did him. And I never felt any better."

She traced a circle on the back of his thumb. "The first time you asked me to marry you, I warned you I was no good. I should have told you the whole then, but since you said it wasn't real . . . if you no longer want to marry me, I won't complain." Aloud, anyway.

This was the safest way. Give him a chance to escape. Say the words for him so she wouldn't have to hear them from his own mouth. But his arms tightened, pressing her close. "Good thing Morris is already dead," he said, his tone flat. "Goodness, Anna. What did he do to you?"

She wasn't spurned, then. At least not yet. Anna curled her fingers, tightening her grip on his fingers. "Married me without any love. Or even liking. I've made plenty of mistakes, but I won't make that one twice."

"No, you won't," he said. He pushed back her hair, dabbed at one damp eye with the loose cuff of his shirt. He kissed one eyebrow, then the other, then drew his finger down the bridge of her nose. "Anna."

"You don't mind?" She needed to be sure.

"I was playing games at that ball, too. I'm not—I haven't

always—well, love is a fine thing, and it took me longer than you to learn not to be careless with it. But I'm not careless anymore, and I won't be with you."

She replied with lips but not words, learning his worn face with soft touches. His stubble was raspy, his cheeks thinner, his skin cool, but her response hadn't changed. And though it came a little late, this was the welcome she'd wanted.

"No more arguing then?" she teased. "Good. Kisses are better."

"You're quite convincing. I'd be a fool to resist. Wish I had all my pieces, though. I'd rather you married a perfect man."

"Perfect!" Anna was scornful. "I couldn't endure that. If such a man existed, just think how insufferable he would be!"

"I'll remind you of that," he said. "Go get Henry. Griggs too—I expect you'll find him lurking at the bottom of the stairs."

She protested, but when he threatened to hop down the stairs himself, she had to give in. Griggs wasn't there, so Anna winged her way outside, expecting he'd gone to find Henry. Instead of a tired town she saw stars. It felt like her head might bump them.

Just as she thought, Griggs was in the tap room, plotting with Henry while Bartolome tiredly swirled his wine.

"How is he?" Griggs asked, looking up.

Smiles couldn't grow big enough to break open, could they? Perhaps so, for it seemed like bits of her own were attaching onto Henry, Griggs, to the bar keep, to Bartolome, and the newcomer nodding from the corner. Color swept into her cheeks.

"He's well," Anna said.

26

FIDELITY

LONDON WAS QUIET AND COLD, with snow-muffled streets and frost-sharpened edges. Lord Fairchild could have gone out for a congenial evening of company, cards and hot punch, but had elected to spend the evening alone in front of the library fire, hoping Georgiana would return from a compassionate visit to her sister. It was late now. The snow would have slowed her progress, if she had set out at all. Georgiana hadn't much fortitude for travel, even under the best conditions, and might have extended her stay.

He shouldn't begrudge the visit. Lady Ruffington's husband was dying, and her son ailing in Spain. There was no one else to help her since Cyril, her eldest son, was traveling to help his brother. Hysterics were a habit with his sister-in-law, invariably over the least consequential issue at hand; it surprised no one that she'd gone into a tizzy about Anna Morris getting her hooks into Alistair when he lay at death's door. If it were up to William, he'd slap some sense into Louisa Beaumaris, but Georgiana would mix up possets and listen, trying to reconcile her to the idea of Anna as a daughter-in-law. It wouldn't be a prudent match, but she loved him. Besides, with Sophy wed to Tom

Bagshot, it might not be a bad thing to have one more shop-stained person in the family. It would give Bagshot someone to speak to at dinners, at any rate.

He was beginning to hope that perhaps there would be some —dinners that is, with Sophy and her lanky husband. Jasper too, sophisticated and discontented, and Henrietta and her Percy, if he could be coaxed away from his books. May as well have Alistair and Anna too—poor, but handsome as a match pair of horses. They'd never lack for conversation. Georgy might pretend to disapprove of whatever unspoken currents swirled around the table, but she'd thrive on it. And if she played at being miffed, then he'd have the pleasure of coaxing her out of it later. He liked this game of theirs, this secret happiness. William sighed and stretched his feet to the fender, smiling because it was good for a man his age to have dreams that might even happen.

He missed her. She'd been gone a fortnight, and—glancing at the clock—it seemed he must await her return at least one more day.

Above the clock, a new oil painting, still smelling of varnish, hung on the wall. He wasn't used to it yet. Every time his gaze flew that way, his eyes stuck on it. The old watercolor was on the floor, propped against the other armchair. He'd wrap it and send it to Sophy. Jasper was visiting her this Christmas—he'd refused flat out to go to Spain.

"Let the Morris woman do it. Not my affair."

It was the only thing William and his son had agreed on for months. William wasn't sure how to fix matters with Jasper or Sophy, but he hoped sending this painting would be a start. He would miss it, though. The picture was an old friend, but it was past time. If he loved his wife, he couldn't cherish this memento of Fanny.

You understand, don't you?

Of course there was no answer. Just an image in his mind, half Sophy, half her mother. They had the same thin little shoulders:

276

sculpted, birdlike, delicate but determined. Though short-lived, it had been a joy to press his lips into those hollows in Fanny's skin and then look up into her astonished eyes.

Yes. I must think about you before I can put you away.

Fanny was young back then, of a family both genteel and poor, connected to a friend of Georgiana's. He and Georgiana both terrified her. She was comfortable with children though, having a tribe of siblings herself. He got used to the sound of her laughing with his children as they came in from the park, hushing as they walked up to the nursery, where the happy sounds resumed again. It made him glad, that muffled evidence of contentment and childhood pleasures—captured frogs, perfect pebbles, running barefoot, and laughing for no reason.

Then Julius died and all turned silent. Henrietta and Jasper recovered first because of Fanny. Occupied with his own torn soul and the nasty assignment of blame between him and his wife, William was mostly blind to the way his older children took shelter under Fanny's thin arms. Then one day, half-angered, half-drawn by their happy noise, he found them in the nursery, crooked paper crowns on their heads and snips of paper littering the floor. Jasper and Henrietta wore untroubled smiles, though Fanny Prescott's vanished the minute she lifted her eyes to his. She said nothing, too afraid to apologize for laughing. That moment, he wanted to shelter in her warmth too.

He and Georgiana weren't a love match, though until Julius died they'd liked each other well enough. She was beautiful and charming, and since he had no brothers, he had to marry relatively young. Georgiana danced delightfully, had a nice-sized fortune, and was brought up to be a gentleman's wife. It didn't matter, much, that they had so little in common. Jasper was born less than a year after their marriage, Henrietta soon after. Three more years and they had another son. They knew how to be polite, to behave as they ought. It was a respectful relationship, until Julius died and sharp words and days of arid silence hammered it apart. Georgiana took herself off to her sister's, leaving him to rage and call her a coward. Of course it was no one's fault but God's, but without Georgiana to glare at . . . .

Fanny was shy and timid, no match for his desperate cunning. He put himself in her way, and naturally she felt sorry for him. She invited him, with twisting fingers and blushing cheeks, to play with his children, to row them on the lake.

"I couldn't do it alone," he said.

So she came along, and he let himself fall into her dreamy world of story books with sticky pages, milk tea and jam sandwiches eaten under the sun on the lawn. He came up to the schoolroom to admire her watercolors and the progress of his children, to smile with her when Henrietta conjured sums quicker than Jasper, and to watch her accept with unfailing grace the gifts his son presented almost daily: pinecones she arranged on the mantle, a snake caught in a smelly lineament tin that miraculously escaped overnight, dead beetles with black backs that shone green in the right light, and a necklace of braided grass she wore for two days straight. She would smile over Jasper's blond head, but she never teased him about the offerings or chuckled at the way his chest swelled when she praised him. Most every day Jasper summoned her down to the stables to watch him ride his pony. She was always properly awed. William came to watch too, stealing her hand when Jasper and the groom disappeared into the stables.

"Oh. You shouldn't." Flustered and pink, Fanny retreated to the house, leaving William and Jasper to walk back alone.

"When I grow up, I'm going to marry Miss Prescott," Jasper confided. William laughed, distracted momentarily from his own shameful thoughts. It should have recalled him to his senses— Fanny deserved a husband, nothing else—but he wanted her, and felt that success was not far off. It wasn't.

"Your French is excellent. I wish you would help me—I've been reading some poems and I don't quite understand."

Pretending an unconcern she didn't feel, she followed him into the library at Cordell, starting just a little when he closed the door. "I have a headache," he explained. The closed door muffled every outside sound. He handed over the book.

Her blushes! Such a delicate stain tinting her cheek as she pointed out his error, such surprise in her eyes as she looked up to see him advance. Confusion, dismay—then bliss!—as she succumbed in his arms at last.

And after, those giddy weeks—not many—of rambles in the gardens, kisses stolen behind corners, of indoor games when they could evade the children. He couldn't remember what kind of weather they'd had, but in memory the days were all drenched with sunlight, the only shadow a little furrow between Fanny's eyes that steadily grew darker and deeper. He chose not to notice. He had tears in his eyes when she told him she was pregnant, though *enciente* was the word she used. She had excellent French, and she wasn't blushing anymore.

He was selfishly happy. Another child—not another Julius, never that—but another little one to watch over, who would toddle and lisp, and climb into his lap and fall warmly asleep.

"No," Fanny said.

He didn't believe it when she said she wasn't going to stay.

"You already have a family. You already have a wife."

She was resolute, impatient with his excuses, defiant when he pressured her.

"I'm going. If you love me, make certain we don't starve."

Though angry and ashamed, he did as she asked. She wouldn't let him do anything else. "I'm not making more mistakes," she told him. "Don't you make any either."

Oh, but he had. This watercolor painting she'd done of his gardens, her last, brought by ten-year-old Sophy when she came to Cordell, shouldn't have gone up on his study wall. He should have mended things with Georgiana long ago—shouldn't have soiled Fanny in the first place. And he should ask forgiveness from Sophy, the daughter Fanny had loved. He should have loved her better, and helped her when she wanted to make her own choice. William looked at the picture propped up on the floor, at the light, melting tints and the play of sunlight and shadow. He would wrap it up now. On his desk he had tissue and brown paper. Jenkins could do it, but he felt he owed it to Fanny to do it himself.

Can't say for certain, but I think Georgiana and I can be happy. I love her.

He thought this was what Fanny had wanted—though not so many wasted years, he was certain. He could only blame his own self for that. Fanny, bless her, had known what was impossible and what was right and best.

He carried it to the desk, laying it on the paper. He fumbled a bit over the corners, unable to make them neat—they stuck out like puppy ears. He was groping through the desk drawer, reaching for a knife to cut the twine when he heard noises in the hall.

"You're still awake?" It was Georgiana, pushing wide the library door.

"Mhmm," he said, unnecessarily.

She glanced from the mess on his desk to the wall and the new picture there. Her cheeks turned faintly pink, though perhaps that was only because the room was warm and she'd been outside in the cold.

"Turned out well, didn't it?" he asked.

"I told you he'd flatter me. I thought you wanted it for the gallery at Cordell." It was where they usually hung portraits.

"I like you a little nearer than that." He smiled. "I think it's a good likeness, though someone should have told him your true feelings about dogs." It must be the fashion, because in life Georgiana would never rest her fingers affectionately on the head of a silky-eared spaniel.

"The dog's just a device," she said, coming into the room and drawing off her gloves.

He'd never been the type to fall into raptures over poetry or paintings. Some were good; some weren't. Didn't really matter why. "Oh? What's a dog mean?"

"It's an emblem of fidelity," she said, intent on smoothing the empty gloves. "I didn't know he was going to paint it in. I didn't ask him—"

"Of course," William said softly. "Yes, I'd say he captured you very well." Like her, he kept his attention on the portrait. "But I meant this picture to be an emblem of mine. You have my fidelity, whether you want it or not."

She nodded, glancing at him fleetingly as she studied the portrait.

"I'd given up hoping you'd return today. I'm surprised Tom Coachman agreed to drive in this dark," William said.

"He didn't drive quickly," she said, the usual lean towards displeasure in her voice. "I wanted to come home."

William wasn't going to argue with that. "Come, you must be frozen," he said, taking her hands and bringing her to the fire. "How's your sister?" he asked, needing some diversion as he pulled her into his own chair instead of the one opposite, sweeping her in his lap. She lifted her eyes to the ceiling, but came willingly enough.

"It was a trying week. I'd rather not talk of it. I didn't realize you meant to redecorate."

"No, just changing that picture."

"It never really suited the room," she said.

"No."

"You'll send the old one to Sophy?" she asked.

"If I can convince Jasper to take it. I'd rather he brought it to her. If she has any words for me in reply, better to have Jasper be messenger. Wouldn't do to have a servant dressing me down."

"Yes, and Jasper will love the chance to singe your ears," Georgiana said.

"You aren't going to?" he asked.

She curled close, seeking warmth, making him flinch when she laid a cold hand on his cheek.

"I like them the way they are," she said, inspecting his nearest ear, running her finger, explorer-like, down the curved edge. "Besides, I'm anxious to hear from her. I thought—perhaps we can try to mend things in the new year."

"I'm going to try," William said, finding her other hand and interlacing their fingers. "It would be nice if we could do it together."

Georgiana didn't say anything. She didn't need to. He understood what she meant when she laid her head on his shoulder and tightened her hold on his fingers. Of course, he couldn't deny himself a little folly. "I missed you, Penelope," he whispered.

"Gah—" was all she managed, before he captured her mouth in a kiss.

27

LEG-SHACKLED

OF COURSE THE one time in Alistair's life that he wanted to rush out and find a minister, he couldn't. It was an ungodly hour of the night and he was missing a leg—hadn't used his crutches for more than hobbling about his room yet.

"Tomorrow's just as good," Anna promised. "Or even the next day." She kissed him and left the room, carrying a heavy-eyed Henry.

Alistair settled into the pillows. It would be tomorrow, even if he had to turn to the Catholics. Oh, he wasn't in any state to inflict a wedding night on her—wished he was, but with his leg gone, the idea was frankly terrifying. His face burned at the very thought.

Get used to it. Not going to happen any other way.

It was a worry that would keep. There were others needing his attention. Anna might be careless of her reputation, but he couldn't afford to be, not when she'd been passing herself off as his wife. And she would be, before the new day got old. Griggs and Jamieson could be witnesses. The cathedral wasn't far if Griggs couldn't roust out a chaplain. If people wanted to talk—he'd never known more inveterate gossips than the men of the army—they could talk about the indecent swiftness of his wedding or the secretive arrangements. Whatever they pleased, so long as they spoke nicely about his bride. With his leg gone and his career finished, he wasn't going to be much of a husband. If he couldn't keep Anna's name clean so she could hold up her head, he may as well put himself to grass.

He'd have to clean up so he wouldn't shame her. Get Griggs to brush out his good coat. Get his hair trimmed. And a shave . . . .

ALISTAIR WOKE in the morning to find Anna sitting in the chair beside his bed. Henry was in her lap, squirming as she drew circles in his palm and whispered silliness in his ears.

"Shh!" Anna said, when a squeal escaped Henry. She glanced up into Alistair's open eyes. "Oh."

"He's awake," Henry whispered needlessly.

"Where's my breakfast?" Alistair said.

Once Henry was dispatched for it, Alistair reached out for Anna's hand. "You can't change your mind, you know. You've got to be married to someone out here, and that sea captain of yours thinks it's me." *Jamieson's too young for you, and besides, he likes the high fliers. Simpson would make a perfect husband if I let him have you —but I won't, cause I'm a selfish lout, and there it is . . . .*

"Mrs. Beaumaris sounds lovely to me," she said.

He looked her over. Plain green wool dress, clean lace collar— she must have been saving it—her hair simply drawn up. The color was high in her cheeks, but it was natural, he knew. She looked happy.

"You'll do," he said.

"You won't. I'll marry you in your nightshirt if I have to, but I insist you shave!"

So he banished her, shouting for Griggs.

. . .

ALISTAIR WAS FORCED to ask Major Simpson to witness the ceremony since Jamieson was nowhere to be found.

"All right! But I don't like it!" Simpson said, when repeated warnings failed to change Alistair's mind—he was injured, he hadn't gotten his commander's permission, and Spain was no place for ladies.

"Have to get married. Only thing to do with her since she's here," Alistair said blithely, praying Simpson would lose the scowl before his own patience snapped. His leg was wrapped and bandaged, but he was worried all this moving around would make him bleed through his pinned up trousers. He looked gruesome enough as it was. Griggs had rounded up a Scottish chaplain, who was waiting with Anna downstairs in the landlady's sitting room. They'd been waiting at least a quarter hour, while Simpson tried to talk him out of it.

"You'll have to help me with the stairs," Alistair said, before Simpson could list his objections again. Simpson, nearly as broad as he was tiresome, let Alistair prop an arm around his shoulders. Alistair hopped down the steps, resolving that tomorrow they'd find new lodgings on the ground floor. He wasn't going to have Anna doing this every time he had to venture out of his room.

The sitting room wasn't a church, though it was almost as cold and austere as one. The landlady, disapproving of English heresies, had dusted off a crucifix and placed it right in the middle of the table on top of a yellowing piece of lace.

"Anna, this is Major Simpson."

She curtsied. Simpson nodded stiffly. She'd have softened anyone else with that demure dress and those downcast eyelashes, but Simpson was a stickler and this was highly irregular. Oh well. If it were Jamieson, he'd have taken one look at Anna and begun groveling like the puppy he was. Alistair didn't care overmuch, so long as they got the thing done. And Anna kept smiling.

"Mr. Fraser says he'll marry us," she said, her lips twitching.

Once the chaplain started speaking, Alistair understood why. His Scots rumble was like a mouthful of gravel.

"I'd have understood more Spanish," Anna whispered, when Alistair moved to her side, leaning onto his crutches so he could take her hands in his own. They were rougher now. He was glad she wasn't wearing gloves.

He stood through the whole thing, stiffened by crutches and his own will, worried the distraction of keeping his balance and ignoring the pain in his missing leg would make him miss his cue. He didn't, though. He might not have caught the exact words binding him to Anna Fulham Morris, but he got his affirmative in the right place, confidently, like a man with both feet on the ground. If he needed clarification later about the forsaking of others or remedies against sin and fornication, he'd ask another priest. Despite the Scot's burr, Alistair caught the heart-stinging part about sickness and health, but it came as a balm to him, sunk as he was in Anna's shining eyes.

They kissed, chastely, because even he was cowed by those stern Scottish eyebrows. Then they accepted the congratulations of the chaplain and the skeptical well-wishes of Major Simpson. Alistair decided he'd been wrong—the man would make any woman a terrible husband. Before Alistair could send him to the devil, the Major made his bows and took himself out. The Divine waited a little longer, baffling Anna with conversation until her eyes grew round, while Alistair wished for Jamieson, or any of his other friends, who'd have sense enough to invite the man to join them for a drink.

After Alistair thanked him for the fourth time, he made an exit. Alistair lowered himself gratefully into a hard chair—if he dropped himself into the sofa's gaping mouth it would swallow him. Across the room, Henry sat in the matching chair, his feet dangling above the floor.

"Well, Henry. I think when that priest gave me your mother

he must have forgotten she was already yours. Do you think we can share?"

Henry considered.

"Maybe I could have her on Tuesdays." Alistair suggested. "Or after eight o' clock."

"What do you want her for?" Henry asked.

Alistair laughed, watching Anna turn pink out of the corner of his eye. "I think everyone must want her," Alistair said. "She's wonderfully brave."

"She wasn't afraid of the ship at all," Henry conceded. "So are you my papa now?"

"If you'll have me. We said all the right words."

"Good. I couldn't tell," Anna interjected, dropping into the sofa and raising puffs of dust. She brushed once at her dress then settled back, filling up the space and motioning Henry over. He sped across the floor and into her lap.

"Is that how you become a papa? Saying the right words?" Henry asked, incredulous.

"For you and me, yes. You don't mind?"

"Not really, though I should have liked a sword."

He hadn't won a French one, and there'd be no chance now. Griggs could find one, of course—he could source out astonishing things, when asked, but—

Grimacing, Alistair twisted around his sword belt. Silly of him to wear it today, but it completed the uniform and he'd wanted to look dashing. Or approximate it, anyway. "You're too young now, but would you like to have mine? I'm leaving the army."

Henry's eager face was answer enough.

"Come help me with the buckles. You can have a look at it."

Anna said nothing, perhaps not entirely pleased with the gift, though it brought Henry close to him, drawing their heads together.

"You'll need a trifle more height before you can try it," Alistair said, but he slid the blade an inch or two out of the scabbard so Henry could see his face on the gleaming metal. Before Henry finished drawing in an ecstatic breath, Alistair slid it home again. "It's a real sword, not for fooling," he said, tickling Henry's chin with the silk tassel.

"And it belongs on the mantel," Anna said, plucking it away from them.

Henry leaned after it longingly, but Alistair tethered him by his hand. "We mustn't argue with the commander-in-chief, you know." He slid a hand into his pocket, pulling out a few coins. "Ask Griggs to help you buy your mama a wedding gift."

Henry scampered off.

"What do you think he'll find?" Anna asked, leaning back on the mantelpiece.

Alistair wanted a lace mantilla, if one could be found, but it was possible the best that could be managed might be a pair of gloves—not such a bad thing, in winter. Dull though. Not the kind of thing a man wanted to give his bride. He didn't even have a ring for her, so she was wearing his own, which had to be wrapped with string to stay on her finger. "Nothing as rare as you are," he said, which was the simple truth. He meant only to look at her with warm eyes, but she came to his side, glowing like a candle, looking at him in a way he could scarce believe. It was enough to flummox a man, to make him a fool, but he'd lost his leg, not his wits. Incredulous stammering wasn't the thing to do when presented with your heart's desire. No. You took her—carefully, if you had to—and held her close, because all the world was now in your arms.

AFFAIRS OF HONOR

"IT'S TOO FAR," Anna said, but her pleading tone told Alistair he'd already won. The journey to headquarters in Freineda wouldn't kill him, though he might be too white-lipped to speak. There was going to be a ball, and it was time he and Anna were seen.

"Let me be the managing one for a change," he said.

Anna frowned, and for a moment he feared she'd scald his ears. She'd done it to Griggs, Bartolome and the doctor. Even Jamieson, who stopped in regularly to take note of Alistair's progress and gawp at Anna, took care to mind her gentlest suggestions. Only her son and her husband were allowed to give any trouble.

"Come on. I want to see you dance," Alistair said. There would be music and wine and jollity; though he didn't mind keeping Anna to himself, he didn't want people thinking he was ashamed of her. "If I can't endure a few miles in a wagon, how will I manage the trip to England?"

"A few miles! It's at least fifteen."

"That's not many. How far is Oporto?"

Her answering parry was feeble. "I've nothing to wear."

True, her trunks had only yielded up practical clothing.

"Doesn't matter. If you wore a feed sack you'd still outshine them all." The gloss on her hair and the shine in her eyes might be the effect of his own mind, but the smiles weren't. They fluttered across her face and lighted on her lips, too many and too often to count. He'd never seen a woman more beautiful than Anna smiling. "Wear the blue muslin and your black mantilla." Griggs, wonder that he was, had procured hair combs too.

"I don't like leaving Henry."

They'd be away overnight if they went to Freineda. Unless he drank much more wine than he intended, Alistair didn't want to endure those fifteen miles in the hours before dawn. A friend had offered to put them up so Alistair could sleep for a few hours and make the return journey once it was daylight. "Nothing will happen to Henry," Alistair assured her. "Not with Mrs. Orfila, Bartolome and Griggs to look after him." She knew it was true, but wouldn't relinquish the worry. She was never entirely easy without her son near, which was understandable, he supposed. "He's safe here, so long as he stays out of Mrs. Orfila's sitting room," Alistair reminded her. "You'll never see a party like this again."

It would be filled with smart uniforms and threadbare ones, wives and women given that courteous assumption. The food would be awful—had to be, since it was being driven over from the depot in Ciudad Rodrigo once it was cooked—but there would be plenty of wine, plenty of toasts, plenty of boasting and blustering. There might be a hole in the dance floor and bare plaster on the walls, but the guests would dance until they were too fuddled to find their way across the floor. His friends would congratulate him on his wife and commiserate over his leg—rotten luck, Beaumaris!—and he'd wish them well too, knowing come spring, they'd be on the march again and he wouldn't be here to see it. Before much longer, he hoped to be off, if the weather didn't make the journey to Oporto impractical. The trip would be easier if they began before Anna's money ran out—it would be nigh impossible to pry his back pay from the quartermaster.

"I don't—"

"Anna," he interrupted. "Unless you've lost your legs, there's no reason not to go."

As he'd predicted, Anna looked lovely in her blue gown, but neither he nor the mirror could convince her. She still wore a worried frown. Attempting to steer her away from the mirror (if she wasn't satisfied now, she'd never be), Alistair heard a voice from the sitting room.

"Henry Morris? Good. Where's your mother?"

Anna rushed past him before he could blink. He followed after, his crutches clumping on the scarred plank floors.

They found Cyril, struggling to free himself from the sofa. He looked from Alistair to Anna to Henry, who was sidling into the corner by the fireplace and glaring suspiciously at Cyril.

"Cyril." Alistair greeted him with a nod. "Anna, I think you've met my brother. Cyril, my wife and my stepson, Henry."

Cyril swallowed, a gulp that seemed to encompass the entire room. "So it's done, then?" He played nervously with a button on his waistcoat.

"A week ago. Shame you missed it."

Cyril exhaled, ruffling the hair so carefully disarranged about his forehead. He rocked back onto his heels, feebly insisting how pleased he was to see Anna and to find his brother married.

"Nice to see you out and about," he said, blinking again at the space where Alistair's foot used to be.

"Let's have some tea," Anna said, seating herself grimly on the sofa.

"Wo-wonderful!" said Cyril.

Alistair inquired after his journey, unsurprised that his travails were considerably more acute than Anna's had been.

"I can't believe you managed it, ma'am," he said, looking at Anna with some trepidation.

"I expect you have a softer skin," Anna said, setting aside her spoon.

And a softer head, Alistair thought.

"Well, the important thing is everyone's still breathing and in one piece—" Cyril drew to a strangled halt.

"Nearly," Alistair said. "Have you a place to stay?"

"Oh, I'll stay with you." Cyril didn't notice Anna's dark look.

"We're going to a party tonight in Freineda," Alistair said, with an apologetic glance at his wife. "You really must come."

CYRIL ATTIRED himself from his numerous boxes in putty-colored breeches and a dark blue coat he'd never have been able to don without Griggs's assistance. It molded to his shoulders much more closely than Alistair's uniform. He was thinner than he used to be.

"Well, it'll be a pleasure to dance with such a handsome sister-in-law," Cyril said, as they set out. Alistair tried to swallow his irritation, but it wasn't easy, with Cyril riding beside the wagon on his own horse. He'd lent him the black. It hurt less than seeing Cyril on the other one. Just looking at the mare made him ache for everything he'd lost.

"Go on ahead," Alistair urged after a few miles. Cyril was growing impatient with the wagon's pace, and he was impatient with Cyril. Anna, her face closed as a clam, hadn't said anything for several minutes.

"You see why I had to marry you so quickly," Alistair said, before Cyril's hoofbeats were out of hearing. "If you'd acquainted yourself with more of my family, I'd have been jilted." He grinned. "Once was enough for that."

"We're going to have to bring him back to London," Anna said.

"Yes, and the whole way he'll be trying to steal the services of Griggs. I mean, I don't particularly like managing without one, but Cyril's near helpless without a valet."

"I used to feel bad for cutting you off from your family."

"I don't think you have, but even if you did, I'd consider it a gift, I assure you."

She settled herself firmly under his arm. "Tell me the future," she said.

It was a game they'd started the last few days, to stop Alistair from gasping and biting through his lip when Anna changed his bandages. Usually he tried to appall her by predicting a shabby set of rooms redolent of boiled cabbages, with darned stockings hanging in front of a miniature fire. "We'll have to ration out the coal mighty carefully, you see." This time they begged a home with her parents, until they threw Alistair out for making love to Anna in the middle of the day.

"I'd follow you," Anna promised.

"You might like a rest," Alistair teased. "It was every day, you understand."

"Practically persecution," Anna murmured.

"Quite." Alistair pushed his head into the cowl of her hood. "Mmmn."

But when he tried to draw away, Anna whispered, "Persecute me some more."

He gave her a quick peck. "Not a chance. It's not full dark yet. I don't want the driver rolling us into the road. And what about the officers and their ladies that pass? I, at least, have a reputation to maintain."

Anna laughed. "I expect the sight would do wonders for your reputation. They'll toast you all night long."

It was slow, traveling like this, but it wasn't so bad with Anna's company. "We might be the last to arrive, but we can be sure dinner won't start without us," Alistair said, spying the lights of Freineda glimmering ahead.

Anna sighed. "Must we go? I'm happy right here."

"I'm hungry," Alistair said.

"Supper is right beside you," Anna said. "You should have taken some before, when it was halfway warm."

"I can only eat off the best china," he said loftily.

"I'll remember that. For the cabbages," Anna retorted.

He picked up his crutches and shifted to the back of the wagon.

"Be there in a minute, Captain," called a batman, pressed into service for the evening. He helped Anna down first, then Alistair, standing by as Anna brushed down their clothes. He'd never seen Anna give her clothes such care since she'd arrived. While she tried to look at the back of her skirts, he pointed the batman to their case of overnight things, directing him to take it to tonight's temporary lodging. Anna was still fussing with her dress.

"I'd hate to have to tell Henry your courage failed you," he said.

She lifted her eyebrows in challenge. "Unlike you, I haven't a talent for humbling people with a glance," she said.

Promising to do it to everyone but her, he swung forward on his crutches, wishing it were possible to take her by the arm. She stayed close though, and he didn't think it was only because she feared for his stability. They were only a yard or two through the doorway, clustered with other guests removing cloaks and over-coats when Cyril pushed his way through the crowd.

"Don't take her in," he said, speaking low in Alistair's ear.

"What do you mean?" Alistair said, annoyed now. "Of course I'm bringing her in. We came all this way." The only advantage of crutches was that people tended to give him a clear path. "Come on, Anna," he said, pausing with the crutches propped under his shoulders so he could stretch out his hand. She moved to his side again, not looking to see if Cyril followed behind them.

At first he noticed nothing. The room was too full, packed with golden epaulets and gleaming boots, lace and plumes and the gloved arms of ladies. Nodding at the faces he knew, they penetrated a little way into the crowd, into the hot, heavy-scented air. The dark timbered ceiling pressed down on them.

"People are staring at me," Anna whispered under her breath.

"Of course. You're the most beautiful lady here." They moved a little further, sidestepping a scowling man with heavy side whiskers. "Evening, Kelling," Alistair said. The man gave a loud harrumph.

"That's not why," Anna said, sounding half-strangled.

"Nonsense," Alistair said, but it wasn't. Anna was drawing stares. Not kind ones either.

"Let's find Jamieson," he said, squeezing her hand. They just needed to find a corner with friends in it, where they could visit until supper. The lady in front of them drew her skirts aside with a sniff.

"Please. Let's go," Anna whispered, putting her hand on his arm.

He stopped. Anna's face was white, her smile gone. The moment he relented, a black clad shoulder turned toward them, opening a circle of avid faces and revealing Frederick Morris, his smooth hair gold in the candlelight.

Anna started, her hand closing around Alistair's arm. Frederick gave Anna a long look, then turned deliberately back to his listeners. "It was a gruesome journey, but what could I do? The worries for my nephew were ten times worse . . . ."

"Take me out of here," Anna said.

Alistair complied, all gentle solicitude, inwardly carving out Morris's entrails. His heart beat loud in his ears, overpowering the whispers that trailed them.

"What about Henry?" Anna gasped, clutching Alistair's arm at the door of his friend's lodging.

"Probably playing cards with Griggs," Alistair said. "Wait here. I'll see to it. Sleep if you can." He kissed her wet cheek, then returned to the festivities.

"What's happened?" he asked Cyril, who he found lurking by the door.

"Fellow was here when I arrived. Said he'd come to Spain to find your wife, though he claimed he was surprised you'd gone and married her. Said he feared you were a victim of her deceits. There's plenty of people amused with the idea that you've finally been taken in. And a good number who are downright angry you had the bad manners to bring her. Morris has come to reclaim the boy. Says she can't be trusted with him."

"Any number of army wives travel with their children," Alistair said, tense as a coiled spring. "Ladies, even."

"I'm just telling you what he said," Cyril said.

"It's all over the room?" Alistair asked.

"What do you think?"

Following on the heels of his broken engagement over the summer, this story topped anything else, even the rumors of Lord and Lady Westing's divorce. Well, he knew what to do. Standing as proudly as he could—a difficult thing, with crutches—Alistair moved into the room. Finding a prominent place, well lit, well-spaced, he glared at Morris, who was laughing scurrilously with a couple of riflemen. One of them nudged Morris with his elbow, directing him to look at Alistair. Ignoring the rifleman's cautious tilt of the head, Morris let his face fall into a sneer.

"You can't challenge him," Cyril whispered at his elbow.

"Can't I? What provocation would you think appropriate?"

"I'm not saying you don't have cause—"

"I can still shoot," said Alistair, silencing his brother.

He didn't let himself be distracted by conversation or the friends who approached, trying to draw him off. He was polite, exquisitely so, but his eyes never left Morris for long.

"Where's your wife?" asked a cocky infantry lieutenant as Alistair sat down for dinner.

"She felt unwell," Alistair replied.

The lieutenant smirked.

"Anyone would, with Morris for a brother-in-law," Alistair said blandly, serving himself from a dish of peas.

"What about the child?" a woman down the table asked.

"My stepson is a remarkable boy," Alistair said. "Nearly as brave as his mother. She came to Spain to escape Morris as much as for my own sake—the boy was taken from her when only an infant. He inherited her fortune when her husband died, and Frederick Morris can't afford to be without it."

"No!" gasped the long-faced lady.

Tempted to strike the round eyes off their faces, Alistair dabbed his mouth instead. "It's a nuisance, but it seems I must remind Morris to be careful of the way he behaves to my wife. But enough of that. Dawlish, you're late of London. How does my cousin Jasper?"

He didn't plan to wait out the dancing. Tonight's cross and jostle work was nearly done.

"Ask Morris to come speak with me," he said to Cyril after dinner. "Do it kindly. If he demurs, tell him I would cross the room, but my leg pains me."

Cyril gave a silent whistle, but he went. He returned a moment later, bringing Morris.

"And your friends!" Alistair exclaimed as he approached. "Really, this is most convenient."

"Is it?" said Morris, his lip surly.

"Indeed. I should like them to hear your apology." Alistair shifted on his crutches. After leaning on them for hours, his arms hurt. It was important in the next few days to take good care of them.

"I won't apologize to you, Beaumaris," spat Morris. "Where's Henry? You've no right to him."

"Gently, my friend. You're making a scene. Dueling isn't illegal here, but Wellington doesn't like it." Which didn't stop affairs of honor. Over the years Alistair had heard any number of cock and bull stories about 'shooting accidents.'

"Are you challenging me?"

"Yes, if you don't see your way to an apology. I'm not going to stomach insults to my wife."

Morris swore, twisting his head when a flock of ladies moved further away.

"Was that necessary?" Alistair asked.

"I'll tell you what's necessary! Give me back my nephew. And keep an eye on that jade of yours. If she didn't let half the county into her bed, it wasn't for lack of try—"

Alistair leaned closer, laying a hand on Morris's shoulder. He squeezed. Hard.

"My dear friend," he whispered. "I advise you to be careful. And to unsay those words. If not for your own sake, you should think of Henry."

Morris tried to shrug off Alistair's hand.

"We are in company," Alistair warned him. "It is advisable for others to think we both know how to behave. Do you accept my challenge?"

"Yes, and I wish you well of it!" Morris said, red-faced.

"Then I wish you good evening. Cyril, you will do me the favor of meeting Morris's friends tomorrow, won't you?"

"I'll walk you home," Cyril said.

Once they were outside, the headiness of the challenge evaporating into the deep sky, Cyril allowed himself to swear long and fluently. "You can't mean it. It's impossible. I'll fix things with Morris's seconds tomorrow. Of course you couldn't ignore such provocation—"

"Morris won't relent," Alistair interrupted. "He wouldn't meet me before. Now he thinks he has a chance. He wants me dead because I'm a trouble to him, but with my leg gone he can't issue a challenge himself."

"I should dashed well think so! How do you propose to meet him? With one leg!"

"It only takes one hand to fire a gun. I can sit on a chair—or if Morris is unwilling to agree to that, I can have a crutch under my left shoulder."

"I'm not letting him put a hole in you! Is life so cheap, that you'd fling it away?"

Alistair stopped, then swung himself forward again. "I've risked my life any number of times the last ten years. Made a career of it. You never got exercised over it before."

"War's different," Cyril countered.

"However it comes, I expect death is the same."

"You were close enough recently to have some idea," Cyril said. He kicked a loose stone, sending it skidding across the narrow street. "I'll be your proxy," he muttered.

This time Alistair halted so abruptly he nearly flew off his crutches. "You can't shoot," he said, steadying himself.

"I don't expect Morris is very good either," Cyril said.

"You mean it?" Alistair asked, still stunned.

"I do," Cyril said.

"It's good of you. I never expected—" Alistair shifted on his crutches. "It's a princely offer, Cyril, but I can't accept. Promise me this—act as my second. And look after Anna if Morris snuffs me. Don't let him take Henry." This wouldn't have happened if he hadn't threatened Frederick in the first place, back in London.

They walked up to the house. A chink of light escaping through the shutters fell on Cyril's pained face. "Let me," he begged. "I'm expendable."

Alistair pulled his hand away from the latch. "You are not." He met his brother's eyes. Temporized. "All right, you can be something of a trial, but you don't need to be. Besides, I'm a better shot. I'll win. Just please don't say anything to Anna."

29

ON ALERT

Waiting was difficult at the best of times. Tonight it was impossible. When she finally heard the scraping latch, Anna flew to the door.

"What happened?" she asked, taking Alistair's hands as if she could pull answers out of them.

"I've spoken to Morris. I've taken care of it."

"Thank God." Anna sagged into herself, limp and drained.

"Are you cold?" Alistair asked.

"No." Numb perhaps, but not from cold.

"Then why the cloak?"

Anna followed his gaze to the lantern waiting on the table, the undisturbed bed. "Anna," he began carefully. "Were you going to walk all the way home from Freineda?"

"Not alone. I didn't know what else to do," she admitted. "You were such a long time and I was so afraid." She was dreadful at coping with uncertainty, a victim of relentless imagining that smothered her until she could think of nothing but rushing to her child.

Alistair hauled himself across the floor and sank onto the bed, propping his crutches against the wall. He looked tired as a rained out parade. "I don't like to stand in your way, but I can't manage a fifteen-mile walk in the dark."

Anna flinched. "I didn't think. I'm sorry." She moved to his side, contrite yet still needing reassurance. "You're sure Henry's all right?"

"He is. And we can leave first thing in the morning."

Anna nodded, ducking her chin, but Alistair wouldn't let her hide. He nudged up her chin and studied her face with probing eyes. "As long as I live I'll keep you both safe."

Primed for tears already, she was too worn to hold them back. Alistair pulled her into his shoulder, letting them soak into his coat. "There now," he said, in the first decent pause. "Let's get some rest. You're so ghastly pale you'll frighten Henry."

Anna laughed shakily as Alistair worked on the fastenings of her cloak. He got her out of her dress, but her fingers were too clumsy to return the favor.

"I can manage," he said, smiling into her bleary eyes. "Go to sleep."

DESPITE ALISTAIR'S REASSURANCES, it was a relief to get home and to lay her eyes on Henry, who greeted them with a quick smile and a torrent of questions. Did they get any pudding? See many generals? Was Napoleon there?

Griggs murmured that luncheon was waiting.

"I want to go outside," Henry said.

"We can go walking after we eat," Anna replied, momentarily forgetting her resolution to barricade Henry in the house. "Papa and I are hungry." Cyril was pale and fidgety, which probably meant he needed a drink.

He downed three, shifting in his seat and staring at his brother.

"What's the matter?" she asked, glancing between them.

"Nothing," Cyril said.

"Griggs makes better soup than this. Out of shoe leather even," Alistair said, pushing away his bowl.

Henry's head jerked up.

"Finish your potatoes," Anna told him.

"I want to know what's the matter too," Henry said.

Alistair buttered another slice of bread. "I'm afraid we saw your Uncle Frederick last night."

"Is he the matter?" Henry's voice seemed to fade.

"No, darling," said Anna.

"Yes," Alistair said at the same time. "He has terrible manners. Don't you grow up like that."

"Yes, sir," said Henry, his anxious creases gone. Anna was not not so easily appeased.

"Will Frederick mention the matter to your commanders?" she asked tentatively. Cyril was jumpy, which didn't help her worries that Frederick might show up at their door, accompanied by a pair of armed sergeants.

"No," said Alistair.

"You seem very sure," Anna said, turning her water glass around on the table.

"Trust me, Anna. I've taken care of this."

Yes, but what did you do? His assurances meant less each time he refused to explain. "How?" she asked finally, staring at him until he had to look up from his plate.

He set down his fork. "You don't think I'm capable of managing a coward like Frederick Morris?" His fierce look ought to have toppled her chair.

"Of course I do!" It was a lie, but the only thing she could say when he looked at her like that. "I do," she insisted, trying to budge the scowl from his face.

"Then you should trust me." He picked up his fork, and though he finished his meal the picture of complete unconcern, Cyril wouldn't look up from his plate.

. . .

UNEASY, Anna wanted to defer walking with Henry, but Alistair told her not to be foolish and hurried them out of the house. She and Henry wandered through the empty market and into the cathedral, where Henry liked to sit in the back and make ghoulish whispers. When he growled 'dead dog' (they'd seen several since leaving London, but Anna was glad it was merely these frights that stuck with him, because it could have been worse) just a little too loud, she whisked him back outside. His flagging steps said he felt as tired as she did, so they returned to their lodging.

Alistair was gone.

Anna contained her uneasiness until Henry went down for a nap. By the time he was asleep, rest for her was impossible. She decided to tidy their rooms. She did trust Alistair. When he said he would handle Frederick, she believed him. But he had revealed nothing to her, nothing at all. It wasn't unreasonable, expecting an explanation.

If she were Frederick, she'd be banging down the door by now, or dragging Henry to the nearest port. Why hadn't he come?

Anna brushed yesterday's ball dress with unnecessary force and attacked the mending as her mood soured. Alistair had an alarming number of fraying stockings for someone who could only wear one at a time. Anna sighed. It was probably time to get rid of the left boots. It was depressing, shoving them aside every time they had to get anything from his trunk. Jabbing her needle into torn cuff as if the shirt might be coerced into revealing information, Anna stood up and threw back the lid of the trunk.

They couldn't travel with this jumble, that was certain. And it wouldn't hurt, now that Frederick was on the loose, to be ready. Anna picked up two left boots and tossed them on the bed, setting aside the packet of her letters and discarding a broken pen. Henry's dit (she'd been looking for that), a knife, a jar of ointment: she kept all those. The ointment was smelly, but Alistair must have it for a reason. Anna tossed the dit on top of her heap of mending, then moved the rest aside so she could sweep out the dirt that had sifted to the bottom of the trunk.

She stopped. Something was missing. A case that usually rested at the bottom of the trunk, beneath the superfluous boots. Blood rushed to puddle at her feet and she pressed a hand to her stomach. Dear God. She'd opened that case once, looking for scissors to trim Alistair's bandages. It held two identical pistols.

He couldn't mean to—surely he wouldn't—

He wouldn't dare. Not on crutches. She'd come all this way, bargaining for his soul with death. He'd mended—and married her. In Anna's book, both these indicated that ownership of his soul had passed, at least in part, to her. She had a life interest in him, a dependence . . . she cleared her head with a shake. Silly legalities were no way to describe the hole she felt widening in her chest. What about his missing leg? Sucking air through her fingers, which were clapped stupidly over her mouth, Anna blinked away the sting in her eyes. It couldn't be.

She glanced again at the chest. Yes, they were gone.

Without knowing how, Anna found herself sitting on the edge of the bed, clutching her hands to stop their shaking. Frederick wasn't coming for Henry. Not yet. He was going to kill her husband first.

"Are those—"

"They're mine now," Alistair said, lifting out one of the pistols and inspecting it in the slanting winter sun. "You can load for me." He reconsidered. "Better not. I'll do it." Alistair had thought about practicing in a tumbledown house down the street—he could chalk a mark on the wall—but had changed his mind. Better to practice like it was the real thing. A walk outside the town walls to tire him and standing on uneven ground. Of course sunlight was better than shooting indoors, but today it came with a wind.

"Morris insists on going through with this," Cyril said, gingerly lifting out the second pistol. Squelching the thought that one of these guns might kill him, Alistair found a spot approximately the right distance from a slanting tree that had almost managed to survive the latest assault on the town.

"Friday, you said?"

"Yes."

"And pistols."

Cyril groaned. "If his seconds hadn't talked him out of it, he'd have insisted on swords! He means to kill you."

"He's not the first one to try," Alistair said mildly.

"You never stood still for the French."

"No, but I did when I faced Renton. And Galloway."

"You met him?" Cyril said, turning in surprise.

"My temper was quicker back then."

Cyril grunted. "What did you do?"

"Watched him shoot first. Then I told him to hold up his hand. Shot the pistol right out of it."

Cyril laughed. "No wonder he avoids me."

"You should avoid him. Bad lot. Doesn't do to mix with those."

"I daresay," Cyril said, mocking him.

"I mean it. You'd save yourself a lot of trouble if you cut yourself free of that bunch. If you're going to be looking after Anna, you'll have to—"

"You're going to win, remember? Want this?" he asked, holding out Alistair's camp stool.

"Not yet." He would eventually, but he must practice standing for as long as he could.

"Where's Morris?" Cyril asked, as Alistair positioned his crutch and aimed.

"Right there," Alistair said, and fired. "Damn. Missed him." He'd have to adjust his stance.

"Did Morris shoot you?" Cyril asked.

"Nope. Missed by a yard. He will, you know. See my sideway stance? He's got a narrow target."

"Yes, and it wobbles."

"I won't by Friday," Alistair said.

An hour later he wasn't so sure. He'd have fallen today, if Cyril hadn't been close by. He shot Morris in the chest perhaps four times in ten—not nearly enough. He was tired.

ANNA WAS pale and unsmiling when he returned, and mute until they sat down to dinner.

"I noticed you got out your pistols," she said, with frightening calm.

"Just to keep in practice. Something to do," interjected Cyril.

"I see," said Anna. The anger pulsing through the air was bad enough, but the hurt in her eyes was intolerable.

"I need to speak to Griggs," Alistair said, rising from the table and fleeing the house, knowing he'd find Griggs at the tavern across the square. Griggs listened, nodding seriously as Alistair emptied two bottles of wine and instructed him on the necessary preparations for their journey home.

"Thank you, Captain, I'm sure I'll manage," said Griggs, keeping a straight face. "Just as I have a time or two before."

Alistair blinked, his scowl late in coming. "Dash it, Griggs, you aren't supposed to let me play the fool."

"And when did you ever listen to me?" Griggs sighed. "Let me help you to bed."

Anna was there, huddled under the blankets. Waving away Griggs, Alistair lowered himself onto the bed. The door clicked shut. Anna lurched another foot away from him, no small feat in a bed this narrow, hauling the blankets with her and leaving him to wiggle his five toes in the cold. Impossible to sleep in this charged silence. Even her breathing made no sound. Tentatively, Alistair rested his hand against the wall of her back.

"I want you to tell me," she ground out.

Fear took him then, like rushing water in the spring thaw. He closed the space between them, sliding his arms under her own, stifling a groan that pushed against his closed throat. "Please don't make me. You already know."

"Can't we run away?"

He choked. "I can't run."

"Can you shoot?"

"Yes." If he was lucky.

Her face, when she brought it to his, was wet, though some of the tears might have been his own. His leg ached and his head swam, heavy with the knowledge that he might not get to keep her. Two days left.

"Is there another way?" she asked.

"He's not going to trouble you," he said.

"I hate this," she said—or at least, he thought so. Her face was half in his shoulder, half in the pillow.

"No more crying," he said, to himself and to her, as he laced his fingers together behind her back. He wouldn't be able to bear it else. It was all right now, when he was drunk and tired, but tomorrow he must think only about shooting straight, and where he wanted to put his bullet.

30

RECKONING

FRIDAY MORNING GRIGGS arrived to dress him before dawn. "I thought the black coat today, Captain," he said, holding it out.

"What did you do to the buttons?" Alistair asked.

"Must be this damp air. They've tarnished," Griggs lied. He'd clearly blacked them. Alistair was about to ask for another coat, unwilling to humble himself before Frederick Morris, but then he caught Anna's shadowed eyes, peering at him over the edge of the sheet. The blacked buttons were her and Griggs's doing. Steadying himself with a hand against the bed, Alistair bent down to kiss her forehead. "Thank you." He'd wear the black coat and sacrifice pride. He was a husband and a father. No need to make Frederick's aim easier.

"I'll be back soon. Don't forget that I love you," he said. He downed a cup of coffee and ordered Griggs to move a sleeping Henry into bed with Anna. Better if she had a warm body to hold. He'd asked her not to get out of bed.

Griggs came with him when he stepped outside, waiting for Cyril. He arrived in fine style, driving a well-sprung gig.

"Lord knows what it will cost me, but I won't have you bounced from here into Hades," Cyril said.

"Where did you find it?" Alistair asked, accepting Cyril's hand and Griggs's shoulder.

"Some fellows helped me borrow it. They wish you their best."

"I hope we won't have an audience," Alistair said.

"They know we're just going for a drive," Cyril said.

They drove from the town, winding down the hill, passing a pinched-looking boy and his gathering of goats—too few to call a flock. A stand of bare trees clustered in the low ground. On the other side was the chosen field, a flat space screened from the town by the trees.

"Lovely spot," Alistair said.

"I'm glad you think so." Cyril settled the horses, then helped Alistair with his awkward descent, keeping hold of Alistair's shoulders even after he was on the ground. "You're certain I can't do this? I'd consider it a great honor."

Alistair wiped a drip from the end of his nose. The air was cold. "I'll always remember you offered. And that you meant it."

Alistair found himself a convenient tree to lean on, wanting to spare his arms. Cyril paced back and forth across the grass. "They'll be late," he said.

The air felt sharp and chill and clean, with only a hint of distant smoke. Alistair swung his arms, working blood into his flexing fingers, shaking out the tightness in his shoulders. He breathed long and slow, watching the sun blunt the frosty edges of the grass until he felt languid and easy. These things didn't take long. He didn't want to kill Morris and wasn't entirely sure he could. Perhaps blowing a hole in his shoulder would be enough. It would be, in most cases, but there was a fortune at stake. If the Morrises were as profligate with Henry's money as Alistair suspected, giving Frederick a wound in the shoulder was only raising the stakes. If Frederick didn't kill him today, the idea of paying someone to do the job for him would soon cross Frederick's mind, if it hadn't already—his own fault again. He should never have mentioned killing back in London. Such threats could never be unsaid or forgotten. He hadn't thought, back then, as he'd prodded Morris, that it would lead to today, to Anna's scared eyes.

Alistair waited until the sound of rattling wheels stopped before turning his head. Morris, buttoned up and determined, jumped down from a rackety cart. Alistair swung his arms again, waiting for Cyril to say the necessary things to Morris's seconds.

Should tell Cyril I'm glad he's standing up with me.

They examined the case of pistols, their motions scrupulous and refined, their low voices a pleasant rumble. There was something about this air, Alistair thought, drawing it in slowly. He wanted more and more of it, as if inflating his chest enough would float him up into the pale sky. He shut his eyes and smiled, letting the sun wash over his face. He was an eye and an arm and a ball of lead, nothing more, with one task only: shoot straight. He'd aim for the shoulder. They were reasonable men. Morris just needed a reminder not to trifle with him.

Cyril came back, carrying one of the pistols.

"They like 'em. No reason not too. Cost a nice round sum, as I recall."

"I never thanked you for the lovely present," Alistair murmured.

"Save it for later," Cyril said, his mouth drawing tight.

"You have the other one?"

Cyril nodded, confirming he had Alistair's army pistol concealed under his greatcoat.

"Keep it ready. Just in case he doesn't stick to his ground. He might try to run."

"Don't let him shoot first," Cyril began.

"I like to take my time," Alistair said. He preferred to load his own gun, but today he had to leave it to the seconds. No matter. Cyril had shot with him enough this week to do a proper job. A fellow couldn't allow any qualms—if he fretted about one thing, he'd invite in a host of worries. You couldn't shoot straight with fear piled on your back. Planting his left crutch with care—he'd left the other one in the gig—Alistair angled himself away from Morris, presenting his right side. He squinted at Morris, who was shaking his hands, squaring his hips.

Alistair imagined his foot, his knee, his crutch planted in the earth, steady as stone. He stared a moment at the backdrop of branches, outlined in the sunlight.

"Ready?"

Alistair nodded, picking a point on Morris's chest. He wore a dark coat too, with dull silver buttons, denying him an easy target. Alistair stood with his hand relaxed at his side, reminding himself to be perfectly still. From the corner of his eye, he saw one of Morris's seconds raise his hand, lifting a handkerchief into the air. It waved up, then fell, instantly succeeded by a sharp retort. Alistair flinched, his stomach clenching, his heart instinctively galloping forward before he could rein it back. No time to examine himself or his surroundings, to think where the shot may have gone.

"Give me my shot!" he barked, as Morris began to move. The other seconds jerked in surprise, Cyril shouting for Morris to hold to his ground. Morris was coming for him, leaving wet footprints on the frosty grass. Alistair raised his arm. "Give me my shot!" he shouted again. Much harder to hit a moving target. Morris reached behind his back, but by then Alistair already knew. Morris was closing the distance because he had another pistol.

The other seconds were shouting now, but no one wanted to step into the line of fire. Morris wore an ugly snarl and now Alistair could see the glint of his second gun. His own shot got easier, the closer Morris came, but if he waited until Morris raised his gun—

One breath in. Let it halfway out. Pull.

His pistol cracked, jumping in his hand, the sound splintering their little drama.

"Damn it!" Morris said, clapping a hand to the corner of his neck. He hadn't killed him. A scratch on the skin and a torn neckcloth when he'd been aiming for the chest. Cyril seized his chance, rushing to Alistair's side, yelling at Morris to back away, waving his pistol ineffectively, but still managing to look threatening. As Cyril slid his free arm around him Alistair realized he was listing sideways.

Was he shot? He didn't feel anything. He probed his stomach, finding nothing.

"Give me that," he said, holding out a hand for the other pistol and adjusting his crutch. Morris might still use his second gun. He'd clearly given up any of his remaining scruples. Alistair watched warily, not raising the pistol yet. He didn't want to tire his arm. Morris was still holding his shoulder, spitting out curses.

"You all right?" Cyril asked. Alistair probed his stomach again. It seemed he was. All he felt was the urge to vomit.

"Let me," Cyril said, moving his arm under Alistair's shoulder, helping him step aside.

"Nicked me is all," Morris said, to no one in particular, letting go of his shoulder and raising his gun. But halfway Morris frowned, looking down at his shoulder and then at his hand. It was washed red, and something was dripping off the end of his gun. His dark coat was shining. Alistair raised his own gun, just in case, but he no longer feared Frederick's fire, watching the way he stepped, lurching a little in the knees.

"Good God," Morris said, half cursing, half in wonderment. He took another step, but his fingers were lax, his head swaying.

"Frederick!" One of the seconds came running, mouthing a steady stream of disbelieving recriminations. Morris swam into the fellow's arms, his legs too soft to keep him standing.

"Staunch it quick," shouted the other second, falling to his knees and clapping his hand over Morris's wound. Together Alistair and Cyril stumbled across the grass.

"Here!" Cyril said, throwing down a wad of lint and a roll of cotton from his greatcoat pocket. These were snatched up and swiftly applied, but Alistair knew from the way they drank up blood that it wouldn't be long. Morris's eyes were wide, searching the sky. His breath dipped quick and shallow, a stone skipping across water for a few exhilarating seconds before it sinks and falls.

Alistair shut his eyes. "God, I'm sorry." It was the wrong thing to say, a terrible lie that was painfully true—all week he'd meant to kill Morris, until this morning, when he'd decided to shoot for the shoulder. Then, with Morris advancing, he'd unthinkingly aimed for the chest and gotten him between the neck and the shoulder instead. Strangely enough, it was a killing shot. He wanted to leave, to get away from the smell of blood, but he must wait for Morris's steaming blood to spread over the grass, and for his breaths to finally rattle to a stop. And then for Cyril to help Morris's seconds carry his body to the cart. He knew how it would happen, but it didn't make it go any faster or quiet the thudding in his ears.

He and Cyril drove back, fighting silence.

"It was a lucky shot," Cyril said.

Alistair supposed it was. Unlucky for Morris though. They had blood on their boots and brown crusts under their fingernails. Alistair hadn't been able to help the futile attempts to stop the blood, or to compose the corpse. He'd put a hand on the ground though, still surprised to see so much blood. It mingled with the melting frost, staining the dead grass.

"You won't have to worry now. That's a good thing," Cyril said, guiding the horses round the last curve on the hill.

"True." He watched as the gate came nearer. "Do you think Griggs can bring me clean clothes?" He could, of course, but how to get word to him without alerting Anna? Impossible. She was probably making herself sick, waiting for his return. He wanted to see her, just not stained with Frederick Morris's blood.

"Don't get maudlin," Cyril said. "Ghastly business, but it had to be done. I'm just thankful we didn't load you in the wagon. Hungry?"

"Enormously," Alistair said. How lowering.

"We'll get you a drink, some breakfast, and let your wife weep over you. You'll feel better then."

Of course he would. Ten years of campaigning had already proven so. One remembered the chill of watching a life expire, but one didn't always shiver. Thank God. He had time to let warmth work its way into his fingertips again.

Anna burst onto the step before he'd been extracted from carriage. She fell upon him, crying and scolding, clinging to him and feeling for hurts. Henry hung back on the step, troubled and silent.

"Henry is worried," Alistair whispered into Anna's ear.

She rubbed off her tears, clamped her lips shut, forced her face into a trembling smile. Draping his arm over her shoulders, they made shaky progress to the door.

"Are you all right?" Alistair asked Henry, leaning down, steadying himself on the door frame.

"Mama was afraid you wouldn't come back," he said.

Alistair slid his hand through the boy's soft falls of hair. Perhaps there was no excuse for what he'd done, but right now, Henry seemed like a good one. Anna too, could be quite compelling.

"Were you?" Alistair asked.

"A little." Henry bit his lip.

"I'm well, Henry. As well as may be, but I would like my breakfast. Are you hungry?" Alistair knew him well enough by now to know he always was.

Tears came, when he saw Anna had laid out breakfast in the sitting room, though he gave only cursory attention to the tablecloth, the smell of warm bread and the evergreen branches gathered in a glass on the table. The threadbare cushion she'd procured last week was waiting for him in the sturdiest chair. Two more places were set, one on each side.

"I didn't think," she sniffed. "I'm so stupid this morning. I never laid a place for Cyril."

There were times when looks had to suffice for words. Alistair gave Anna one, hoping it could spare him from having to think too much about what he was feeling. It was too painful to hold. "You better get another plate."

31

THE SMELLS OF APRIL AND MAY

ANNA SAID LITTLE OVER BREAKFAST, brimming with too many watery emotions to speak. Miser-like, she quietly stored every moment: his hands dabbing his napkin to his mouth and spooning up egg for Henry, his tired smile and his shadowed eyes, the weary look that silenced Cyril when he began talking about their morning.

"We can tell it another day," Alistair said.

Anna didn't mind. She'd lived through his death so many times this week all she could do now was cling to his hand and look at him.

"You haven't eaten," Alistair said, when Mrs. Orfila came to clear the plates.

"I can't," she said, amazed his own breakfast was gone. His hand had hardly left hers, because each time it did, she felt a spurt of panic that didn't fade until his fingers slid back into her own. Somehow though, he must have managed his fork, for only crumbs and smears of butter remained. Anna hovered at her husband's side as he maneuvered his way into the sitting room, steering him to the sagging sofa. It would be a struggle for him to get out of it, but that suited her purposes. She had no intention of letting him move beyond her reach anytime soon. Later, when she wasn't trembling inside. Perhaps.

They slid in one warm lump to the hollow in the middle of the seat, nudged together by the sofa's worn velvet and decrepit springs. Alistair winced as Henry clambered aboard, bumping his left leg, but kept him close.

"Let's stay here and never move," Anna said, too exhausted to do more than tether herself to her family through touch and listen to their breathing.

"Never?" Henry asked.

Anna shut her eyes, knowing he was wondering how they'd manage without a chamber pot. "Maybe once in a while," she conceded.

"Señora Orfila doesn't allow food in here," Henry added.

"We'll just stay for a little while then," Alistair said. "We'll get up in time for supper."

That satisfied him. Anna moved her cheek away from Alistair's coat buttons. Cyril lit a fire and found himself a chair. He and Alistair were talking, but Anna couldn't open her eyes, couldn't even follow the words. All she could hear was the cadence of their talk, the regular thump of Henry's feet waggling against the sofa. The room grew warmer, the sounds smoother, until they stopped her ears.

WHEN SHE WOKE, the sitting room was dim and quiet. She was curled into Alistair's side. He was stretched out half-beside, half-beneath her, his head resting on one arm of the sofa, his good leg propped up on the other.

"What time is it?" she asked, sitting quickly and wiping a hand across her lips.

"No idea." He picked up her hand and brought it to his cheek. "Are you all right?"

"I will be, since you are." He didn't seem uncomfortable, despite the sofa's shortcomings, so she wriggled back into the narrow space she'd just left. Might as well. It was still warm. She didn't sleep though, just lay beside him while he toyed with a wisp of her hair. The knot she'd twisted on the back of her head this morning was squashed and listing toward her shoulder. "What happens now?" Anna asked.

Alistair didn't immediately answer. "Frederick Morris is dead, Anna." She wanted to squeeze his hand, but one of hers was caught between their chests. She couldn't reach his with her other, never mind her instinct that it would be wrong to arrest the idle movements of his fingers, winding and unwinding her loose hair. She burrowed her chin closer and waited.

"I didn't want to kill him. Probably couldn't have done it if I tried, but—" His words came quickly now, a muddy rush of confession, both guilty and painfully glad. Frederick Morris wouldn't trouble them again. Wouldn't trouble anyone. No more wrangles over Henry and his money, no more slurs hurled at Anna. They were free, so long as she could stand to live with him.

Anna licked her dry lips, warned by his desperate tone that she must choose her words with care. She must not be flippant. He wouldn't be the man she loved if he could exterminate another and walk away without a backward glance. And yet she was glad Frederick was dead, so horribly relieved she felt dizzy. Frederick couldn't take Henry or steal his money or fill him up with his own consequence and teach him to despise her.

"You let him have his shot," she said, tracing her fingers around the lapel of his coat, afraid of saying more. If she wept, he might not understand. She could tell him that he was the truest, best man she knew, but he wouldn't agree with her, not now. She must save those words for another time and face the problem of blame instead. He needn't shoulder any of it. "You will forgive me, I hope, for forcing you into that duel," she said.

"Anna . . . . "

She didn't allow him to contradict her, though he tried more than once. "No, love. It can't be your fault. And if you knew how my heart is flying because Henry is safe, you'd think me a remorseless baggage."

"No, I wouldn't."

"Then why should I think differently of you?" She shifted her cheek against the soft wool of his coat. "I'm just glad you came back." Better to examine other ideas later; she couldn't see them very well when relief kept bumping to the forefront.

He heard her covert sniff and swept a gentle thumb over her eye.

"So am I."

Spring was slow in coming that year, or perhaps it only seemed that way because they were journeying north. Progress was slow, and they lingered in Oporto, waiting for a ship. It did no harm though, having ample time for quiet, for there was none to be found on the ship. No space either, but the Gallant was swift and sound, carrying them across cold seas. They were making straight for London.

Anna took well to the sea. She took well to everything, even her hop-along husband, who had to be helped across tilting decks, rough gangplanks and, at last, London's crowded docks.

"Beaumaris!" It was Jasper, waving at them over the crowd as he fought his way toward them. "Another ship brought word the Gallant was coming in. I've been waiting two days for you in the seamiest taproom you'll ever see!"

"And never enjoyed anything more, I'm sure," Alistair said.

"The words I've learned! It's like another language," Jasper said. He looked Alistair up and down. "Well, you're a pretty mess. What's to be done?"

"Not much, I'm afraid," Alistair said, reaching out to collar Henry before he could wander.

"You're family now, so you'll have to let me kiss you," Jasper said, bowing and saluting Anna's hand. As he looked up, he realized she'd offered him her cheek. "Oh. I will, thank you."

"I warned you about him, but there aren't words fit to explain how annoying—" Alistair began.

"I have my uses," Jasper interrupted. "Cyril, you've got to attend your father—you too, Alistair, but it would be a nice thing to let him chew Cyril apart first. And Anna, your parents are waiting. I'm to deliver you."

"What about Lord and Lady Fairchild?" asked Anna, feeling guilty.

Jasper shrugged. "Haven't seen 'em. Bolted to Cordell at Christmas without a word to anyone. Haven't been seen since."

THOUGH TIRED FROM THE JOURNEY, the happy greetings of her parents revived Anna enough to see to the unpacking. She supposed they would find their own home eventually, once they liberated Henry's inheritance from Frederick's mother, but Anna didn't feel any hurry. She'd missed her parents, and liked having her family under a friendly roof. Alistair didn't seem to mind.

"You'll have to get used to middle class ways, love. My parents only gave us a single dressing room," Anna said, popping her head into the room in question.

"Perfectly acceptable. Even when I had both legs, I depended on Griggs. You're almost as helpful, you know. Wouldn't trust you with my boots, though."

"Why not? There's only one!"

He tried to catch her with one hand but she darted out of reach, back into the bedchamber where she was supervising the bringing up of their trunks. She'd let him catch her next time. He was quicker and steadier every day. Soon they'd get him a wooden leg, which the doctors said would permit him to walk with only the aid of a cane.

Alistair had already written to Frederick's mother, but they would need to arrange a meeting, now they were come home—a dreadful prospect, but it had to be done. She felt as wretched about it as he. Perhaps more even, for if she'd never married Anthony, the other Mrs. Morris might have both her sons. And she would have married someone else, borne different children and probably never met Alistair. She had regrets by the bushel, but she wouldn't wish away her choices if it meant losing him and Henry. If there'd been any way for things to have happened better . . . .

It would probably be best, Anna thought, if she and Mrs. Morris only peered at each other through a fence of lawyers.

One couldn't bemoan these tragedies all the time though, any more than one could constantly remember them or permanently forget. She'd have times of sorrow and regret, which was only just. But she would have happy moments too, laughter and soft embraces and looking into understanding eyes. The best thing to do seemed to be to hold onto her own happiness and wish some for Mrs. Morris.

Anna smiled, listening to Henry chasing his grandfather up the stairs and Alistair humming in the dressing room. She knew the tune, so she hummed breathily along, lifting out her crumpled gowns. Alistair didn't care that her voice wasn't nearly as fine as his; he liked music when he was happy, and cared more that she felt happy with him than for the quality of their song. Anna hummed a little louder, glad to be home with her mother and father, her husband and son. Tomorrow, if the weather was fine, they would buy a new boat for Henry to sail in the park.

Alistair's humming floated closer. Before his hand could steal around her waist and his lips land in the vicinity of her ear, Anna dropped her grey pelisse and and shut the lid of her trunk. Creased gowns and musty linen . . . no reason they couldn't wait.

ALSO BY JAIMA FIXSEN

Fairchild

Courting Scandal

The Reformer

A Holiday in Bath

The Dark Before Dawn

ABOUT THE AUTHOR

Jaima Fixsen is the author of the popular Fairchild regency romance series. She would rather read than sleep and though all her novels take place in the past, she couldn't live without indoor plumbing or smart phones.

When she isn't writing or child wrangling, she's a snow enthusiast. She lives with her family in Alberta, Canada, and most all just tries to keep up.

Made in the USA
Las Vegas, NV
28 November 2022

60561392R00192